"*We Hope for Better Things* has it all: fabulous storytelling, an emotional impact that lingers long after you turn the last page, and a setting that immerses you. I haven't read such a powerful, moving story since I read *To Kill a Mockingbird* in high school. This book will change how you look at the world we live in. Highly recommended!"

Colleen Coble, *USA Today* bestselling author of the Rock Harbor series and *The View from Rainshadow Bay*

"A timely exploration of race in America, *We Hope for Better Things* is an exercise of empathy that will shape many a soul. Erin Bartels navigates this sensitive topic with compassion as she shifts her readers back and forth between past and present, nudging us to examine the secrets we keep, the grudges we hold, and the prejudices we may help create even without intention."

Julie Cantrell, *New York Times* and *USA Today* bestselling author of *Perennials*

"It's not easy to weave three time periods into a cohesive narrative, each with its own story and intriguing characters. Erin Bartels has accomplished the difficult. She's woven together black and white silk threads into a braid so well crafted that a reader will carry forward the braid of love and separation, race and reconciliation, long after the last page is read. I applaud her courage, her authenticity, her beautiful turn of phrase, the freshness of her imagery, and the depth of her story that speaks to a contemporary world where understanding is often absent. *We Hope for Better Things* is a remarkable debut novel that every reader will see was written by a skilled writer telling a story of her heart."

Jane Kirkpatrick, award-winning author of *Everything She Didn't Say*

"Erin Bartels's *We Hope for Better Things* shares the joys and sorrows of three women from different generations. Beginning with the turmoil of the Civil War through the race riots of the sixties to modern day, the story peels away excuses and pretensions to reveal the personal tragedies of prejudice. A roller coaster of emotions awaits as you share the lives of these women and hope along with them for better things."

Ann H. Gabhart, bestselling author of *River to Redemption*

"Storytelling at its finest. Erin Bartels delivers a riveting story of forbidden love, family bonds, racial injustice, and the power of forgiveness. Spanning multiple generations, *We Hope for Better Things* is a timely, sobering, moving account of how far we've come . . . and how much distance remains to be covered. A compulsively readable, incredibly powerful novel."

Lori Nelson Spielman, *New York Times* bestselling author of *The Life List*

"There is the Detroit we think we know, and there is the Detroit full of stories that are never brought to the forefront. With *We Hope for Better Things*, Erin Bartels brings full circle an understanding of contemporary Detroit firmly rooted in the past, with enthralling characters and acute attention to detail. It's a must not just for Detroit lovers but also for those who need to understand that Detroit history is also American history."

Aaron Foley, city of Detroit's chief storyteller and editor of *The Detroit Neighborhood Guidebook*

WE HOPE *for* BETTER THINGS

WE HOPE *for* BETTER THINGS

ERIN BARTELS

a division of Baker Publishing Group
Grand Rapids, Michigan

Published by Revell
a division of Baker Publishing Group
PO Box 6287, Grand Rapids, MI 49516-6287
www.revellbooks.com

Printed in the United States of America

Library of Congress Cataloging-in-Publication Data
Names: Bartels, Erin, 1980– author.
Title: We hope for better things / Erin Bartels.
Description: Grand Rapids, MI : Revell, [2019]
Identifiers: LCCN 2018020852 | ISBN 9780800734916 (pbk. : alk. paper)
Classification: LCC PS3602.A83854 W4 2018 | DDC 813/.6—dc23
LC record available at https://lccn.loc.gov/2018020852

This book is a work of fiction. Names, characters, places, and incidents are the product of the author's imagination or are used fictitiously. Any resemblance to actual events, locales, or persons, living or dead, is coincidental.

Martin Luther King Jr.'s speech in chapter 20 is taken from The Martin Luther King Jr. Research and Education Institute, https://kinginstitute.stanford.edu/king-papers/documents/address-freedom-rally-cobo-hall.

19 20 21 22 23 24 25 7 6 5 4 3 2 1

For Calvin,
whose compassion gives me
hope for the future

Speramus meliora; resurget cineribus.
We hope for better things; it will rise from the ashes.

Detroit city motto

ONE

Detroit, July

The Lafayette Coney Island was not a comfortable place to be early. It wasn't a comfortable place, period. It was cramped and dingy and packed, and seat saving, such as I was attempting at the lunch rush, was not appreciated.

Thankfully, at precisely noon as promised, an older black gentleman in a baggy Detroit Lions jersey shuffled through the door, ratty leather bag slung over one drooped shoulder.

"Mr. Rich?" I called over the din.

He slid into the chair across from me. I'd fought hard for that chair. Hopefully this meeting would be worth the effort.

"How'd you know it was me?" he said.

"You said you'd be wearing a Lions jersey."

"Oh yes. I did, didn't I? My son gave me this."

"You ready to order? I only have twenty minutes."

Mr. Rich was looking back toward the door. "Well, I was hoping that . . . Oh! Here we go."

The door swung open and a tall, well-built man sporting a slick suit and a head of short black dreads walked in. He looked vaguely familiar.

"Denny! We're just about to order." Mr. Rich set the leather bag on his lap and slid over in his seat to accommodate the newcomer.

The man sat on the eight inches of chair Mr. Rich had managed to unearth from his own backside, but most of him spilled out into the already narrow aisle.

"This is my son, Linden."

Something clicked and my eyes flew to one of the many photos on the wall of famous people who'd eaten here over the years. There he was, between Eminem and Drew Barrymore, towering over the smiling staff.

I sat a little straighter. "The Linden Rich who kicks for the Lions?"

"Yeah," he said. "And you are . . . ?"

"This is Elizabeth Balsam," Mr. Rich supplied, "the lady who writes all those scandal stories in the *Free Press* about corruption and land grabbing and those ten thousand—eleven thousand?—untested rape kits they found awhile back and such. She covered the Kilpatrick trial."

I offered up a little smile, one I'd practiced in the mirror every morning since college, one I hoped made me look equal parts approachable and intelligent.

"Oh, yeah, okay," Linden said. "I see the resemblance. In the eyes."

"I told you," Mr. Rich said.

"You did."

"I'm sorry," I broke in, "what resemblance?"

A waiter in a filthy white T-shirt balancing ten plates on one arm came up to the table just then and said, "Denny! Whaddayawant?"

We ordered our coney dogs—coney sauce and onions for me, everything they had in the kitchen for Linden, and just coney sauce for Mr. Rich, who explained, "I can't eat onions no more."

"And I need silverware," I added in an undertone.

When the waiter shouted the order to the old man at the grill, Linden was already talking. "You are not giving her that camera."

"You said the photos—the photos should stay for now," Mr. Rich said. "Why shouldn't I give her the camera? It ain't yours, Denny."

"It ain't hers either."

"No, she's going to give it to Nora."

Linden took a deep breath and looked off to the side. Though probably anyone else would have been embarrassed to be so obviously talked about as if she wasn't even there, years of cut-throat journalism had largely squelched that entirely natural impulse in my brain.

I jumped on the dead air to start my own line of questioning. "On the phone you said you'd been given a few things that were found in a police evidence locker—that belonged to a relative of yours?"

"No, they belong to a relative of *yours*. Maybe I should just start from the beginning."

I resisted the urge to pull out my phone and start recording the conversation.

But before Mr. Rich could begin, our coney dogs were plunked down on the table in no particular order. We slid the plates around to their proper owners. The men across from me bit into their dogs. I began to cut mine with a knife and fork, eliciting a you-gotta-be-kidding-me look from Linden.

"I've been reading the *Free Press* over the years," Mr. Rich began, "and I kept seeing your byline. I don't know if I would have noticed that all those articles were by the same person if I didn't have a connection to your family name."

I nodded to let him know I was tracking with him.

"And I got to thinking, maybe this Elizabeth Balsam is related to the Balsam I know. It's not a real common name in Detroit. I don't know if I'd ever heard it outside of my own association with a Nora Balsam. Now, is that name familiar to you?"

I speared a bit of bun and sopped up some sauce. "Sorry, no. I don't think I know anyone by that name."

Linden lifted his hand up to his father as if to say, "See?"

"Now, hold on," the older man said in his son's direction. "You said yourself she looks like her."

"I'll admit you do look like her," Linden said. "But—no offense and all—you do kind of all look the same."

I laughed. As a white person in a city that was over eighty percent black, I was used to occasional reminders of what minority races had to contend with in most parts of the country. I didn't mind it. It helped me remember that the readership I served wasn't only made up of people just like me.

"I wouldn't say you're the spitting image," Mr. Rich said, "but there's a definite resemblance in the eyes. If you had blonde hair, maybe a different chin, it'd be spot-on."

I took a sip of water. "I still don't know who you're talking about. Or what this meeting is all about."

Mr. Rich shut his eyes and shook his head. "Yeah, we're getting ahead of ourselves again. Now, you know well as anyone lots of things have gone by the wayside in this city. We got too many problems to deal with them all. Well, I been looking for something that's been lost for a very long time. I knew the police had to have it, but you try getting someone on the phone who knows what they're talking about in an organization that had five police chiefs in five years. And I get it. They got way more important things to do than find some old bag collecting dust on a shelf." He paused and smiled broadly. "But I finally found it. Got the call a couple years ago and got it back—and a bit more I hadn't bargained for." He tapped the bag on his lap, still miraculously free of coney sauce. "This camera belongs to Nora Balsam. And I have a box full of photographs for her as well."

I realized I'd been squinting, trying to put the pieces together in my head as to what any of this really had to do with me. I relaxed my face and tried to look sympathetic. "And you think I'm related and I therefore can get them to her?"

"That's what I hoped."

I wiped my already clean hands on my napkin. "I'm sorry, Mr. Rich, but I think you'll have to look elsewhere. I've never heard of her."

The old man looked disappointed, but I was relieved. I had bigger fish to fry and a deadline that was breathing down my neck. I didn't have time to courier old photos to someone. I glanced at my phone. I didn't even have time to finish lunch.

"I'm so sorry not to have better news for you. But unfortunately, I have to get going." I started to pull some bills from my wallet.

Linden held up his hand. "It's on me."

"Thanks." I drained my water glass, pulled my purse strap onto my shoulder, and pushed back my chair a couple inches, which was as far as it would go in the tight space. "Just out of curiosity, why was this stuff at a police station? What are these pictures of?"

Linden looked at his father, who looked down at his plate as if the answer were written there in the smear of coney sauce.

"They're from the '67 riots."

I felt my heart rate tick up, scooted back up to the table, and leaned in. "Did you bring them?"

"Denny didn't think I should."

"Why not?"

"Because of that," Linden said. "Because you weren't interested until you knew what they were, and I knew it would play out this way." He turned to his father. "Didn't I tell you? Didn't I say she'd only be interested in getting her hands on the photos?"

I sat back, trying to play it cool, trying to put that approachable-yet-intelligent smile back on my face. "Why shouldn't I be? I've built my entire reputation on exposing corruption and neglect in this city. Photos of historic significance left to rot in a police station are just one more symptom of the larger problem. And I'm working on a big piece right now on the riots. Those photos have never been published—I assume. I'm sure the *Free Press* would pay handsomely to have the privilege of sharing them with the world."

Linden pointed a finger in my direction. "There! There it is! Just like I said."

Mr. Rich placed a hand on his son's forearm. "Okay, okay. Just calm down and let me talk a moment."

Linden withdrew the accusative finger and leaned back on his half of the seat, his million-dollar foot stretching out past my chair, blocking me in even as I knew he must want me out.

His father looked at me with tired eyes. "Miss Balsam, I'm burdened. I been carrying something around for fifty years that I got to let go of. This camera and those photos have to get back to Nora. Not to the paper, not to a museum or a library. To Nora. Now, I can't take them. But you could. Are you willing to just look into it? Do a little poking around to see if you're related like we think you are? And if you are, would you be willing to make contact with her? Kind of ease her into the idea slowly? These photos will stir up a lot of hard memories for an old lady. But I know it in my heart—the Lord laid it on my soul—I need to get these to her."

One of the most important lessons I learned in my first couple years as a professional journalist was not to get emotionally involved with a story. There was simply too much heartbreaking stuff you had to write about. To let yourself empathize with the boy who was being bullied or the man who had lost his business or the woman whose daughter had been abducted, when there was nothing you could do to help the situation beyond making a voice heard—it was just too heavy a burden to bring home with you every night. So I built up a wall around my heart and stayed within it at all times when it came to work.

But there was something about this man's eyes, the crooked

lines on either side of his mouth suggesting he had found as much to frown at in life as to smile about, that chipped away at that wall.

I tapped my finger on the table. "Why do you have them if she's the one who took them?"

"She didn't take them. My uncle did. But he's gone. They belong to her now."

"Why?"

"She's his wife."

An interracial couple in the 1960s? This was getting interesting. Maybe I could work this into my larger series of articles about the riots and the time surrounding them. It had a great human angle, a larger cultural-historical angle, a connection to a beloved NFL player. I could even frame it as a personal family story if I truly was related. The question was, would I have the time? I still hadn't been able to crack the protective shield around Judge Sharpe, the white whale of my investigative series, and time was running out.

"Okay, let's say I am related to her. I still don't know her and she doesn't know me, so why would she even listen to me?"

"Miss Balsam, do you believe in God?"

The question caught me off guard. "Yes."

"Do you believe he works all things together for his glory?"

My parents believed that. My sister did. I had once. Before I'd seen just how chaotic and messed up and out of control the world was. If journalism had taught me anything, it was that we were all just out there flailing and stumbling through a minefield of dangers and predators and dumb blind chance. But it was obvious that Mr. Rich believed God had given him a task—return these items—and that he would get no rest until the task was completed.

Instead of answering his question, I asked one of my own. "Why don't you just ship it to her?"

"No, that ain't the way."

I waited for a logical reason why not, but clearly none was forthcoming.

"Would you just look into it?" he said.

Those beseeching brown eyes tugged a few more bricks out of my wall.

"Sure. I'll look into it," I said.

Mr. Rich nodded and slid a business card across the table. I avoided Linden's sharp gaze as I pocketed the card and squeezed out of my chair.

"It was so nice meeting you," I said. "Thanks for lunch."

I walked out into the windy, sun-drenched afternoon, handed a dollar to the homeless guy who paced and mumbled a few yards from the door, and headed down the street to the old Federal Reserve building, which had housed the shrinking *Free Press* staff since 2014, and where a pile of work awaited me.

I tried to concentrate on the unending march of emails marked *urgent* in my inbox, including one from my editor—*My office, ASAP*—but my mind was spinning out all the directions this new story idea could go. This was decidedly inconvenient because I needed to focus.

I'd been stalking Judge Sharpe through his affable and unsuspecting son Vic for months, and I finally felt like a break was imminent. Vic had texted me last night to set up a meeting after he, in his words, "discovered something big I think you'll be interested to know." I had to get these photos off my mind for the moment, and the best way to do that was to get the research ball rolling.

I slipped out to the stairwell and pulled up Ancestry.com on my phone. A few minutes and thirty dollars later, I was clicking on little green leaf icons that waved at me from the screen. I found my parents and then began tracing my father's branch back to the family tree. Grandfather Richard, Great-Uncle Warner, and *ping*, just like that, a great-aunt born Eleanor Balsam.

I typed a quick text to my sister in L.A.

Hey, long time, no see. Family question: have you ever heard Mom or Dad talk about a great-aunt Eleanor or Nora? Let me know. TX.

I waited a moment for a reply. She was probably with a patient. It was also possible she had no idea who was texting her because it had been at least two years since we last talked. I walked back to my desk, pulled up my piece on a black cop who worked the 1967 riots, and gave it one last read before sending it on its way to my editor. It would join my piece on a white firefighter I'd sent him two days ago. The piece on Judge Sharpe, who'd been a National Guardsman during the riots, would complete the triptych. If I could get it written.

It was 1:14 p.m. If I left in five, I'd have time to freshen up before meeting Vic for coffee at the Renaissance Center Starbucks.

My phone buzzed. My sister.

She's Dad's aunt. Why? Is she okay?

Leave it to Grace to immediately worry.

I want to visit her. Do you know where she lives?

I stared at the screen, waiting.

As far as I know, she still lives in the old Lapeer house.

She said it like I should know what it was, like The Old Lapeer House was a thing. Even after all this time, it still irked me that my unplanned birth nine years after my sister's meant that I so often felt like an outsider in my own family, never quite in on the stories or inside jokes.

Address?

Pause.

Mom may have it.

Great. My parents had been medical missionaries in the Amazon River Basin for the past eight years. It wasn't as if I could just call them up any time I wanted. Mom called on my birthday and Christmas and any other time they happened to be in a town for supplies, but that wasn't often.

My phone buzzed again.

Or call Barb. 269-555-7185

I didn't bother asking who Barb was, especially since it was apparent I should already know. I'd cold-call her no matter what. The prospect of getting my hands on those never-before-seen photos of the riots was too tempting to wait for proper introductions.

I looked at the clock again. If I was going to make it to the RenCen Starbucks on time, I had to leave. Now. I grabbed my purse and my bag from my desk and headed back to the stairwell.

"Liz!"

My editor was the one person in the world who called me Liz.

"I'm out the door, Jack. I'll stop in when I get back. Three o'clock. Four, tops."

I pushed through the metal door, put the box of photos out of mind, and got on with my real work: getting the notoriously circumspect Judge Ryan Sharpe to open up about his involvement in the 1967 riots. Because no matter what image he liked to project to the public, my gut told me that beneath the black robe lurked a man who had something to hide.

TWO

Detroit, March 1963

Nora was finding it difficult to breathe. The man in the photo wore the same hat, the same suit and tie, the same shoes shined to reflective brilliance. She recognized the nose, the mouth, the eyes, though they were distorted. The high forehead drawn into deep furrows. Lips twisted into a shout. Left hand packed into a fist at his side. Right hand reaching out, clawlike, and wearing a familiar ring. He was lunging at the camera. Or rather, at whoever had held it.

"That's the last photograph I took with that camera," came a silky voice behind her.

Nora spun around to find she stood eye to chest with a man in a loose white button-up shirt tucked into black pants. She took a step back. The man smiling down at her was lean and striking, with skin the color of dark mahogany and deep brown eyes. A badge clipped to his breast pocket proclaimed "Exhibitor."

"You took this picture?"

The man nodded and held out his hand. "I took all the photos on this wall."

"Where did you take this?" Nora asked, ignoring the proffered hand. She certainly wouldn't shake it.

"I took that outside the GM building a few months back. That fellow was mad. Right after I took that photo he smashed my camera on the sidewalk. You believe that? I grabbed it up quick and took off. Saved the film, but that thing ain't never gonna take no more pictures, that's for sure."

"What did you do to him?"

The man held up both hands in surrender. "Hey, I didn't do nothing to that guy."

"Well, you must have done something. Why was he so angry? Why would he attack you?"

The man shook his head. "Men like that don't need a reason."

"Like what?"

"You know. Big men. They don't need a reason for anything they do. Do whatever they want, no consequences."

Nora could tell she was scowling. She relaxed her facial muscles. Scowling at twenty meant wrinkles at thirty, or so her mother reminded her with some regularity.

"I just don't understand what would cause him to do that. He's not—" She stopped short and saw something click in the man's mind.

He opened his mouth, but before he could ask the question, Diane slid up, already speaking.

"Did you see that series with the enormous twins on little motorbikes down the south hall? It was hideously creepy. I mean, twins are disturbing anyway and—" She suddenly seemed to realize that no one was listening to her. "Hey, what's the deal?" She turned to look at the picture Nora was attempting to block with her petite frame. "Oh my word, is that your dad?" Her voice echoed in the stark hall.

"Keep your voice down." Nora tipped her head toward the lanky photographer.

"Oh," Diane said. She pulled the strap of her purse over her head.

"He took the picture," Nora said under her breath.

The man lifted one hand in greeting, then put both in his pockets.

"Serious?" She let out a little snort, then stifled her laughter at Nora's disapproving glare. "Well, I guess you two must have something to talk about. I'll just be over . . . somewhere."

She scuttled off, leaving Nora to face the awkward situation alone.

"Listen, miss, I'm sorry about that. I didn't know."

Nora shook her head rapidly. "No, no. No need to apologize. But of course I must ask you to take it down."

He frowned. "Take it down? It's the best one of the bunch. Judging doesn't happen till three o'clock. There's no way I'm taking it down before then."

Nora clenched her fists and manufactured a smile. "Please? Lots of people know my father. Someone will recognize him."

"So?" He shrugged.

"So?"

"Yeah, so what if he's recognized? I hope he is. Why shouldn't he be?"

Nora felt herself scowling again. "Because that's rude. It's incredibly rude to take a picture of someone when they are upset and then plaster it all over for the world to see."

The man's eyes widened. "Rude? Ain't it rude to attack someone? To destroy someone's property? You know how much overtime I had to work to afford that camera? I need that prize money. That prize money's gonna buy me a new camera."

Nora opened her mouth but couldn't find anything to say.

"That's what I thought," the man said. He turned to walk away.

"Wait! I'll buy you a new camera."

He turned back, mouth twisted, eyebrows raised.

"I'll buy you a new camera," she said again, "if you give me that photo right now."

A bemused little smile crept over his face. "You'll buy me a camera?"

"Yes."

"*You* gonna buy *me* a camera?"

"Yes, if you give me that photo."

The man laughed. "You ain't gonna buy me no camera."

She took a step forward to show she was in earnest. "Yes, I will. You give me the name of the camera you want and I will go straight out right now and buy it for you. All I ask in exchange is that you take down that photo immediately and give it to me when I give you the camera."

Nora felt her insides squirm as the man bit his lip and looked her up and down, considering.

"All right, little lady. You got yourself a deal. But you got till just 2:30 to get me a new camera. If you don't show, that photo's going back up before the judges come around."

"Fine." She dug in her purse for a pen and piece of paper. "Write down what you want—exactly what you want. If you're not specific, you'll just have to take what you get."

He smirked as he scribbled out *Nikon F* and then held the paper out to her. She took the slip and looked pointedly at the photo.

"All right, all right," he said. "It's coming down." He lifted the framed print off the wall and looked from it to Nora and back again. "I can see the resemblance now."

She pressed her lips together for a moment and breathed slowly through her nose. "Very funny. Where will you put it?"

"I got a box, don't worry."

She stuck the slip of paper into her jacket pocket and looked at the delicate silver watch on her wrist. "I'll try to be back in thirty minutes or so."

He gave her a mock salute. "Hey, you know that's an expensive camera, right? It's what professionals use. You sure you can afford it?"

It was Nora's turn to smirk. "I wouldn't worry about that."

THREE

Detroit, July

I didn't remember the trip back to the office. I knew that at some point, after a disastrous meeting with Vic Sharpe, I had stepped onto the People Mover platform at the Renaissance Center station, careful to keep away from the yellow caution line lest I pass out and fry myself on the electric monorail. Then somehow I was standing at Jack McKnight's door.

"Almost didn't recognize you in that getup," he said. "Come in and close the door."

I did as directed. "I'm sorry, Jack," I began. "I made a mistake."

He held up his hand. "No, I'm sorry. I got wind of that video footage late last night. I tried to catch you before you left. I knew what was coming."

"I can still fix this," I said, knowing it wasn't true.

Jack shook his head. "I hate to do this. I wish there was another way, but I have the integrity of the paper to think about. I'm going to need you to sign this."

Still in a fog, I took a pen from his hand and moved toward the papers he was indicating on his desk.

"You'll have a decent severance," he said.

I took a step back. "Severance?"

"Of course. We wouldn't send you away empty-handed."

"Wait, why would you be sending me away? Because of one botched story? Are you kidding me?"

"Liz, I'm sorry, but Ryan and Vic Sharpe are powerful men, and someone needed to take the blame."

Another step, this one forward, toward my boss. "And you laid that on me? That was on you! You told me to—"

"Liz, it's done. You need to sign this statement and—"

"I'm not signing any statement!"

"If you don't sign attesting to the fact that you investigated Judge Sharpe under false pretenses and an assumed identity and release the *Free Press* from any liability, you'll get nothing in severance. Nothing."

I don't remember throwing the pen. It bounced off Jack's chest and clattered to the floor. We stood for a breath in that awesomely empty space, and I contemplated how suddenly my life had changed in the space of just two hours. Then I thrust open his office door and stalked to my desk. Heads swiveled. Eyes stared. I pulled the last two reams of paper from a box beneath the printer table, plopped it onto my chair, and commenced packing.

"Elizabeth?"

I shoved a photo of my parents into the box.

"What's going on? Why are you dressed like that?"

A coffee mug I hadn't cleaned with actual dish soap in four years.

"Elizabeth."

An ugly paperweight I'd received from an interviewee who wanted to thank me for not misquoting her.

"Elizabeth!"

I scanned the rest of the desk. Was that it? Was that the extent of me? Three measly personal items? I scraped the change from the shallow tray in my middle drawer and dumped it in the box as well. A familiar hand caught my arm. I finally looked at Desiree, who was looking at me like my mother had the first time I got dumped.

"Did you get fired?" she said.

I started to shake my head.

"Did you quit?"

Did I?

"I can't talk about it now," I said. I looked in the pitiful box, pulled out the photo of my parents, and stuffed it in my purse. "I'll text you later."

Leaving everything else on my chair, I kicked off the horrible three-inch heels I was wearing in place of my normal sensible flats, pushed my way past the gawkers, and rushed down the back stairs barefoot. At the bottom, I threw my body against the crash bar and stared down at the parking lot. It had been soaking up the summer heat all day and was littered with bits of gravel and broken glass. I half ran, half tiptoed the thirty feet to my car, sat down hard, flicked the stones out of the balls of my feet, and slammed the door.

My breath came in shallow gasps. The last two hours had felt less real than any dream I could remember having.

Three months ago, Jack had summoned me to his office, shut the door, and leaned against his desk. "I'm pulling Roger off Judge Sharpe," he said. "I want you on him."

"Absolutely."

"But not you."

"Excuse me?"

"I want you to go in as someone else, not a reporter. Just as a woman."

"Like, undercover?"

"Yes. We're getting nowhere with tying him to the riots. I want you to see if you can get inside using the back door. His son Vic is a developer."

"I know that, Jack. His name is on every empty building in town."

"He's also single."

So I invented Dana Bowers, bought her a wardrobe I'd never be seen dead in, and set her on a collision course with the judge's son, convinced it would result in a breakout story.

Becoming Dana had felt a little like getting ready for church as a kid, except then it was my mother curling my hair and makeup was limited to tinted lip gloss. The sweat was the same, as was the sense that I was putting on someone else's identity in hopes that the real me wouldn't be recognized.

My alter ego had met Vic Sharpe at a lavish wedding reception—one to which she had not been invited—at the Detroit Athletic Club, slamming into him outside the men's room. He was going in. She was coming out.

"Oh! I'm sorry, miss," he said as he steadied Dana with two warm hands on her bare arms. "Please excuse me. I thought this was the men's room."

"It is," Dana said saucily. "The ladies' had a line."

She tossed a brazen smile over her shoulder as she walked to a nearby mirror and reapplied her lipstick. Vic hesitated a moment, then walked into the men's room and immediately back out again.

"What are you doing after the reception?" he said.

Just like that, Dana was in. It was so easy.

There had been no reason to think today's coffee date would be any different than any other time Dana and Vic had gone out. But when Dana arrived at the RenCen Starbucks, Vic was already there, an unusually serious expression on his face. She focused on staying upright in those shoes until she reached the table, where her usual—an Americano—already steamed next to a poppy-seed muffin. Not half a muffin. Vic hadn't cut it in two as he normally did so they could share. In fact, as Dana looked closer she saw that there was nothing on the table in front of Vic other than his folded hands.

She smiled anyway as she sat down. "Sorry I'm a bit late."

Dana was always a little late.

Vic nodded. "We need to talk."

"What's wrong?"

"I know what's going on here."

My blood froze. I was no longer Dana. I was Elizabeth. And I didn't like the way Vic Sharpe was looking at me—as if he knew it.

He unfolded his hands, revealing his phone. He swiped the screen, turned it toward me, and tapped a play button. A shot of his home office came up. At the bottom right-hand corner of the screen was last Saturday's date. I already knew what would come next. I watched with a growing sense of dread as Dana came into the office, sat down behind the desk, and began going through drawers and tapping away at a laptop that wasn't hers.

"This video was brought to my attention on Sunday. I was going to ask you about it, but then I thought I might do a little snooping of my own, and you know what I found?"

He waited for my answer, but I couldn't give it. It felt as if the entire poppy-seed muffin was lodged in my throat, though I hadn't taken a bite.

"I discovered that you are living a bit of a double life."

I found my voice. "I can explain."

"I'm sure you can, Elizabeth, but there's no need. I've spoken with your editor. He explained everything to me. I imagine he is waiting for you back at the office."

The email. The attempt to talk to me as I rushed downstairs to become Dana. Jack had been trying to save me from this moment.

"Before you run off," Vic continued, "I want to ask you something, and I want an honest answer. Why is everyone in this town suspicious of anyone who cares enough to make a real difference?"

"Vic, this isn't about you."

"Look, I get it that some investors are predators. They're just looking to make a profit. Some people are wolves. But some people are shepherds."

I tried to break in, to tell him that I wasn't doing a story about him, but he barreled on.

"I was straight with you about my business. I don't have some secret diabolical plan to suck the city dry. I'm pouring money into this city in the slim hope that it can rise from the ashes and live again."

"Vic, I know. That's not what this is about. It's about your father."

"My father."

"I—I was hoping to get some insight into your father. For a story."

"What story?"

"About his time in the National Guard."

He stared me down. "You mean the riots."

"I'm doing a series on law enforcement and city services involved in the riots. He refuses to talk about anything that happened before he enlisted and went to Vietnam. Everything hinges on getting him to open up about that time."

He sat back in his chair. "So you've just been using me to get to him."

I bit the inside of my mouth. *Yes, Elizabeth. That's what you have been doing.* "It's not like that," I said, because I didn't know what else to say.

He stood up and dropped his phone into the inside pocket of his suit coat. Then he pushed in his chair and leaned on it. For an instant a look of disappointment passed across his face. Then the stony anger returned. "You have a nice day."

Then he walked out.

And now I was out. Out of a job. Not quite out of my mind, but getting there. How fast would word of my failure travel? How much time did I have to get my résumé out? Where could

I go? I didn't want to work anywhere else. This was my paper. My family. My family had disowned me.

I turned the key in the ignition. I needed air. Cold air. I was going to throw up. I opened the door and leaned over the blacktop, but nothing came out. This sick feeling would not leave me. It was settling in my gut like the film on cream soup that needed stirring.

I shut the door, threw the car in reverse, and went anywhere but there. I drove aimlessly, taking the path of least resistance, until I found myself in a mostly empty lot near the Riverwalk. I pulled on the black pants and flats I had been wearing earlier, wrenched Dana's body-hugging red dress off over my head, and slipped my arms into the sleeves of my white blouse.

I got out of the car and walked slowly down the Riverwalk, trying to stay out of the way of cyclists. I passed playgrounds and artwork and the calm blue carousel with its beautiful carved fish and frogs and water birds. The fountains danced in front of the gleaming towers of the Renaissance Center. Across the river, Canada lay flat and placid and modest, tied to Detroit by the umbilical cord of the Ambassador Bridge. And somewhere under my feet—it was rumored—lay the storied corpse of Jimmy Hoffa.

So much history. So much commerce. So much pain and beauty and restlessness. Detroit was a city that vibrated with pent-up feelings looking for an outlet—ambition and desire, greed and rage, suspicion and deep love of community. Everyone looking for a break, looking for a second chance, looking for the next big thing.

I sat down hard on the stone steps.

It had taken me three years of hit-and-miss freelancing after college—along with some concentrated stalking—to land a full-time position at the *Detroit Free Press*. Like all newbies, I got put on fluff pieces. It was a start. Then, by sheer chance, I was in the right place at the right time and got sent to the courthouse to cover the civil trial of Mayor Kwame Kilpatrick's alleged affair and unlawful dismissal of the bodyguard who knew too much. I started filing stories Detroiters actually read.

The mayor became my bread and butter, staying in the news for six years as scandalous text messages, corruption, abuse of power, assault, tax evasion, and fraud came to light, one after the other. When the sentence came down in the fall of 2013—twenty-eight years in federal prison—I wondered how I'd be able to keep my momentum going without him. I needn't have worried. He was just one canker on Detroit's body. If I dug around long enough, I'd be sure to unearth another one.

And I did. City council members, police officers, businessmen, and predatory lenders. Arsonists, drug dealers, and pimps. Scrappers who stripped vacant houses of every bit of metal they could sell. And plain old garden-variety neglect—sins of omission—which did as much damage to the city as the corruption and greed of the people bent on taking advantage of a place where nearly everyone was down on their luck.

I became known as the woman who exposed people, who showed them for what they really were. And I loved it. People from all over the city sent me tips to follow up on. Wherever I went, I was either respected or feared, depending on which side of the story you found yourself on.

Vic Sharpe wasn't a bad guy. He owned a firm that was doing good work, investing in small local-business start-ups rather than simply buying up defunct properties in order to sell them at a premium to outsiders looking to make a killing on others' misfortunes. I actually admired him, liked him even, and I'd started feeling uneasy with the way I was using him to get to his father, even if it hadn't been my idea. And even if Judge Sharpe was another one of those cankers that needed to be excised.

I stood up and paced a few steps. I couldn't let this stop me. Detroiters didn't quit. When the whole city burned to the ground in 1805, we rebuilt. When white flight robbed the city of its tax base in the 1960s and '70s, we struggled on. When it became the largest municipal bankruptcy in US history, it came out leaner, meaner, stronger. It rose from the ashes, facing every challenge with grim determination.

And that's what I would do. I'd get my job back. All I needed was a story no one else could get. All I needed was a box of old photos no one else had.

I felt my pocket. The card was still there. I dialed Mr. Rich's number and waited while it rang three times.

"Hello?"

"Mr. Rich, this is Elizabeth Balsam."

"Oh, yes. Good to hear from you so soon."

"Sir, I just wanted you to know, Nora Balsam is my great-aunt."

"She is, is she?" His voice was bright.

"And I will return those photos for you."

FOUR

Detroit, March 1963

Nora stalked off to find Diane. It didn't take long, as she was eavesdropping just around the corner and pounced on Nora the minute she laid eyes on her.

"Oh my word," she whispered loudly, "I can't believe that guy! And frankly, I can't believe they've allowed someone like that to enter this contest. Deplorable."

Nora ignored her friend's outrage and pulled her keys from her purse. "Let's go. I have to buy a camera and you're coming with me."

"We can't just leave. I told Mrs. Rasmussen we would help with the reception afterward."

Nora grabbed Diane's elbow and began steering her toward the front door. "We'll be back before anyone knows we're gone. Come on."

"Ooh! Are we going to Hudson's?"

"If you can get your feet to move, yes."

Nora shoved the exhibit hall doors aside and hurried down the sidewalk to where she had parked, Diane trailing her. She pulled into the traffic on Woodward Avenue and headed downtown. Several minutes later they were standing at the elevator bay near the northwest entrance of the twenty-five-story department store that covered almost an entire city block.

During the drive, Diane had not ceased talking. Now she was silent as the elevator operator took them to the correct floor. But once the doors closed behind them again, the barrage picked up where it had left off.

"Nora, you're not really going to buy that guy a camera."

"Yes I am."

"You can't buy those people nice things. They don't take care of them."

Nora pressed Diane forward. They turned a corner and nearly collided with a woman in a fox fur coat. Nora didn't even slow down to make a proper apology.

"Why do you think your father was so angry?" Diane went on. "The guy obviously insulted him or something worse. You shouldn't reward him for that."

They drew up to a long glass case filled with cameras. Lens filters hung from a spinning rack on the counter. Behind them stood an older gentleman in an impeccable suit and bow tie.

"Hello, sir, I'm in need of this camera." Nora slid the piece of paper across the counter. "Do you carry it?"

The man smiled. "Of course, miss. We carry all top-of-the-line models." He fiddled with a lock, slid open the cabinet, and reached under the counter for the floor model.

"Do you have a box?" Nora asked.

"Well, yes, of course it comes in a box, but allow me to show you—"

"I'm so sorry, sir, but it's not for me. It's a gift. Could you simply ring it up? I'm in a terrible hurry today."

The man seemed irritated by the interruption, but relented at her constant smile and fluttering eyelashes. "Of course, miss."

Nora exchanged a stack of cash for the camera, money she had planned on using to purchase a painting at the exhibit. A few minutes later, to Diane's keen disappointment, the women were back outside pushing through the sea of Saturday shoppers. The sun was shining, but the March wind was still bitter and promised snow. By the time they got back to the Detroit Artists Market, parked, and walked back to the exhibit entrance, Nora's face matched her pink suit.

She was patting her hair back into place as they came upon the hall with the handsome and infuriating photographer. She turned to Diane. "Stay here."

At the quick clicks of Nora's heels on the floor, the photographer looked up. "Well, well. That was fast. You change your mind?"

She thrust the bag at him. He eyed it a moment, took it, and pulled out the box. He chuckled and shook his head.

Nora felt her heart rate tick up. "What? Is it the wrong one? It's what you wrote."

"No, it's the right one."

She let out a relieved sigh. "Then why are you laughing?"

"Because you just bought me a new camera."

He was so pleased it almost made Nora smile. Then she remembered the photo. "Where's the picture?"

He stopped smiling and looked at her thoughtfully. "You want to know what happened? Why he was so mad?"

Nora wanted to get the photo and get out of there as fast as possible. Yet she had to know. She gave a little nod.

"It was an accident. I wasn't watching where I was going 'cause I was looking through the viewfinder up at the GM building. I was backing up and backing up, trying to get more in the frame, and I backed right into him. I stepped hard on his foot and he dropped a bunch of papers. I said I was sorry and I tried to help him pick it all up. Then he called me a stupid nigger."

Nora winced.

"Now, I understand being upset," he went on, "but there's no call for that. And I told him so. Well, that made him real mad.

He got so mad he started spewing things I wouldn't repeat in your presence, even if he wasn't your daddy. I knew I could either get mad or do what my mama always tells me to do when someone's like that."

"What's that?"

"Laugh it off. Just laugh and they know they ain't got you. So I laughed. And the more I laughed the angrier he got, which started to get funny for real. He looked like a cartoon, face all screwed up and red and sweating. You understand, I had to take a picture. And that's when he came at me and smashed up my camera."

Nora wasn't sure what to say. She knew her father was an impatient man who did not tolerate incompetence in any form, whether from his staff, his tailor, or his family. However, she had not imagined he would use such crude language, let alone physically attack someone. To even consider it seemed ludicrous.

The man removed the print from the frame, rolled it up, and handed it to her.

"Thank you," she almost whispered.

"No hard feelings?" he said, catching her eye.

Nora managed a small smile, her first genuine smile of the day. "No."

He grinned. "Now don't you go and burn your fingers when you destroy that, okay?"

She laughed in spite of herself. She would have turned around and walked off just then, but for some reason she hesitated, caught in his steady gaze.

"Hey," he said, "before you go, I better test this thing out, make sure it works. Wouldn't want to get scammed by a pretty girl. Never hear the end of it."

Again Nora failed to suppress her smile. "Go ahead."

He opened the box.

"Oh!" Nora said. "I didn't get you any film."

He reached into his pocket, producing a roll of 35mm film. "Never leave home without it."

"Even with no camera?"

He shrugged. "Habit."

In less than thirty seconds, the man had the lens on the camera body and had loaded the film. He closed one eye and looked through the viewfinder, scanning the hall for a subject. He stopped on Nora.

"No, not me," she said, holding up a hand toward the lens.

"What else? We're in a hallway. There's nothing here but you."

He snapped a photo and advanced the film.

"Please don't."

"What?" he said with feigned surprise. "I didn't take your picture."

"You did."

He snapped another.

"No, stop!" she protested through laughter.

The shutter clicked again. She could see him grinning behind the camera.

"Knock it off," she said, putting a hand to her face, more to cover her own smile than to ward off further pictures.

"Aw, that wasn't of you. Don't flatter yourself."

Click. Twist. *Click.* Twist. *Click.*

"Stop." She rushed up to him and covered the lens with her hand.

"Oh, hey, hey, hey now. Don't do that," he said with a laugh. "That's what your daddy did right before he threw it to the ground."

Her smile disappeared. She adjusted her purse on her shoulder and stalked off.

"Wait! I'm sorry. I'm sorry. I shouldn't have said that. That was stupid. I didn't mean it." He caught up with her and put a hand on her arm.

She pulled away from his touch and turned to face him. "Thank you for keeping your promise," she said stiffly.

"Don't do that. Don't leave angry. I got some great shots of you. Don't you want to see them when they come out?"

She pressed her lips together.

"Of course you do," he went on. "So you give me your number and I'll give you a call when I develop them. Maybe you'll want one for your boyfriend."

"I don't have a boyfriend."

Why had she told him that?

"Well then, you might want copies for your friend over there."

Nora turned and saw Diane's face disappear behind the corner.

"Okay, fine," she said, though she wasn't sure why. She tucked the rolled-up picture under her arm and pulled out her pen, but no amount of digging in her purse produced any more scraps of paper.

"Give me the Hudson's bag to write it on."

He held out his hand to her. "Just write it here."

Nora's cheeks flushed as a self-satisfied half smile touched the man's lips. She reached out, cradled his hand in hers, and wrote her name and phone number across his palm in black ink. Then she dropped the pen in her purse and shoved her hands into her coat pockets.

"Nora Balsam. That's a pretty name. All right, Nora. I'll see you later."

When he waved, Nora could see her own precise penmanship on his hand. She gave a little return wave and started to walk down the hall. Then she turned back. "Wait, what's your name?"

"Will."

"Just Will?"

"William Rich."

"Oh," she said. "I like William better than Will."

"Then you can call me William."

FIVE

Lapeer County, August

I spoke toward the phone sitting on the console. "Am I out of my mind? I'm in the middle of nowhere here."

"No way," came Desiree's voice over the speaker. "This will do you good. You're doing a good thing, for that guy *and* your aunt. And anyway, in the end you're going to have a great story."

"Maybe."

"You will"—her voice crackled—"and then you can sell it to anyone you want. Forget Jack."

"I guess. I mean, yeah. This could be good. Get away for a while. Breathe some clean air."

"Exac . . . you sh . . . b . . . f . . . otally je . . ."

"You're breaking up."

". . ."

"Desiree? Can you hear me?"

I stared at the phone. Call dropped. One bar flickered in. Then out. I sighed and looked back out at the road, only to see that I was inches away from the craggy edge of a drainage ditch. I cranked the wheel. Straightening out life should be so simple. No matter what Mr. Rich believed, God was not in control. My situation was incontrovertible proof of that. The frightening thing was that I wasn't in control either. I should be in Detroit. Instead, I was driving north on a deserted county road, squinting through the colorful remains of dead bugs on the windshield.

I'd called the mysterious Barb the moment I got home the day I lost my job. As it turned out, she was my father's cousin, which, in her rather convoluted explanation, seemed to make her one of Nora Balsam's nieces. She remembered me as a five-year-old, but she had moved to Arizona and rarely got back to Michigan.

"You're an answer to prayer," she'd said. "I didn't know there was anyone left in Detroit since your parents and Grace moved. I just assumed you had too. I've been worrying about what to do about Nora and here you call me out of the blue."

"What needs to be done about her?"

"Oh, she is such a sweet, independent woman, and she's done just fine on her own. But I had a letter from her a few months ago, and there were just one or two things she wrote that had me concerned."

"How?"

"I'm not sure how to describe it. It was more a feeling I got. Like she seemed . . . different. Maybe not quite as sharp. A little out of step. Her handwriting was a little shaky."

"She's old. People slow down."

"Yes, they do. And that's why your call comes at such a perfect time. You can run up there and check on her and let me know if you think she needs assistance."

"Like live-in help?"

"That, or perhaps—and I hate to even suggest this—but perhaps she needs to move into an assisted living facility. She's out in the middle of God's country. The nearest hospital is thirty minutes away."

"Well, I was hoping just to visit her for a day or maybe overnight." I didn't intend to tell Barb anything about the camera or the photos or Mr. Rich.

"Oh, can't you get away from work longer than that?"

Work. That's right. I had all the time in the world. I had no job. And if I couldn't get a new job—which I was sure Judge Sharpe and Vic could make very difficult for me—I would have no money. No money, no apartment. Or food. Why hadn't I just signed that stupid paper so I could get the severance?

I told Barb about losing my job. "You think she'd be up for a houseguest for a bit longer? Maybe I could use it as time to strategize about my next career move."

"You're not worried about losing your apartment?"

I laughed. "It's not like I won't be able to find another place when I get back. Limited housing stock is one problem Detroit doesn't have."

"If you're sure, I think it would be great if you could spend some extended time there. As I said, she's very independent. If she thought I'd sent you to check up on her, she might be offended. But if you're going up there for a little R & R while you figure out what's next for you, that paints a different picture. I can make all the arrangements with Nora—just give me a week."

Barb had come through. Nora offered an open-ended invitation to come stay with her. The rest—determining her ability to take care of herself, finding the right time to talk about her husband's lost property, developing a show-stopping personal interest story around the emergence of the photos, oh, and looking for gainful employment—was up to me. Within just a few weeks I should be back in Detroit putting together the article that would accompany the rare photos and redeem me in the eyes of the journalistic community. This was temporary. A favor. Nothing more.

After an hour or so of driving, the GPS announced, "You have reached your destination." But just where I had arrived seemed almost arbitrary. The only thing that even indicated human habitation at this spot was a rusty mailbox, a narrow gravel two-track, and a broken line of boulders that might have been a wall in another century.

I crunched along the gray ribbons of stones into a dense grove of towering evergreens planted too close together and too close to the driveway. Needles scraped at the car, trying to push me back out. But I would not be deterred. I could not go back to Detroit. Not yet.

I emerged from the tunnel and was greeted with what would be my interim home. The white two-story farmhouse was simple and forgettable and half strangled by Virginia creeper. I killed the engine and stepped out into the heavy summer air. The wide porch extended like a friendly handshake, but with my first move toward it I felt ill. This was a mistake. There was no way a normal person would agree to having a stranger come stay at their house with no definite end date. Would she resent my presence there? What if her memory failed and she had no idea who I was or why I was on her doorstep? What if she had a shotgun?

As I stood at the bottom step wondering just when it was I had lost my nerve, the faded orange front door swung open and a petite, white-haired lady smiled at me from the doorway. But the smile did not reach her clear blue eyes.

"You must be Elizabeth."

"Yes, hi, Nora!" I said in a chirpy voice I had never before used to speak to another human. "It's so nice to meet you. I can't believe we've lived this close all this time and I never knew it."

She raised her eyebrows at that but stopped short of rolling her eyes, and I got the distinct impression that the unintentional estrangement was somehow my fault.

"Come on in. I'll show you to the powder room."

A few minutes later I found myself seated at a round kitchen table topped with sunny yellow placemats and a sweating pitcher of iced tea. My great-aunt lifted the full pitcher with thin arms. No shaking, no tremors. She appeared healthy, strong, and, so far, in possession of her wits.

We sat and sipped in awkward silence as I searched for something appropriate to say. I was so rarely at a loss for words, even around total strangers. But how did one begin such an impossible conversation? When was the right time to bring up the camera and the riots, to test the waters so I could report back to Mr. Rich and get him to loosen his grip on the photos that I now needed more than ever? I lost myself in my glass of tea, and the silence thickened around us until that was all there was.

Finally Nora spoke, perhaps signaled by the hollow clink of ice in my empty glass. "Now that you've had a chance to catch your breath, you can bring your things up to your room. I'd help, but I don't do stairs anymore when I can avoid it. I've had William freshen up the back bedroom for you."

I sucked the slim remains of an ice cube into my mouth and followed her to the grand staircase in the front hall.

"You see that door up there? That's the bathroom. The door you want is just to the left. If you go up those last few steps around the corner, you've gone too far."

I half dragged two suitcases up the stairs. The higher I climbed, the hotter and heavier the air around me became, and when I reached the landing, beads of sweat sprouted from my forehead. In that one horrifying moment I realized that Nora did not have air-conditioning.

I swept the wet hair from my face and opened the door, surprised to find not a bedroom as I expected but a cramped hall with two more doors and a second staircase, this one steep and narrow and leading back down to some unknown spot on the first floor. I tried the door to the left and found yet more stairs, these leading up, presumably to the attic. I tried the door across the hall. It swung open with a creak, releasing a torrent of yellow sunlight that flowed into the dark hall and kissed my sandaled feet.

The room was hot and musty—a far cry from the fresh and immaculate kitchen. I set my suitcases down and pushed back the brittle sheer curtains at the closest window. The sash relented with an angry crack of protest, and oxygen flowed into the room like CPR. I ran my fingers along a dresser, leaving undulating trails in what had to be years of dust. It was clear that, despite Nora's assertion that someone had freshened up the room, no one had been in here for a very long time.

But there were some redeeming qualities to this stuffy space. The bed was magnificent. Slender curves of light and dark wood wound themselves around one another at the head and foot like tangled roots, framing a quilt done in every rich hue of yellow I could imagine. Each tiny piece of fabric was artfully arranged so that one shade blended into the next. The pieces right next to each other looked almost identical. It was only when looking at the whole you noticed they were different shades.

Sitting primly between two windows was a small fireplace. The thought of hearing the cozy crackling of a fire while falling asleep made me almost giddy. But no. I wouldn't be here in the winter. I had a job to do.

I had met up with Mr. Rich on a heavy, clouded August day that whispered of tornados. Thankfully, his suspicious son was too busy to join us. He relinquished the camera, reminded me once more not to mention his name, and advised me to take things slow. The one thing I still didn't have from him was the box of photos. Linden had seen to that. I was to contact Mr. Rich once I had determined that Nora would accept them, and we'd go from there.

"When I knew Nora," he said, "she was spoiled and stubborn. We parted on very bad terms."

"I'll be careful," I said, and I braced myself for an unpleasant trip.

The next week, I brought most of my furniture and my housewares back to the same thrift store I'd purchased them from in my first month of employment at the *Free Press*. Desiree took in my houseplant—singular—which she had given me three years earlier. Everything else—clothes, some books, and childhood mementos I couldn't part with—I'd packed into the car with a speed that astonished me. I had never imagined I could be erased from Detroit so efficiently.

After two more trips up and down the stairs with all my worldly possessions, I found Nora puttering in the kitchen.

"That bed is amazing," I said, happy at least to have found something safe to say. "And that quilt is incredible."

"I thought you might like it. Yellow is cheerful. That's why I put you in that room. I've always been proud of that quilt."

I ignored her intimation that I might need cheering up. "You made that?"

"Oh, sure. I made all the quilts upstairs."

The craftiest thing I had ever constructed was a single knitted washcloth in drab brown yarn. I had learned from my mother, at her insistence, and retained enough knowledge and skill to complete the one project. It took me an entire summer.

Nora took my arm and led me back out to the front hall. "There are four bedrooms upstairs. Yours was my bedroom before I moved down to the first floor. Did you see the back steps?"

"Yes. I wondered about those."

"A lot of old houses have them. So the help could move around unseen while you entertained guests in the parlor. I always used them because the first place I wanted to go in the morning was the kitchen to make coffee."

My inner nosy reporter perked up. Perfect. If I could get her talking about the house, it wouldn't be long before she was talking about herself, telling me about her husband, giving me the in I needed to bring up the camera and the photos.

"So what's the story with this place? When was it built?"

"I was told 1859. But there's no one story in a place this old. Everything in this house has a story. You'll have to look around upstairs on your own, but I can give you the grand tour down here."

For the next hour I moved through each room of the main floor, struggling to stick to my great-aunt's glacial pace but entranced nonetheless. I gazed at antique furniture, oil paintings, and rugs as she relayed what she knew of their origin. With every room I felt weighed down by a new layer of guilt. This woman clearly loved her home and did not know that Barb had given me the thankless task of determining whether she was capable of continuing to live there on her own.

Eventually we came to her bedroom. If I thought the quilt on my bed was nice, the one on Nora's was exquisite. A kaleidoscope of color, it was formed from varied patches of jewel-toned velvet and silk, each piece edged with multicolored embroidery thread in a hundred different patterns. I wanted to run my fingers along it, but it looked like something you'd get your hand slapped for touching.

"Wow." I felt like I had said that a lot during the tour, but it was the one word that kept coming to mind. The house was packed full of wow. "Did you make this one?"

"No. My great-grandmother Mary did. It was the only quilt she made that I know of. Takes a long time to make a quilt like that. All handwork. A lot of Victorian crazy quilts don't hold up well. The dyes in the silks eat away at the fabric over the years, and it gets worse if you're not careful with them. Collectors would faint if they knew I slept under it, but I sleep like the dead, so I don't do much tossing and turning. And I never sit on it."

This last statement seemed to be added for my benefit—or admonishment. I leaned over to examine the varied stitches. Vines and flowers, geometric designs, ribbons and feathers, something that looked like bird tracks.

"Did she teach you to quilt?"

"Heavens, no! How old do you think I am? She died in 1875. She's buried out back."

I straightened up. "She lived here?"

She looked at me as if I should have known that. "You've never heard of Nathaniel and Mary Balsam before?"

I shrugged. "Those names don't ring any bells."

Nora shook her head. "I guess I shouldn't be surprised."

"Why's that?"

"Because history is written by the victors."

SIX

Lapeer County, April 1861

Mary Balsam felt the morning sun streaming in through the east windows. Though it had been spring for close to three weeks already, there was something about the light on this particular morning that told her the new season was finally real, that they'd seen the last of the snow and planting time had arrived. She stretched out her hand to touch her husband's face. Her fingers found his pillow and nothing more.

Mary rose to an elbow. A newspaper lay beside her on the bed where Nathaniel should have been. It took just a moment to read the headline, but in that moment her entire world trembled. The trouble had been fermenting for so long she had ceased to note it, turning instead to the society pages for lighter fare. But this was different. This was the headline that would take Nathaniel from her.

She sat upright, her eyes darting back and forth down the slim columns of type. With every sentence, the floor dropped away a little more.

Nathaniel marched into the bedchamber, his mouth a determined line, his eyes locked upon some object across the room.

He retrieved a bottle of ink and was nearly gone again when Mary said, "Where are you going with that?"

"Oh, Mary, I'm sorry I woke you. I'm just gathering up a few things." He took the newspaper from the bed. "You're finished with this?"

"You're not enlisting."

"We can talk about it over breakfast."

He walked out the door and Mary scrambled after him, gripping the banister as he disappeared around a corner one flight below.

"Nathaniel? Nathaniel, please," she called out, but he was either out of earshot or ignoring her.

She hurried back to the bedchamber and threw on her dressing gown and slippers. It would be so like Nathaniel to jump headlong into a conflict that wasn't his. All those abolitionist meetings and paraphernalia lying about the house had seemed harmless enough—just talk, and talk never hurt anyone. Anyway, it wouldn't take long to persuade him to stay at home where he belonged. He could hardly leave her now.

By the time she entered the dining room he was already seated, newspaper held up to catch the light from the large bay of windows behind him. Mary wanted to snatch the thing out of his hands and tear it to shreds, but at that very moment Bridget came in with the tray. The girl stopped short when she saw her disheveled mistress.

At the sound of the clinking china, Nathaniel looked up. "Ah, here we are," he said. Then he saw Mary and frowned. "You're not dressed."

Mary pulled at the sides of her dressing gown, but she could no longer button it over her stomach. Bridget flushed and set the tray on the table. She quickly distributed its contents then disappeared into the kitchen, no doubt to report Mrs. Balsam's unprecedented state of undress to Mrs. Maggin.

"You cannot enlist, Nathaniel," Mary stated as she dragged a chair close to him and sat down.

"Of course I'll enlist. Those rebels cannot continue to go unchallenged while they trample our flag and defy our president. And you know how I feel about slavery. I thought you felt the same."

"You know I do. But there are plenty of young men who can fight. Men who are not mere months away from becoming a father."

"My brothers will be enlisting. My father was a military man. My grandfather fought in 1812. My great-grandfather fought in the Revolution. They did not balk at serving their country because the timing was inconvenient."

"But they lived in towns and had family nearby," she countered. "What am I to do when you're off to war? Run the farm by myself? Give birth to our child alone?"

Nathaniel laughed. "Don't be ridiculous, Mary. You're not alone. We're just a short train ride from Detroit. You could stay with my mother there if you like, or I'm sure she would come up to keep you company. John will run the farm and hire any extra help he may need, and there's time to get the corn planted before I leave. You needn't worry about that."

"John should go to war rather than you."

"Enough, Mary. I must go. It will only be a few months." Nathaniel patted her hand. "I may even be back before this baby is born." He turned his attention back to the newspaper.

The meal before them was consumed in silence as Nathaniel read and Mary argued with him in her head. But she could think of no angle that seemed to her to be more important than the impending birth of his firstborn child, which he had so easily dismissed.

Each day of the following week, preparations were made. The trunk was packed, food was prepared, corn was planted. They spoke little. Mary tried on several occasions to write a letter that might convince him to relent. But each one, so carefully reasoned in the first two paragraphs, devolved into begging by the third. And begging was something she did not do.

Mary did not go with Nathaniel when John Grouse drove him to the train station. Indeed, she could scarcely remove herself from the bed that morning to relieve her bladder. After she had crawled back under the covers, Nathaniel came to say his goodbyes. He leaned in close and whispered words of love and promises of his safe return, but she could do little more than nod.

All that day she drifted in and out of fitful sleep and stared at the new wallpaper, following the pattern from one end of the room to the other. When the failing light suggested evening, she heard the door creak open.

"For you, ma'am," came Bridget's tentative voice.

The girl walked in, a small piece of paper in her outstretched hand. Mary took the paper and glanced over the short message. Then she sat up.

"No," she whispered.

"What? What's wrong?"

"John Grouse has decided to enlist as well. He's sending back the carriage but is not coming with it."

Bridget's hand shot to her mouth. "Would you like me to send for Mrs. Balsam?"

In her distress, Mary almost said yes. But she looked into Bridget's wide blue eyes and put on a smile. "Mrs. Balsam has her own affairs to tend to, and I'll not tear her away from them out of my own apprehension over the days to come. We shall face this problem ourselves." She folded the note and handed it back to Bridget. "There is no reason I shouldn't be able to manage everything with some assistance from you and Mrs. Maggin. The corn is planted. We shan't need to do much with it until harvesttime, and by that time Nathaniel assures me he will have returned. He'll certainly be back by the time the winter wheat must be sown in October."

Bridget twisted the paper in her hands. "But what about the baby?"

"You may summon the midwife for me when it's time."

Bridget looked doubtful.

"My girl," Mary continued, "I would rather have a stranger deliver this baby than have my mother-in-law anywhere near me when the time comes. She would undoubtedly let me know everything I was doing wrong. Now then, Bridget," she said as she threw back her shoulders, "I'm famished. What does Mrs. Maggin have planned for supper?"

Later that evening, after a lonely meal of roasted rabbit in onion sauce, Mary retired to the library to look over Nathaniel's ledgers. He kept meticulous records, and Mary was determined that when he came home he would find that she had managed the farm well in his absence.

The sun was below the horizon when she heard the bell at the back door, then footsteps hurrying down the back stairs. Voices floated upon the still air, including a masculine one the likes of which Mary had never heard. It was understated and slow and yet somehow urgent. She stood at the library door and listened. Then she remembered that Nathaniel and John were both gone. All who were left in the house were three unarmed women, one of them carrying a child.

She cursed John Grouse under her breath, then scanned the library for some implement. She settled on one of the heavy silver candlesticks sitting on the mantel, a gift from her mother-in-law.

Outside the kitchen door she could distinguish Mrs. Maggin's gruff voice.

"You must leave this house at once."

Then that low, round, masculine voice again. "Please. Just a drink of water and a bit a bread for the journey."

"Not a crumb, and you're lucky I haven't called the master of the house down on your head." It was an empty threat, but the man needn't know it.

Mary pushed the oak door open a crack. Mrs. Maggin stood wielding a large knife with Bridget behind her, grasping at her skirts. A man stood just inside the back door, silhouetted against the twilight sky. His head was bare, his arms tight against his sides, his hands wringing some item in front of him. Then he brought a hand to his face in a gesture of tired despair. The movement apparently startled Mrs. Maggin, and she pointed the knife at him.

Mary burst in. "Mrs. Maggin, what is the meaning of this?"

The old cook kept her weapon trained on the man in the door. "This fugitive has come begging from your household, and I am simply sending him on his way."

"Fugitive?"

She took a closer look at the man. Tattered clothes, crumpled hat in his hand, no shoes despite the cold, damp night. But the man's most striking feature was his skin. It was dark brown, deep as midnight, and glistening with sweat.

"Get him inside this instant!" Mary commanded.

When no one moved, Mary hurried past the bedraggled man and shut the door against the coming night. She gave Mrs. Maggin a severe look. The woman lowered the knife but would not relinquish it.

"Please sit down," Mary said to the man. "Bridget!"

Bridget sprang into action, pulling out a chair before retreating once more behind her protector. The stranger turned fearful eyes upon each of them, and finally sat when Mary nodded at him.

"Mrs. Maggin, please get this man a glass of water at once. And get the leftover rabbit from supper."

Mrs. Maggin let the knife clatter onto the countertop and crossed her arms. "I'll do no such thing."

Mary met her cook's hard eyes. "I beg your pardon?"

"I'll serve Satan himself before I serve one of those—"

Mary raised a finger in the air. "Don't say it! Whatever vulgar slur is on your tongue, don't say it. Not in this house, not within these walls. If you are so high and mighty you won't serve one of God's children, I shan't have you serve me either. You may stay the night, but I suggest you use the short time you have left in this house to pack up your belongings." She pointed to the door.

Mrs. Maggin's arms dropped to her sides. "You don't mean that!"

"I surely do," Mary said, hands on hips. "Mr. Balsam would be livid with me if I kept you on after such a heartless display. You'll have your wages. Good night."

The old cook stood speechless, Bridget still frozen in place behind her. When she saw that her mistress was in earnest, she stalked out of the room, leaving Bridget cowering behind nothing at all.

"Bridget, water and food," Mary said.

As the girl hurried to do her bidding, Mary looked at the man who would not raise his eyes to meet hers. A jagged scar ran down his cheek and neck and disappeared under a filthy shirt that had perhaps once been white.

Bridget set down a glass of water from the basin and a plate of leftover rabbit and a slice of bread.

"The butter, Bridget," Mary said. Then to the man, "I'm sorry it is no longer hot."

"No, ma'am," he said into the plate.

"Please eat your fill and excuse me a moment." Mary pulled Bridget into the hallway. "Go upstairs and retrieve a set of clothes for this man. I'm sure there must be something old that Nathaniel left behind. Britches, shirt, stockings. If you don't see his old boots, they may be in the barn. Fetch them."

Bridget scuttled away and Mary stared at the kitchen door. It was one thing to read articles in the *Liberator* and listen to speeches, quite another to be imposed upon by a fugitive slave in the flesh. While she may not agree with the vile practices of her Southern countrymen, Mary did not care to be implicated in such a messy business as harboring an escaped slave. She needed to send him on his way as soon as possible.

When she entered the kitchen again, Mary found that the man was already cleaning the last bits of cold onion sauce from the plate with a crust of bread. The terrified expression she'd seen earlier had been supplanted by utter exhaustion.

"Bridget is gathering up some clothes for you."

The man stood up, bowed his head, and commenced wringing his defeated hat. "I couldn't take—"

She held up a hand. "Nonsense. You knocked at our door for a reason. The least you can do is take the charity we offer."

He nodded and looked at the floor.

Mary searched for something more to say. "Where are you from?"

"Don't know as I should say."

She nodded. "I understand."

He was taller than Nathaniel, broader in the shoulders and chest, and in all ways an imposing individual. Mary had heard that Southern whites were so afraid of slave uprisings that they prohibited groups of slaves from meeting together—even for church—without a white man present. Looking at the man before her, she understood why. What she didn't understand was why her Nathaniel was asked to sacrifice his life for people who seemed to lack only weapons. Slaves had numbers. They had motivation. Surely they had opportunities. Couldn't they be armed and allowed to fight for their own freedom as the Haitians had?

Then she heard Nathaniel's voice in her head. *What of the Union? What of honor? What of Christian duty?* Mary tried to believe in these things. But one of the people her husband sought to liberate now stood in her kitchen while Nathaniel was in Detroit, quite possibly preparing to fight in the very state from which this fugitive hailed. By the time Nathaniel got there, this man would be in Canada—free, no one shooting at him. And he hadn't even fought for it. Simply took an opportunity and ran away from home.

Mary fought back a tremble of resentment. "Is it quite terrible there?"

He looked her in the eye at last, and she was stunned by the depth of sorrow she read across his face.

The door swung open, and Bridget entered behind a pile of patched-up clothes and well-worn boots.

"Ah, here we are," Mary said with forced cheer. "Please take these things for your journey. Take them out to the barn to change. You may sleep out there for a few hours, if you must. I only ask that you leave before dawn and be careful that no one who may happen by on the road sees you. It's only fifty miles east to Port Huron. Go around the city to the south to cross the river. If you go north you'll run into Lake Huron and be trapped. On the other side of the river is Canada. You will be safe there."

"Yes, ma'am. Thank you."

"And of course you mustn't breathe a word of this to anyone."

The man nodded. "God bless you."

Mary hurried to the library, Bridget on her heels. Once they were inside, she shut the door and leaned on it. "Make sure he's out of the house and lock all the doors or I'll never be able to sleep."

The girl nodded.

"I know this is much to ask of you," Mary went on, "but you must keep watch out your back window as I can't see the barn from my room."

The girl looked frightened. "What should I watch for?"

"I'm not sure, but I feel it would be foolish not to watch."

If possible, Bridget's eyes grew even wider. "You don't suppose he'd steal a horse?"

Mary felt the blood drain from her face. "I hadn't thought of that. Let us pray he doesn't."

Mary tossed all through the night, questioning every decision she had made. Would Nathaniel have done the same? Perhaps she should go to Mrs. Maggin's room and apologize, ask the cook to stay. But by the time gray morning peeked through her windows, Mary had resolved to stand firm.

She found a weary Bridget alone in the kitchen. "Has Mrs. Maggin been down?"

"She's already left," Bridget said. "She gave me an address for you to send her pay."

"Good. And our . . . guest?"

Bridget shook her head. "I don't know. I haven't seen him this morning." She looked at her hands. "I fell asleep."

"Never mind that, Bridget. Of course you should sleep." Mary looked around the room. "Hand me those extra biscuits."

Bridget put a biscuit in each of her mistress's hands. Mary walked out to the barn with more poise than she felt and slid back the heavy door with an elbow. "Hello?"

When no one answered she checked the stalls. The horses stomped. The cow waited to be milked. The pigs were all accounted for. From outside she heard the quarrelsome sound of chickens. The clothing she had asked Bridget to gather sat in a neat stack upon a bale of hay. The old boots were nowhere to be found.

All at once, Mary became aware of the smell of manure and the restless stirrings of hungry animals. Inside her womb the baby moved. She put the biscuits in her pockets, took up a pitchfork, and squared her shoulders. Then she squeezed her eyes shut and tried to remember what she'd seen Nathaniel do with a pitchfork.

SEVEN

Lapeer County, August

Nora pointed toward a half-open door on the west wall of her bedroom and said, "Here's my workroom."

I dutifully followed her into a small back room. Three sewing machines of varying ages—none of them new—sat upon tables. Long metal racks, bowed by the weight of the many clothes that hung on them, crouched over the machines like buzzards. Pins encircled the cuffs of pants and the arms of jackets, emerged from pincushions, clung to magnets. And everywhere there was fabric. Piles and piles of it.

I took one experimental step into the crowded room and tripped. My hand found a stack of fabric and pulled it all onto the floor with me.

"Hey!" Nora yelled.

I looked up, mortified, only to find that she was yelling not at me but at the swiftly retreating orange cat that had tripped me. I picked myself up off the floor and began re-creating the stacks I'd demolished.

"I'm so sorry!" I said.

"Never mind that. That cat. He knows he's not allowed in

here." Nora looked at the wobbly tower I'd constructed. "I'm not sure just what to do with all of this."

"You must sew an awful lot."

"No, I don't sew anymore."

I glanced around what was so obviously a sewing room, tiny alarm bells ringing in my head on Barb's behalf.

She looked hopeful. "Do you sew, Elizabeth?"

"No. I can barely tie my shoes. I'm a lost cause when it comes to the domestic arts."

"Everyone has different gifts. I understand your gift is with words."

"Maybe. But it's kind of hard to use it when you don't have a job anymore."

"Perhaps," she said in a doubtful tone. "Let's eat some dinner and you'll see what gift I don't have."

I would have liked to help prepare our meal—there was nothing else to do, after all—but Nora insisted I sit at the kitchen table while she cooked spaghetti with marinara sauce. She toasted white bread, buttered it, and sprinkled it with a little garlic salt. It was a simple meal, but I was happy to see that the woman could still manage to feed herself. And it was better than the microwave dinners and fast food I had been eating so often of late.

"When you cook for just one you kind of lose the knack," she said.

"I wouldn't know. I never had the knack. This is perfect."

"You won't think so when you get it three times a week." She laughed.

"I hope you don't think I came here expecting you to be slaving over a hot stove for me all day. I'm here more to look after you than for you to look after me."

The moment I said it I wished the words back into my mouth. Nora's expression soured.

"Elizabeth, I was under the impression that you had lost your job and you needed a place to stay and some time to think about what you'd like to do next with your life. Did Barb lead you to believe I needed a nursemaid?"

I shook my head. "No, I don't know why I said that just now. She never said anything to me of your situation except that you lived alone far from town and could probably use some help around the house." I hated lying to her, but more than that I hated how easily lies had rolled off my tongue since I'd started my undercover investigation of Judge Sharpe.

She nodded. "So she didn't tell you about my drinking?"

Drinking?

"Or my sleepwalking?" she continued. "Or the various wanderers I've invited into this house only to murder them in their sleep and bury them in the backyard?"

"What?"

She rolled her eyes. "Elizabeth, I'm a perfectly capable and healthy person in control of my wits, despite my age. Let's agree to treat each other as adults. I don't need a babysitter. The only thing I might be in need of is some company."

I silently cursed Barb for putting me in this position. Nora was just lonely, that's all. I could relate. It was as easy to be alone in a city of 700,000 people as it was in a farmhouse in the middle of nowhere.

The orange cat walked into the kitchen just then, jumped up on the chair across the table, and glowered at me.

"What's your cat's name?" I said to change the subject.

"Matthew. My cats are always Matthew."

The doorbell rang and Nora rose to answer it. When I looked back at Matthew he was gone. I glanced around the room, which was still impeccably clean despite dinner preparations. Nora had washed each dish as she went, leaving me nothing to clean up.

"Elizabeth," Nora said as she reentered the kitchen with a short stack of fabric in her hands, "this is Brenda Morris. Brenda, this is my great-niece Elizabeth Balsam."

I rose to shake the hand of the sharply dressed woman who followed my aunt.

"Brenda's one of my regulars."

My face must have registered blankness.

"I do alterations for her."

"Me and the rest of the county," Brenda said. "You should have been here in the spring. That's when she gets all the prom girls and June brides and all their bridesmaids. It's a madhouse."

I struggled to picture the parlor overrun by tittering girls. This house was a museum and Nora its curator. It seemed that with little effort I might discover velvet ropes tucked in some closet, ready to come out at any moment to keep humanity at bay.

"Ms. Rich did my daughter Kelli's wedding three years ago, and it was gorgeous!"

"That was none of my doing," Nora said. "You have a beautiful daughter who has lovely friends and good taste. I just made sure no one looked sloppy, that's all."

Brenda crossed her fingers on both hands. "It will be Katie's turn pretty soon."

"No doubt about it," Nora said with a pat on the woman's shoulder.

"I better get moving," Brenda said. "I'm running late."

"Your jacket is hanging on the workroom door."

"Jacket? I thought you were hemming that teal dress for me?"

Nora looked momentarily confused but recovered. "Yes, yes. The dress. That's what I meant."

Brenda smiled. "It was so nice to meet you, Elizabeth! I hope you can use that fabric, Nora."

They disappeared through the swinging door.

"I thought you didn't sew anymore," I said when Nora came back into the kitchen.

"I don't. I just do alterations and mend things."

"That's not sewing?"

"There's sewing involved. But it's not the same. Sewing is making something from scratch. I don't do that anymore. I just do repairs these days. The quilt in your room was my last true creation."

"Why?"

She gave her head a little shake. "I just haven't been in the mood. Alterations keep me plenty busy. Between that and my pension from the school system, I should be able to keep the electricity and water on until I die."

Except for my Dana wardrobe, I'd never thought much about clothes. I looked closely for the first time at what my aunt was wearing on this humid August day. Her white pants were long, cuffed, and pressed to a crisp crease down the center of each wide leg. Her lightweight blue button-up shirt was tucked securely into her waistband and held there by a stylish belt. She was entirely too well dressed to live in the boondocks.

"Were you a teacher?"

"No. Secretary. Thirty years. Would you mind taking this fabric up to the big closet in the blue room? There may be a smidge more space in that one."

Upstairs I found a room with pale blue walls. The bed was covered with a quilt made of strips of blue fabric in washed-out stripes, checks, and plaids, and the closet was filled to the gills. I slid Brenda's unwanted gift into place and quickly shut the doors to keep it from escaping. Then I went snooping.

Beautiful quilts graced every bed in every room. I pulled open each dresser drawer, peeked into every closet, and found stacks and stacks of fabric like ancient layers of sediment. If she didn't sew, why did she have all this fabric? It appeared that Nora was a prime candidate for one of those hideous reality TV shows about demented people who amass great hordes of stuff for no apparent reason.

"Elizabeth," I heard my aunt call from somewhere below. "Did you get lost?"

I found her just outside the back door of the kitchen, silhouetted by the beguiling light of early evening.

"I wanted to show you the gardens before the sun goes down," she said. "I'm afraid the formal garden is all but gone. It's been so long since I had the time or inclination to fuss with it. But the field is pretty and it takes care of itself."

I followed her through the screen door and onto a wide lawn that ended where the field began.

She motioned to the wildflowers nodding in the light breeze. "All of this used to be planted with crops. When it was a functioning farm, those trees weren't there. There was corn and wheat and an apple orchard way, way out there." She waved at the twisted remains of a dilapidated wooden structure surrounded by bent and rusted wire. "That's the old chicken coop. And that pile of rubble out a ways in the field was the barn. It fell down about ten or fifteen years ago."

I shielded my eyes against the sinking sun as we ambled on to a large square of weathered wooden fencing.

Nora rested her wrinkled hand upon a picket. "This was the herb garden. Mostly perennial herbs, but some you have to plant every year—or they seed themselves. Nowadays, they're so grown over with weeds you can't tell what's what, and my eyes aren't as good as they used to be, so I stick to buying dried herbs from the store. There's a lot out here that's not for cooking. Some medicinal herbs. I've never known what to do with any of those. Some of them you probably shouldn't mess with."

I looked over the sad, tangled patch of ground.

"Do you like gardening?" she asked.

"I like gardens," I said. "I never had a real one. I like the idea of gardening."

Nora gave me an appraising look. "I'll tell you what, Elizabeth. I'm going to give you a job to do. You can't sit around the house doing nothing while you wait for a job offer, and I doubt you want to. So here's your project. Look through the books on the dining room shelves and find the ones on gardening and herbs and such. I know there are some there. You start studying those, and then see what you can make of this herb garden."

Did everyone in the world have a special task for me? Mr. Rich and his artifacts, Barb and her busybodying. Still, I couldn't spend every waking moment on those things, and I was here to help out, after all. It would be nice to expend some energy on a project with a positive and palpable end result rather than simply helping with laundry and cataloging all the reasons my great-aunt shouldn't be living alone. I could work in the garden by day and work on my résumé and my story by night.

"That sounds fun."

"It won't be any fun pulling those weeds." She laughed. "They've been there a long time and the roots run deep." She headed toward the house.

"Hey, what's the story with this tree?" I asked, hanging back.

Nora stopped walking and looked at me with eyes that had lost their sparkle. "I noticed it struggling a few years ago. I got a man out here to treat it. It's a catalpa tree. William planted it. They always leaf out late, so this spring I had been holding out hope it would make it a little longer, just until I was gone. But it's pretty clear to me that it's dead now."

The colossal, denuded tree stood a little to the south of the herb garden. Not far from the ground, its immense trunk had split, looking like two massive arms lifted up to the heavens. I squinted at the topmost branches. One trunk was most definitely dead. The other clung tenuously to life.

"I think there's still one branch with leaves."

Nora trained her eyes skyward and adjusted her glasses, and while she didn't smile, she no longer looked quite so dismal.

"Still," I said, "that's too bad. It looks like it was a beautiful tree."

"It sure was a messy one," she said, "but yes . . . it was beautiful."

EIGHT

Bloomfield Hills, April 1963

"It looks like the artist found a garbage can, glued its contents to a board, and used a dead cat to smudge some paint on it. I could have made this—if I were a lunatic."

Nora let the mixed media painting in her hands drop a little and felt her ire rise.

"What did you pay for this monstrosity?" her father asked.

"It was very reasonable."

"If it were anything other than free, it couldn't be that."

Nora let out an exasperated sigh. "You told me to choose things that were less pedestrian, more eye-catching. I was trying to follow your advice. Anyway, I like it." She looked around at the bare walls of her new apartment. "Though I'm still not sure where to put it."

"How about the dumpster out back? Send it back where it came from. I cannot believe you would use the money I gave you for investing on this junk."

Nora would not tell her father that she had spent most of that money on a camera for a stranger, whom he apparently despised, and so had less than she'd hoped to spend on an actual piece of art.

"What kind of a gallery would display something like that?" he continued.

"It was at the Detroit Artists Market. They just opened a special exhibit of Cass Corridor artists. It's very avant-garde. Very cutting edge."

Daniel Balsam shook his head. "I don't know where I went wrong with you."

The phrase had been uttered so many times since she'd turned thirteen, she had begun to take it as a compliment.

"Anyway, get your clubs. We'll be late for our tee time."

Nora sighed and thought that perhaps she could enjoy golf if she played with anyone other than her father.

"Stop choking the club, Nora. It's not a baseball bat."

"Your feet should be farther apart."

"You're slicing, Nora."

"Too much power. Look how close you are to the hole. Lightly, lightly."

She endured it all in silence as it was the only time they spent together without her mother. Nora preferred her father's disapproval of her taste in art or her backswing to her mother's brand of criticism, which tended toward the very personal.

Just two weeks earlier, as they shopped for a new Easter dress, Mallory had frowned at her daughter's hips in the mirror and declared, "I'm sorry, honey, but you just can't wear sheath dresses. You'll have to get the yellow one with the full skirt even if it does make you look washed-out." Nora had wanted to sew her own Easter dress that year, but a heavy schedule of volunteering and social calls made it difficult to find the time, so it hung unfinished in her closet.

"Your mother wants you to come back to the house with me when we're done here," Daniel said as they left for the golf course. "Something about some charity event or other."

"I have plans with Diane tonight."

"It will just take a moment."

It wouldn't, and they both knew it.

Nora finished their eighteen holes two under par and slid her putter back into her bag. Her father loaded the bags on the cart, and they headed for the clubhouse.

"Nice job out there today," Daniel said.

"Thanks." Nora looked out at the lush green grass and smiled.

"Hey!" her father shouted. "Ray!" He lifted a hand in greeting to his favorite groundskeeper and slowed the cart to a stop.

"Mr. Balsam, Miss Balsam," Ray said as he tipped his hat to reveal a head of tightly curled black hair that had just a little more gray in it than last year. "Good to see you both out here this fine afternoon."

"Been waiting for weather like this," Daniel said as he shook Ray's weathered hand.

"You and me both, sir." Ray gave Nora a nod. "Glad to see you survived the winter, miss."

Nora smiled. "Barely. I thought I might go mad in February."

"Mm-hmm. We're all a little mad in February." Ray laughed.

"I thought you were supposed to be managing this year, and here you are out raking the sand and trimming the bushes," Daniel said.

Ray glanced around. "Boss just don't think a Negro can do the job, I guess."

Daniel scowled. "I've half a mind to write a letter."

Ray put up his hand. "Don't go doing that. I like my job and I'd like to keep it. I'll see you two again soon, right, Miss Balsam?"

"Probably next week."

"Excellent. You both have a good evening now."

Ray went back to his duties and Daniel drove on, frowning the entire way.

"What's the matter?" Nora asked.

"Ray's been here fifteen years. He should be a manager by now."

Nora tried to reconcile the egalitarian before her with the angry man in the photo. "You think *he* could be a manager?"

"Of course! If a man has the experience, the color of his skin shouldn't matter."

Nora scoffed at his hypocrisy.

"What?"

"Nothing."

"Don't be such an elitist, Nora. It's unbecoming."

Nora bit her tongue all the way to her parents' house. The garage was empty when she and her father pulled in.

"Where's the Corvette?"

"Your mother has it."

"I thought you said she needed to ask me something."

"She'll be home soon."

Nora rolled her eyes and trudged into the kitchen.

"Hello, Miss Nora. Good to see you. How did you do your first time out this season?" Wanda pulled a clean glass from the cupboard and began running the cold water before Nora even had time to ask for a drink.

"Two under par."

Wanda flashed a grin. "Nice job, girl." She set the water down in front of Nora and wiped her hands on her apron. "Having roast tonight."

"That seems pretty elaborate for just Mom and Dad."

"That's what your mother wanted. She's expecting guests." Wanda pulled open a drawer and counted out four forks, four knives, and four spoons. "I assume you're one of them?"

"I have plans tonight."

Wanda laughed. "Your mama got plans too."

She rarely slipped into such informal speech anymore—and never in the presence of Mallory Balsam. As a child Nora had been fascinated by the maid's two personas.

"Why do you talk like that?" she'd asked when she was five years old.

"Like what?"

"All funny like that. Like you don't know how to talk."

Wanda laughed. "Honey, I speak two languages."

"You do?"

"Yes, I do." She leaned down to Nora's height and whispered conspiratorially, "Sometimes I forget where I am and I use the wrong one. What you just heard there was my home language."

Little Nora chewed on this a moment. "Where do you live?"

"I live in Detroit."

"Don't they speak English there?"

"Sure do. And here in Bloomfield Hills they speak Snobbish."

Wanda had laughed at her own joke, thinking perhaps that Nora was too little to understand it or repeat it. And she was. But later in life that conversation resurfaced in Nora's memory and she did understand. She lived in a city divided. There was us. And there was them.

"Do you need help with anything?" Nora asked as Wanda arranged the silverware on the table.

"You can take these flowers into the kitchen and cut off the dead ones if you want."

Nora retrieved the vase from the center of the dining room table and set it on the kitchen counter. She opened and closed three drawers before finding the scissors.

"You've rearranged everything."

"Your mother thought it made more sense this way."

"But you're the one who uses it."

Wanda muttered something Nora couldn't quite make out. The sound of a door opening put an end to Wanda's commentary, whatever it was. Mallory Balsam's arrival in the kitchen was like a wasp visiting a picnic. Maybe if they just kept still, she would get bored and go away.

"Evening, Mrs. Balsam."

Mallory's answer to this greeting was a heavy sigh. She plunked her purse onto the counter and tossed a set of keys next to it. "Wanda, I wonder if you would be a dear and see if you can get the box out of Mr. Balsam's car. The shop boy somehow got it in there, but I can't get the infernal thing out now. I don't know why he couldn't have gotten an Impala."

"Yes, ma'am." Wanda disappeared into the garage.

Mallory patted her hair and looked at her daughter with disapproval. "Nora, what are you doing?"

"I'm just freshening up the centerpiece."

Mallory waved her away. "Wanda can do that."

Nora continued to trim browned petals and leaves from the arrangement.

"Oh, never mind," Mallory said, pinching the bridge of her nose with two perfectly manicured fingers. "I can't argue with you right now. I've had a trial of a day. Where is your father?"

"He went up to shower and change."

Mallory took hold of her daughter's shoulders and spun her around. "You're not wearing that to dinner, are you?"

Nora looked down at her cropped pants and golf shirt. "I hadn't planned on it, no. Diane and I are going out tonight, but Dad said you had to ask me something about a charity event."

Mallory waved her hand. "We can talk about that later. Why didn't you bring other clothes?"

Nora went back to the centerpiece and lopped off the head of a dying rose. "I didn't even know I'd be coming here today."

Mallory's nails drummed on the counter. "I guess there may be something suitable left in your closet you could wear."

Nora closed her eyes and turned her face to the ceiling, bracing herself for what was coming. "For what?"

"For dinner, of course."

"I told you, I have plans."

A buzzer sounded. Nora walked over to the stove and turned it off, then opened the door to the garage. "Wanda? The buzzer went off! What should we do?"

No answer. Nora walked back into the kitchen, but Mallory guided her out the other way.

"Go on up to your room and see if you can find something to wear. And do something with your hair."

"But—"

"Diane will understand. I need you here tonight. Now go."

Nora headed for the stairs. On her way up she met Wanda coming down. "A buzzer went off."

In her old bedroom, a few forgotten dresses hung limply in the dark corners of the closet. Nora flipped through them and considered the four places Wanda had been setting at the table. A few minutes later, her hair brushed but not particularly becoming, Nora walked down the stairs in a too-formal green taffeta dress just as the doorbell was ringing. Now she wouldn't even have time to call Diane to apologize for standing her up. Balsam house rules were unbending when it came to entertaining, and the primary one was that you never leave your guest. When Nora opened the door, she was met with a tall, handsome, undoubtedly eligible young man, and everything became clear.

"You must be Nora," the man said, his eyes roaming her body. "I'm Michael."

The next two hours traveled the spectrum of boring to embarrassing, as Mallory Balsam attempted to sell Nora to a potential husband and Daniel Balsam tried to determine how much of his great-uncle's fortune Michael Kresge might have at his disposal.

When the roast and potatoes and pie and coffee were all consumed and a lull developed in the conversation, Nora jumped in. "Mother, I need to get up early tomorrow. Can you take me home now?"

"I can take you," Michael offered.

"Lovely." Mallory beamed before Nora could utter a word. "That's so kind of you, Michael."

The drive was made in awkward silence, and Nora wondered if Michael realized the plans her mother had for him. When he stopped in front of Nora's apartment, she put her hand on the car door and said a quick but polite thank-you.

"That's it?" Michael said.

"What do you mean?"

"Thank you, good night, and then you're gone? No time for a little good-night kiss?"

"I hardly know you."

He leaned closer. "How about you get to know me then?"

Before Nora knew what was happening, he'd grabbed the back of her neck and captured her lips with his. She pushed on his chest until he released her.

"Come on!" he intoned with a playful leer.

Nora slipped out of his grasp, escaped to the sidewalk, and slammed the door shut. Her rejected chauffeur sped off in anger, tearing the hem of her taffeta dress where it had caught in the door. Nora stomped up the steps to her apartment, ready to throw the dress in the garbage can the moment she got inside. Then she remembered that her golf clubs were in Michael Kresge's trunk. She stifled a scream and pounded on her door in frustration. The phone rang inside.

Nora scrambled for her keys and made it to the phone on the fourth ring, expecting to hear Diane's irritated voice wondering where she'd been and what was so important that she stood up her best friend.

Instead a vaguely familiar silky voice awaited her on the other end of the line.

"William?"

NINE

Lapeer County, August 1861

The barn door squeaked, drawing Mary from the dark precipice of sleep and back to the light.

"Ma'am?"

Mary pushed herself up on one elbow and swiped at a piece of hay that stuck to the trail of drool on her cheek. "Yes, Bridget?"

"I have letters for you."

She sat up as straight as she could, resting her pregnant belly upon her thighs. "Anything from Mr. Balsam?" The question was automatic, uttered without much thought to the answer that would follow. It was nearly always no.

"Yes." Bridget reached out for her mistress's hand to help her up, but Mary waved her away.

"Where is it?"

The girl fumbled through her apron pockets and produced a small envelope. "But it's not the only thing."

Mary snatched up the envelope, aching to hold anything Nathaniel had touched. "My girl, all I want in this life is a word from my husband. It's been two weeks since that horrendous battle was in the papers, and this is the first certain sign I've had that he is alive."

"But there's a package. A trunk. A man brought it for me on his wagon, and he is waiting at the house to take it down. It's very heavy."

Mary struggled to her feet. "What on earth can it be?" But in her mind she feared she knew. Letters might be delayed in times of war. Was it possible that the trunk was Nathaniel's? That it contained his effects, sent back after his death, and that the letter in her hand had been penned in haste the night before battle? That he might be dead even now? With every step toward the house, Mary's heartbeat quickened, both at the effort it now took to do such a simple thing as walk twenty yards and at the dread that was building in her chest.

As she rounded the front of the house and the wagon came into view, her knees buckled. It was Nathaniel's trunk.

Bridget caught her arm and slung it around her own sturdy shoulders. "This is too much strain for you. You need to sit down. You've been working too hard for any woman, let alone one in your condition."

Soon Mary found herself seated in the parlor as Bridget helped the man drag in the heavy trunk.

"I trust you have the key?" the man said as he wiped the sweat from his brow.

"I do. Thank you, sir. Bridget, please find this nice man something to eat in the kitchen and pay him from my reticule."

"I thank you for the pay," the man said, "but I'm afraid I must pass on the food. I need to get back to town."

Moments later, the two women sat staring at the trunk as the sound of the horses' hooves faded.

Mary forced her breath into an even rhythm. "Fetch the spare key from Mr. Balsam's desk drawer, please."

Bridget hurried off, and Mary looked at the envelope in her shaking hands. Which should she open first? The letter that was surely meant to arrive before whatever heartache the trunk held? Or should she save the last words of her husband to her as a small comfort after facing the reality of his death?

Bridget returned too quickly and Mary was still undecided. With the letter in one hand and the key in the other, she felt on the brink of tears.

"Perhaps you should read the letter first," Mary suggested, holding it out to Bridget.

"Heavens, no! I wouldn't dare."

"I don't know—" Her voice cracked. She breathed deeply. "I don't know how I could bear it if he—which should I open?"

"The trunk."

The answer came in a muffled voice that didn't belong to her maid.

Mary's eyes locked upon the trunk, then flashed to Bridget's. She slid to the floor, thrust the key into the lock, and flung open the lid. The act released the foul stench of urine into the parlor, but it was the sight of the contents rather than the smell that shocked the senses. Both women screamed.

Inside the trunk, folded up into a grotesque shape and littered with bloodied straw, was the lacerated body of a Negro man. His eyes squinted against the sudden light, and he took a shuddering, groaning breath. Bridget was still screaming.

"Stop, Bridget! Stop!"

The girl clapped her hands hard over her mouth and exchanged her screams for shallow wheezing.

Mary attempted to gather her scattered wits. "Wh-who are you?"

The man groaned again and twisted in the cramped space. Scarred brown fingers curled over the edge of the trunk.

Mary reached for them. "Bridget, help!"

Together they extracted the man and laid him out upon the floor. He moaned as joints that had been bent at severe angles for who knew how long struggled to straighten themselves.

Straw was everywhere, stained red and sticking in clumps. Mary snapped her fingers at a pillow, and Bridget helped her slide it beneath the man's bleeding head, then ran for water.

"Who are you?" Mary asked again.

The man coughed. "Mr. Balsam . . ."

"You've seen Nathaniel? Where? Where was he? When did you see him? Were you in the battle?" Then she remembered the letter. She tore open the envelope and unfolded three small pieces of paper, all graced with her husband's distinct penmanship.

My Darling Mary,

I know you are anxious for news of how I fare, but before I share with you my adventures south of the Ohio River, I must mention a practical matter. I've sent you a large package, and I hope that this letter reaches you ahead of it. I've devised a clever way of keeping my belongings in a smaller space and so have sent my trunk home to you. Please open it immediately and remove the contents, for nothing could abide such confinement for long, and its contents are precious to me. They came to me here in Maryland from parts south, and though they were damaged I vowed to myself that they should find a place in our home, even if just for a time. They will surely be a help to you, and I know that you will take good care of them.

I am sure you read in the newspapers of the Union's troubles at Bull Run. I did as well. I was not there and, as you can plainly see, am very much alive and well. However, our cause is floundering. Thus—and I know it will come as a cruel disappointment—I have decided to reenlist. I know you expected me home at the end of my three-month enlistment, but I've not yet had the opportunity to fight for the cause, and I would feel disgraced coming home with nothing to show for my time beyond a few amusing stories of our training camp. I am sure that when you see what I have sent you, you will not begrudge me the chance to fight. Do not despair. God has seen the end of this war—indeed, He has written it.

Now, my dearest one, it is with tears in my eyes that I close this letter to you. I know it is a bitter thing to hear that I will not be home to kiss our baby when it is born. But I want this child—and all the many children we will have—to live in a country that is united in truth and justice, and to know that their father did not retreat in the face of the great evil of slavery but fought to destroy it. That is the legacy I desire for our family. And I must, for a time, put this above my desire to see you and touch you again.

Your Loving Husband,
Nathaniel
August 1, 1861

Mary looked up from the letter, her vision clouded by tears. Bridget was steadying the broken man before her as he attempted to slake his thirst. He was shorter and slighter of build than the fugitive slave she had met back in the spring, but Mary still did not see how he had managed to fit into the space of the trunk. What terrors could possess someone to commit himself to what might become his coffin, to risk death as nameless cargo aboard a northbound train? What if someone had opened the trunk en route? What if delivery had been delayed and the man had suffocated? Any number of dreadful things might have happened in this desperate escape.

Mary felt a sharp pain in her abdomen and pressed her hand against her side. She wanted the full story from this man—to hear every word he had exchanged with Nathaniel—but even in times of war one must attempt to retain some sense of decorum. Perhaps especially in such times.

"Bridget, will you please prepare a bath for . . . I'm sorry, what is your name?"

"George," the man said in a still-parched voice.

"Please prepare a bath in the kitchen for George and then freshen the pitcher in my bedchamber for me. And we must take this trunk outside at once."

George attempted to stand.

"No, no. You stay there. We can manage it now that it's empty. Bridget?"

The girl helped her off the floor. They closed the lid to suppress the rank odor and each grasped a handle.

"Let's take it straight back through the kitchen," Mary said, "and leave it open in the yard. We'll deal with it later."

When Mary hoisted up her side of the trunk, the sharp pain in her belly returned and she sucked in a breath between clenched teeth.

Bridget looked at her with concern. "Ma'am?"

"It's fine, Bridget. Come, let us dispense with this task."

They hobbled down the hall and through three doors before they reached the backyard. Mary dropped her end.

"What is it?" Bridget asked. "Are you okay?"

"Yes, fine. Just a little discomfort. Though I'm sure it is nothing compared to what that man went through. Do you think the trunk can be saved?"

"I'll have to rip the lining out," Bridget said. "Then it can be scoured and aired."

"The lining can be replaced. I've a green silk gown I'm sure I'll never have the shape or the occasion to wear again. We can use that. Be sure to remove the bottom panel. There is a hidden compartment beneath it for important papers. If you don't clean it out, the smell will haunt the trunk forever. Draw the bath and fetch me some fresh water for the pitcher. Then you can start on this."

The girl ran off to gather supplies, and Mary crept back to

the parlor, keeping one hand on the wall for balance. George was standing, two fingertips touching the very edge of a table to steady himself. They were snatched back up the moment he noticed her in the doorway. He clasped his hands and seemed to be awaiting instruction.

She lowered herself onto the settee. "Won't you sit down?"

"No, ma'am. I'd soil it."

She nodded. Of course. The man's clothes would have to be boiled.

She was unsure what to say next. If she had previously thought that her first interaction with a fugitive slave was the most uncomfortable conversation of her life, she knew now that it was infinitely more difficult to find something appropriate to say to a man who had been delivered to her house in a trunk.

"We'll get a meal ready for you as soon as we can after you've had a chance to clean up. You can rest a bit and then be on your way tonight."

George nodded. "Thank you, ma'am." He was silent a moment, then said, "Mr. Balsam say you have a man name of John Grouse can loan me a set of clothes. Said he about my height."

Mary gritted her teeth, still as angry as she ever was about John Grouse's abandonment. "We did have a man here by that name, but he enlisted. I haven't heard from him since. I'll have Bridget fetch you something from Mr. Balsam's wardrobe when she's drawn the bath."

"Just you and the girl and the cook, then?"

"No," Mary admitted with a regretful tone. "Mrs. Maggin was dismissed in April."

"That ain't no good. How you farmin'? You's lucky I come when I did."

Mary was about to respond to this bold pronouncement when Bridget entered.

"The bath is nearly ready."

"Then I think we shall all retire for a time. Bridget, please get a set of clothes for George and take his outside. I'll be down to help with dinner once our guest has had a chance to clean up."

She walked out to the front hall and took a long look up the staircase. She grasped the banister and took the first step, then the next, then the next. Each was a study in self-control. She had hidden the pains from Bridget for a month, despite the fact that they had been building in frequency and intensity, and now she was determined to make it up those steps.

"Mrs. Balsam!" Bridget exclaimed from behind her. "You're bleeding!"

Mary turned to look. Drops of blood led from her left foot down the stairs to the parlor door.

"I just stepped in some of that straw, Bridget. I should have been more careful. Now you'll be scrubbing blood out of the carpet here too. But not now. I could use your help. I'm very tired."

Bridget scrambled up the steps to her mistress. After a few steps more, she looked back. "If you'd stepped in something, there would be less and less of it as you walked, but the spots are getting bigger."

"Just a little further, Bridget." But even as she said it, Mary felt her head swim. The heat, the climb, the trunk, the man, the blood. All of it circled around until it coalesced into a leaden weight.

Then the world went black.

TEN

Lapeer County, August

Whoever had amassed the library in Aunt Nora's house was certainly interested in horticulture—though not, it would seem, in organizing things in any discernible way. After scanning every spine in the bookshelves, I found more than a dozen volumes about plants and gardening. I was delivering this tower of tomes to my bedside as Nora was retiring for the night.

"I rarely manage to make it past eight o'clock these days," she said. "You'll be on your own at night. I hope you don't mind."

"Not at all."

Upstairs I deposited the books on the bed, but reading would have to wait until I unpacked. I opened the armoire, ready to hang up my clothes, and a waterfall of fabric came pouring down at my feet. Of course.

I dumped my clothes on the bed and transferred the fabric into my now empty suitcases. I hung up some clothes, tucked the camera bag in the back corner of the armoire, and faced the dresser. Drawer by drawer, I purged it of its contents. Most fit into the boxes that had transported my books, my laptop, and a few tokens of childhood I kept for nostalgia's sake.

I still had one drawer left to go when I ran out of boxes. I thought of the steep stairs I'd seen earlier that must lead to the attic. If Nora no longer sewed, I could just bring all of this up there. And if I was lucky, I might find another box.

I pulled one suitcase, step by awkward step, up the attic stairs and ran my hands along the walls. No switch. A sudden tickle on my forehead had me ducking before I realized it was a light chain. My fingers found it swinging through the air and pulled. The light flickered on, throwing a weak yellow glow under the eaves to reveal—were those . . . beds?

Yes, those were definitely beds. Perhaps a dozen or more narrow wood-framed cots topped with dusty mattresses were lined up on either side of me, all the way to the far wall, where a large window framed the sky. Beneath the window was a steamer trunk.

Intense curiosity overriding any respect for Nora's privacy, I knelt down and tried the lid. Locked. Disappointed, I tucked the suitcase neatly between two beds and went down for the rest. By the time I pushed the last box into place, my face and back were slicked with sweat. I reorganized some old Christmas decorations, freeing up one box for the last of the fabric.

Piece by piece by piece, I emptied the last dresser drawer of its contents until my fingernails scraped the wood bottom. And then they scraped something else. Something metallic. I looked in the bottom of the drawer and there, to my great delight, was a key.

With the last box in my hands and my heart in my throat, I climbed the narrow stairs to the attic. I shoved the box into place beside the others and knelt down before the trunk. Despite the duplicitous activities in which I'd recently taken part at the behest of the spineless Jack McKnight, I had never felt so like a spy. I pulled the key from my pocket and braced myself for the moment of revelation I knew was coming.

But it didn't fit.

In fact, it wasn't even close to fitting. One critical glance revealed why. The key I held was modern; the keyhole in the trunk was shaped for one of those old-timey lever lock keys you might see hanging from a medieval jailer's comically oversized key ring.

Disappointed and exhausted, I settled into bed and checked my phone out of habit. Oh yeah. No service. No Facebook. No Twitter. No news. No nothing. I experienced a brief moment of panic, akin, I imagine, to any other kind of addict realizing that he was out of cigarettes or booze or heroin. Then I turned my phone off for the first time since I'd bought it. I didn't need the outside world. Not tonight. I had no schedule, no deadline, no responsibilities. I could relax. I just had to work at it.

I flipped through the pages of an old herbal encyclopedia of various useful, if sometimes deadly, plants and imagined what I would find growing within that weathered picket fence out back. It didn't take long for my eyes to get so heavy that I couldn't focus. I shut the book, turned off the lamp, and was asleep within minutes.

"William cuts the grass every couple weeks," Nora said over oatmeal the next morning, "but the gardening tools haven't been used in quite some time. I think the clippers are down in the cellar. And a shovel and a few other things. If you need something and can't find it, just let me know. I'll give you some money and you can go buy what you need."

"Is that a neighbor?"

Nora looked out the window. "Who?"

"The guy who cuts the grass."

"No. He works for a landscaping company."

That would explain why he did such a poor job "freshening up" my bedroom. Thoughts of my dusty room became thoughts of the dusty old cots in the attic.

"Hey, what's the deal with the beds in the attic? Was this place a hospital at some point?"

Nora stared blankly at me for a moment, then the shutters on her eyes lifted. "Oh, the cots? I'd nearly forgotten about those. That's a bit of a long story. Why don't I tell you about it some evening after dinner? We both have work to do right now."

And without another word, she was gone.

The cellar was cobwebby and damp, and I had to duck to clear the jerry-rigged network of pipes and ducts along the low ceiling. A dead light bulb stuck impotently out of its socket, and weak daylight struggled through small transom windows streaked with grime. The floor was nothing more than packed dirt, and the walls were just stones heaped upon each other and slathered with crumbling mortar. I had never been claustrophobic, but I was certain that prolonged time in this space had the potential to make me so.

A rusty shovel and hoe rested against the wall near an old washer and dryer, hedge clippers and a trowel hung from nails in a joist. I rattled through an old gray toolbox and came up with a pair of pruning shears. Then I noticed a door beneath the stairs. Perhaps there might be something useful behind it.

But the room was locked. With a padlock. Last night's discovery of the key rushed back to the front of my mind. It was upstairs in the bedside table drawer. I filed this away for later and walked out into the gathering sunlight of late morning.

I breathed in the clear blue sky, the dancing pollen, the dew-wet grass. It smelled invigorating, not at all like the fog of exhaust I was used to. When I tried the garden gate it stuck firm, kept in place by a rusty latch and drifted dirt and the spiny, grasping tendrils of some creeping vine. After some pounding and yanking, it opened just wide enough for me to slip through sideways.

For the next hour I brought specimen after specimen over to the plant encyclopedia I'd been looking at the night before, flipping pages and setting them in piles of like things. Cooking herbs, medicinal herbs, herbs for tea. They rapidly all began to look the same, especially the largest pile: unidentifiable. With nothing else to go on, I decided these were the weeds that I'd need to eradicate. And though I didn't know much about gardening, I did know that it wasn't easy to get rid of weeds. Most would grow back if cut off at the surface. If I wanted to eliminate the weeds from this garden for good, I would have to dig deep.

I thrust my spade down and pried up a section of earth at a time, shaking the soil from each uprooted weed and tossing it on an ever-growing pile to be destroyed. It was dirty, sweaty, backbreaking—perfect. Every weed removed felt like an accomplishment. Like cutting a bloated column from a thousand words to five hundred.

While working at a particularly stubborn dandelion, my trowel hit a stone. I widened the hole to find the edge so I could pry it out, but it wouldn't budge. The stone was flat and straight and seemed to have a right angle. Something man-made. A paving stone that had sunk into the soil after years of neglect?

I made the hole bigger and bigger and finally dragged the stone out with bare hands that were now black with dirt. Wiping away the soil, I saw faint numbers. A one, then a six, then an eight, then a one. Then a comma. A date. I swiped and clawed to reveal the rest. *August 5, 1861*. The cornerstone of some long-forgotten building? No. It was far too thin. A gravestone. It must have broken and toppled long ago, then been reclaimed by the garden.

I looked at the shovel stuck in the ground mere inches from where a casket might lie. What if I had disturbed the final resting place of a Civil War soldier who had died of gangrene due to a botched leg amputation? Visions of horror movies popped unbidden into my mind. I looked around the tangled mess of weeds that remained. Hadn't Nora said something about a woman being buried in the backyard?

I tiptoed out of the garden, shutting the gate behind me to keep the ghosts in.

Inside, Nora was at her sewing machine.

"Um . . . I have a question for you."

The whirring of the machine ceased.

"I found something strange and I'm wondering if you could check it out."

"Something you can't identify?" she said, getting to her feet.

"There are plenty of those, but that's not my problem. I think I found a headstone."

"Oh, yes. Mary Balsam is buried there. Didn't I tell you that?"

"You did, but I don't think that's what I found."

She looked perplexed. "Hers is the only grave out there."

"Well, this stone said 1861 on it. And I think you told me she died in the 1870s, didn't you?"

She nodded. "In 1875. I'm certain of it. I've seen her stone. Not for years, but when William was first working in the garden, he found the grave and called me out to see it."

I led Nora to the stone resting at the edge of the hole. She adjusted her glasses. "One date," she muttered.

"I don't know if I should keep working out here," I said. "What if I damage something? Or . . . unearth somebody?"

"Nonsense. I'll show you where Mary's grave is. Then you'll know to be careful there." She started to pick her way across the weeds. "Let's see."

"Watch your step."

"It's just right here." She pushed at a clump of mint, releasing its fresh scent into the air and revealing the top half of a larger, more ornate stone. "You used to be able to see the whole thing. It's sunk over the years."

Mary Elizabeth Balsam. Born October 15, 1840. Died June 23, 1875. Thirty-four years old.

"Mary Elizabeth," I said. "Am I named after her?"

"I don't know, dear."

"I have to say I'm a little spooked. What if there's something else out here? Her husband maybe?"

Her expression darkened just a bit. "He's buried in Detroit."

"Why not here?"

Nora took a slow breath. "It just so happens, for good or ill, that parents have only so much influence over their children. I can see yours did a fine job with you, but sometimes kids just don't turn out the way their parents hoped they would."

"My parents tried," I said, unsure of how that answered my question at all. "But I don't think I turned out as they hoped. I certainly haven't turned out how I hoped, in any case."

"I'm sure you are quite a bit closer to the mark than Mary and Nathaniel's eldest son was . . . Or than I was, frankly."

Then, as if she knew she'd opened a door she'd meant to keep closed, Nora turned and walked back to the house, leaving me kneeling in the dirt with the mystery grave and all of my unanswered questions.

ELEVEN

Detroit, April 1963

Nora hoped her nerves didn't show as she walked into a diner on Twelfth Street. It had been her suggestion to meet in William's neighborhood to avoid running into anyone she knew. Now as the bell overhead rang and patrons looked up from their meals, she felt like an exhibit at the zoo. Most turned their attention back to their food or their companions, but a few kept their eyes on the white girl in the doorway.

She scanned the room, hoping to spot the winsome photographer she'd met at the art exhibition. It had been a month, and she worried she wouldn't recognize him at all. When she didn't see any familiar faces, she lost her nerve and pushed back through the diner door, slamming it into a man on his way in.

"Oh, I'm so sorry!"

The man recovered and smiled. "I know I'm a little late, but there's no call for that."

"William! I'm sorry! I didn't see you and then I didn't know what to do."

He knit his brow in confusion. "It's a restaurant. You just sit down at a table."

She laughed to cover her discomfort.

He sighed as he eased past her and headed for a booth in the back corner. "You'd be happier back here than by the windows, am I right?"

Nora felt shame rising but slid into the secluded booth without a word. She thought she detected a hum of whispers filtering through the room. William nodded at a couple people who nodded back. But Nora couldn't tell if they were friends of his. They were watching her like one might watch a strange dog that had wandered into the neighborhood, waiting to see if it was friendly or not.

"That's a pretty dress," William said.

Nora shook off her paranoia. "Thank you. I was hoping it would be done by Easter, but I ran out of time."

"You made it? Hmm."

"What?"

"You make all your clothes?"

"Some, why?"

"I dunno. You don't strike me as the frugal type." William handed her a menu.

"I'm not hungry," she said. "I'll just have a Coke."

"It's eleven o'clock. You already ate lunch?"

"No."

"Then eat. It's on me."

"I had a big breakfast."

"No girl your size ever had a big breakfast. Just order something."

She read the menu in silence as the waitress approached the table. Once they had ordered, Nora studied the salt and pepper shakers and searched for something to say.

"I was beginning to think you never intended to call, you know," she said.

"Yeah, sorry about that." He rubbed the back of his neck. "Took me longer than I thought to get enough time in a darkroom. I can't develop on Sundays—church and all—and I'm on the line at Detroit Assembly six days a week making Cadillacs."

"And how did they turn out?"

"The Cadillacs? Real good."

She laughed and rolled her eyes. "The photos, of course."

"Oh, those!" he said with feigned stupidity. "Beautiful."

Nora tried not to seem too eager as she said, "Can I see them?"

William nodded. "Absolutely."

She waited for him to produce something—a box, a folder, she didn't know what. But something. "Well?"

"Oh, I don't have them here with me now."

"I thought you said—"

He held up a hand to stop her. "I've got them, don't worry. They're back at my house."

"But isn't that why we're here?"

William shook his head. "I didn't think it would work to show them to you here. They're not real . . . portable."

"They're photos. They'd fit in your pocket."

"No, I sized them up a bit. They're bigger than you're thinking."

Nora couldn't hold back a sigh. "Then why did you suggest we meet at a diner rather than just meeting at your house?"

He shrugged. "Because I wanted to have lunch with you."

William smiled at her and Nora realized she'd been tricked into a date. She narrowed her eyes. "Why didn't you just ask me?"

"Would you have said yes?"

Nora stopped to consider. Across the table William raised his eyebrows and waited for her answer.

"I don't know."

"I guess we'll never know. But in the meantime, here you are."

The waitress glided up to the table, glanced nervously at Nora as she set down their meals, and then disappeared again. William pounded on the bottom of a ketchup bottle.

"You're doing it wrong," Nora said. "You only have to shake it a bit."

"No, you have to hit the bottom of the bottle." He demonstrated it for her. "You can't just shake it." He shook the bottle mockingly.

She held out her hand. "Give it to me. You're not doing it right. You're shaking it too much."

"Okay, you try."

Nora positioned the bottle over his hamburger and shook. Nothing came out.

"See? Give me that thing. My food's getting cold while you're 'just shaking it a little bit.'" He reached for the bottle, but she pulled it away.

"No, this works."

"I don't think so."

"It does."

"It don't work. Look at it."

Nora shook the bottle a little harder and a little harder, but still nothing came out.

"Can I have that ketchup now, please?" William said in a tone that suggested he was talking to a child.

"No." She was determined now.

"Then can you at least try it my way so maybe I can eat sometime today?"

"Fine." Nora smacked the bottom of the bottle hard with her right hand, and half of its contents emptied out onto William's burger. She gasped as she righted the bottle too late.

"You see? I told you," he said.

"I'm so sorry!"

"Nah, don't worry." He smashed the bun down. Ketchup oozed out the sides and onto the plate. "But now we know, don't we," he said through a smile, "that just shaking it up a little doesn't work. You gotta smack it."

"I'll buy you a new burger."

"That your solution for everything?"

"What? No, I just—"

"Look, it's fine." He scraped the excess ketchup onto the lip of the plate. "Now eat your sandwich."

Nora and William ate in uncomfortable silence for a few minutes.

"So where do you live?" she finally thought to ask.

"Just down the street off Seward."

She nodded, though she wasn't quite sure where that was.

"What about you?"

"I live in Bloomfield Hills."

"Of course you do."

She put down her sandwich. "Why 'of course'?"

"Beautiful, well-bred white girls always live in Bloomfield Hills."

"That's not true."

"True enough."

She wiped her fingers on her napkin. "Do you dislike white people?"

A few heads at neighboring tables swiveled her way.

"I like you," he said.

"That's not what I asked," she said, quieter now.

"Do you dislike black people?" he said.

"No."

"None of your daddy rubbed off on you?"

"What? No! I would never—" She lowered her voice to a whisper. "I would never use that word."

"Don't matter if you'd never say it. It's what's in your heart that matters." He gave her a look of challenge. "What's in your heart?"

She looked him straight in the eyes. "Do you think I'd come to this neighborhood and meet you for lunch if I was a racist?"

"Does your father know you bought that camera for me?" he said with a provocative smirk.

She hesitated. "I'm an adult."

"So you didn't tell him?"

"It's none of his business."

They were both quiet for a moment. In her mind, Nora traced the conversation in reverse, trying to figure out where she'd made a wrong turn. She had been looking forward to this all week, remembering William's charm and ready smile. But it was obvious that this was not going well. She picked up her sandwich again but couldn't bring herself to take another bite.

William regarded his burger. "So what did you do with that picture? You burn it?"

She wanted to say yes, but the truth was that hardly a day had gone by that she had not unrolled the print and stared at it. She kept hoping she would see some minute detail that had previously escaped her notice, one that would prove to her that it wasn't her father, that perhaps it was just someone who looked like him. But each examination only confirmed his identity.

"No, I didn't burn it. I'm not sure I'd ever do something so dramatic as that."

TWELVE

Lapeer County, August 1861

Before anything else, Mary was aware of a strange, low voice mumbling in the dark. Then the suffocating sensation of an enormous stone upon her body. Every muscle seized. A groan escaped her lips, and the voice stopped its murmurings and drew close to her ear.

"Mrs. Balsam? You hear me?"

Mary groaned again.

"Ma'am, you gonna be all right."

The events of the day began to trickle back through Mary's mind. The letter. The trunk. The man. Then they came in a rush of fear. The straw. The blood. The blackness. Nathaniel was reenlisting and she was having their baby too soon.

"You want some water, ma'am?"

She opened her eyes then. The dark face of the man from the trunk hovered at the side of the bed. What was his name?

Mary nodded and the face was gone. She glanced around the room to get her bearings. The curtains were drawn, but in the weak candlelight she saw the red damask wall coverings, the fireplace, the armoire, the table by the window, the walnut bedstead. Her room.

The man—what was his name?—appeared at her side. He set the water on the bedside table and gathered up a couple of pillows. Grasping her sweating body under her arms, he lifted her like a child and propped her up to drink. It was then, as she felt his hands upon her bare skin, that Mary realized that she was wearing only her chemise and her petticoat.

She gasped and fumbled for the sheet. "My dress!"

"It's hangin' up over there. Didn't think you wanted to ruin it with birthin', but I can get it if you want."

She lessened her grip on the sheet but kept her arms crossed over her chest and shook her head. He held the glass of water out. Mary took it in shaky hands. Water sloshed over the side and onto the bed.

"I got it, I got it," he said as he took it back. He held it to her lips. "There, now. You feelin' better, ma'am? You'll be all right."

But Mary could tell by the tone of his voice that he was trying to convince himself of this as much as her.

"Where is Bridget?"

"Your girl gone to get the midwife."

She was alone with this stranger, this unexpected and unwanted delivery from Nathaniel.

"How long has she been gone?"

Then the pain returned and Mary clenched her teeth. The man caught her hand in his and she squeezed it hard. The pain settled in, lingered too long. When Mary was sure she could not bear it another moment, it stopped.

"How long has she been gone?" she asked again.

"Don't you worry. She'll be back soon. Midwife's comin'. On her way."

"How long?"

He looked at the curtained window with troubled eyes. "Not too long. They'll be here soon."

Mary noticed that she was gripping the man's deep brown hand in hers, which was deathly white from the effort. She unfurled her fingers and pulled her hand away, tucking it underneath the sheet. He rubbed at the deep indentations where her nails had been.

"What time is it?" she asked.

He got up and turned the clock face toward her. Eleven? But the trunk had been delivered in the afternoon. What could be taking Bridget so long? Mary didn't have much time to consider the question as pain swept over her once again. Now, though, it was not as a stone suffocating her. This pain was sharp, pointed, fiery. It pulsated from between her legs. She emitted a long, low growl that became a yell.

The man sprang up and began to pace. He looked to the door as if he were debating whether he could make a nighttime escape from the house as he must have from his ramshackle slave quarters. Mary trembled at the thought that he likely had no experience with delivering babies, perhaps not even any experience with helping livestock with the task. Probably all he knew how to do was to pick cotton as fast as possible from the dark of morning to the dark of evening.

Mary screamed again and writhed upon the bed. The man tore the covers from her and seemed about to lift her petticoat when he stopped cold. She clawed at her petticoat at the same time he scrambled to cover her once more, but his efforts were too late.

Her bloomers were pink with blood and water. A sinister wet circle crept out from beneath her. Mary had no notion of whether this was normal. Why hadn't she called upon her mother-in-law, Catherine, to come stay with her? Where was Bridget with the midwife? A glance at the man's shocked face revealed that he too was at a loss.

The pain throbbed, relentless. She screamed, shaking him from his stunned trance.

"You gonna have a baby, ma'am. Women been doin' it since Eve. You okay. You okay."

He mumbled something to the ceiling and pulled the soiled bloomers from her body. Mary was in too much pain to care about the scandalous indecency of it all.

"I see him now. He comin' now. You almost there."

She clenched every muscle she had, bearing down hard until her body went limp.

"No, no!" The man leaned up over her exhausted form and slapped her cheek. "Don't you go faintin'!"

Mary was brought back from the brink by a rush of indignation. She would have chastised him had she been able to squeeze an intelligible word past her throat.

"Come on, now, ma'am."

She let out a tortured holler as she bore down hard once more.

"Here he come!"

Another breath. Another push. Another scream. And suddenly the fire was quenched, replaced with a throbbing ache.

"You done it!" the man yelled from the end of the bed. He met her eyes with a relieved smile and then looked back at the child who had emerged from her body. His smile faltered.

"What?"

He schooled his features and would not meet her eyes.

"What?"

Then she realized that the baby did not cry.

The man leaned in and wiped at the baby's face with the sheet. He put his ear to the baby's chest. Then he squeezed his eyes shut and a tear tumbled down his cheek. He wrapped the tiny child in part of the bedsheet and laid it, still bound with the cord, on Mary's heaving chest.

"A girl."

Mary looked at the silent child, almost the same color as the sheet in which she was wrapped. She placed a shaking hand on the baby's head, nearly obscuring it. It was so small. Then she wept bitter tears until she was delivered of the afterbirth and exhaustion overtook her.

When Mary came to, the light of dawn crept through a crack in the curtains. There was no baby on her breast. Her once round stomach was flaccid. The midwife was closing up her bag while Bridget hovered nearby. The man from the trunk was nowhere to be seen.

"I'm so sorry, my dear," the midwife said. "Rest now. Your girl will call on the town doctor if needed, but I'm afraid my work here is done." She disappeared into the hallway.

Bridget burst into tears. "I'm so sorry it took so long. Anna was already attending someone else. I didn't mean to leave you to go through this trial all alone."

Mary hushed her. "I was not alone. Where is the baby?"

"In her cradle. Just there. Poor little thing."

"Please bring her to me and then go find that man."

Bridget carried the dead child like an overfull cup of tea. Mary took the baby in her arms, and her maid rushed from the room.

Looking at the small, cold face poking out from the blanket, Mary thought she might cry again. Instead she felt a frightening void in her heart. As she traced the features of her baby's face, Mary traced the hollow feeling back beyond the events of the night before, beyond the delivery of the trunk and her fear for Nathaniel's life, beyond the months of laboring to feed the animals and keep the house, beyond the loss of Mrs. Maggin, beyond the telegram about John Grouse enlisting, beyond the sound of the carriage disappearing as it carried her Nathaniel away. She traced it all the way back to the newspaper article declaring that war had begun.

For years Nathaniel and Mary had read abolitionist newspapers, prayed for the cause, encouraged others to take up the banner of freedom. Nathaniel had declared that she should not buy cotton for her dresses, and so she walked about in silk and wool and sewed him shirts of linen. They had done what they could from afar. And she had been satisfied.

Nathaniel had not, and that terrible headline in the *Detroit Free Press* back in April had stolen him from her. Some reckless man at a printer's tray had wantonly placed a lethal string of letters together, rolled the poison ink across, and stamped out a death sentence. Nathaniel may yet be alive, but that headline had killed his child just as surely as it had already killed thousands of young men in battle. Had he been home to work the farm, had he not sent an escaped slave curled up in a trunk to her doorstep, had he not sent word of his reenlistment, her baby would still be safe in her womb instead of lying dead in her arms.

At that moment she hated them all. The Southern slaveholders, the power-hungry Confederates, the Northern men all too happy to rush off to war. She'd been wrong to resent the fugitive who had shown up at her kitchen door. It was not the fault of those wretched souls. It was pale, blue-eyed men who were ripping her world apart, whether they had in their hands the slave driver's whip or the liberator's rifle.

Finally a tear overflowed from her eye. The door opened and she looked up to see the man from the trunk standing in the doorway. She wiped the wetness from her cheek. "Please sit by me."

He moved a wooden chair to the side of the bed and sat, but he did not look at her.

"I want to thank you for being there . . . with me."

He nodded.

She examined his face. It was haggard and exhausted. "Have you slept?"

He shook his head.

"Where have you been? Why did you leave?"

"I heard the midwife comin', and I run out and hid in the barn."

"Why?"

He shook his head. "Shouldn't a been in here with you."

Understanding dawned. "I see." After a moment of silence she said, "You couldn't sleep out there?"

"I's busy."

"Doing what?"

He looked at the baby. "Gettin' things ready."

Mary shut her eyes tight to hold back her tears.

"I hear that midwife tell your girl she gonna tell the minister to come see you. I got a spot dug and a box made. But I'll make myself scarce when he comes."

"I want you to stay. Please?"

He nodded. "Yes, ma'am."

Mary placed a tender kiss upon the baby's small, cold lips. "Please take her away. I'm sorry, what is your name again?"

"George."

"Thank you for not leaving me alone, George."

He took the child from her. "I's never going to leave you alone, ma'am."

THIRTEEN

Lapeer County, August

That evening after dinner, I expected to be regaled by the story of the cots in the attic, but Nora apologized, saying she was quite tired and thought she'd go to bed.

"Are you feeling okay?"

"Oh, I'm fine. Just tuckered out. I had a lot of orders that needed working on. Everyone's digging out their fall clothes and realizing they'd meant to get something fixed or they've lost weight and everything needs to be taken in."

"If you're sure."

Nora waved a dismissive hand. "I'm perfectly fine. And I'll tell you all about the cots tomorrow."

My initial disappointment at the deferment was quickly supplanted with excitement. Now I could take a look behind that locked door in the basement—provided the key worked.

I tidied up the kitchen and imagined what I might find. A wine cellar, locked since the days of Prohibition? The Balsam family fortune, perhaps in gold bar form? Or—and this macabre thought began to encircle my brain like the Virginia creeper on the house—perhaps the bodies Nora had joked about?

I stood at the apron-front sink and took my time washing and drying our two plates, two forks, and two glasses. I put them in the cupboards, moving the plates to the bottom of the stack and the glasses to the back of the cupboard, according to Nora's precise instructions.

"That way they all get the same amount of use," she'd said after lunch.

When I was sure she was asleep, I crept into the dining room with the key and a working light bulb I had pilfered from one of the unused upstairs bedrooms. I silently slid open the drawers above the linens and found dozens of tapers and a brass candleholder. A kitchen drawer yielded a box of matches. I fitted the holder with a tall red candle, struck a match, and set it ablaze. It may still be light outside, but the cellar would be dark.

The door to the cellar squeaked open. I held my breath and listened for footsteps. When nothing happened, I started down the stairs and shut the door most of the way. There was no way I was going to shut it completely and risk getting stuck down there. Leaning forward into the space below me to get a better look, I let the light bulb slip from my hand and stifled a gasp. I waited for the sound of breaking glass. Instead I heard a dull plop.

At the bottom of the stairs, the ground reflected my meager flame. The light bulb had landed in a little puddle. I crept downstairs. Directly above the puddle a pipe dripped what must have been the remains of the dishwater. How long had it been leaking? I'd have to call a plumber.

I fished the bulb out of the water and dried it on my shirt. The ground directly beneath the light socket was not wet, but I wasn't taking any chances. I hadn't done extensive research into electrocution, but I did know that electricity and water didn't mix. I imagined Nora finding me there in a smoking heap the next morning and dying from the shock of it, our bodies not to be found until they had been reduced to skeletons. I'd stick with candlelight for now.

I placed the light bulb on the bottom step and made my way to the door with the padlock. I would have prayed for success, but I was pretty sure God disapproved of invading someone's privacy. Anyway, no prayer was needed. The key slid into the lock and the mechanism released with a click.

The small space was packed with objects, but not the ones I might have hoped for. No gold or precious stones winked back at me—but also, thankfully, no skeletons. One wall was lined with a narrow countertop, upon which a row of bottles stood watch over three shallow trays. The bottles were labeled, but they may as well not have been, as I could make no sense of their polysyllabic contents. The trays were empty. In the corner of the counter was a metal object whose purpose eluded me. Was someone doing perfidious science experiments down here?

I turned around and found myself eye to eye with a beautiful young woman. Or rather a picture of a beautiful young woman. A thin clothesline strung with black-and-white 8x10 photographs spanned the length of the room. The same striking blonde with large eyes and perfect skin was in every photo. I wanted to take them to Nora and ask who she was. But of course I couldn't. Nora didn't know I was down here. And the last time I went snooping into someone's life without permission, it didn't turn out so well.

I looked over the trays and chemicals again. There was something familiar about it all. It reminded me of when I first toured the offices at the *Free Press*. Though everything had gone digital, there were still vestiges of an analog past here and there in dark corners.

Then I got it. A darkroom.

Did it belong to Mr. Rich's uncle? Had these photos been taken with the camera that now sat in the bottom of the armoire?

Who had locked that door? The photographer? What was he hiding? I plucked a photo off the line. Was he hiding her?

At that moment, a motor started up just outside.

"What in the world?" I said out loud.

I double-checked that the key was in my pocket, replaced the lock, and headed up the stairs. My first step shattered the light bulb into a zillion pieces. I would have to clean it up tomorrow when I could get some real light shining down here.

I burst out the back door just as a red riding lawn mower driven by a black man in a baseball cap zipped by. I waved and shouted, but it wasn't until his third pass that the driver noticed me and cut the motor.

"Are you William?" I asked, glad to finally lay eyes on this mysterious figure.

He smiled and got off the mower. "I'm Tyrese."

"Are you at the wrong house?"

He frowned behind his sunglasses. "No, this is Eleanor Rich's house. Has been for years. Are *you* at the wrong house?"

"Sorry. No. I just—I thought your name was William." I extended my hand to him. "I'm Nora's great-niece, Elizabeth."

He shook my hand. "Yeah, sometimes Ms. Rich calls me William. I assume she's home? I have to apologize for coming so late, but I knew I wouldn't get a chance later in the week."

"She's asleep. Or she was. She might have woken up at the noise." The wheels in my head began turning. "Hey, did she ever ask you to do anything in the house? Air out a room or clean things up or anything?"

He shook his head. "I've never been in the house."

"Oh. Weird. Why does she call you William?"

He shrugged. "I don't know. Just started calling me that last summer. I figured she was getting old and maybe a little confused."

"Doesn't that make cashing your checks a little difficult?" I joked, trying to ignore the bad feeling I was starting to get from all this.

"*Ms.* Rich doesn't pay me. *Mr.* Rich does. He's down in Detroit. But she doesn't know that," he added quickly. "He told me when I first started this job that Ms. Rich wouldn't accept it if she knew it was him paying for it."

I felt myself frowning. Why was James Rich going through all this trouble for a woman he was on bad terms with? "Who does she think is paying for it?"

"I told her it was her taxes."

I gave him a doubtful look. "She seems smarter than that."

Tyrese smiled. "She is. It took some serious convincing, and for a while she tried to pay me anyway. But a friend of mine is a staffer for a state representative, and he corroborated the story for me with some official stationery. Convinced her it was a pilot program for helping rural seniors stay in their homes."

"Lucky for you she doesn't get out much, or a bunch of other rural seniors would be wondering where their free lawn care was."

"Yeah." He laughed. "Listen, I've got to get going on this lawn. Sun's going down."

"Right. Sorry. Go right ahead."

I went inside and watched through the kitchen window as Tyrese zipped back and forth across the yard on the lawn mower. If he wasn't William, then who was?

I wished the house around me would open up and talk. Of course I knew that houses were merely wood and plaster and brick. But it felt like this particular house had a memory and it was hiding something from me. The crumbly cellar walls had been there when the photographer dipped photos of a beautiful woman into chemical baths and strung them up to dry. The walls of my bedroom had witnessed someone bringing in the incredible carved bedstead. The house had looked on as graves were dug and headstones were placed and herbs were planted.

Yet all stood silent but for the creaking sounds that all old houses make. Were the answers to my questions there in those groans and snaps, waiting for an interpreter? Or would I have to slip into full reporter mode in order to pry the information out of my reluctant hostess? Mr. Rich had warned me to ease into talking about Nora's past. But how did one ease into a topic that never came up?

FOURTEEN

Detroit, April 1963

William gave a low whistle. "Dang. Now that's a car." He circled the little red Corvette. "That this year's model?"

"Yes, it is," Nora said with pride. "I got it for my birthday."

"You kidding me? This was a present?"

"Well, my father . . ."

"Oh, I see. Daddy's a car man."

"Not exactly. He's an ad man. At GM. Corvette is his main account."

"Yeah, well, listen, I don't know if I could fit these legs of mine in that little thing. It isn't far. Let's just hoof it."

Nora gave the car an anxious look but followed William as he began walking down the street. Beautiful cars were everywhere in Detroit, as much a part of the landscape as the striking Art Deco architecture or the rows of flowering trees lining the streets. But as she walked down Twelfth Street she could see that her car was outclassing everyone else's. And there were no stunning buildings in this neighborhood, no prim cherry trees with their delicate pink blossoms. The houses hunched close together and all fell somewhere along a spectrum of disrepair that ranged from dirty to dilapidated. Paint peeled from siding, shingles curled on roofs, smoke stains peeked from beneath boarded-up windows.

"What?" William said.

"Hmm?"

"What are you shaking your head for?"

"I didn't shake my head."

"Yeah you did. What's the problem?"

"Nothing."

He stopped walking a moment. "Come on."

Nora took a deep breath. "It's just . . . I was just wondering why these people don't keep their houses up very well."

William gave her an incredulous look. "You serious? You think the people who live there own those houses? They don't own them. They're rentals. Landlords don't keep them up."

Nora felt a little stupid, but only for a moment. "Don't they complain?"

He started walking again. "Don't do much good."

"Why wouldn't the landlord maintain them?" Nora said from behind him.

"No money in it."

"But why don't they just move somewhere else, somewhere nicer?"

"Where?" He laughed mirthlessly. "Bloomfield Hills?"

She shrugged. "Why not?"

William stopped again. "Oh, please. When was the last time you saw a black person in Bloomfield Hills who wasn't just working in some white man's home?"

Nora searched her memories and came up empty. "Is it just too expensive?"

"For most," he conceded, "but there's black people in this town could afford it."

"Then why live here?"

"You live under a rock or something? You ever heard of Dr. Sweet?"

"That wasn't Bloomfield Hills."

"You're right about that. It was Detroit. So how do you think he'd have fared in lily-white Bloomfield Hills?"

Nora put her hands on her hips. "That was almost forty years ago."

"May as well have been forty minutes ago. Some places are just off-limits. Bloomfield Hills is white. If you think any Realtor in this city would sell a house in Bloomfield Hills to a black family, you're out of your mind. And if they did, just watch how fast the rocks start flying."

He started walking again. In her hurry not to be left behind, Nora caught her heel on a broken piece of sidewalk and pitched forward. Her knee connected with the pavement.

"Oh, man. You all right?" William said as he rushed back to help her up. He brushed at tiny stones that were embedded in her knee. "You're bleeding."

Nora's stocking was torn, and a trickle of red was beginning to drip down her left leg.

William pulled a handkerchief from his pocket and dabbed at the blood. "We're just a few houses away. Can you walk?"

Nora sucked in a breath and nodded gamely. William's hand hovered at her elbow, ready to steady her, as she hobbled forward, holding the handkerchief against the wound with her other hand and feeling very much like a broken marionette. Every few steps, Nora felt William's warm fingers brush the inside of her arm, which only increased her embarrassment at the whole situation.

In another minute, he ushered her up a set of creaky front steps and inside a house.

"Have a seat." He pointed at a tan couch. "I'll be right back."

Nora lowered herself to the couch and examined the injury. William came back into the room holding a bottle of hydrogen peroxide, a cotton ball, and a box of adhesive bandages.

"It's nothing," Nora said.

"No, no. You don't want a nasty scab on that knee."

He knelt before her and dabbed her exposed flesh with the solution. It bubbled up and dripped down her leg. He caught the drop with the back of a finger, which he ran up her shin.

"Um . . ." He hesitated. "A bandage isn't going to stick with those stockings on."

Nora felt herself blush.

"Here." William handed her a bandage. "Bathroom's just back there." He motioned to a dark hall and stood up to give her some room.

Nora hurried into the bathroom and shut the door. She hiked up her dress, slipped off her stockings one by one, and wadded them up into a ball. Should she throw them away there? She imagined what her mother would say if she ever found out she'd left her stockings at a man's house. She stared at herself in the mirror. What *was* she doing here?

With the bandage secure and her heartbeat returning to normal, Nora walked back to the living room and discreetly pushed her stockings into her purse. She needn't have worried about discretion, however, as William was nowhere to be found. In his absence, Nora looked over the room. It was sparsely furnished but tidy. Fluffy pillows sat at pleasing angles. Houseplants showed no brown or dying leaves. A photo of a man in an Army uniform graced a side table. Nora absently ran her hand over the top of the small television. There was no dust.

The front door opened and shut.

"Um, hello?" came a feminine voice. The voice had an edge to it, like it was daring her to answer.

Nora was startled to see a tall, thin black woman with fashionably straightened and flipped hair accompanied by a boy of about twelve. The two of them seemed just as surprised to see a strange white woman standing in their living room.

The woman narrowed her eyes. "And just who are you?"

Nora struggled to find her voice. "I'm Nora," she practically whispered.

The woman bit the inside of her cheek. The boy was looking at her like she'd just taken his ball and wouldn't give it back. Nora's mind was racing for the right thing to say when William walked in holding a large brown portfolio.

"Oh, hey," he said. "Bianca, this is Nora."

"Mmm," Bianca said, clearly unimpressed.

To Nora he said, "This is Bianca and J.J."

"Go on upstairs, J.J.," Bianca said.

William tried to rub J.J.'s head as he slipped by, but the boy ducked.

The woman squared herself to face William. "I don't know what this is, Will, but it looks like trouble to me."

"Relax," he said.

Bianca sighed. "Listen, I gotta get some sleep before my shift. J.J. should be fine in his room till dinnertime."

"Okay." He kissed her cheek. "See you in a bit."

Bianca gave Nora one last long look, then said to William, "You better sort this out, and fast." Then she disappeared down the hall.

William sat on the couch and placed a large brown portfolio on the coffee table.

Nora shook herself out of her stunned silence. "I should go."

William looked up. "Say what?"

"I need to go."

"What? Why would you go now? The pictures are right here."

Nora lowered her voice to a harsh whisper. "This is not appropriate."

William looked around the room. "What?"

She took a couple steps in the direction of the door, and he shot up from the couch.

"Hey, what?"

"How can you ask that? I thought you were . . . you know . . . how could you ask me to lunch when you're—" Nora gestured at the hall down which Bianca had disappeared.

William's face was blank. Then he laughed. "Bianca's my sister. We look almost exactly alike. She's me in a wig. Didn't you see? And J.J.'s my nephew."

"Well," Nora said, recovering, "whoever she is, she does not want me here."

"So what? She ain't the boss of me. Now sit down here and look at these photos, please." He guided her back to the couch.

"No, really," Nora said. "Maybe I shouldn't be here."

"But you are here. So you may as well have a look, right?"

At his insistence, Nora sat gingerly on the couch.

"Okay, are you ready now?" he said.

She nodded.

"No more craziness first?"

"I'm ready," she said sternly.

William opened the portfolio to reveal the first black-and-white photograph. It was 8x10 and mounted on stiff black cardstock. In it, Nora was looking down and to the left, the smile she had not been able to suppress dancing on her lips. Even though the moment had been spontaneous, her eyes were in perfect focus and the play of light and shadow across her face seemed almost intended.

It had been some time since she'd seen a photo of herself looking happy. There were many from the time when she was the same age as she imagined William's nephew to be, but after about age thirteen her smile was replaced by closed lips that seemed to grow tighter as the years marched on. The distance between her and her older brothers had grown as they discovered far more interesting girls to hang out with. Her father had become so engrossed in his work that Nora found she rarely spoke to him. Her mother's ever more obvious attempts to find fulfillment in her daughter's accomplishments became a heavy chain of expectation around Nora's neck. Her friends had become more competitive, more catty. Life no longer sparkled.

Now, as Nora turned each page, she could see a bit of that

lost spark, hinting at a different girl lying there underneath the severe young woman she had become. As she flipped through the portfolio, Nora became aware that William was looking not at the photos but at the side of her face. She felt her eyes begin to tear up as she turned over the last one, but she reined in her emotions and looked up at the artist beside her.

"They're lovely. You're very talented."

He smiled and sat back. "I knew you would like them. Those are yours to keep."

"Thank you. Though I'm not sure what to do with them. It would be strange to hang photos of myself in my apartment. You don't want to keep them?"

"I got the negatives. I can make more of you whenever I want."

"I'm pretty replaceable, then?" she said, raising her eyebrows.

He tipped his head. "You know that's not what I mean."

Nora felt her stomach flutter at his intense gaze. There was something in his eyes she had never seen in any of the guys she'd dated. Like Michael Kresge, they had all been from wealthy families much like hers. Their eyes had appraised her like a new car, determining whether others would be jealous enough when they saw her on their arm.

William's eyes had seen past her brittle shell and were drawing out the carefree girl she wished she could be.

And at that moment, on a nondescript tan couch in an impeccably clean living room at Twelfth and Seward, Nora fell in love with the wrong man.

FIFTEEN

Lapeer County, January 1862

Mary hung back in the sanctuary as the rest of the congregation filed out into the snow. Men and boys drove their horses and sleighs up to the shoveled path at the church door, tucked their women in under furs and blankets, and headed for home where the fires waited to be stoked. Each month it seemed another young man was missing from their midst, sucked into the growing maelstrom to the south. The joy of Christmas faded, and though it was the dawn of a new year, there was a palpable lack of cheer.

Bridget handed Mary her cloak. "Are you ready, ma'am?"

"Nearly. Fetch the sleigh. I'll only be a moment."

Bridget shook the minister's hand and disappeared through the door.

Reverend Whittaker turned to Mary. "Well, Mrs. Balsam, it seems you are reluctant to leave. Is there something on your mind?"

"Very perceptive, Reverend, as always. There is something about which I should like to speak with you—briefly. I won't keep you from your Sunday dinner."

"Of course, my dear. What can I do for you?"

Mary lowered her voice despite the empty room. "As you know, I am currently housing an escaped slave at my husband's behest. He is an upright and God-fearing man, and you can't imagine what a help he was to me during the harvest. Indeed, I find that he is indispensable."

The minister nodded in a noncommittal manner. Mary couldn't tell if he was agreeing or if he simply wanted to get home to the hot meal Mrs. Whittaker was preparing.

"George has been learning to read, which he had been forbidden to do by his former master, and he longs to come to church. He knows Bible stories that were passed down verbally, but now that he is reading the very Word of God, he's encountering things he doesn't understand, and I'm not so sure I'm the best person to interpret them. He'd so benefit from sitting under your preaching, and he is starved for Christian community."

Reverend Whittaker held up a hand, and Mary realized she had been rambling. "Mrs. Balsam, are you asking to bring him with you to church on Sundays?"

"I guess I am. I know that not everyone here is for abolition, but I can't imagine why anyone would deny a fellow human being the chance to worship."

"Indeed." The minister appeared deep in thought, and Mary held her tongue to allow him to consider her appeal. "Mrs. Balsam, I believe your request comes from a kind and generous heart. I can't say how he will be received by some, but I do believe it would be against Christian teaching and Christian charity to exclude someone from worship. Were there a Negro congregation close by, it wouldn't be an issue, as he would just go there. But we cannot expect that out here in such wild country."

Mary allowed her hopes to rise. "Then I may bring him with us?"

Reverend Whittaker smiled. "Yes, you may. And I will preach on Paul's letter to the Galatian church in support."

"Oh, thank you, Reverend." Mary grasped his hand. "George will be so thrilled." She threw her cloak around her shoulders, and Reverend Whittaker walked her to the door. A sprinkling of snow peppered Bridget and the horses as they waited by the shoveled pathway. Mary turned back once more to her minister. "Thank you again."

Reverend Whittaker nodded. "Oh, Mrs. Balsam?"

"Yes?"

"It may be best if you came in rather late and sat in the back row."

Mary's smile faltered. "Of course."

She felt like someone had offered her a slice of apple pie and then handed her nothing but burnt crust. But then, George could learn as easily from the back row as from the front row.

The smile on George's face when Mary relayed the news to him at dinner an hour later was the brightest she had yet seen. With each passing week since his arrival, Mary had detected changes in George. His external wounds had healed and faded. He had put on some much-needed extra weight. His subservient manner had changed so that he no longer seemed like a chastened dog but a partner in the work on the farm. And now, five months into his stay, he had truly smiled.

In that moment, Mary realized that he was a handsome man. On the heels of that realization was another—that he was indeed a man. She counted up the months that Nathaniel had been gone and recognized with unsettling clarity that she did not simply miss her husband; she longed for a man's touch.

Mary, Bridget, and George had been eating at the same table without discomfort for months. But during Sunday dinner, as she caught herself staring at him, Mary wished he were eating in the kitchen. The meal could not end fast enough, and as soon as she could do so without seeming rude, Mary excused herself and fled to the library, leaving Bridget to clean up.

With the return of the weekly routine the next day, Mary

felt back to normal. When George came in to breakfast after feeding the animals, he was once again just George. And when the two of them sat down in the library for his lessons, she was merely the teacher and he the student.

"I'm quite happy with your progress reading," Mary said after he had read aloud a passage from Acts. "And now I think we must focus on writing for a time. You've progressed as far as you can with the slate. We must get you to write your letters smaller and work on your script. If you are ever to have a business for yourself, you cannot write out orders or receipts with such a shaky hand. I've decided to let you try paper and ink."

Mary pulled some supplies together from the desktop and gave George a quick lesson in dipping the nib in the ink and applying the correct amount of pressure to create a bold line with no splotches. "It will take a good deal of practice, so please don't get discouraged."

He stared at the paper. "What should I write?"

Mary thought but a moment and then retrieved the Bible from the library table. She flipped to Philemon. "Copy this entire letter. You may only use one piece of paper."

George looked dubious. An hour later he stood up and brought the paper to where she sat reading. "I can't get that whole letter on just one sheet of paper."

"Yet," she corrected. "You can't do it *yet*. Your letters are too large. You will have to write smaller. Try it again on the back."

By the end of the day, George had attempted the feat five times. Each time he could fit more words on the paper, until finally all he was missing were Paul's greetings at the end.

"Nicely done," Mary said. "And now you have the back side of that paper to fill."

"Could I write a letter of my own?"

"To whom?"

"I have a sister."

Mary hesitated. She couldn't allow George to write a letter

to someone he knew in the South and risk alerting his former master to his whereabouts. Perhaps it was foolish to have taught him to write at all.

"Can she read?"

"No, but one of the girls she looks after does."

"I don't know," she said slowly. "Wouldn't that be dangerous for you both?"

George's face fell, but he nodded his understanding. After a moment's thought he said, "Could I write a letter to you?"

SIXTEEN

Lapeer County, September

A downpour began Thursday night—a heavy, constant flow of water from sluggish clouds. The next morning it was still coming down at the same steady rate, now peppered with lightning and thunder. I couldn't work outside in the garden, which was okay by me. Every muscle screamed for rest.

Nora and I were playing gin at the kitchen table when a flash of light and a crack of thunder got me thinking of power outages and flashlights and flooded basements—all those things that were exciting as a child and irritating as an adult.

"Do you lose power much out here?"

"On occasion."

"Where do you keep a flashlight?"

"I have one by my bed, and there are candles in the drawers above the table linens."

"Yes, I've seen those."

Nora looked up from her cards. "Been snooping around?"

My breath stopped. "What?"

She smiled. "I don't mind. I'm not hiding anything."

I thought of the locked trunk and the locked room and had

to stop myself from snickering out loud. "I was looking for matches," I said, though I already knew where they were. "I thought I'd burn up that weed pile."

"You'll find the matches in the kitchen, in the drawer by the phone. But I don't think you'll be burning anything out there anytime soon with all this rain."

The card game continued until I'd lost track of the number of times Nora had won. Finally she went to her sewing room and I tried to distract myself with reading. I was getting stir-crazy in this house in the middle of nowhere. Back in Detroit, I sometimes went a dozen places in a day. I didn't have to think about how to fill downtime because there was no downtime. All I did was work.

I felt more urgently than ever that I needed to bring up the camera and the photos, get the story, and get the heck out of here and back to Detroit. What was I waiting for anyway? Mr. Rich had probably blown the whole thing out of proportion. I should just call him and tell him I was ready for the photos.

As I drifted off to sleep that night, I resolved to do just that.

I woke Saturday morning to an emptiness. It took a moment for me to realize that it was the lack of the constant drum of rain on the roof. Outside the air was cool and wet and invigorating. The plants in the garden looked greener than they had two days ago and showed signs of new growth. A glance at the bare dirt I had left when I pulled out the weeds revealed a sprinkling of seedlings that I would need to eradicate.

I retrieved my spade and turned the earth to smother this newest generation of weeds. Deprived of light, the unwanted growth would soon die off. That's what the books said, anyway. But if I didn't fill those spots in with good plants and some mulch, the weeds would take advantage of the empty space and fill it up themselves. A trip to the nearest garden center seemed in order. If nothing else, it would get me out of this house.

"That would be lovely!" was Nora's response to my suggested outing. "We'll go grocery shopping as well. We're starting to run low on most everything."

I hadn't driven in a week, and I guess hadn't really missed that aspect of Detroit life. No traffic jams. No long red lights. No angry honking. No near misses with jaywalkers and cyclists. And I was getting less twitchy about not having internet access. I didn't exactly miss hearing the constant beeps notifying me of texts and tweets and status updates. Out here it was just the ambling, quiet life of the country. A comfortable obscurity.

It wasn't exactly thrilling—nothing like seeing my byline on the front page. But at least I felt needed. I was watching over someone. Someone who didn't particularly want to be watched over. But still.

We pulled up to Perkins Nursery not long after they opened and had the place practically to ourselves. Once we had come within range of a cell tower, my phone had begun to buzz with activity. When Nora wandered off to browse, I flipped through the texts, notifications, and emails until I saw one from Desiree.

Before we'd been cut off by the sheer density of nothingness in the atmosphere of rural Lapeer County, she'd offered to follow up on a few leads I'd managed to scrounge up on Judge Sharpe. There was still a chance that I could salvage my reputation if I could prove he was hiding something nefarious about his service during the riots. Now my heart sank as I read the email she had sent a day earlier.

> I know I promised to come through for you on this, but I'm just not sure there's a real story here. He seems clean. Congressional Medal of Honor in Vietnam, lots of service to the community, no one seems to have anything bad to say about him. And there's just nothing out there about him in particular in connection to the riots. All we have

> is a little info on where his unit was, but with the chaos of that week, who knows if he was ever where you think he was. I'm sorry, but I'm going to have to back out. Jack is getting suspicious. Good luck with your aunt. Catch a lightning bug for me!

Desiree was a good researcher. Was it really possible that the reason we hadn't found anything was that there wasn't anything to find? But I was good too, and I had good instincts. The only reason I could think of for someone to avoid talking about a particular time in his life was that he was hiding something. There were a lot of people involved in those riots who did terrible things, assuming they wouldn't have to answer to anyone for it. So far, most of them hadn't.

I grabbed an oversized metal cart and shuffled off to drown my frustrations in herbs. The plants looked unhappy to still be in their little plastic pots this late in the summer. I filled up my cart with end-of-season deals and pushed thoughts of Judge Sharpe out of my mind. Instead I focused on how pleased my new plants would be when I gave them room to breathe in the great wide open and found myself smiling in spite of everything.

"Elizabeth, right?" said a voice from across the aisle.

I looked up to see a man watching me. His khaki pants and green polo shirt were soiled, and each hand gripped the edge of a large pot of some sort of evergreen shrub. His eyes were hazel, almost green, striking against his dark skin.

"Tyrese," he said. "Remember? I met you at your aunt's house."

"Of course. I didn't recognize you without your hat and sunglasses."

He closed the space between us and looked at my cart. "Herb garden?"

"Yes. My aunt has me revamping hers. It's the little fenced-in area near that big tree. I guess it's been around since the nineteenth century, but it's been neglected for a long time."

He put down his pots and wiped his dirt-encrusted hands on his pants. "I never really took the time to look at it. What sort of plants are in there?"

I searched my memory. "Mint, dill, some roses—"

"What sort of roses?"

I shrugged. "I have no idea. There are no blooms on them now. And I guess I wouldn't know even if there were." I leaned in and said in a conspiratorial whisper, "I don't actually know what I'm doing."

He laughed. "Would you mind if I took a look at them? I breed some of our roses here, and it's always good to introduce heirloom stock into the mix, but it's hard to find old varieties that are still viable. The roses you have may not be original to the garden, but I might get lucky and find something rare."

"What would you do with it?"

"I could show you how to prune it and help it perform well—rejuvenate it a bit. Different types of roses require different care. And, if you were willing, I could take a few cuttings back with me. What do you think?"

"You'd have to ask Nora. It's not my garden."

I called Nora over and watched her closely as Tyrese explained his request. I was waiting for her to call him William so I could correct her. But she never called Tyrese anything at all.

"Certainly, you could come look at our roses. So long as it's okay with Elizabeth. It's her garden."

"She said it was your garden." He smiled at me as he said it.

"Oh, no. It's Elizabeth's garden."

We worked out the details as Tyrese followed us to the checkout. At the car, he opened the passenger door for Nora and loaded the plants. He shut the trunk and turned to me. "I'm looking forward to coming out tomorrow."

"Yeah," I said casually. "Should be fun."

We stood there a moment, both of us nodding slightly and

looking for the conversation's natural end, which you only ever do when you are hoping the other person will prolong it.

"Okay, well . . . we'll see you tomorrow then," I finally said. I got in the car, wondering why Dana was so much better at these things than I was.

Tyrese shut my door for me and waved. From the rearview mirror I could see that he was still watching us when I made the turn onto the road to head home.

"He's nice," Nora said a little too innocently.

I gave her a look.

"What? He is."

"Yes," I agreed. He was nice.

Maybe I didn't have to rush back to Detroit just yet.

SEVENTEEN

Detroit, May 1963

"Let's sit out on the porch." William nodded toward the front windows where the evening flirted with twilight.

"Go on," came Mrs. Rich's voice from the head of the table. "Bianca and I'll wash up. J.J., don't you slink off now. You know you need to clear this table first."

Nora had eaten dinner at William's house five times in the past four weeks. William's mother was a perfect hostess, and Nora could tell the older woman was trying to make her guest feel at home. Bianca had warmed to her a little but was still guarded. J.J. hadn't said word one despite William's efforts to get him to talk.

"Holler when the coffee's done, Mama," William said as the screen door closed behind him.

The setting sun was warm, the slight breeze was cool, and the night was young. Nora settled herself in a creaky wicker chair and folded her arms across her stomach. She could make out movement and voices in the shadows of other porches. A laugh echoed down the street.

"I thought you'd want to sit on the swing." William settled himself on one end of the faded green swing hanging from the rafters. He patted the spot next to him and Nora joined him. Encircled by his arm, she felt more relaxed than she had in a very long time. In less than a minute, her eyes were closed, her head rested upon his shoulder, and their breathing fell into sync with the gentle movement of the swing.

The sudden sound of footfalls tearing up the front porch steps startled Nora to attention.

"J.J. here?" The voice was raspy and breathless.

"He's inside, Arnold," William said.

Arnold rapped at the door. "J.J.!"

"Just go on inside."

The boy disappeared into the house. Nora's heartbeat was just returning to normal when another voice drifted out of the shadows beyond the yew bushes.

"Will Rich, how you been?"

William extracted himself from Nora, leaving her side suddenly cold and empty. "Not bad, Derek. You?"

The men exchanged a handshake. Then Derek looked toward the swing.

"This is Nora," William said.

Nora stood and held out her hand.

Derek shook it, but he was looking at William. "You must be outta your mind," he said.

"Oh?" William said. "And why's that?"

"You gonna get yourself in a heap a trouble, Will Rich. And not just you."

Nora shrank back a step, but William gripped her arm and pulled her to his side. "No trouble," he said.

"You watch," Derek said. "You watch. You shouldn't be messing around with no white girl."

"My girl ain't none of your concern."

Nora's tight muscles loosened a little.

"Your girl is everyone's concern," Derek said. "Your girl is gonna get someone killed."

"Derek!" Mrs. Rich said as she came out the front door with the coffee tray. "I haven't seen you in weeks. How's your mother?"

Derek's no-nonsense demeanor changed instantly as he took the tray from her hands, set it down on a wicker table, and kissed her on the cheek. "She's good, she's good. She was asking about you the other day."

"I have to get up to see her soon. So busy with work, you know."

"I know it," he said cheerfully.

"Give her my love."

"Will do, will do."

Mrs. Rich went back into the house, and the smile melted from Derek's face. He leaned in toward William. "Listen, man. I'm telling you this as a friend. You playin' with fire."

At that moment, Arnold and J.J. burst through the door and hurried down the stairs.

"J.J.!" Bianca shouted from the house. "Get back in here!"

But the boys were gone. Derek drifted off into the night in the direction Arnold and J.J. had run.

William squeezed Nora's shoulders and gave her a quick kiss on the forehead. "Never mind that." He stirred cream and sugar into Nora's coffee, and they sipped in tension-laden silence.

"You called me your girl," Nora finally said.

"Yeah."

"I like that."

"Yeah?"

She nodded behind her mug. Nora followed that "my girl" a few steps down the road. Dates, kisses, professions of love. Then she stopped. Where did they go from there? The path into the future with someone like Michael Kresge was wide, well marked, and lined with well-wishers. The path with William Rich was a gauntlet.

"Should I stop coming here?" Nora said. "I mean, I don't want to make trouble."

William took a moment to think. "Derek's just watching out for me like a good friend should. In this neighborhood, the only white people you see are cops and landlords and people from the bank who are repossessing your car. He thinks it's safer to stay separate. I get where he's coming from." He took a long gulp of coffee. "I just don't think separate is the answer."

"What is the answer?"

"If anyone knew that, don't you think we'd a tried it by now?" William put his mug down on the tray and took her hand in his. "Actually, I think this here is the answer."

Nora smiled at him. "That's easy to say."

"Folks just need to see it work."

He put a warm hand to her face, the same hand on which she had written her name and phone number two months before. He leaned in. She met him halfway. When their lips touched, nothing else mattered.

"I want it to work," she said when the kiss ended.

"Well, that's a start then."

EIGHTEEN

Lapeer County, July 1863

Mary stood at the door of her bedchamber and assessed the space. There would be room on her bed for Bridget, but didn't the girl warrant her own? Perhaps George could make something for her. Now that the north chamber slept three men and the smallest one had to accommodate the entire Dixon family, the house was getting crowded and concessions would have to be made.

Where they kept coming from was anyone's guess. Mary began to suspect that Nathaniel was directing people her way. It would be just like him to tell liberated slaves trailing the Union Army that they would find shelter and provision at the house he had so blithely abandoned.

After that first lesson with paper and ink, George had written Mary a letter most days. Mary kept each one safely tucked away, but the last one she had kept on her bedside table. She'd read it a dozen times and still wondered what to do with it. At the very bottom of the page, after his beautiful signature, George had added a postscript requesting a letter in response. It had now been a week with no further letters, and Mary realized with some consternation that if she did not respond to his request, he may not write her again. He certainly no longer needed the practice.

She considered putting her request for help with the sleeping space problem in a letter. But George had become a good friend in addition to a good farmhand, and his request warranted a more personal response than a work order. Indeed, Mary could think of page upon page of things she should like to tell him—how she could not have survived without his help, how she appreciated his attention to every detail of the household, how she believed him to be the most extraordinary and courageous man she had ever met. But to put pen to such personal musings, and to a man not her husband? The very thought of it shamed her.

She heard footsteps behind her and turned to find George tucking in a clean shirt as he walked out of the bedroom he shared with Jacob and Thomas.

He nodded her way. "Morning, Mrs. Balsam."

"Good morning, George. I wonder if I might ask a favor of you." She waved him over to the doorway. "Could you make a slim bed for Bridget that we could put there under the window? I think we will need to make the back bedchamber the men's room now that Mrs. Dixon is to have another child. They will need the larger room, and since you and Jacob and Thomas are always coming and going out the back door, I thought that would be a better place for you. Then the Dixons can have your room."

"Why not give Bridget the room the Dixons are in now?"

"Didn't I tell you? We've had a new arrival. Her name is Loretta and she has a baby just weeks old. I can't imagine how she kept that child quiet on the journey, but miraculously, she has made it here." She started down the stairs. "How are we on tomatoes now? I've a request from Mr. Hathaway for more. Seems everything anyone can do to keep up with the demand from the troops."

"I should have another few crates ready to go on the wagon today."

"I don't know what I'd do without you."

Bridget emerged from the library with an armful of new shirts in blue checks, plaids, and stripes. "I got the buttons on all these. Who should get them?"

"Just give them to me," Mary said. "I'll distribute them."

"I'll get Loretta's tray," Bridget said as she handed them over, "then give you a hand in the kitchen." She started up the steps.

At the back door, Mary turned to George with a smile and a light touch on his arm. "You really have come a long way since you showed up in my parlor."

"I guess we both have."

Even after nearly two years under her roof, he still rarely looked her in the eye. Though Mary had noticed of late that every time she looked at him, he seemed to have already been looking at her. Always his eyes would snap away to some task. Now his eyes held hers steadily, and Mary saw something in them she had not noticed before.

She dropped her hand and looked away. "Yes, I suppose we have."

Martha Dixon walked into the kitchen followed by her daughter Angelica and her husband John.

"Good morning," Mary greeted them, happy for the distraction.

John nodded at her, grabbed a biscuit from the basket on the table, and followed George out the door.

Mary laid the shirts across the back of a chair and tried not to look at Martha's round belly. "Martha, shall we get started on the pies for tomorrow's celebration?"

"What's tomorrow?" Angelica asked as she climbed onto a kitchen chair and plucked her own biscuit from the basket.

"Independence Day," Mary answered.

"What's that?"

"It's when we celebrate independence from Great Britain."

"What's Great Britain?"

"It's a country across the ocean. Many years ago, people came to America from other places, and the king of England controlled this land and the people who lived here."

"What's England?" Angelica interrupted.

"Hush!" her mother admonished her. "You listen, you learn."

Mary gave a gentle laugh. "England is a part of Great Britain. I guess. It's a bit confusing, I know."

The girl screwed up her face and looked about to question further, but a look from her mother silenced her.

"Well," Mary continued, "the people who lived in the American colonies wanted to be free. They didn't want others to control their land and their destiny, to tell them how to live, and so they fought a war to win their independence."

Angelica looked thoughtful. "That the war going right now?"

Mary shook her head. "No, child. This was almost one hundred years ago. It was a different war."

"Don't seem different."

"Quiet, girl," Martha said. "You get outside and let me and Mrs. Balsam get to work."

Angelica leapt to her bare feet and streaked out the door.

"And you stay away from them chickens!" her mother shouted after her. Then she said in a quiet tone, "Sorry 'bout that."

Mary shook her head. "No need. I suppose she is right."

Martha poured herself a cup of coffee. "Same fight, different folk." Then the women silently took up their tasks of making pie crusts, rinsing berries, and measuring out flour and sugar and cinnamon.

"That baby is beautiful," Bridget said as she came in with a tray.

Mary was happy to see that the plate was scraped clean. "I see our new guest likes your biscuits, Bridget."

"I think she would have eaten twice as much."

The three women bustled about in the kitchen for much of the rest of the morning, leaving only to pump fresh water for the pot or go to the outhouse or check on Loretta and her baby.

At lunchtime, every spot at Mary's dining room table was filled. She marveled at the change from those first few months after Nathaniel enlisted, when it was just her and Bridget scraping by. Six months after George arrived, Jacob had appeared at the back door, terrified and frostbitten. He had lost two toes and part of an ear but had otherwise made a full recovery. The Dixons came the next spring, escaping from their plantation mere hours before the master planned to sell off Martha and Angelica to another owner. Thomas made it the previous fall, claiming to have covered the last three hundred miles clinging to the underside of a train car. Mary wasn't sure she believed that, but the story of his escape had captivated them all.

Mary looked around the table and made a mental note to find a chair for Loretta for dinner. For now, the woman lay in Bridget's room, hidden away while the terror of her escape left her little by little, breath by free breath. But she would soon be welcomed with open arms into this convocation of friends.

After lunch, the wagon was loaded with vegetables and socks the women had knitted in the evenings. Mary handed George a list of necessary dry goods. "Please bring back the mail and the *Free Press*. Of course it will be nothing but bad news, but we must keep abreast of it nonetheless."

"Yes, ma'am," George said.

"I wish you wouldn't do that."

"What?"

"Call me ma'am."

"It's a habit. You don't object when Bridget says it."

Thomas walked in then.

"Thinking of Bridget," Mary said, "do you want her to go with you to town?"

"Yes," Thomas said at the exact moment George said, "No need."

Thomas gave George a look, which Mary read clearly. She would have to watch Thomas and Bridget. Now seventeen, the girl had become quite a beauty. It wouldn't do to allow the two young people to develop any sort of attachment when it could only lead to heartache.

"Mr. Hathaway knows me well enough," George said. "We'll do our business, pick up the mail and the paper, and come straight home. That time was just bad timing, is all."

Mary recalled her horror at George returning from town a few months prior with a black eye and a bloodied lip. His only offense had been the unfortunate coincidence of going to town when news was breaking of the draft riots in Detroit. After that, Mary went to town herself or sent Bridget along.

"If you're sure," she said. "I feel silly for even asking as I'm sure there are none to be had, but do see if you can bring back some lemons for lemonade."

George and Thomas tipped their hats and with a snap of the reins were on the move. Mary watched them drive out past the low stone wall and down the dusty road. What could she write to George that would be true and yet safe?

It was when she was sweeping flour from the counter into her hand that it dawned on her: she had lived with George longer than she had lived with Nathaniel. She felt disloyal even thinking it. But the fact of the matter was that while Nathaniel was tramping all over Virginia, the one who planted their crops and mended their fences and mucked out their stalls was George. He was the one who had been there for her at her darkest hour. He was the one who might soon walk into the kitchen with a crate of tangy lemons. He was the one she thought about upon waking and the last one on her mind as she drifted off to sleep.

At the burbling sound of a baby, Mary turned to see Loretta standing at the door to the kitchen, tiny Simon in her thin arms.

"Loretta! I'm so glad you feel well enough to come downstairs. Please sit down." Mary pulled out a seat. "Can I get you a cup of water?"

"I'll get it."

Mary put her hands on the woman's shoulders and guided her to the chair. "Certainly not. Sit down here and I'll fetch it for you." She poured a cup of water from the pitcher and placed it on the table. "We'll have supper soon, once George and Thomas have returned."

Mary gazed at the mother and child before her. How could she have looked at any of these individuals as undeserving of the sacrifice the Union was making on battlefields all over the South? It seemed to her now that the lives of the Negro and the lives of the white man were placed upon an enormous scale, and that soldiers would continue to die until the misery and grief had been balanced.

The baby gurgled again.

"May I?" Mary asked, indicating the child.

Loretta pulled back a bit.

"I won't hurt him, I promise. I just . . . I haven't held a baby in a long time."

Loretta's face remained suspicious, but she held out the boy to Mary's waiting arms. The moment the baby changed hands, Loretta slumped, exhausted, in her chair.

Mary gazed at Simon's little round face and wide brown eyes and smiled despite the pain in her heart. She cooed and soothed the already content child. Then she looked at Loretta. The young mother seemed on the verge of collapse.

"Loretta, you may stay here as long as you like. As you can see, several souls have joined my household to work the farm. Others have stopped for a night or two and moved on. If you stay and help around the house, I can offer little pay beyond a place to lay your head and food for your belly. I do manage to pay the men who work the farm, and I will see what I can do for you."

Loretta smiled weakly but said nothing.

"Would you like me to take care of the baby for a little while so you can get some sleep?" Mary said. "I can wake you when he's hungry."

Loretta nodded, finished her water, and drifted out the door. For the next hour, Mary marveled at Simon's every detail—his wise eyes, his perfect bow of a mouth, his wavy hair that tended toward brown more than black, his silky light brown skin. She showed him the books in the library and tickled his nose with a quill pen. But the spell was broken when his empty belly made him call out for food, which she could not provide.

Mary walked up the stairs and entered the back bedchamber after a soft knock. Loretta was already pushing herself upright in bed.

Once Simon was suckling, Mary gathered enough courage to ask the question that had been plaguing her since Loretta arrived. "Where is his father?"

"Back on the plantation."

Mary frowned. "I'm so sorry. It is a pity he couldn't have come with you."

Loretta looked at her with confusion. "He the master."

Mary glanced at the child upon Loretta's breast, as much white as he was black. And yet, if Loretta hadn't escaped, he would be a slave in his own father's household.

Mary was searching for the right thing to say when George's voice filtered up the stairs. "Excuse me." She hurried down to the kitchen and found George talking to Bridget.

"Did you manage any lemons?" Mary asked with a hopeful smile.

"It's this you'll be most interested in seeing."

He pointed at the newspaper on the table in front of Bridget, who was as white as cream. The horror leapt out in cold black letters. Tens of thousands killed. Whole regiments lost. Carnage unimaginable.

Gettysburg.

NINETEEN

Lapeer County, September

I'd shaken the habit of going to church back in college. It wasn't that I was mad at God exactly. He'd just slipped a bit in my estimation. I found him less dependable, so I got less dependable too.

Still, I wanted to make a good impression on Nora. By nine o'clock Sunday I was bedecked in Dana's red dress—the only dress I owned—my hair was curled, and I even put on a little makeup. I tugged the dress's neckline up a few times, then added a black cardigan, which did nothing to help the problem but seemed to me to indicate that I had at least made an effort to be modest.

I went down to the kitchen expecting to see Nora dressed similarly—albeit with a higher neckline—so I was surprised to see her still in her robe and slippers, nursing a cup of coffee.

"You're awfully dressed up," she said.

"I figured we'd be going to church."

She stroked Matthew's fur. "Not this morning."

"Aren't you feeling well?"

"I just don't think I'll go today. But since you're all dressed up, you could."

"Without you?"

"Sure. Don't let me stop you."

Before I stopped going, Sunday church had been part of my weekly routine from my earliest days. Yet the thought of showing up alone at a new church did not appeal to me in the least.

"I wouldn't know where to go."

"There's a phone book in the drawer under the toaster. I'm sure they're all listed."

I hesitated. "How about I make us breakfast this morning and we stay home?"

"Breakfast would be nice."

I pulled out the pancake mix we had bought the day before and whipped up a batch, all the while wondering why Nora didn't want to go to church if she wasn't sick. All old ladies went to church. That was part of the old lady deal.

"Tell me about your parents, Elizabeth. I've lost track of my nieces and nephews over the years."

"They're medical missionaries in Brazil. They work with people who still get their living from the Amazon River. Raise pigs and farm in the dry season. Then when the river floods their land in the rainy season, they do a lot of fishing. And that's when Mom and Dad get visitors from all along the river. They paddle in to the clinic to get help with medical issues."

Nora had a faraway look in her eyes. "Have you ever been there?"

"I've never been anywhere."

"Me neither. We moved not long after we got married, and I haven't really left since."

Marriage. I was in. But I had to be careful.

"When was that?"

"1963."

I nodded and waited for her to say more. But she didn't.

"Were you married in Lapeer?" I prodded.

"No, Detroit. Like Mary and Nathaniel were. Then they moved out here to build where there was lots of land."

And just like that, we were talking about Mary again, Nora's favorite subject. But I needed to keep this train on the tracks.

"Tell me about your husband," I said.

Nora looked at her empty coffee cup. A minute dragged by, but I didn't speak to fill the silence. One of my journalism professors had told us to just wait in these situations. "No one can stand empty space in a conversation for very long. Your interview subject will speak eventually if you give them time."

Finally Nora stood up. "I've got a terrible headache. I'm sorry. I'm going to go back to bed."

So much for that.

It was only ten o'clock by the time I got breakfast cleaned up. Tyrese wasn't due until noon. Two empty hours stretched out before me, so I kicked off my sandals and headed barefoot to the garden. A flock of noisy blackbirds rose as one from the field as I approached the trays of discounted plants from Perkins just outside the gate. I positioned the pots here and there, consulting a drawing I had sketched the night before. I tried to imagine them all at their full height and spread. How did anyone know what a garden would look like in the future?

Then I noticed some dandelion leaves poking up near a fence post. Then some more. Then some more. Crouching in the dirt in Dana's red dress, I started digging. The leaves continued several inches down into the soil, having sprung from some small portion of root I'd failed to remove. I dug deep, gripped the offending root, and pulled, but the soil was still wet and my fingers slipped. I dug deeper, grasped more firmly, and tugged. The root snapped off in my hand. I tried again. Another little bit broke off. On the other side of the fence, Matthew smirked at my futile efforts.

After this irritating scenario repeated itself with every bit of dandelion root I found, I gave up in exasperation, back aching and knees sore from squatting. I pulled my cardigan off and used it to mop the sweat from my forehead and the back of my neck. With one blackened bare foot, I pushed the soil back over the last bit of root, vowing to forget about it and telling myself that I'd done enough. Surely it wouldn't grow back again. It was time for a shower.

Matthew took off in an orange streak, and I spied Tyrese walking toward me.

"A little overdressed for yardwork, aren't you?"

I gave a little laugh to cover my embarrassment. I must look ridiculous. "Yeah, I wasn't planning on doing all this when I came out here. It kind of got away from me."

"Looks like you've made a lot of progress." He motioned to the wet, rotting piles of weeds and vines I'd pulled earlier that I still hadn't burned.

"That's what I've been doing all week. And they're already coming back."

"Weeds do that. Gotta keep on top of them." He put his hands on the fence and surveyed the battlefield. "So what are your plans?"

I picked up my sketch and brushed the dirt from it. "This is what I was thinking, though I'm having a hard time seeing what it would all look like in real life."

He examined the paper, mouth twisted in thought. I pulled at the neckline of Dana's dress, leaving an obvious smudge of black dirt on my chest.

"Can I suggest a few revisions?"

"Suggest away. I'll take all the advice I can get."

For the next few minutes he explained why what I had planned wouldn't work. By the time he was done, my plans lay in ruins.

"I told you I don't know what I'm doing."

He laughed. "Good thing you've got me, eh?"

"Did you want to see the rosebushes?"

At the mention of the roses, he snapped into action, looking under leaves, lifting branches, examining the little green, orange, and red balls left after the petals had dropped, which I would later learn were called hips. He even searched the ground around the plant.

"What are you looking for down there?"

"Just seeing if there are any dried-up petals so I can try to guess what color the flowers are."

"We could ask Nora. Let me run inside a minute and see if she remembers."

I rinsed my feet off in the cold stream of water from the pump and dried them with my defeated cardigan, then took a detour through the main floor bathroom to survey the damage. My hair hung in limp clumps, my cheeks were flushed, and a streak of dirt ran across my forehead like tire tracks. I washed my hands and rinsed the dirt from my face. I ran a brush through my hair, but it only seemed to make things worse.

I knocked on Nora's bedroom door and opened it a crack when she didn't answer. She was still in her nightgown, lying in bed beneath the crazy quilt. In a moment of panic, I put my face near hers. Not dead. Just asleep. She must be coming down with something after all.

I crept back out of the room and shut the door. Matthew was sitting in the hall, staring daggers at me. I left him there, changed into jeans and a T-shirt, and went back out to the garden.

"She's taking a nap."

"That's okay. I think I've got a few clues to go on here. But I'll want to take some cuttings with me if you don't mind. Just to be sure."

"No problem. I have some shears. Let me go grab them."

"Not just yet. I'll make the cuttings right before I leave, and we'll put them in some wet paper towels so they'll keep until I can get them in water."

"Okay." I was pleased beyond reason that he was not leaving right away. "Do you want something to drink?"

"Sure. Why don't we sit down and see if we can draw up some revised plans?"

I narrowed my eyes. "Am I going to get charged some sort of consulting fee for this?"

He laughed. "No, ma'am. Just helping out a friend."

"My friends don't call me ma'am."

He kept smiling. "No, I guess they probably don't."

My own smile faltered, though. Did I even have any real friends? My job had kept me so busy, I'd hardly taken time for anyone the past several years. I had Desiree, I guess. But I doubted we would stay in touch without the *Free Press* to bind us together.

Inside, we sat at the kitchen table, sipping lemonade and talking herbs. Tyrese drew out two garden plans, one formal and symmetrical, the other with a winding path and haphazard—or so it seemed to me—placement of plants.

"See, we've got the same plants in each of these, but a totally different look and feel. Which one speaks to you?"

"I like the geometrical one."

"It's a little formal for this type of house and setting, but I have to say I'm a fan of that one too. It would take more upkeep."

"Then maybe that's not the best idea. I don't think Nora's up to that."

He frowned. "I thought this was your garden."

"That's what she says, but I don't really live here. I'm just visiting."

Tyrese swirled the ice in his glass. "That's too bad."

"Why's that?"

He shrugged. "You may not have noticed this, but there's

not a lot of people our age in Lapeer. I kind of liked the idea of hanging out a little with someone over eighteen and under forty, you know?"

I smiled. "Yeah, I guess so. Well, I'm here for now. So let me know if you ever want to hang out."

"I sure will."

TWENTY

Detroit, June 1963

Nora slid past nine sets of knees, gripping the backs of the chairs in the row ahead to keep her balance. She could sense William's hand at the small of her back, ready to steady her, but not touching. Haunted by the warning she had felt in that man Derek's voice, Nora had suggested that they maintain a platonic facade in public. William had agreed, so that while they might kiss tenderly behind curtained windows, they avoided eye contact in certain parts of town. It kept things simpler, even if it didn't stop the sometimes quizzical and often disgusted looks they got from strangers when they walked down the street or sat in a movie theater together.

Now as they found their seats by Bianca and J.J. in the packed auditorium of Cobo Hall, Nora felt eyes upon her. It was an odd sensation to be the minority—one she still wasn't used to. There were other white people there, but they were outnumbered more than ten to one, and in an auditorium that seated twenty-five thousand people, that ratio was on full display.

It had taken William some time to convince Nora to attend the speech, let alone to take part in the freedom march down

Woodward. It was one thing to break with convention in the privacy of her own apartment or William's house. It was quite another to make a public spectacle of herself.

"It's just walking down a street," he'd said through playful kisses.

"It isn't and you know it."

"I know you got legs."

"Yes, but—"

"Then you can do it."

"No," she said, getting to her feet. "I'm sorry, but I just don't see myself marching—for anything. It's not this cause—you know it's not. It's any cause."

William sighed. "No one's asking you to hold a sign or chant a slogan or do anything but walk."

"Balsams don't march. We mind our own business. We don't protest. We don't make a fuss."

"That's because you've got nothing to make a fuss about."

Some variation of this conversation had occurred three evenings in a row. Most nights now, when William got out of work, Nora would put together a simple meal of sandwiches or soup and salad. They'd eat, drink, listen to records, and share their most intimate thoughts, digging themselves ever deeper into a love from which they were helpless to escape. But when news of the march and the rally filtered through William's community, it brought with it cold reality, unwelcome and unavoidable.

She finally broke down the night before at the Rich house when William said, "Listen, this *is* your business because I'm asking you to do it for me, not for everyone else or the cause. For me. If I'm going to photograph this event, I need you to be another set of eyes and hands. Gonna be all sorts of stuff going on and I don't want to miss a good shot. I've got a good chance of selling some photos of this event. Will you help me?"

And so she had reluctantly submerged herself in the river of souls flowing down Woodward from the headwaters at Adelaide to the restless, eddying pool at Cobo Hall. She settled into the seat next to Bianca and leaned toward her rather than William. Few in Detroit would look askance at a white woman and a black woman who were casual friends. And she had to believe that this crowd would be as sympathetic as they came. The hubbub continued as people found their seats, then the lights dimmed, twenty-five thousand voices hushed, and a kind-eyed, impeccably dressed man strode on stage to vigorous applause.

"That's Reverend Franklin from New Bethel Baptist Church," Bianca said over the clapping.

Nora nodded blankly.

"Aretha Franklin's father," Bianca clarified.

That name Nora could identify. The new singer was making some waves in Detroit, and her powerful voice could often be heard coming from the Riches' record player. But Rev. Franklin wasn't who they had come to see, and he seemed to know that, wasting little time introducing the man of the hour.

"And now, my friends, let the trumpets sound, let the bells ring, let the drums roll. Lay out the red carpet. Here he comes: America's beloved freedom fighter, Martin Luther King!"

The crowd erupted. Nora fixed her eyes upon the man. He seemed to fill the hall with a quiet dignity that was larger than he was. His voice had a leisurely, plodding cadence only acquired in the South. It was difficult for him to say much more than a sentence or two without interruption from the jubilant audience. Nora tried to settle into the steady exchange of carefully chosen words and rapturous applause. From all directions, the powerful thrum of clapping resonated, so different in quality than the measured applause at the symphony. Voices called out "All right" and "Uh-huh" and "Mm-hmm." To her right, William leaned forward, his forearms resting on his knees, eyes fixed on the stage. To her left, Bianca nodded rhythmically in affirmation. Beside his mother, J.J. slumped back in his chair, hands dangling off the armrests.

And as King's words rolled over her, Nora found herself nodding in her heart, if not her head.

"We've got to come to see," he said, "that the problem of racial injustice is a national problem. No community in this country can boast of clean hands in the area of brotherhood. Now in the North it's different in that it doesn't have the legal sanction that it has in the South. But it has its subtle and hidden forms and it exists in three areas: in the area of employment discrimination, in the area of housing discrimination, and in the area of de facto segregation in the public schools. And we must come to see that de facto segregation in the North is just as injurious as the actual segregation in the South."

Nora was still trying to process these words when pounding waves of applause engulfed her.

"That's right," William said.

"All right," Bianca said.

Even J.J. sat up straight and shouted, "Yeah!"

"And so," King went on, "if you want to help us in Alabama and Mississippi and all over the South, do all that you can to get rid of the problem here."

He went on to speak of marching on Washington; of sacrifice, imprisonment, and death; and of dreams and dignity. On all sides, bodies shifted in their seats, hands clapped, and heads nodded until the entire mass of people seemed to vibrate in anticipation of something big. Each wave of clapping and shouting pushed the words deeper into Nora's heart.

As King came to the end of his speech and quoted a song she had never sung in her reserved Presbyterian church, Nora felt that someone had turned on a light. She understood the rundown houses in William's neighborhood, the cautious kindness his mother had shown to her during the past six weeks, the way J.J. looked at her when she parked her Corvette in front of their house. She knew why that Derek fellow had been so opposed to her presence in William's arms. She knew without a doubt that she would not have said yes if William had asked her on a date. She knew that the reason she had not told her parents she was seeing him was more than that he was a particular man who had angered her father. She had been afraid of the judgments they would make about her intelligence, morals, and common sense. She knew she was a coward.

And she knew she had to make it right.

Late that night, when she and William lounged on the couch listening to Chico Hamilton on the hi-fi, Nora gathered her courage.

"William, where do you think this is going?"

"I think it's going to Washington's where I think it's going. I think we're finally going to see some real change."

She sat up and turned to face him. "That's not what I mean. I mean us."

"Oh." Concern settled on his face. "Well, I hope it's going somewhere. Hope it's not going away."

She smiled to reassure him. "Me too."

"Good."

She leaned back in his arms and talked to the ceiling. "Only that speech got me thinking."

"If it didn't, I'd be worried about you."

"I think we should get married."

He sat up. "Say what?"

Nora frowned at him. "You don't think we should?"

"Well, no. I mean, I do. I just thought maybe I'd be the one to do the asking. Eventually."

She smiled, relieved. "When?"

"I don't know. Didn't think you were ready for that question yet. And I sure don't think your family's ready for it."

Nora shook her head. "They'll never be ready. We can't wait for that."

"Fair enough." He took her hands in his. "So what you thinking?"

"How about tomorrow?"

His eyebrows shot up. "Tomorrow? Are you crazy?"

"No. I just don't see a reason to wait. My parents aren't going to pay for it no matter what. There's no planning needed. All we need is us and a couple witnesses."

"For real?"

"Yes."

He looked at her sideways. "You sure you're not just high on Martin Luther King?"

She tugged at his hands. "I want to marry you. I don't care what my parents say. I don't care what other people say. I just want to be with you."

"Stop and think a minute, Nora. Think of what you'd be giving up. No wedding dress. No cake. No dancing. No gifts."

"I know."

"And that's just that day. What about your parents? Are they going to be Grandma and Grandpa to our kids? They even going to talk to you anymore?"

She couldn't let herself think about that. "They'll come around if they're forced to."

"Psh. I bet they said the same thing about the Confederates when they lost the war, and those white boys down South still ain't come around in a hundred years."

Her confidence faltered, but just for a moment. "William, every hour I'm with you, that's the best hour of my day."

He pulled her into his arms. "Mine too, baby."

They sat for a moment, lost in silent thoughts of an uncertain future.

"Okay, Nora," William finally said. "Let's get married."

The next afternoon, Nora stood in a pale pink dress beside William before a justice of the peace, vowing to devote her life to a man she had known for three months. She pushed every anxious thought from her mind, but her hands were still sweating and her stomach churned. Behind them, Bianca and Diane witnessed the proceedings, both looking apprehensive and skeptical.

As they were waiting in the lobby for their turn, Diane had pulled Nora aside. "Are you out of your mind? You are committing suicide here. Social and familial suicide. Do you know what people will say about you?"

Nora fiddled with the corsage William had affixed to her dress. "Diane, I need your signature, not your opinions."

"And if I give you that, how am I not also giving my blessing on this whole sordid affair? Your parents will hate me. *My* parents will hate me. You're dragging me down with you into the gutter. Guilt by association."

"Diane, I'm going to forgive you for that because we've been friends so long."

"Don't forgive me, just don't do this," Diane pleaded. "You'll regret it the rest of your life."

Nora looked Diane in the eye. "I love him. If I don't marry him, that's what I would regret." But she was talking more to herself than anyone else.

Diane had looked like she was about to respond when the clerk called out their names. They filed into the chamber, made their simple vows to one another before a sour-faced judge, and exchanged the simple gold bands they had bought that morning.

When the papers were all signed, Diane said, "Wish I could be a fly on the wall when your parents find out about this." Then she turned and walked away, her footsteps echoing in the hall like a fading heartbeat.

Bianca was more subtle. "I sure hope you two know what you've gotten yourselves into."

William kissed her on the cheek. "We know."

Bianca shook her head and looked at her brother the same way she looked at her impossible son. "I'm late for work."

When it was just the two of them in that cold, empty hall, William tipped Nora's face up to meet his. "Now then, Mrs. Rich, how about I take you back to your apartment—"

"*Our* apartment."

"—our apartment, and you let me show you just how much I love you."

Nora turned the shade of her dress and looked around to make sure no one had overheard.

"Don't worry, baby. There's no one here but us. It's you and me against the world."

Nora smiled. As long as she kept looking into those eyes, everything would work out just fine.

Wouldn't it?

TWENTY-ONE

Lapeer County, December 1863

In the soft gray before the dawn, Mary awoke but did not open her eyes. She could still see Nathaniel coming up the road toward the house, could still feel the cold wind on her face as she rushed out to greet him in the snow, could still hear the yells and clapping behind her as everyone called out their jubilation. But if she opened her eyes, it would all be gone, replaced by a cold room and the final dying embers of last night's fire. Then she felt a warm hand on her cheek.

"Good morning, my love." Nathaniel's sleepy blue eyes lay inches from hers.

"So you are real," Mary said. "I thought I might wake up to find that yesterday had been a dream."

"I am here," he whispered as he stroked her cheek. "And so happy to be waking up next to you in my own bed."

Mary tested the air outside of the covers with one foot. "I'll stoke the fire."

"No, stay. Let's just stay here in bed all day."

She laughed. "I have a houseful of people who might wonder at such behavior."

Nathaniel frowned, then stood and walked over to the hearth. His nightshirt hung limply on his angular frame. He was thinner, his face drawn, his gait uneven. He poked at the ash, added a bit of paper and a few slim pieces of kindling, and blew on the embers.

"You're not upset, are you?" Mary asked him.

"Upset?"

"About how many are living here. I thought I had written you about each of them, and so I had until Loretta came. But she just arrived in July, and when we heard the news about Gettysburg, of course it slipped my mind."

"I'm not upset, Mary. I think it's wonderful. I've been so happy to know you've not been alone. I do wish you'd told me about John Grouse and Mrs. Maggin a little earlier. I'd have sent you to live with Mother."

Exactly, Mary thought. "But then what would have happened to George? You couldn't have sent him to your mother's house. She might have had an attack if it were her opening that trunk."

Nathaniel looked grave. "But perhaps then you wouldn't have lost the baby."

"Perhaps," she said softly. "But what of the Dixons and Jacob and Thomas? And Loretta and Simon? I know it was wrong to keep the business about John and Mrs. Maggin from you, but perhaps God used my deception for his own ends."

Nathaniel smiled then. "Anyway, what's done is done, and I am certain God is using this house for his purposes. It is his safe haven for the oppressed. And you are his instrument of love and care."

"Hardly," she demurred. "George is more his instrument than I. I don't know what we'd do without him."

"Let's hope we don't find out. Now, can we get this starving soldier his breakfast? You can't imagine how I am looking forward to eggs and bacon and flapjacks with maple syrup."

Downstairs the house was abuzz with activity as Bridget,

Martha, and Loretta made breakfast and continued to prepare all of the special dishes for their Christmas celebration. Pots clanged, dishes clinked, and Angelica was shooed out of the kitchen half a dozen times in as many minutes.

"Why don't you entertain Simon in the parlor, Angelica?" Mary finally suggested. "You can let him play with some of these ribbons." She handed the girl a tangled mass of red ribbons left over from the making of garlands and wreaths the day before.

"Okay," Angelica acquiesced, "but if he start stinkin' I's gone."

Nathaniel laughed out loud.

Mary silenced him with a look. "You'll do no such thing," she said. "You'll take him upstairs and change him."

Angelica looked at her shoes. "Yes, ma'am."

"My, my," Nathaniel teased. "You certainly have become a force to reckon with."

Mary picked up Nathaniel's dishes and paused at the kitchen door. "When one is suddenly left in charge of an entire household, one does what one must to keep things running."

Thus chastened, Nathaniel followed the men into the library to get an update on the farm and the finances. Mary was still in the kitchen when they all filed through to the backyard to feed and water the animals and chop more wood. She measured flour and butter and cinnamon, sliced through apples, crushed walnuts—each movement precise, each result of her efforts predictable. She had done more than manage without her husband. Here she reigned supreme and unquestioned. Until now.

It felt good to have Nathaniel in the house again. Yet Mary had to admit that it wasn't the same. She wondered if it ever could be. She could tell by the way his sharp eyes lingered on the woodpile and the pantry and the people living and working in the house that he was assessing. Mary hated that she wondered how she measured up.

For his part, Nathaniel seemed distant despite the proximity, lost perhaps in thoughts of the soldiering life. So accustomed was he to the constant company of men and lack of women that she overheard him tell more than one crude joke she had never imagined he would make. The rest of the men stopped their chopping and stacking outside the kitchen and laughed. Except George. She had not heard his familiar low, sweet laugh among the voices.

That evening, they made the trip to church for the Christmas Eve service. Mary was grateful that Nathaniel would be with them. Reverend Whittaker's acceptance of her ever-multiplying houseguests at worship services each Sunday had held for many months. But when Loretta and Simon had been added to the group, the minister had taken Mary aside after service one day with concern written in his eyes.

"I wonder if I might have a quick word with you, Mrs. Balsam."

"Of course, Reverend."

"As you know, we are all impressed at your fervor for abolition and your willingness to aid the escape of Negroes from the South. And I know that I gave you permission to bring George to services. But I must pass on a concern that has been brought to my attention."

"What is it?"

He furrowed his brow and hesitated as though he were not sure he should tell her after all. "There are some in the congregation who are beginning to wonder why some of these folks are not moving on. Most seem to use our town as a resting point on a longer journey, and we've seen them once or twice. And I don't believe I have heard concerns about them particularly. But people are questioning those who have been under your roof for more than a year—and in George's case, more than two years. Isn't it time they moved on?"

"Is it?" she asked in surprise.

Reverend Whittaker looked uncomfortable. "Well, some would say so."

"Would you?"

"Mrs. Balsam, I know you mean well, but on one end some are complaining about having these Negroes at our services at all and about them doing business around town in your name. I'm not among them. I believe as you do that they are God's children the same as you and I. But there is that sentiment. And on the other end, some of your former supporters are now comparing your farm to a Southern plantation."

Mary gasped. "But—"

"I know that you pay them what you can and that they are free to leave whenever they choose. But I wanted you to know that there has been murmuring about it."

"I won't turn them out of my home, if that's what you're suggesting."

"Of course not. But I wonder if it would be best to limit their contact with certain members of the church."

After that unsavory conversation, Mary had suggested to George that they hold their own services in the parlor on Sunday mornings. She framed it as a way to give the horses a Sabbath of their own by sparing them the long trip pulling a wagon full of people, but she was sure that they all suspected otherwise. She was certain that Reverend Whittaker had meant for her to continue coming with Bridget and leave the others behind. But this she would not do.

Now, as they all stomped the snow from their boots and filed into the little church for this special service, Mary examined the faces of the parishioners to determine who might be standing in judgment of her. It was difficult to tell, as most were preoccupied with Nathaniel and the few other soldiers home on a rare furlough.

So many families had been touched by grief, and it seemed

that every battle was worse than the one before it. These survivors were claimed as evidence that all had not yet been lost. Mary looked at those who had lost a son or husband or brother at Gettysburg or Chancellorsville or Antietam and was ashamed of her pettiness. Why should it matter if some disapproved? Her family was still untouched by war's deathly finger. Even Nathaniel's brothers had managed to stay alive thus far, though one had sacrificed a leg.

"Why so gloomy?" Bridget said in her ear.

"Not gloomy. Humbled."

Later that evening they were gathered around the hearth in the parlor as Nathaniel read from Luke. Little by little the crowd thinned. Loretta went up with Simon, Martha retired with Angelica and her new baby, Elwin, and Bridget tumbled exhausted into her cot, which had been moved into Loretta's already small room while Nathaniel was home. Soon it was only Mary, Nathaniel, and four emancipated men who were eager for a backstage look at the war effort.

Mary pulled out the quilt she was working on. Not long after losing the baby, she had begun cutting up some of her fine dresses and remnants from pillows and curtains she had made for the house when they first moved in. Stitch by stitch, she had pulled these colorful scraps together until she had enough to cover her bed. Now she chose from varied colors of embroidery thread to embellish it as Nathaniel commanded the room.

"It is hard to bear the bitterness of the Southern women whose houses we often use as our headquarters," he said. "And well I understand it. While this farm is enjoying prosperity in the Union's efforts to supply the troops, Southern farms are stripped bare of every conceivable useful thing. Soldiers take meat from smokehouses, flour and sugar from barrels, onions and potatoes from the root cellar, pigs and chickens from the fields, fence rails for firewood, and every scrap of leather or piece of silver is pocketed."

"How terrible," Mary said.

"You could not imagine it unless you were there."

Mary threaded a needle with red embroidery floss and pushed it into a patch of green silk left over from the dress she had dismantled to replace the lining in Nathaniel's trunk.

"The night after a skirmish the field is covered in the dead. And once the sound of cannons and rifles dies down, you can hear the moaning of the wounded out among the corpses. You can't sleep for the groans and screams. But if the battle has not yet been won, you dare not go out to them and draw fire."

Mary shivered as she pulled the needle toward her, the long red trail of thread making a shushing sound as she drew it through the stiff silk. She didn't want to hear of the horrors of war, especially since Nathaniel must soon return to them. Neither did she want to leave the faces glowing in the firelight for her dark, empty room.

"I made the mistake one night of looking out to see if I could identify the source of a voice I thought I knew. The moon was almost full and I could see the field. It was moving, like waves on a lake after a boat has passed by."

Mary put down her needle and looked up. Jacob's face was frozen in hypnotic terror.

"What was it?" he whispered.

"The wounded. Hundreds of them. Maybe thousands."

"Nathaniel, I don't think we should talk about this so late at night," Mary admonished. "And on Christmas Eve, after all."

Nathaniel rubbed his hands over his face. "You're right. I'm sorry."

The spell was broken. The other men sat back in their seats. Jacob shook his head, perhaps to dislodge the frightening images from his brain.

Thomas, who had been uncharacteristically quiet, slapped his knees and got to his feet. "I gotta get some sleep," he said. "Good night."

"Good night, Thomas," Mary said.

Jacob rushed after him with a hasty good night, then John stood and took his leave.

Mary tied off the red thread and pulled the knot through the fabric with a popping sound.

"What is this you're doing, Mary?" Nathaniel asked.

"I'm making a quilt. It's quite popular now. And it gives me something to do in the evenings."

"Mrs. Balsam has been working on that almost since the day I got here," George offered.

Nathaniel leaned closer. "My heavens," he said, pointing to the stitching she had just completed, "it looks like a river. How is that accomplished?"

"A river? Oh dear. It's supposed to look like a ribbon. Why would a river be red?"

"Oh, I see. It does look like a ribbon."

But now as she examined it, Mary did see a river. A river running red with blood.

"It's deceptively simple," she said, pushing the image from her mind.

Nathaniel yawned. "Perhaps you can show me tomorrow. I must retire. Are you coming up?"

"Soon," she said. "I just want to do a little more while I still have the firelight."

Nathaniel nodded and stood. "Don't be too long. It can't be good for your eyes. Good night, George."

"Good night, sir."

He disappeared beyond the ring of light around the hearth.

Mary threaded her needle again. "I wish now I hadn't made this red. I'll never be able to look at it again without thinking of the blood of those dying men. What a dreadful story to tell us."

George nodded. "But I suppose in the telling a man gets some relief of his burden."

"I suppose."

"It's terrible hard to carry around a secret pain all by yourself."

"Yes. Yes it is."

Mary thought of her stillborn baby. But no. That was not secret. Thousands of other women suffered such pain, including some of those who had given her love and support after her own tragedy.

She looked at George, who was staring into the fire. "Do you carry such a pain, George?" It felt like too intimate a question, but there was no getting back the words. "How stupid of me. Of course you all do."

"The pain of slavery is no secret."

They were both quiet.

"But I do carry one," he said.

He met her gaze in that same sad and tender way he had at the kitchen door the day they learned of the devastation at Gettysburg, the day she felt she might have lost Nathaniel for good. It was the same expression she'd seen in Nathaniel's face when he had looked at her that morning.

Love.

At that moment, Mary knew she must write her long-tardy response to George's request for a letter.

TWENTY-TWO

Lapeer County, September

"Cardinal de Richelieu, Charles de Mills, Hénri Martin, and Rosa gallica officinalis. Those are my best guesses." Tyrese stood near the center of the garden and pointed at each of the four rosebushes in turn.

"Cardinal Richard, Charles de Mill, Henry Martin, and Rosa gallifinakus," I said.

He laughed. "I'll write them on the map." He pulled out two pairs of long leather gloves and handed one to me. "You're going to want to get some of these."

"Another trip to the nursery."

It had been three weeks since he'd taken the cuttings, weeks during which I had been to the nursery at least half a dozen times. I'd buy landscape fabric and gravel, then realize I didn't have any stakes to keep the fabric in place. Then there wasn't enough gravel. Then I remembered the edging to keep the tiny gray stones corralled. Then it seemed like I needed more plants. I always decided to make do, but Nora would push some cash into my hand and send me on my way.

"May as well do things the right way," she'd say. "If you rush things, they don't always turn out as good as they might have if you'd been just a little more intentional about them."

Sometimes Tyrese was there and sometimes he wasn't. But each time I saw him he would assure me he was "working on it." After stopping at the nursery, I'd sit for a half hour or so in the Kroger parking lot and follow the trail of little green leaves on Ancestry.com. I found Nora's parents, Daniel and Mallory, and discovered that while Daniel was my great-grandfather, my great-grandmother was not Nora's mother but a woman from an earlier marriage. More importantly, I found Nora's husband—William Rich—and the tumblers in the lock on my brain all fell into place and things started making sense.

Nora had said that William cut the lawn, but of course that was Tyrese. She'd said that William had freshened up what was the mustiest room on the planet. She'd said that William had planted the nearly dead tree in the backyard. That one might be true. The scanned marriage license proved that they had indeed been married in Detroit in 1963. But why had they moved? And when had William dropped out of the picture? So far my research had uncovered no death certificate.

"Why would someone plant roses in an herb garden?" I asked as Tyrese gathered up the thorny canes he'd pruned and slipped them into paper yard bags I held open.

"People used to make rose water to freshen their linens. You can use the hips for tea. And they just look and smell nice and give the garden a little height. Not everything in an herb garden is for eating." A look of concern came over him. "You do know what you're doing with this stuff, don't you? There are some plants that you just shouldn't mess around with. There are a number of dangerous plants that look a lot like edibles. Or sometimes one part of a plant is okay to ingest, but another is not. Like, you might eat rhubarb stalks, but the leaves are toxic."

He was looking around the garden, I assumed for all the

things that would kill me. He walked over to a patch of what I had determined was either Queen Anne's lace or caraway.

"This is water hemlock. You need to get it out of here. It's in the carrot and parsnip family—the roots even smell like carrots—but it's not edible. In fact, it's quite deadly."

Oops.

"Isn't that what killed Socrates?"

"That's the rumor. Wear gloves when you pull it up, make sure you get the roots, and wash your hands well afterward." He dumped some more clippings into the bag.

"Hey, how do you know so much about this stuff?"

"I majored in plant sciences at Michigan State. I planned to work for the Department of Natural Resources when I got out, but they didn't have any spots available and Dad needed me at the nursery."

"Your dad works there too?"

"He's Anthony Perkins. He owns it. Well, we own it now. He made me his partner last year."

I tried not to look surprised. "Why are you mowing lawns if you own the place?"

He tossed a full bag into the bed of his pickup. "I started mowing the lawn here right when I got home from college. The nursery got a call from that James Rich guy and I happened to answer it. He gave me his spiel, told me how much he'd be paying me, which was ridiculous for just mowing a lawn, and I took the job. Had to repay my college loans, you know?" He tossed another bag in. "Then I just got used to doing it. Now I put all that lawn money into a savings account and don't touch it. That way when I have my own kids maybe they won't need student loans for school."

When the last of the bags was in the truck, he got into the cab, shut the door, and then leaned out the open window. "I'm working tomorrow from ten to five. Want to come out and I'll get you hooked up with some rose gear?"

"Sure. I think that would work."

"Great! See you then."

He drove off, leaving a cloud of dust behind him, and I headed back into the kitchen where Nora was wiping the counter.

"Was that the young man from Perkins?" she asked, though I was pretty sure she knew it was.

"Yes. He came to tell me more about the roses. You know he owns that place? Him and his dad."

"Yes, of course. Tony Perkins bought it from Frank Wilson in the late 1980s."

I wondered why she didn't think it was strange for a business owner to be mowing her lawn. But it was none of my business. If I started to pry, Mr. Rich's cover might be blown.

"Think we'll see him again soon?" she asked.

"I'll see him tomorrow if I go in to get the gloves I need. Want to come with me?"

She draped the wet dishrag over the edge of the sink. "No, no. You go. I'd just get in the way. I have plenty to do here."

"It's not really like that, Aunt Nora. I've seen him five times and he's hardly talked about anything but plants."

She looked out the window and seemed to be remembering something pleasant. "Sometimes you just need the right moment."

The next day was cold, gray, and rainy, a day when you must accept that summer is truly over and done with. I drove down the county highway past fields of high corn and the occasional maple tree turning an intense orange.

I'd always had mixed feelings about maples. While others pointed them out as happy harbingers of the cozy season to come, they had always seemed to me to be reckless—the first small flames of fall, each dropping leaf a burning ember that spread the fire until every tree was bare and dead and the November snows came like ash. I'd learned not to share this opinion with others, as it was universally judged as incomprehensible. Everyone loved fall.

I couldn't say exactly why it depressed me. Maybe it was because winter in Detroit was the opposite of charming and fall was the warning sign that it was coming. Or maybe it had something to do with going back to school as a kid. Mom called it seasonal affective disorder. I didn't know what to call it. I just knew it always brought me down.

I parked the car in the dirt lot at Perkins and rushed through the raindrops. Scanning the ever-shrinking selection, I found what I needed too quickly.

"Can I leave these here?" I asked a clerk as I put my items on the end of a closed checkout counter.

"Sure. Can I help you find something else?"

No, not some*thing*. "Do you know if Tyrese is here today?"

"Mr. Perkins is around here somewhere. Want me to page him?"

"No, that's not necessary. I'll just look around."

"Be sure to check out our patio pots. Everything's on sale right now."

I walked down a ramp into the enormous greenhouse with metal tables that stretched on for fifty yards or more. Most were empty, but the ones near the front were crowded with chrysanthemums, that ubiquitous fall flower I had never cared for. A few workers milled about with hoses, but no Tyrese.

I slid open a heavy door and looked down at the tree and shrub area outside and saw no one at all. Then a fantastic notion popped into my head. A tree. I should buy a tree. A tree to replace the one by the garden. What had Nora called it? I put up my hood and walked down a long concrete ramp to the tree section.

Despite the rain, I started down a row of trees, looking at each plastic tag. Surely if I read the name I would know it.

Crab apple, cherry, pear, serviceberry. Another row. Oak, maple, birch, ash. All of them were on clearance, but none of them were what I was looking for.

"Can I help you find something, ma'am?" came a familiar voice.

I looked up. The rain dripped off Tyrese's hair and down his cheeks and soaked into his green fleece jacket.

"Elizabeth! I didn't recognize you with your hood up."

"Hi." I hoped I did not look too pleased to see him.

"Looking for a tree?"

"Sort of. There's that tree out back that's just about dead and I thought I'd replace it for my aunt, but I can't remember what she called it. I'd like to get the same kind. I thought I'd know it if I read the name, but nothing's sounding familiar."

"Our selection's picked over this time of year. Why don't you come into the booth over there out of the rain and I'll grab a book."

I was getting drenched, so I agreed at once. A moment later, we stood at a rough wooden countertop in a tiny booth barely big enough for two people. I could hardly turn the pages of the thick binder without elbowing Tyrese in the ribs. He smelled of earth and rain, and I turned the pages of the book slowly, more to extend the time we were stuck in that little shed than to study the pictures. Something about him made me feel relaxed, at ease, and yet all keyed up at the same time.

"That's it," he suddenly said, leaning close. "The catalpa."

I examined the page. The picture was of a tree with large, teardrop-shaped leaves. "Are they messy? She said it was messy."

"Oh yeah. Those seed pods can be over a foot long and they all fall to the ground, and not at the same time the leaves do, so you have to rake them all up in the spring. Well, I have to." He laughed. "They make a huge mess. And they get to be very big trees. They've sort of fallen out of favor. People mostly seem to want smaller flowering trees and statement foliage trees that give good color in fall, like maples. We don't typically carry these."

"Oh."

"But I could order one for you."

I turned to face him. "Really? You can?"

"Sure. It would come in the spring. I'll put in the order today." There was that killer smile again. "I got you covered."

An awkward silence descended as the eye contact lasted longer than the conversation.

"Well, okay then." I turned away. "I guess I'll just go buy my stuff at the front and see you later."

He stopped me with a hand on my arm. "Hey, would you ever want to go see a movie sometime?"

I almost didn't answer, so sure I was that he hadn't actually said it. But he was looking at me as though he were waiting for a response.

"That'd be nice."

"Why don't I give you a call tonight and we'll figure it out."

"Okay. I better go." I had to leave before the spell was broken and he changed his mind.

"Want me to walk you up?" he said.

"That's okay." I put my hood up. "Wouldn't want you to get wet."

He laughed and looked down at his already rain-soaked clothes.

I trotted back up the hill with a stupid smile fixed on my face. Maybe fall wasn't so bad after all.

TWENTY-THREE

Detroit, August 1963

Nora's steps on the gray tile floor echoed off the bare walls. She tried to see past the cosmetic failings to the potential that might lie beneath. Torn wallpaper, water-stained ceiling, gouged door frames, dirty carpet in the next room. The place smelled like an ashtray left out in the rain. William tapped her on the shoulder and, with an almost imperceptible shake of his head, expressed the same sentiment she felt. *This won't work. This isn't for us.*

They weren't quite out of options yet. There were other apartments in other neighborhoods. Though it seemed to Nora that she'd been in this same apartment a dozen times already. Why should the next one be any better?

"And this is the kitchen," came the voice of Mrs. Wendell from down the hall. "The appliances are in working order, and I think you'll like the spice rack."

William leaned in close to Nora's ear. "Let's get out of here. She's just wasting our time. We can't live here. It's a terrible neighborhood. No insurance company is going to cover us here."

The overly coiffed head of their Realtor appeared in a doorway. "Come, come, we haven't time to dillydally."

William pushed ahead of Nora and into the kitchen. "When are you going to show us some places in Southfield or Warren?"

Mrs. Wendell offered a condescending smile. "That's not in your budget, I'm afraid."

"Okay, fine, but there's better neighborhoods in Detroit. What about the East Side?"

Mrs. Wendell's mouth became a hard line. "I don't think so."

"You'd show it to my wife if it was just her."

"But it isn't just her, is it?"

William took a step back. "I'm out of here," he mumbled. In the next moment he was gone, and Nora stood looking at Mrs. Wendell's disapproving scowl.

"You see, that's why I can't show you places in white neighborhoods. Colored people are just too emotional. No one wants a neighbor who will fly off the handle at every little thing."

"Thank you," Nora said. "I don't think we'll be needing your services anymore." She spun on her heels and caught up with William, who was pacing up and down the hallway outside the apartment. "Let's go."

On the long ride back to Seward Avenue, Nora stared out the window and fiddled with an errant thread on the skirt she had hemmed the night before. The scene at her parents' house two months earlier played back in her mind. A slack-jawed Wanda had pointed to the veranda, where Nora found her parents with drinks in hand, her father reading the paper, her mother staring into the trees. William waited in the house as Nora painstakingly paved the way for the revelation, leaving out any mention of the photo of her father that had started it all.

"I met him when Diane and I were volunteering at the Detroit Artists Market back in the spring. He told me his camera had been damaged, and I could see that he had a lot of talent but not a lot of extra money—I mean, he does have a job, but you know good cameras are so expensive—so I offered to buy him a new one."

"That was very generous," Mallory said with eyebrows raised.

"Important to support the arts," Daniel said without looking up from the newspaper, "though I'd prefer you did so through some decent acquisitions."

"He took some photos of me to test it out," Nora continued, "and then I met up with him to see them when they were developed."

Her mother frowned, guessing at the trajectory of the story. "And?"

"And we hit it off, of course. He's charming and intelligent and loves his family. I've spent quite a bit of time with his mother and sister. They're very nice people. His father was killed in France during the war."

From behind the newspaper, Daniel nodded his approval of this sacrifice.

"They're not as well-off as we are, but they are polite and well-mannered and hardworking people."

"Then they will go far in life," her father declared. "Our family was not always so well-off. We had to work for it. That's what makes this country great."

"We'll have to meet this William someday," her mother said noncommittally.

"Actually, he's here now."

Her father finally looked over the top of his paper. "Where?"

"In the kitchen. I wanted to tell you a little about him before I sprung him on you."

"The kitchen?" Mallory said. "Why on earth did you leave him waiting there? Call him outside, Nora."

Nora walked back into the kitchen to beckon William from the cool shadows of the house into the soft light of the perfect June evening.

As they walked hand in hand onto the veranda, Nora examined her father's face to see if he recognized William. He didn't seem to. But the matching expressions of shock on her parents' faces told Nora that the next twenty minutes would be painful anyway.

William walked up to the man who had attacked him in the street and held out his hand. "Good evening, sir. I'm William Rich."

Daniel Balsam struggled past his incredulity, got to his feet, and shook William's hand. Nora would have taken this as a good sign had it not been for the steady change in the color of her father's face. She had no sooner opened her mouth to preempt whatever he might say than her mother's strangled gasp stopped her short.

"Oh, Nora! What have you done?"

Nora covered her left hand, but it was too late.

"What?" Daniel asked.

"Mom, don't get hysterical."

But the snowball was already rolling down the hill, and nothing could stop the avalanche of angry words that followed.

"How could you do this to us?"

"What is wrong with you?"

"You can get it annulled."

"Where will you live?"

"Does he even have a job?"

"Are you pregnant?"

"Why would you go and pull such an idiotic stunt?"

"You have ruined your life."

Nora weathered the barrage of disapproval, gritting her teeth like someone receiving surgery with no local anesthetic. At her side, William stood stoic and silent.

When the comments slowed enough that she could get a word in, all she could think to say was, "You seemed to like him just fine before you saw the color of his skin. And it shouldn't matter. We're in love."

"No you're not," her father said. "You're just trying to make some stupid statement. All you kids, all brought up with everything you could ever want. Most ungrateful bunch of idiots I've ever seen. Marching around town creating problems where there were none."

"I hope it does make a statement," Nora said with more boldness than she felt. William squeezed her hand in support. "There are problems. Real problems that can't be ignored. And I'll have you know I was in that march. I saw Martin Luther King speak at Cobo Hall, and he was amazing."

"Amazing? I guess any huckster can amaze an audience of simpletons."

"He's a well-respected minister."

"He's a Baptist."

Nora threw up her hands. "What's wrong with that?"

"Nora, I'll give you my solemn blessing on this farce if you can name one Presbyterian minister other than our own."

Silence grew between them.

"You know why you can't do it? Because we know how to mind our own business."

Nora's stomach turned as her own words to William rushed back.

"Francis Schaeffer," William said in an even tone.

"No one's talking to you, boy," Daniel spat.

"Watch it!" Nora practically shouted. She caught the look of shock on her mother's face at this and said in a more respectful tone, "Ending segregation is everyone's business."

"No it isn't. That's the South's business. We were on the right side of the war. A black man can do whatever he wants up here." He looked at William. "And he obviously does."

Nora let out a mirthless laugh. "Maybe our ancestors were on the right side a hundred years ago, but it seems pretty obvious whose side you're on now."

Daniel's eyes snapped back to his daughter. "I'll tell you what side I'm on. I'm on the side of folks who don't skulk around behind people's backs and fill their daughters' heads with propaganda.

I'm on the side of decent people who do their jobs, earn their keep, and don't rabble-rouse. And it's apparent you're not."

"Maybe not. But I'm on the right side." Nora looked at William, who nodded his support. Then she had an idea. "What about Ray?"

"Ray?" her father said incredulously. "The groundskeeper? What does he have to do with any of this?"

"You like Ray."

"Ray is not trying to sleep with my daughter!" Daniel appeared on the verge of erupting. He closed the gap between them, stopping a few inches from Nora's face. "Black people already ruined this family once, young lady."

Nora's breath caught. "What?"

"You will get this marriage annulled."

"I most certainly will not!"

Daniel clenched his fists, white knuckles delineating the end of every bone. His cheeks trembled in what seemed to be a herculean effort to keep from exploding. "Fine. I want nothing to do with you or him." He raised a finger and began to wave it at her face. "No more apartment. No more clothes. No more restaurants. No more money to waste on junk art. And you can leave the Corvette here and call a cab to get back to whatever slum this guy's been living in. He won't get his grubby paws on even a cent of Balsam money. Not a cent. Now get out of my house."

Whatever cold reception she had anticipated from her father, Nora had not been prepared for this. The magnitude of her hasty marriage began to accumulate like a great weight on her chest. Her mother sat in stony silence, her face an emotionless mask.

Stunned, Nora led William into the house. She veered off to the kitchen as he kept going out the front door. She picked up the phone to call a cab. Her mother appeared in the doorway and took it out of her hand. "I'll take you."

The long drive was silent beyond the giving of directions.

When they pulled up to the Rich house, William got out of the car without a word and went inside.

Nora hung back, fighting tears. "Mom, I wish you would be happy for me."

Mallory looked at her daughter, her own eyes shining with unshed tears. "How could I be happy for you when I know what your life will be like now? What was wrong with Michael Kresge? Or Kenneth Lowe? Or any of the others?"

Nora shook her head. "How can you even ask me that?" She started to open the car door, but her mother squeezed her hand.

"Call me when you're settled and give me your new address."

That night and all the next day Nora and William emptied out her apartment, shoving her clothes and shoes and coats into every closet in the Rich house until they spilled out onto the floors. Boxes of her books and keepsakes filled the basement. Her makeup, brushes, and curlers littered the bathroom counter and jammed the drawers. The house she had admired for its cleanliness and spare ornamentation had been inundated with the clutter that came from a life where money was no object.

Though Mrs. Rich was welcoming, Nora could tell she was uncomfortable with the situation. Bianca too was courteous, but sighed constantly and closed curtains whenever she found them open. Even William seemed on edge, and Nora wondered if he regretted their decision to get married.

But J.J. was the worst. Nora began to suspect that he was sabotaging her. An expensive shoe turned up missing. A favorite blouse had an unidentifiable stain. A lipstick was smashed. A coat lining was torn. One night at dinner, Nora pondered aloud the disappearance of a diamond-studded bracelet, and J.J. said what everyone must have been thinking.

"Man, I wish you would disappear. Just get outta here. This ain't your house."

"J.J.!" Bianca whacked him on the back of his head.

Everyone looked at their plates, but Nora could see the truth in their faces. She and William needed to find a place of their own. Fast.

Yet two tedious months later they were no closer to success.

As she and William neared the house, Nora was stunned to see her mother's car on the street in front of it. She was even more surprised to see Mallory Balsam sitting next to Mrs. Rich on the couch, sipping a cup of tea.

"What are you doing here?" Nora asked.

"Hello to you too. I came to see what happened to you. You were going to call when you found an apartment."

"We're still looking."

"So Louise tells me."

Mrs. Rich rose. "Give me a hand in the kitchen, Will."

They left Nora staring at the empty spot next to her mother.

"Are you going to sit down?"

Nora rounded the coffee table and sat. "Don't say I told you so."

"That's not why I'm here, Nora." Mallory folded her hands. "I'm sorry about what happened. We were both quite shocked. You can't pretend that we shouldn't have been. But I want you to know that I don't share your father's view on cutting ties. That's why I'm here."

They were silent a moment. Nora felt herself begin to unravel like the hem of her skirt.

"Anywhere they'll even show us an apartment it's horrible." She took a slow breath and stifled the tears that threatened to spill forth.

Her mother said nothing.

Nora stared out the front window and tried to understand. Why did people care about what she did with her own life? How did her marriage affect anyone else? How was it any of their business at all? Then she voiced the question she had been brooding over for the past two months. "What did Daddy mean when he said black people ruined this family?"

Mallory shook her head. "I don't know, honey. You'd have to ask him."

"I'll do that," Nora said bitterly. "On our next golf outing, perhaps."

Mallory ignored this. "I do have a possible solution to your problem of where to live. It would mean a lot of changes. But perhaps that would be a good thing."

Nora gave her mother a quizzical look.

"There is a house that has been in the family for generations. A big house. Your Grandma Rose told me about it not long before she died. There's no mortgage. Your father and Uncle David have kept up on the taxes. All the furniture is still there, though I'm not sure what shape it's in. It hasn't been lived in for thirty years, so it may need some work."

Hope rose in Nora's heart. "Where is it?"

"That's the catch. It's not in town."

"So where is it?"

Mallory sipped at her tea. "Up north a ways, just outside of Lapeer."

"Lapeer! We can't move to Lapeer. What about William's job?"

"I said it would mean changes. But you said yourself that you don't have many options here. If you lived out in the country, at least you wouldn't be bothered every day by people on the street."

"But what is William supposed to do? Become a farmer?"

Mallory shrugged. "It's not far from Flint. I'm sure he could find another job. He does have a car, doesn't he?"

"Of course he has a car."

"Okay, okay. No need to get defensive."

They were both quiet a moment.

"You could make some extra money sewing if you needed to," Mallory suggested.

Nora's heart sank at the thought of having to take in sewing for other people. It was just something she did for fun. "Does Dad know you're here offering this house to me?"

"No. And there's no reason for it to concern him. If he's intent on pretending this whole situation doesn't exist, then he won't go looking into where you're living."

Slowly, the thought of being where prying eyes would not see her—where no one would even know she was there—caught hold of Nora. A house just for her and William. And their children. Children who would never need hear their parents jeered at. A yard for them to play in away from the dangerous streets. Just their own little family, insulated from the world. Protected. Secluded. Safe.

"I'll think about it."

But she didn't need to. In her heart, she was already there.

TWENTY-FOUR

Lapeer County, March 1864

Not long after Nathaniel returned to his regiment, Mary had resumed writing him letters. For nearly three years she had written regularly, keeping him abreast of developments on the home front and wishing him a safe return. Now the renewed distance helped erase the resentment she had felt toward him when he was home. In January, she had added a new step to her routine. Once she signed off on Nathaniel's letter, she began one to George.

Her first letter began with an apology for having taken so long to reply. She added some observations about the weather and a funny thing Angelica had done. She was just about to close with a line about her hopes that the war would soon end and Nathaniel would come home—almost identical to a line she had written in Nathaniel's letter—when something stopped her. She did not want Nathaniel's name in this letter. Instead, she wrote, *I thank God every day that you came to this house and relieved my loneliness.*

The moment she placed the period she wished she could

erase the sentence. The sentiment was true, but much too forward. She considered crumpling it all up and starting again.

George's voice from the door interrupted her thoughts. "I have to go into town. Do you have any letters?"

"Yes, I do." She folded Nathaniel's letter and slid it into an envelope. She wrote in the proper address and blew across the ink.

"What about that one?" George motioned to the sheet of paper still at the center of the desk.

"Oh, that's—that's not going just yet. I haven't finished it."

"I don't mean to rush you. Take your time and I'll come back when you're through."

"It's nothing . . . I . . . well, actually, it's for you, George."

His eyebrows rose. "For me?"

"Yes. It's quite late in coming, I'm afraid."

He walked behind the desk and leaned over her shoulder to look at the small rectangle graced with fine script. Mary could smell the soap from his bath the night before.

"It looks like it just needs to be signed."

"That's what I was about to do."

What could be the harm, after all, in that one sentence? It didn't say anything inappropriate. A friend could relieve someone's loneliness. She dipped the nib in the ink pot and let it hover a moment over the page. How should she close this letter? She signed Nathaniel's letters with an automatic *All my love, Mary*. George must have noticed her hesitation, as he backed away from her chair. Finally she settled on *Sincerely, Mrs. Balsam*. She blew on the ink, folded the paper, and slid it into an envelope.

"There you are, George," she said brightly to mask her nerves. "And I promise the next one will not take me six months to write."

George responded the very next day, ending the letter once again with a question: *Which is your favorite season?* Mary responded the day after that, claiming to enjoy late summer the most and early spring the least, and asking him a question of her own: *What is your favorite hymn?*

Each day these notes passed between them. George learned that Mary adored the color green but disliked pink, that she preferred fruity desserts to chocolates, and that she harbored a secret love for reading novels that she kept under the bed. Mary learned that George enjoyed milking but not gathering eggs, that he liked building things, and that he wished they might someday plant an apple orchard on the farm.

Those first exchanges reminded Mary of carefree childhood days when her parents were still alive and she exchanged notes with schoolmates. It was not long, though, before the tone of the letters turned more serious. George asked about her family, and Mary relayed the sad tale of influenza claiming her parents and baby sister. Mary asked about the sister he had once spoken of, but he knew little of her current situation beyond the battles that raged nearby.

Then George asked a question Mary had not allowed herself to consider. *What will you do if Mr. Balsam is killed in the war?*

The letters stopped as Mary debated how to answer. George came to the library as usual to collect her other letters and left with an excuse from her. She had a headache. His letter would be written the next day. But it wasn't. Nor the next, nor the one after that.

Then one evening when George and Mary found themselves alone in the library, he looked up from the newspaper and said, "I shouldn't have asked that question, Mrs. Balsam. It's none of my business."

"It's not that, George. It's just a difficult question to answer."

"You don't have to answer it."

She sighed. "The problem is, I don't quite know myself. It's not that I haven't thought about it."

In fact, she had lately thought of almost nothing else. She had known for some time now that she carried another baby within her, conceived when Nathaniel was furloughed. What would she do if he didn't come home? With a child, she would have to remarry, despite the fact that she could run the farm by herself. She recalled the pricks of bitterness she had felt at Nathaniel's comments and calculating expressions when he was home. What did it matter if he would have done things differently? She had managed fine in his absence. And what might a new husband think? Would he put her back in her place? Exclude her from decision making? Might Nathaniel do that as well when he was home for good?

With George, she felt an equal. They conferred about plantings, harvesttime, and pricing. They examined the finances together and made joint decisions on purchasing everything from a new plow to that month's supply of flour and sugar. They looked to each other for wisdom and affirmation that they had made the right choice.

Finally she spoke again. "George, no matter what happens—if Nathaniel comes back whole, or without a leg or arm, or in a coffin—I want you to stay. That is all I know for sure."

George set the newspaper down. "Good." He held her gaze. "Will you write to me tomorrow?"

TWENTY-FIVE

Lapeer County, October

"Is this too dressy for a movie?" I stood in front of Nora and pulled at the hem of my knee-length skirt. "What am I saying? Of course it is. No one wears a skirt to a movie."

"They did in my day."

"Well, they don't anymore."

Nora sighed. "Yes, it's all blue jeans and hooded sweatshirts now, everywhere you look. You know, I blame John F. Kennedy. If that man would have just worn a hat . . ."

"So, you think I should wear it?"

She assessed me with a critical eye. "Yes."

"But what if Tyrese is wearing jeans and a hoodie?"

"Run the other way."

I couldn't tell if she was serious.

"It's not too dressy," she assured me with a smile. "You're wearing tights and boots with it, not nylons and stilettos. You look very well-put-together."

"You're the expert," I said as I put on my wool coat.

She laughed. "I may have been long ago."

"I don't know what you mean. You're the most stylish person I know. Of course, I was raised by missionaries, who aren't known for their fashion sense. But still. I hope when I'm your age I look half as good."

"That's nice of you to say."

"It's true. Every word."

"Oh, go on," she said, clearly pleased. "Have a nice night."

Driving toward town, I couldn't help but think of my first date with Vic Sharpe. I'd bought this outfit for Dana. It kept Vic's attention throughout dinner at a swanky new restaurant I later found out he'd invested in. I made up a vague backstory for Dana and kept the conversation focused on him. I gave up so little personal information that at the end of the night he immediately asked me out on a second date while apologizing for monopolizing the conversation. I could hardly believe how easy it had been.

This time would be different. I had nothing to hide and no agenda. It would be nice to be completely in the moment instead of being preoccupied with playing a part and gathering information.

Looking over the people milling around the theater lobby, though, I regretted my apparel decision. Movie night in Lapeer was even more casual than in Detroit. I spotted Tyrese. He was in jeans, though not a hoodie. When I caught him do a little double take I changed my mind about my attire.

The movie was good enough, as far as movies go. But I knew before it was over that I would not remember it six months later. After the credits rolled, we walked out to the lobby.

"Give me a second," I said. "Just have to use the ladies' room."

After washing my hands, I fixed a few stray hairs, straightened and smoothed my skirt, and pulled out my phone to turn it back on. No calls or texts. No notifications from any of my social media accounts. I'd been so out of touch that everyone forgot I existed. I guess in some way, I didn't. If I wasn't online, I wasn't really anywhere anymore. For just a moment this hurt—until

I realized that I hadn't really missed anyone from my past life, my life before I became a rural eccentric who did nothing but garden and snoop around someone else's house.

I was about to return the phone to my purse when my thumb grazed the *Detroit Free Press* app. Before I could shut it, the headlines caught my eye. They were all about the same thing, just from different angles. And that always meant it was something bad.

White Cop Kills Unarmed Black Teen

Police Chief Claims No Wrongdoing in Slaying of Black Teen

Death Threats to White Cop—"We know where you live . . ."

Protesters Dispersed with Tear Gas

Property Destruction at Site of Police Shooting

I popped back over to my Facebook feed and scrolled through the last twenty-four hours of news. Every other post was about the incident. I felt a small twinge of regret. I should be the one covering this story.

Out in the lobby, Tyrese was staring at his phone. In that moment I realized he was the only black guy in the theater.

"You hear about this thing in Detroit?" he said, more serious than I'd seen him before.

"Just saw it."

I felt like I should say something else, but I didn't know what. Were I back home, I'd know exactly what tone to take as a reporter relaying the news of a tragedy to my majority black city. But here . . . what was the right thing to say?

"They're blaming the cop, of course," said a guy standing a couple feet away.

"I didn't read any of the articles," I said. "Just saw the headlines, so I don't know what happened." I took Tyrese's arm and started to turn toward the door.

"Here's what happened," the guy continued. "Another police officer was doing his job, just trying to stay alive in the line of duty. And now he's going to lose his job because apparently you can't shoot criminals anymore."

Tyrese stopped my forward motion and looked at the guy with the unsolicited opinions. "How do you know that kid was a criminal?"

The guy straightened up, trying to match Tyrese's height. "If he wasn't, he wouldn't have been in the line of fire."

"You don't know," Tyrese said forcefully. "You weren't there."

The guy took a step in our direction. "Neither were you."

"Let's go," I said in Tyrese's ear.

Tyrese shoved his phone into his pocket and muttered something indecipherable under his breath. He turned and headed for the doors. I followed, glancing back once to see the guy with the opinions watching us leave.

"I kind of wish we'd driven together," I said to lighten the mood once we were out in the dark parking lot. "Then we could chat on the way home." But really it was because I didn't want Tyrese on the road alone.

He cracked his neck and seemed to shake off the ugly almost-incident. "How did your aunt end up way out in the middle of nowhere anyway?"

"I don't know. She's lived there a long time. But she's from the Detroit area." We sat down on a nearby bench and I tugged at my skirt. "Most of my family is from Detroit."

"You too, eh?"

"Yeah."

"Must be hard to get used to living out in the country."

"I don't know," I said, looking up at the star-studded sky. "I like living here more than I thought I would. It's quiet and green. It feels good to take a mess and sort it out and make it beautiful again. I feel like maybe I'm keeping something important from vanishing. I guess that's a little silly, though. No one would care if that garden disappeared."

He looked thoughtful. "Someone might. Someone obviously worked hard at it in the past. What if they can still see it from where they are?"

I considered this. Could the dead look down and see the living? Could Mary Balsam see me kneeling in the dirt by her grave? Did it bring her pleasure to see that someone was remembering her? Did it pain her that I didn't know who the other grave belonged to?

Tyrese was looking at me with a half smile. How long had I been lost in my own thoughts? His eyes flicked down and then back up to my face. I almost laughed. How did any guy think a girl didn't notice that?

"You look really nice tonight," he said.

"Thanks. I feel a bit ridiculous."

"Why?"

I gestured toward myself. "A bit overdressed, don't you think?"

"Seems about right for someone who pulls weeds in a cocktail dress."

"Har-har," I said, rolling my eyes. "I told you I hadn't planned on doing that when I went out there."

He smiled and shook his head. "I'm kidding. Like I said, you look really nice. You looked good that day too."

I stood up. "It's late. I better get going."

Tyrese got to his feet.

"Are you going to be okay?" I asked.

He screwed up his face. "Why wouldn't I be?"

I shrugged. "You're not going to go back in there and argue with that guy, are you?"

"What would be the point? Anyway, I've got a business to think about." He smiled ruefully. "And the customer is always white."

TWENTY-SIX

Detroit, September 1963

"Nora, I just don't think running is the answer." William shut his car door and handed her a red and white paper tray filled with fries.

"It's not running," she said, placing a napkin across her lap. "It's a new start. Think about it. The house is paid for. It's furnished."

"It's your father's."

"Not exactly."

"What, 'cause your uncle owns half? Psh. Don't you want a place of our own?"

"But that's what makes it so perfect. We would be on our own—no judgment, no commentary from anyone else." Then she added loudly for the benefit of the couple in the car next to them, "No staring." They turned their heads back toward the expansive movie screen, where cartoon food advised them to visit the snack bar before the feature started.

"If you think they stare in Detroit at a black drive-in, just wait till a bunch of white country bumpkins get a load of us." William dropped a fry into his mouth.

Nora sighed. "You're not getting it."

He swallowed. "Yeah, I am. I get it. I get that you want to escape. I know you're not used to jeers and sneers and name-calling. But I am. I been getting that my whole life one way or another."

"William, not two days ago a complete stranger said you should be lynched!"

"No one's lynching a black man in Detroit. Anyway, how am I gonna change that if I run from it? How we gonna change people's minds when there ain't no people around to change? For that matter, what will I photograph when I'm living in a field with no people around? What are we gonna do all day out there?"

"You could get a job in Flint. We can start a family."

"And what would we tell our kids when they're at an all-white school in the boondocks? That their daddy could have helped get Detroit schools integrated, but instead he hid out in a field 'cause it was easier and so now they're the only black kids in the county?"

Nora had nothing to say. She had thought William would jump at the chance for a fresh start in a new place. She hadn't even considered his photography or the fact that he would be even more of a minority than he was now.

"Look, baby, I ain't saying no, all right? I just need more time to think about it. That house ain't going nowhere."

They turned their faces away from one another and focused on the screen, where a caravan of military vehicles traveled a lonely road that bisected a farm field. Enormous red block letters spelled out *The Great Escape* as a spirited military air played over the speakers. Nora imagined the landscape of Lapeer County must look quite a bit like the German countryside behind those big red letters. It looked so pleasant and green and inviting. But then the trucks reached their destination and the rows of plants were replaced with rolls of barbed wire.

It wasn't long before William leaned over and said, "I'm going to get some popcorn."

He slipped out of the car. A moment later he slipped back in. Then Nora realized it wasn't him at all.

"You have the wrong car," she said to the man.

"You got that wrong, missy. *You* in the wrong car. And you at the wrong theater."

Nora's heart raced. "My husband will be back any minute," she said with conjured courage. "Perhaps you can sort it out with him."

"I'd rather sort it out right now."

The man drew a knife from his pocket and opened it to reveal a short blade. On the screen a German officer told Steve McQueen that to cross the warning wire surrounding the prison camp was death. Then the blade was at her throat.

"I don't want to see you at this drive-in again, you understand?"

Nora swallowed hard and felt the lump in her throat scrape across the blade as it went down.

"You belong up at Ted's or Maverick's. You don't see any of us up there. And we don't wanna see you down here. Got it?"

Nora nodded slightly, her eyes fixed on the screen. She didn't want to look at this man, didn't want to remember his face.

He pulled the knife back. "It's nothing personal. It's just better for everybody that way."

She nodded again, and the man slid out of the car as quickly as he had slid in. Nora's hand shot to her neck and her entire body shook. The car door opened again and she cowered.

"What's the matter with you?" William said. He looked at the screen with confusion, then looked back to his wife. "What're you crying at, baby?"

Through shuddering breaths, Nora managed to say, "Someone told me to leave."

William scowled. "Who?"

"I don't know."

He craned his neck, searching for the source of her terror. Then he tucked her still trembling body beneath his arm. "Baby, don't worry about that. Whoever it was, he's all talk, just like the rest of 'em."

He pulled away and took both of her hands in his. Then they saw the blood on her fingers.

TWENTY-SEVEN

Lapeer County, June 1864

"But why would he want to leave?" Mary stood at the open barn door silhouetted by bright morning sunlight, her loose skirts casting a shadow that reached almost to George's dusty boots.

George stopped hammering. "He says he wants to do his part now that the army is accepting Negro soldiers."

"Mrs. Balsam," Thomas said, coming up behind her, "if we don't do somethin' for ourselves today, why would we think tomorrow will be any different?"

"I wish you'd reconsider and wait to see if you're drafted," she said.

"Mr. Balsam done talked me into enlistin' 'fore his furlough ended. Said they makin' former slaves into spies," Thomas said with a gleam in his eye. "That's what I'm gonna do. I'm gonna spy out the land for Mr. Lincoln. Tell him what I see. Help him end this war."

"He needs all the help he can get," George interjected.

"But what if you should get kidnapped and taken back to the plantation?" Mary asked. "What might your former master do to you then?"

"I 'spect Mr. Charles is too busy tryin' to keep them Yankees away from his farm to worry 'bout me. Besides, I aim my death won't come easy." He walked past her into the barn and leaned his shovel against the wall. "I'm sorry to leave you, Mrs. Balsam. And Bridget too. I know you was countin' on me at harvest now the crop's got so much bigger. But the road for me leads to Massachusetts and then on to Virginia."

Until he said it, Mary hadn't considered the vastly expanded plots of land they now had under cultivation. What if others enlisted as well and she was left in September with no one to bring in the harvest?

"Jacob isn't going with you, is he?"

"Nah. I don't think so. He ain't convinced my road his road. He been consultin' the Lord 'bout it. I guess we'll see what he has to say. But I'm leavin' tomorrow mornin', with or without Jacob."

Thomas walked back out into the sun. Mary sighed.

"You need to sit down?" George asked.

"No, I'm fine. I just . . . I hate this unending struggle. We seem to be no closer to victory than we were in the first month of the war, and yet hundreds of thousands of men are gone, wiped from the face of the earth. For what? What have we accomplished?"

George went back to hammering.

"I don't mean to say it has all been for nothing, of course," she hastened to say. "Were it not for the conflict, there would have been no emancipation. But I just don't see how it will ever end. Is every young man in this land to be offered as a sacrifice? Will we become a nation of women and children and old men?"

"I've thought of it," George said between strikes of the hammer.

"Thought of what?"

"Joining up."

Mary did need to sit down then. "You wouldn't," she said,

one hand on her swollen stomach, the other searching for a bale of hay.

George dropped the hammer. He grasped her hand and guided her to the milking stool. "No, ma'am, I wouldn't."

"Don't do that to me," she said, a little breathless. "And don't call me ma'am. You know I hate that. And don't tell me it's a habit, because you have been here long enough to form a new habit."

Mary put one hand on her heart and then realized that George still held the other. She did not pull it away, did not dare to even look for fear he too would notice and let go. He had not held her hand since that terrible night nearly three years ago.

"Are you okay?" He searched her face.

"I'm fine. As long as you stay here, I'm fine."

"I told you before I ain't never leaving you, Mrs. Balsam." He looked deep into her eyes. "I mean that."

"Then why should you talk of enlisting?"

"I only said I thought about it, not that I was thinking about actually doing it. It would be an honor. What kind of man would I be if I was not willing to fight?"

"I've heard that before. It seems to be the final line of reasoning for every man who ever wanted to do a reckless thing."

George said nothing.

"I'm so tired of this war," Mary went on. "You know that the papers are full of dire news about Lincoln's chances of getting reelected. Some are calling for him to rescind emancipation to get enough votes. What will happen to all who have escaped north should the worst transpire? What would happen to you?"

"Worrying won't change things," he said. "Change happens when the cost of keeping things the way they are is too high. We need to make it so that the South has no choice but to change. That's what Thomas wants to help do."

Mary took a calming breath and fixed her eyes upon his. At that moment she could not conjure up a memory of what her own husband's eyes looked like. "I know you're right. I should not give in to despair. Only do not leave me. I could not survive without you."

Then there was nothing else to say. Nothing that could be said aloud. Nothing even that Mary might dare put in a letter. They held each other's gaze a moment longer, then George looked down to his fingers wrapped around hers and let go.

"I better get back to these beds. Even with Thomas leaving, we still have people sleeping on the floor. You need help getting back to the house?"

Mary struggled to push the words past her throat. "I can manage."

George pulled her to a standing position. When she wobbled on unsteady legs, he put his arm around where her waist had been six months before and walked her out of the barn.

They were halfway up the slope toward the house when three white men on horseback galloped up in a cloud of dirt. George's tight hold on Mary did not abate as he met the eyes of the man who seemed to be leading the group.

"Can I help you?" George asked.

"I sincerely doubt it," the man replied. He turned to Mary. "I would like a word with you, Mrs. Balsam."

"Mrs. Balsam doesn't feel well right now, and you can see she is in need of a place to sit," George said. "I'm afraid you will have to come back another time, gentlemen."

"You'd do good to hold your tongue, boy," one of the other men said.

The leader raised his hand to suppress his companion. "Now, now. I think we can allow the lady a seat." He dismounted and handed the reins to George. "Here, make yourself useful, son."

The man offered Mary his arm. She sent a nervous glance George's way, then took the proffered help and walked toward the house. The man's two companions stayed astride their horses and surveyed the grounds. George stood by, powerless.

The man walked Mary through the kitchen, past Bridget and Loretta, and into the parlor. She sat on the settee and took a long breath. The man before her was tall and humorless, sandy brown hair peeking out from beneath his hat. She couldn't decide whether or not she recognized him.

"Mrs. Balsam, I am Bartholomew Sharpe, and I am here representing a number of people whose names don't matter at the moment."

"Mr. Sharpe, will you please sit down?"

"I shan't be here long. I'm here only to deliver a message."

"Then perhaps a letter would have been a more appropriate use of your very valuable time, sir."

He scowled. "Young woman, I don't think you grasp how serious this message is. I have a warning for you. If you don't send these Negroes on their way and get them out of our town and off of this farm, you're going to be in for a load of trouble."

"Is that so?" she said, holding his gaze. "And what sort of trouble might that be?"

"The kind you cannot afford to have, I assure you."

"Well, sir, it just so happens that I have a warning for you as well." She got to her feet and stood her ground. "If I ever see you on this land again, I will not hesitate to report your trespassing and your threats of violence to the constable. This is my house and my farm, and I will house whomever I wish. I answer to God, and you would do good to remember that you will someday be called upon to answer to him as well. Now leave this house at once and take your friends with you."

Mr. Sharpe appeared to struggle for the proper retort. When none was forthcoming, he stormed to the front door but turned around before opening it, wagging a long finger at her. "This matter is far from settled, Mrs. Balsam." Then he walked out.

Mary heard a yell and then horses' hooves striking the rocks on the long drive. She collapsed into a chair as Bridget and Loretta rushed into the room.

"Mrs. Balsam, are you all right?" Bridget fretted. Loretta fanned her with a tea towel. Seconds later George burst through the door, followed by John Dixon.

"I'm fine. I'm fine." Mary waved them away. "Though I do think I shall lie down for a bit."

George pushed past the women, lifted Mary in his arms before she could protest, and carried her up the stairs to her bedchamber, where he laid her gently on the bed.

"We in for a heap of trouble now," he said, reverting in his anxiety to his Southern way of speaking.

"No, *we're* in for a heap of trouble now," she corrected in a feeble attempt to lighten the mood.

"Trouble either way, ma'am."

"George," she admonished.

He sighed but smiled a little. "Mrs. Balsam."

She shook her head and glanced at the open door. "Mary," she whispered.

He looked long at her, a sadness clouding his face. "No, Mrs. Balsam. You know you can never be Mary to me."

TWENTY-EIGHT

Lapeer County, October

Instead of driving home after my movie with Tyrese, I sat in the back corner of a McDonald's parking lot with my phone, reading everything I could find on the shooting in Detroit. The more I read, the more I disagreed with that theater lobby commentator and his unsolicited opinions. Even if the kid had been hanging around unsavory characters, that didn't make him a criminal. The incident seemed to fall into a disturbingly familiar pattern of tension and violence between the police and the inner-city black community—and this time in the very same neighborhoods that were set ablaze in 1967. How did this keep happening?

Depressed and disgusted, I dropped the phone on the passenger seat and pulled out of the parking lot. When I finally turned off the engine on the gravel driveway and dragged myself up to bed, sleep was slow in coming and poor in quality. When I looked at the clock and saw 3:42 a.m., I let out a desperate laugh and thought of all the times I had wondered how people like Judge Sharpe could sleep at night. The cop who had shot that kid—was he asleep?

Late the next morning, I stumbled down to the kitchen with

a pounding headache and stared at my bowl of cereal until the flakes had expanded into a single goopy mass.

Nora took one look at me, poured me a cup of black coffee, and said in a very businesslike manner, "Elizabeth, I need you to do something for me."

I tried to summon a smile. "Sure. What's up?"

"I have a project I need to work on and it needs a lot of fabric. I'm finally going to be able to get some use out of all of the things people have brought me over the years. Well, not all of it. I can only use cottons. Nothing synthetic, nothing stretchy, no polyester or lycra or rayon. Just cotton. There's a ton of it all over this house. I'm afraid I haven't kept it very organized. So what I need you to do is look in all the closets and dressers and see what you can find that's cotton."

"How will I know it's cotton?"

She looked at me as though I was being willfully ignorant.

"What color?"

"Any color. Lots of colors. Any pattern. Anything you see that you like. It doesn't matter. As I said, this is a big project, so I'll need lots of it. And the sooner the better. I'd like to get started on it Monday."

"I can do that." A new distraction was just what I needed now. "You know, I brought a lot of fabric up to the attic from my room when I first moved in. Should I look through that too?"

"Oh, yes."

"Hey, remember when I asked you about the beds up there? You never did tell me the story."

"Let's talk about it over dinner tonight."

Put off again. Eleanor Rich was indeed a stubborn woman as Barb had said. Or did she simply not remember that she'd said the exact same thing to me when I first asked about the mysterious cots?

Nora looked lost in thought. "Why were you up there?"

"I had to get all that fabric out of my room before I could put any of my clothes away; the armoire and the dresser were full of it. I didn't want to mention it at first, because you'd said the room was all ready for me and it wasn't."

"I said that?"

"Yes, you said William had gotten it ready."

"William? I told you William had gotten it ready?" She looked a little pale. "I can't imagine why I would say that. William's been gone for fifty years."

TWENTY-NINE

Lapeer County, October 1963

The day for the move dawned clear and cool, which Nora took as an auspicious sign. She and William loaded up a borrowed trailer behind his old yellow Chevy Biscayne. They shared hugs and kisses with Mrs. Rich and Bianca. J.J. was conspicuously absent.

An almost tangible feeling of promise hung in the air as the miles receded beneath the tires. Nora couldn't read William's expression, whether he was happy or upset about this new chapter in their lives. But the night at the drive-in had made up his mind. Nora fixed her eyes on the horizon, such as it was in the sprawling city, and felt like she was leaving a place she dearly loved that did not love her back. It took over an hour of stop-and-go driving down Woodward Avenue to get out of the Detroit metro area, but soon after they turned onto M-24, farms and windbreaks replaced parking lots and lampposts and they were flying toward their future.

"I think that's the first time I ever saw a tractor in real life," William noted as they passed a farm. Nora was about to laugh at him. Then she wondered if perhaps it was the first time for her as well.

It was lunchtime when Nora pulled her head out of the pile of maps and directions in her lap and said, "I think this is the turn right here."

"Here?" William asked, pressing down on the brake.

"Yes. Look at the picture." She held up an old photograph that showed three neat lines of baby pine trees behind a low, broken-down stone wall. In the background rose a white farmhouse.

William stopped the car on the side of the road and took the photo from her. "I don't know."

"Look there, at that wall. See the gaps? Aren't they in the same place as on the picture? The trees are just bigger. You can't see the house, but I'm sure it's just behind the trees."

"But there's no driveway."

Nora rolled down the window and hung out of it. "There." She pointed. "Those trees aren't so close together. I bet that's the driveway."

William looked dubious. "No, I do believe that is a bunch of tall grass and rocks that the trailer's going to get stuck in."

"Let's just walk up through there and see what's on the other side of those trees."

Picture in hand, they walked past the line of rocks and through the pines. When they emerged on the other side, Nora smiled. The paint was chipped and peeling and vines had grown halfway up the sides, but it was indeed the house from the photo.

"Let's get the car," William said. On the way back to the road, he scanned the ground and tossed aside rocks and branches to clear a path. Then he inched the car and the trailer through the pines.

On the front porch, Nora and William turned the key together, and the door to their new life opened wide. They crept through dark rooms, pulling dusty sheets from furniture and testing lights and faucets. William ventured into the cellar with a flashlight to turn on the water main. Nora peered into kitchen cupboards full of cobwebs. They reconvened by the back door and went outside, where a weathered barn and a quaint old chicken coop stood in a field of wildflowers, and the ghost of a garden lurked inside a picket fence.

"We've got our work cut out for us," William said in a flat tone.

Nora thought of her once-flush bank account—no, she corrected herself, her father's bank account—and felt like crying. She had so blithely swept aside William's warnings about how her life would change, hadn't counted the cost. But she propped herself up with the thought of the love she had for the man at her side.

"I'm going to see if there's a ladder in that barn," William said.

"It's probably locked. Mom gave me an envelope of keys. Let me get it." She trotted to the car and retrieved the envelope from the glove compartment. She also grabbed the picnic basket Mrs. Rich had packed for them that morning. As she walked back to where William stood staring at the house with his hands on his hips, she decided once again that it was all worth it. This was the place they were meant to be.

"Want some lunch first?" she asked.

He shook his head. "We gotta air this old place out if we're going to live in it."

She handed over the keys and he headed off to the barn. Nora went inside, pulled the large white sheet from the dining room table, and coughed at the dust. She shook it until it seemed as good as it would get, then she brought it outside and laid it on the ground in the backyard. Four stones kept the corners from flapping in the breeze.

William came back with a tall wooden ladder. Together they made their way around the outside of the house, unlatching shutters and securing them to the wooden siding.

"We'll have to paint this place before winter," William said.

Nora thought of all the run-down apartments at which they

had turned up their noses. But of course this was different. It wasn't in a bad neighborhood. It wasn't surrounded by people who didn't want one of them there. It was freedom.

When William descended the ladder for the last time, Nora could hear her stomach growling. "Finally," she said. "Let's eat."

They rinsed their hands in cold water from a pump by the house and settled onto the makeshift picnic blanket. Nora opened the basket and began to pull out the sandwiches and potato salad when she felt William's hand on her hip.

"Do you want ham or turkey?" she asked.

"Neither."

She dug around the basket a little more. "Well, that's what we have. That and potato salad and oranges and some cookies."

"Well, I don't want any of that."

Nora knew that tone. "I'm hungry," she said.

William drew up close behind her and whispered into her ear, "So am I."

She turned toward him to say something, but he caught her cheek in his hand and silenced her with a kiss. "Come on, baby."

She was melting inside, but she pushed him away. "Not out here."

"Why not?"

"Are you crazy? Anyone could be watching."

"Who's watching? Squirrels? Birds? No one's here but us, right? Isn't that the whole point? No one's around for miles, and no one even knows this place is here."

She squirmed. "I just . . ."

He kissed her again.

She wasn't hungry for food anymore, but she pushed him away to speak. "In the house."

He got a playful look in his eye. "Uh-uh. It's all musty in there. Somebody could've died on those old beds." He laid her down with him, then pulled a plate out from beneath his back. She laughed as he tossed it off the sheet onto the overgrown grass.

As her self-consciousness melted away at the tender touch of her husband, Nora felt more keenly free than she could remember. There was nothing else. Just her and William. Two people in full view of the God who had made them both.

That afternoon they strolled through the now bright house, making a list of chores to do and repairs to make. They chose the bedroom off by itself at the back of the house. It had the best view, but it was the incredible carved bedstead that clinched it. They brought in armloads of clothing and boxes. Then, tired and getting hungry again, they unhitched the trailer and drove to town. They needed groceries and a newspaper and to get the phone and electricity turned on. More than a few curious heads turned, but Nora kept her eyes fixed ahead as they went about their errands. There was no need to invite comments by making eye contact. In the future, she'd do the shopping alone.

"I think you should try Flint," Nora said as she skimmed job listings on the way back to the house. "Doesn't look like there's too much in Lapeer. In Flint you'd have your pick of assembly-line jobs."

William was quiet.

"What do you think?" she asked.

"I thought I might not look for work right away and spend some serious time fixing up the house and the grounds. We don't have rent to pay."

"No, but there are the utilities and groceries."

"I saw a room in the basement I could turn into a darkroom. Then I'd be able to develop my own pictures."

"What does that cost?"

"I don't know. We'll see. I could probably get ahold of some used equipment."

She was quiet a moment. "I think I'll put an ad in the paper about sewing."

He nodded. "That's good."

"And maybe I'll make us a quilt for our bed."

"Nice."

Suddenly he swerved to the side of the road.

"What?" Nora asked in alarm. "Do we have a flat?"

"No," he said, straining to look over his shoulder. "We just passed a sign for a plant nursery and I want to check it out."

"What about the groceries?"

He did a U-turn. "We won't be long. I just want to look at their trees."

"Why? There are plenty of trees around the house."

"Yes, but not *our* tree."

THIRTY

Lapeer County, November 1864

Mary sat on Loretta's bed, two-month-old George upon her breast. No one knew that that was what she called her baby boy. When he was born in September, she had written to Nathaniel to give him the news and ask him what he would like to call the baby. As she waited for his reply, the child was referred to as "the baby" by the rest of the household. But in her mind and in private moments, Mary could not help but call him George.

"Still nothin' from Mr. Balsam?" Loretta asked as she tucked Simon in for a nap.

"Not yet." She tried to keep the concern out of her voice.

"They just movin' fast, is all," Loretta said. "They winnin' now. Mr. Lincoln voted back in and there ain't nothin' can stop 'em now."

Mary smiled. Surely that had to be the case. Nathaniel's letters had become a bit more sporadic lately anyway. Though this was the longest she had waited without word in some time.

"You write him more than once, right? Just in case it got lost? You write lots of letters."

"Yes, more than once."

In fact, Mary had only sent two letters to Nathaniel. The rest Loretta had seen her writing were for George. She had taken to writing the body of the letter first, with no salutation, just in case someone should come in unexpectedly or the letter should be misplaced. Only at the very last would she write *Dearest George* at the top and *With Love, Mary* at the bottom. Then she sealed the letter in an envelope, wrote his name on the outside, and handed it directly to him the next time the two of them were alone.

George still started his letters with the formal *Dear Mrs. Balsam*. But Mary had noted with a flutter in her stomach when he had replaced *Sincerely* with *Love*. Thinking of his last letter, Mary felt a warm stirring inside. He had been careful to keep his words guarded, but she could read between the lines. Their ardor for one another grew with each passing week, and the longer it remained contained by standards of decorum, the more fierce it became.

"You hot, Mrs. Balsam?"

"Excuse me?"

"Your face is all red, and your chest." Loretta pointed to Mary's chest, which was indeed flushed with her secret thoughts.

"Maybe I am," Mary said. "This baby gets so hot when he nurses. It's as if I'm holding a big baked potato."

"I'll nurse him for you a bit if you want. Give you a breather."

Loretta opened up the bodice of her dress again and sat down beside Mary. Mary broke the suction and handed the baby to Loretta, who had him resettled and suckling from her breast before he could even manage to get out a cry.

Mary fanned herself with her hand. "Thank you."

The first time Loretta had suggested helping with nursing when the baby was just a couple days old, Mary had been shocked. Coming from the South where slaves routinely served as wet nurses for their masters' children, Loretta found Mary's strong response to her offer shocking as well. Then one night, as the baby was screaming and Mary herself had succumbed to tears of exhaustion, Loretta swept into her room and didn't wait to be asked. She took the squalling infant from Mary's arms and put him on one of her own full breasts. From that moment, Loretta and Mary became friends in the true sense of the word, rather than a desperate woman and her benefactress.

Now Mary tried to recover from her runaway thoughts about George while her pale baby boy suckled at Loretta's brown breast.

"What was it like with Simon's father?" she asked.

"What do you mean?"

"Did you love him?"

Loretta laughed. "Naw, I didn't love that man. That man was a no-good, dirty rascal. He slept with all the girls. Had a whole passel a little half-breed children runnin' round that plantation, pickin' his cotton and servin' his white children like they was royalty."

"Did he . . . force himself?"

"On some, yeah. Rest of us learn it was better to just let him, just wait it out. Went better for you that way. Girls that fought back look like they been trampled by horses the next day. He was gonna get what he came for no matter what. I didn't want to get beat, so I let him do his thing when he came to me. Once he knew a girl was pregnant, he was back most every night. Didn't have to worry 'bout gettin' you pregnant if you already was, so he stick with you till the birthin' pains come. Then he move on."

Mary realized her mouth was hanging open and shut it. "How dreadful. That's what happened to you?"

"Twice. Year 'fore I had Simon, he got me with child, but it died."

Mary thought of her own dead baby girl in the frozen ground outside. "I'm so sorry, Loretta."

"I ain't! I's glad for the thing. When you dead you ain't nobody's slave. You reignin' with Jesus then. And when I had Simon and he was healthy, I got out fast as I could. No child of mine gonna grow up a slave like I did, and for certain not in his own father's fields." Loretta pulled the now sleeping baby from her breast.

Mary took her little son back into her arms as Loretta buttoned up her bodice. "Loretta, you amaze me. You all amaze me. I don't know that I could have made the journey you did. I don't think I would have had the courage."

Loretta regarded her. "I think you would, Mrs. Balsam. You got courage enough. Takes courage to do what you doin' here."

Mary shrugged. "Perhaps."

"And it takes courage to give your heart away like you done."

"I beg your pardon?"

"You all in pieces, Mrs. Balsam. A piece of you is on the battlefield and a piece of you is in your little baby there and a piece of you is in all those letters you writin' to George."

All Mary could manage was a breathy, "What?"

"Don't you worry," Loretta said with a smile. "Your secret's safe with me. I ain't gonna tell nobody."

"But how did you know?"

Loretta gave her a confused look. "I think you been mighty tired with your little bundle of joy here. Don't you remember givin' me that last one to read? You handed it right to me when I asked what you had in your hand."

Mary searched her memory. "I didn't—I don't think I meant to do that. No one else knows, do they? You didn't say anything to George?"

"'Course not. Ain't none of my business anyway. I don't know Mr. Balsam well, but from what I seen of him at Christmas, as far as I'm concerned he's like every other white man I know."

"What do you mean? Wasn't he kind to you?"

"Oh, he's kind, all right. But he ain't no saint."

Mary's mind raced. "Did he do something to you?"

"Not me, Mrs. Balsam. Ain't no man doin' nothin' to me no

more I don't want him to. I'd kill 'im first. But when I was comin' back from town with Jacob one day, I seen Mr. Balsam comin' outta that no-good Margaret's house a shame."

Now Mary truly could not speak. A pitiful cry from the baby told her she was squeezing him too tightly. She came to her senses and loosened her grip.

"I don't mean to be spreadin' no stories, so I ain't said nothin' to nobody. Jacob didn't see it on account a he was facin' front in the wagon. I was in the back facin' where we come from. But I just thought maybe I'd tell you that so you don't feel so bad 'bout lovin' another man."

Mary felt sick to her stomach. "I think I need to go lie down."

Loretta stood when Mary did. "Mrs. Balsam, I'm real sorry. I shouldn't a said nothin' 'bout it. But the world is full of a whole lot of rotten people. You one of the good ones. You can't help who you love."

Mary walked as if in a trance out of Loretta's room and into her own, where she put baby George into his crib. She sat down in front of the portable writing desk she had moved into her room when her letter writing to George had become more intimate. In front of her, upon the leather-covered writing surface, was a blank piece of paper. She stared at it, unblinking.

Could Loretta be telling the truth? Mary had never known her to lie. In fact, she was honest to the point of embarrassment. Perhaps she had just been mistaken and it was some other man. Mary tried to recall the faces of all the men she knew in town. So many were dead now. None of them could have been visiting a house of ill repute. So many others rarely emerged from their homes, deformed as they were from burns and amputations and disease.

She thought back to the short days of Nathaniel's furlough. They had made love the first night and the second, but with each new day she felt his growing judgment of her management of the household and farm. The third night they came together again, but her spirit was not in it. She had hoped he wouldn't notice. But after that, they had not made love again until his last night at home. Had she driven him to a prostitute in the meantime with her coldness? Had he visited that Margaret woman and then come home and slept with her?

At that moment, something snapped inside Mary's brain. If Nathaniel could defile their marriage bed with no thought to the consequences, she would say precisely what she wanted to say to George without thought to the consequences as well. Hands shaking, she picked up her pen, dipped it in ink, and began to write.

THIRTY-ONE

Lapeer County, October

Despite my fears, Nora did come through with the story behind the beds in the attic. In fact, she'd seemed more than happy to tell of the escaped slaves who had found refuge within the farmhouse walls. She'd begun as promised, and without further prompting, after dinner that night. It was indeed a long story—at least the way Nora told it—but I was captivated from the start. To think that some of those brave people had slept in my room, that their hands had worn smooth the same banisters that I touched every morning and evening.

Lying in bed that night, I marveled at how little I knew of my own family. Did my parents know this incredible legacy? Surely they would have passed it on to their children if they had.

Having finally gotten a real taste of the secrets my great-aunt was keeping in her head, I wasn't satisfied with just the story of the beds. What about the trunk in the attic? What about the darkroom? What about William? I needed to learn the hidden history of this place before Nora was in the grave. If I didn't, the stories would be lost—like those nameless bones in the garden marked by nothing more than a date.

Plus I had a promise to keep to an old man with a box of old photos.

But the very next day, Nora threw herself into her new project and asked for privacy as she worked on it. The request stung a little. Was I wearing out my welcome? I knew I would never have wanted a guest to stay more than one week, let alone six. I decided to give her space and spend a little more time and energy on me.

Tyrese and I fell into a pleasant routine of hanging out a couple times a week. A movie on a Thursday night, a high school football game on a Friday, cider and donuts and a corn maze one Saturday, a barn sale on another.

It was all good, clean, wholesome fun. Though I admittedly missed what Detroit had to offer—dining at the best restaurants, visiting posh casinos, or watching outstanding performances at the Fox Theatre. So late one night as I talked to Tyrese on Nora's kitchen phone, twisting the cord around my finger as I had when I was thirteen, I suggested we go to Flint one evening for a performance of *Ragtime* at The Whiting.

"I don't know," he said. "I never go to Flint if I can help it."

"Why not? It's not as bad as the media makes it out to be. Same as Detroit. Some spots you want to avoid, but there are some cool things going on in Flint."

"It's just not my scene," he answered. "Not my people."

I wanted to argue with him. Lapeer people weren't his people. I was struggling to know what to say when I realized that my silence had said volumes to Tyrese.

"Just because I'm black doesn't mean I fit in in Flint," he said. "Or Detroit. Or at a showing of *Ragtime*."

"I didn't say that."

"Yeah you did. You didn't, but you did."

"I really didn't mean—"

"It's okay. I know you didn't."

"Well . . . why don't you come over here for dinner? I'm sure

Nora would love to have you, and it might get her out of her cave."

So he did. And Nora did indeed come out of her cave—and her shell. Tyrese had an uncanny ability to talk with her and asked all of the questions I'd been afraid to ask for fear of shutting her down or tipping my hand.

"Elizabeth tells me you're from Detroit but you've lived here since the sixties," he said as he cut into a pile of mashed potatoes with the side of his fork. "Tell me about that. Why'd you move way out here?"

"There was no place for us in Detroit," Nora said matter-of-factly.

I risked entering the conversation. "There wasn't any housing?"

"Not for us. No one would rent to us in decent parts of town. And I didn't want to stay anyway. I was disowned by my family when we got married. Not long after, we moved out here and sort of retreated from life, I guess."

"Why didn't your family want you to marry him?" Tyrese asked.

"Because he was black."

It was the answer I expected, but to hear it stated so baldly was still a shock to my system. I looked to Tyrese, expecting to see an expression of disbelief. But he was unsurprised and nodding.

"It was not unheard-of," she continued, "but it was certainly not considered acceptable, especially for a young woman of my station in life. So we moved out here to escape the dirty looks and rude comments and redlining in Detroit. We had four beautiful years together. And then it ended."

Four years? That was it? "What happened?" I asked.

She furrowed her brow. "I don't really know."

I didn't know either. I could find no death certificate on Ancestry.com. And now that I thought about it, Mr. Rich never actually said his uncle had died.

"Is he . . . alive?"

She shook her head. "Some days I can believe he is." Then she was quiet.

Tyrese looked at his watch. "I better get going."

He was on his feet and at the kitchen door before I realized he meant to leave. I started to stand up.

"Don't get up." He pointed meaningfully at Nora, whose head was down. "I know my way out. Thank you for the wonderful dinner."

I mouthed *thank you*, and he smiled and disappeared, leaving Nora and me to talk about what I'd been dying to talk about.

"Nora, is that William's darkroom in the basement?"

I couldn't quite read her expression, but I was able to rule out *pleasantly surprised*.

"How do you know about the darkroom?"

I took a deep breath, feeling very much like I had as a child when my parents caught me in a lie. "I hope you won't be upset with me. When I cleaned out the dresser in my room, I found a key in the bottom drawer. I should have brought it to you right away. I saw the door when I was getting tools to work on the garden. I wanted to talk to you about it, but I didn't think I could because I'd gone in there without asking. But then when you started talking about William, I thought . . . I know this is weird and morbid, but I wanted to ask you about it while you could still tell me the story behind it."

She raised her eyebrows. "You mean before I'm dead?"

"Or senile," I offered weakly, as if that were better.

She gave me a long look. "Well, my natural reaction would be to tell you to mind your own business."

My heart sank.

"But I guess you're right," she went on. "We're only given so much time on this earth, and though there are some things I think we all take to our graves, I guess your own family history shouldn't be one of them. I had a great-aunt of my own who was kind enough to share much of the history of this place with me—she's the one who told me about the former slaves who used to live here. I shouldn't begrudge you the same courtesy."

I felt my heartbeat tick up. "So is that where William worked?"

"Yes."

"Why did he lock it?" I thought of the photos of the gorgeous young woman and feared I knew the answer.

"He didn't. I did. I locked it the week after he left. I left the key upstairs in the bottom of my dresser so that if I ever got up the nerve, I could open it. Only I never did."

"Why not?"

She was quiet for a moment. "Once you see something, you can't go back to a time when you hadn't." She shook her head. "You can never go back."

What did she think was in there? Did she suspect what I did?

"How did you know he was a photographer, anyway?" she asked.

Here goes nothing.

"Because I have something of his that I need to give you."

THIRTY-TWO

Lapeer County, November 1964

"Shoot!" Nora winced and sucked at her finger.

"Don't bleed all over that thing, now you found it," William said as he walked into the parlor, camera in hand.

"Yeah, yeah. I'm not sure it would be noticeable anyway."

"Maybe not. What do you call that thing again?"

"A crazy quilt."

He nodded. "That's the truth. That thing is crazy ugly."

"No it isn't."

William snapped a picture of her incensed expression. "Yes it is. Nothing matches. The pieces are all jagged. There are little spiders on it. It's crazy."

"Exactly."

He laughed a little. "Whatever. But that isn't going on our bed, is it? I like the red and white one you made better."

"No, it isn't going on our bed. But I thought if I could fix it up I could maybe use it somewhere."

"You mean somewhere I never go, right? Because that's going to send me into spasms if I look at it too long."

"Shut up." She laughed as she lobbed a spool of thread at him.

"Missed."

"Shut up about that too. And go get it for me."

He fished the thread out from under a chair. "Listen, I'm going to be downstairs awhile, okay? You call me when dinner's ready?"

"Sure, such as it is."

"You make a mean meat loaf, baby. Don't let anybody tell you otherwise."

He planted a long kiss on her lips, looked ready to change his mind about leaving, then waved the desire away and disappeared. Nora heard his footsteps diminish then vanish altogether when he hit the dirt floor of the cellar. A squeak. The muffled sound of a door shutting. Then she was alone.

She tied the thread and snipped off the excess. Then she sat back and assessed her work. The open seam was now shut, her tiny stitches hidden beneath the embroidered bird tracks that some ancestor of hers must have made long ago. She smoothed her hand over the quilt, looking for the next part needing repair. She had been taking in mending for months to earn some extra cash, but she hadn't found any of those projects as satisfying as this one.

They had discovered the quilt the night before, which was a great surprise indeed. Having been at the farmhouse over a year, Nora was sure that its secrets had all been revealed, even if they could not be explained. She had not counted on the trunk, and in fact had all but forgotten the skeleton key her mother had included in the envelope when she and William moved in. It didn't seem to open anything, so it went into a kitchen drawer and inched its way to the very back corner beneath the pot holders. When they found the trunk hidden beneath a sheet, back behind the very last mysterious cot in the attic, William had suggested a crowbar. Thankfully, Nora remembered the key.

"What is that?" William had said.

"It's a quilt," Nora said reverently. "Oh my."

They unfolded it gently, each holding two corners. It hung heavy between them like a giant mosaic bowl.

"We need to take this downstairs."

William craned his neck. "Anything else in there? Pirate gold? Maybe some big ol' bags of money from a bank robbery or something?"

"Just some old shirts."

William looked disappointed.

They brought the quilt down to the parlor, moved the furniture to the edges of the large space, and laid it out on the floor.

"Wow," Nora said. "That's amazing."

William had kept his opinion to himself then. The find had made Nora so happy she had barely noticed he was still in the room.

Now as she carefully laid it out on the floor once more to look over her repairs, Nora breathed a little prayer of thanks that it had survived long enough for her to find it. The mantel clock struck the hour and she went into the kitchen to make dinner. After each step in the recipe, as things simmered and sizzled and baked, she wandered back to the front room to stare at the quilt. Where should she put it?

As she pulled the pan out of the oven, she decided to lay the quilt over the bed in the north bedroom, where there was only a plain wool blanket at the moment. She wouldn't see it unless she purposefully went in there, but at least William wouldn't have to look at it.

"Dinner's ready!" she shouted down the cellar stairs.

"Up in a couple!" came the muffled reply.

Nora put the plates on the table and salted William's vegetables.

"What do you think of these?" he asked as he breezed into the room a moment later. He laid four 5x7 photographs out on the table.

Nora came around to examine them. "They're nice."

"Nice?"

"Yes," she said, looking up at him. "They're nice."

He furrowed his brow and frowned at the photos.

"They're beautiful photographs, William."

He shook his head. "No, they're just nice. You were right the first time." He sighed.

She picked up a photograph of a pale leaf upon a large, dark stone. "This one is very good. I like the contrast."

He was still shaking his head. "I don't know what the problem is. I don't like anything I've done since we moved out here. This place is hell on photos."

Nora looked over the four photographs again. "There are no people."

"No people," he echoed.

"Those were always your best photos. Portraits, pictures of all different kinds of people."

William looked thoughtful. He began to nod, slowly at first, then with increasing intensity.

"Let's sit down and eat," Nora suggested.

William sat, but he did not eat. "Here's the problem. There are no people here. Didn't I say exactly that when you first brought this place up?"

"That's one of the things I love about it."

William speared a green bean. "Nothing happens at this house. I doubt anything ever happened here worth photographing. Maybe I should take a day trip somewhere."

"How about Flint?"

He narrowed his eyes. "Why Flint?"

"It's close, it's urban, lots of people. Seems like the right sort of place. Why not?"

"Are you going to get on me again about getting a job on the line?"

Nora played innocent. "I don't know what you're talking about."

"Yeah, right," he said with a half smile.

"Though if you took a notion to it, you could fill out some applications while you were there."

He shook his head. "See? I knew it."

"Why don't you want to get a job at GM? That's good money."

"What do we need it for? We're making ends meet."

"Barely. We're not getting ahead."

"Ahead of what? If you have enough to live, what do you need more for?"

"Don't you want a bit more? We could get another car. We could go on a vacation."

"But if I don't work thirty miles away, we don't need a second car, and if I don't work fifty hours a week on the line, I don't need a vacation."

"What about retirement?"

"Retirement from what? What do I have to retire from?"

Nora let out a frustrated sigh.

"Look, baby, I want time for my photography. That's where my heart is. And now that I'm not contributing to my mama's rent, I got a little freedom. I want to take some good photos—meaningful photos—and sell some, maybe put them in a gallery. Make a book someday. If we still lived someplace where anything happened, I guess I'd be taking more pictures for newspapers, like those photos from the march. You've got your sewing, I've got my camera, we've got this house. What more do we need now?"

They ate in silence for several minutes.

"Nora," William continued finally, "I just don't want to go back to a life where I'm treated different. Any black man can get a job on the assembly line, sure. But he's still a black man while he's there. Still taking orders from self-important white men in suits. Still don't feel like a man."

She was quiet a moment. Then she buried her face in her hands.

William was out of his chair in an instant. "What's wrong?"

"It's just—I'm pregnant."

"What?"

"And there'll be hospital bills and clothes to buy and a crib and all sorts of things and we're not going to be able to afford it so the baby will have to sleep in a—"

He tipped her face to look at his. "Nora, are you serious? Are you really going to have a baby? Our baby?"

She tried to get control of herself. "Yes."

Tears started to form in William's eyes.

"I'm sorry." She sniffed, wiping at her eyes with her sleeve. "I don't know what's come over me."

William laughed lightly and pulled her close to his chest. "It's okay, baby. It's okay." He held her for a long time, swaying back and forth. Finally he said, "Okay. I'll look for a job in Flint."

"Really?"

"Really. I'll start looking tomorrow."

Nora blew her nose in her napkin, and William settled back down into his chair.

The rest of the meal was consumed with talk of what sex the baby might be, which room would be best for a nursery, what color the walls should be, and what names they each liked.

"What about Bernice?" William said.

"Bernice? What? No."

"Why not?"

"Bernice?"

"Yeah."

"No."

"Okay then," he said with a roll of his eyes. "How about Beverly?"

"Maybe."

William sat back, satisfied.

"But if it's a boy," Nora said, "I want to name him Matthew."

THIRTY-THREE

Lapeer County, April 1865

Bridget fastened the last button on Mary's bodice and handed her a black wrap. The two women descended the same staircase George had run up only days before with the jubilant news of the war's end. It had been the first unguarded moment Mary and George had shared in months. He had not responded to her impulsive and passionate letter, and with every day that had passed since she'd written it, it was harder to be in the same room with him. Now Mary grasped her black skirts to keep from treading upon them as she went down to eat the evening meal in a room full of silent, grief-stricken friends, with George at the head of the table.

She imagined they must all be thinking the same things she was. How could it happen? Just when victory had been secured? The gross injustice and tragedy of it was more than she could bear. But as mistress of the house, Mary knew she had to set the example of strength and fortitude despite grief. They could not give way to despair. The war, after all, was still won.

"Little George didn't vomit on me once this morning, Mrs.

Balsam," Angelica announced as she handed the wriggling baby boy to his mother.

"That was very sweet of him." Mary laughed in spite of herself. She liked the nickname her baby had been given by the household to differentiate him from his namesake. It made it much easier to understand who someone was talking about. Not that Mary might suppose that Big George made a habit of throwing up on Angelica. But still, the word *little* seemed apt. He was her little angel child, her solace.

After Loretta's revelation about Nathaniel's indiscretions, Mary had announced to everyone living in the house that the baby's name would be George. He was baptized the next week, Mary and Bridget attending the service with Big George but none of the other residents of the house. Reverend and Mrs. Whittaker had frowned at the name, but she would not be swayed.

When everyone was seated, George prayed over the meal. While their eyes were all closed and George thanked the Lord for his provision, little Simon toddled into the room and yanked at the tablecloth, nearly pulling an entire place setting onto his head. His hand was caught at the last moment, and everyone in the room seemed to let out the collective breath they had been holding.

"Thank God for children during dark days," John Dixon said as he shooed Simon away.

"Yes, indeed," Mary agreed. "I pray these little ones will never suffer the horrors our nation has undergone these past four years."

There were solemn nods of affirmation all around the table.

"Any word yet from Mr. Balsam when he be comin' home?" Jacob asked.

Mary shook her head. "I imagine it may be some time yet. And now with President Lincoln's murder, I fear it may take even longer. I'm sure he will send word when he can."

She still had not heard from Nathaniel since before Little George was born. She checked the lists of names every week to see if he had been killed, injured, or captured. His name never appeared and so she tried not to worry. As angry as she was, she didn't wish him ill. It would be better for him to return home safely, even if she could hardly think of him without lapsing into bitterness.

Soon breakfast was consumed and plates were in the kitchen being washed. The men went out to their various tasks at far-flung corners of the Balsam farm. Bridget and Angelica took the small children out to the front porch for some fresh spring air. Mary was pushing in the last chair when George came back into the room for his hat. It was the first time in months she could remember being alone with him.

"Where have you been lately, George? I feel as though I've hardly seen you."

"We've both been busy, I suspect."

"It's obvious what has occupied my time—a baby is a lot of work—but what about yours? What have you been doing in the barn until all hours?"

He looked at her in surprise.

"Little George has me up all night," she said. "If I look out the kitchen window I often see the lantern light seeping through the crack in the barn door. What has you so occupied?"

George appeared to be considering his response. "I've been carving."

"Carving? Goodness, carving what? You could have carved Noah's ark by now."

A smile crept across his face. "It's nothing like that. It's almost done, though. Would you like to see it?"

She felt a warm sensation in the pit of her stomach. The months of no letters vanished, and Mary felt as though she were reconnecting with a friend. "I'd like that very much."

"Come down to the barn when I'm working on it tonight

and I'll show you." He tipped his hat to her and walked out of the room.

The rest of the day, Mary was the picture of distraction. She didn't notice people speaking to her. She misplaced her letter opener and spilled a pot of ink. What could he have been carving in secret? Why should it be something he must show to her under cover of darkness? Was this an invitation to something more? Could this be his answer to her letter?

When night came, Mary tossed while little George snoozed in his cradle and Bridget snored on her cot. She did eventually fall asleep, and when Little George woke her with his crying, she found it difficult to return fully from unconsciousness. It wasn't until she was putting his sleeping body back into the cradle that she remembered her evening errand. She looked over herself in the glass, fixed her hair, then put on her best dressing gown and slippers. She tiptoed down the stairs and out the back.

A soft and steady light spilled through the crack under the barn door. Heart pounding in her ears, she hurried across the wet lawn and stepped out of the dark night into the warm glow of a lantern. She heard wood being sanded but could see no one.

"Hello?" she whispered.

The sanding stopped.

"Mrs. Balsam?" came George's soft voice.

"Where are you?"

"In the loft."

Mary looked up and saw George looking down at her. She pulled herself up the ladder and crept through scattered bits of hay to the place where George knelt by a large wooden structure.

"This," he said, "is what I have been making."

Mary examined the object. It appeared to be made of undulating branches, some light, some dark, sanded to a smooth polish and locked in a sensuous embrace.

"This isn't all of it," he said. "There are a few more finished pieces that go with it. But I have those stored out of the way."

"What is it?"

"It's a bed. This is the foot. I've done the headboard already and the two sides. I'll put them together on a frame once it's in the room, and then I'll put the ropes through for the feather tick. When I got done with the cots, I couldn't stop. Thought I'd make something real special."

Mary inched closer and ran her hand along the smooth surface of one branch. Only this close she could see that it was not a branch. The entire piece appeared to be carved from two separate but intertwined pieces of wood, one light, one dark. Mary followed one with a finger, but she could not see how George had managed to get the two together.

"There must be a trick to it," she said in wonder.

"There is, but I won't tell you what it is."

"It's like nothing I've ever seen. I had no idea you were an artist."

He laughed. "You and me both."

"Amazing."

"I'm glad you like it. I made it for you."

Her eyes grew wide and her lips parted. "Oh, George," she started, then faltered. "I . . . I don't know what to say."

"You don't need to say anything. I would have rather just gotten it set up in your room without you knowing, but you never leave the house. Anyway, this is better. Now I know you like it."

"George, I . . . I do like it. Only . . ."

This felt wrong. Very wrong. How could the man she loved make a bed in which she would conceive children with another, one she felt she hardly knew anymore?

"Oh, George. How can you give me this?"

His face fell. "I thought you'd be pleased."

"I would, but—oh, it feels so evil to say it, but I cannot deny that there is a part of me that is not looking forward to Nathaniel coming home. I have known you twice as long as I knew him before he enlisted. You have been here with me all this time, in my very darkest moments. Nathaniel has not. How can I know we will ever really love each other the way you and I—" She snapped her mouth shut.

"You know this cannot be anything more than it is," George said softly. "I can never be more than a friend to you."

He spoke the truth. Even if Nathaniel had died in the war, she could not have married George. She'd heard rumors of the races intermingling in the bonds of marriage in Boston and New York. But this was not Boston or New York.

Tears welled up in her eyes. "Why did you make this for me? Why did you ask me to come out here in the dark of night?"

"I didn't think—"

"No, you didn't," she said fiercely. "First I pour my heart out to you in a letter I never should have written, then you all but ignore it—ignore me—for months. What am I to think, then, when you present me with a bed?" She made a move to go.

"Mary, wait."

Tears spilled down her cheeks. "Why? Why should you call me Mary now?"

George pulled her toward him. She held tight to him for a moment and then pushed away.

With a gentle hand on her chin, he turned her face up toward his. He wiped away the wetness on her cheeks with the back of his finger. "I never got such a letter. If I had, of course you know I would have written back."

"But . . . I know I wrote it." Mary tried to recall that terrible day when she had learned of Nathaniel's betrayal of their marriage vows. She remembered putting the letter into an envelope. She remembered writing *My Love* instead of *George* on the envelope. She remembered seeing Bridget as through a fog the next morning after being up all night with Little George. They had spoken, but Mary couldn't recall what was said. She couldn't determine what had been reality and what might have been a dream.

George's hand on her cheek brought her back to the moment. "It used to be that there was nothing in life I wanted more than my freedom," he said, "and for a very long time that was the one thing I could not have. Now I have it, and there is nothing in life I want more than you, and yet you are the one thing I cannot have."

Mary knew at that moment that if he asked her to, she would give herself over to him, no matter the consequences.

As if he could see her desperate desire, George dropped his hand and backed up. "I think it's time for you to go back to the house, Mrs. Balsam."

Somehow Mary made it down the ladder and out of the barn. She rushed across the wet grass to the house, tore up the stairs, and flung herself on her bed. She buried her face in her pillow and poured her sorrows into its downy softness. It was not long before she felt a hand on her shoulder.

"Ma'am, are you okay?"

Mary snapped her head around. "Bridget, did you send a letter for me?"

"A letter?"

Mary gripped Bridget's hand. "Months ago. The envelope said *My Love*."

"Oh, yes, that was some time ago. I did send it to the last address we had for Mr. Balsam, but you never can tell if letters will make it to soldiers. Don't fret, ma'am. I'm sure that Mr. Balsam is safe and will be home soon."

THIRTY-FOUR

Lapeer County, November

I could feel my redemption in the journalistic community slipping out of my hands like autumn slipping into winter.

The night Tyrese had dinner at the farmhouse, I'd retrieved the camera bag from the armoire, moved Nora's plate out of the way, and placed it on the table in front of her. I could see immediately that she recognized it. For a long moment, she didn't touch it. Then she tugged lightly at the leather strap and it snapped open. She reached in and pulled out a black and silver Nikon manual-focus camera. Though I'd worried what to tell her about how I came into possession of her husband's property without implicating Mr. Rich—there was no explanation I could fathom that wouldn't somehow come back around to him—she was so absorbed by the object itself that I felt it best to leave her alone and answer her questions later.

But later never came. The next morning she acted as though nothing out of the ordinary had occurred, and I found myself wondering if she just didn't remember or if she was deliberately avoiding the subject.

Now the camera was returned to its rightful owner, but I'd

gotten almost nowhere when it came to learning more about Nora and William's life together, however short it may have been. Was she ready to see a box of photos William had taken of the Detroit riots? I didn't want to go through this awkwardness again. Maybe I should just tell Mr. Rich I was ready to give her the photos now and get it over with. But then, if she just put them away in her room and refused to talk about them like she had the camera, would I ever get a chance to write the story that might save my career? It just didn't work without the photos. Without this story, there was no reason to think I'd have a chance at what few journalism jobs might come available in Detroit. And I had no desire to live and work anywhere else.

Days later, November blew into our midst like a beast, with howling winds, stinging rain, and more news of unrest an hour south. September and October had been so pleasant and mild that I'd all but forgotten that time for the garden was running short. Then one cold Sunday morning when I went out to inspect it, every leaf, twig, and thorn was coated in fine frost. A glance at the field of wildflowers, which had been so recently bedecked in goldenrod, asters, and teasel, revealed the same. The stiff brown remains of summer's lusty beauty sparkled in frosted brilliance.

When I returned to the house, Nora still hadn't come out for breakfast. She'd been holed up in her room for days, emerging to eat or use the bathroom, but for little else. The stream of alterations customers, fairly steady since I'd arrived in August, had slowed to a trickle despite the upcoming holidays. The phone continued to ring, and I overheard Nora putting off would-be customers. Her big project, whatever it was, consumed her.

With no Nora to talk to, no garden to tend, no judge to expose, no amazing story about racism and love and riots to write, I began to think that maybe I needed to go back to school or join the Peace Corps or hike the Appalachian Trail. Something to give me direction, put me on a path that would lead toward some purpose, some end bigger than just this day-to-day living with no prospects in sight.

Dad's cousin Barb had been worried over nothing. Nora didn't need help living on her own, and she didn't belong in a nursing home. So she got a little confused once in a while. She didn't pose a danger to herself or anyone else. She was perfectly content with her life and didn't need me interfering.

And Mr. Rich? Maybe he needed to do his own dirty work. Maybe he needed to man up, get his butt up to Lapeer, and give those photos to Nora himself.

Maybe I needed to move out, get back to the city. But the moment the thought occurred to me, my heart felt sick. What was there in Detroit for me anymore? Nothing but dead ends and burned bridges. And no Tyrese.

"Where's this going?" I asked him on the phone one evening in late November as I watched the first snowfall. "Should I stick around here? Am I supposed to live with Nora the rest of my life? Am I ever going to get another job in journalism?"

What I really wanted to ask was whether we were doing anything beyond killing time. But somehow I just couldn't. It sounded so presumptuous.

"I don't have any answers for you, Elizabeth. You've got to do what's right for you. It's your life."

Was it? It didn't feel like it. My life was in Detroit. This was someone else's life out here. Someone else's house. Someone else's garden.

"Tyrese, I have no idea what I'm still doing here. I'm thinking of getting back to Detroit."

He was quiet a moment. "Maybe you should."

"Oh."

"It's not like that. I love spending time with you and I want to see if this goes somewhere. I don't want you to leave. Not at all. But the worst thing you can do is stay somewhere for someone else. I mean, I love my dad and I stayed in Lapeer for him, and now I've got the nursery and all, but . . . honestly, I never wanted to own a business. I wanted to work for the DNR. I wanted to be a scientist. I didn't want to be a salesman who sometimes cuts lawns and plows driveways. And you don't want to stay in Lapeer for me or even for Nora if what you really want to do is be a journalist. 'Cause you'll never be happy that way. You've got to do what's right for you."

He was right. The only problem was, I had no idea what that was.

As the sun slipped down behind the tree line on the last night of November, I sat at one of my bedroom windows, looking down at the large stones that had appeared in the back field just two days earlier. They must have always been there, but it wasn't until the rain and snow had pulled back the curtain of wildflowers that I could see them. Six dark gray stones, all of a similar size, evenly spaced, stretched in a line. How had something so obvious escaped my notice for three months?

As evening faded and the stones merged with the darkness, I turned to find Matthew sprawled on my bed. His increasing friendliness toward me was the lone positive effect of Nora's prolonged sessions in her workroom. Starved for attention, he had come to see me as a possible substitute in the affection department. It also helped that I seemed to be the only one remembering to feed him now.

I stretched out next to him and stroked his fiery fur. Then I heard the rain start. It whispered at first, a soft, lulling sound. But it soon grew louder and more insistent, battering the house and streaking down the windowpanes in sheets. I tried not to think about the crumbling foundation of my life as I drifted off to sleep with Matthew tucked in the crook of my arm.

When I woke the next morning the room was glowing. I pushed Matthew off my chest where he had relocated in the night, took a cat-free breath, and looked out the window. My whole world was encased in ice—every twig, every blade of grass, every dead flower. An unclouded sun rose over the frozen expanse and I squinted against the glare. Then I noticed I was shivering.

Downstairs the thermostat in the hall read fifty-two degrees. I flicked the light switch on the wall. Nothing. The house was heated with gas, but the thermostat that told it when to turn on was electric, as was the fan that forced the warmed air through the ducts. No power meant no heat.

"Nora?" I knocked on her bedroom door and peeked in. She popped her head out of her workroom. "Oh, there you are. The power is out."

"Yes, I know. Perhaps you'd be a dear and make a fire in the parlor for us. Or wherever you think you'll be spending the most time today."

"Where are you going to be?" I asked, though I could easily have guessed.

"I'll be back here."

"How can you even see?"

"There's light from the window. I've just switched to the old treadle machine so I can keep working. Can't waste a day."

"Couldn't you just ask for an extension on that project? You're running yourself ragged."

"No, I don't think so. It's something that needs to get done."

"Is there anything I can do to help? I'm concerned about you. You don't seem like yourself lately."

"Nonsense. I'm just fine."

Stubborn woman.

"Aren't you cold? I could help you move the sewing machine out to the parlor and we could sit there together in front of the fire."

"No, it's much too heavy. You could make a fire in here, but then you better keep my bedroom door shut to keep the heat in. And it might be easier for you to heat your bedroom than the parlor with those tall ceilings."

"I could hang out in here," I offered.

She frowned. "You don't want to be stuck in here with me. I'll be no fun at all."

She wanted me gone. Just when I was actually needed.

"I'll get dressed and bring in some firewood," I said.

"Thank you, Elizabeth," she said. "Oh, and I nearly forgot. Someone called for you yesterday." She retrieved a piece of paper from the top of her dresser and held it out. "Some woman from some newspaper."

I scanned the note, my heart beating faster. Just a name—Caryn—and a number.

"Shoot," I said, trying not to sound upset. "Now I can't call back until the power's on."

"Sure you can. The phone still works."

"During an outage?"

Nora nodded. "The phone lines are buried, so if it's just the power supply to the house that was hit, the phones should be fine. Enough power comes through the copper wires. Go try it out."

I folded the note, trying not to appear too eager. "Just as soon as I get the fires going."

I layered leggings under my jeans and piled on shirts and a sweater and two pairs of socks, my mind running through wild tangents about who Caryn was and which newspaper she worked for and how she had gotten Nora's number. The water that had been rushing out through the downspout when the rain began the night before had turned to a sheet of ice right outside the door. I skidded a moment, caught my balance, then shuffled over to the woodpile. After a dozen or so careful trips in and out, I had filled the north wall of the kitchen with wood. I made Nora's fire and brought in wood for her to add to it as the day went on. Then I made several arduous trips up and down the back stairs with wood for my own fireplace.

When I was gathering the last load from the woodpile, the breeze picked up and an ominous creaking sounded from above. I looked up to see the branches of the catalpa tree swaying and chafing like an enormous crystal chandelier. Somewhere in the woods, a tree gave up a branch, a shower of glass punctuated by a great crash. I slipped back inside, safe from the elements, and picked up the phone. I nearly cried for joy when I heard a dial tone.

After two rings, a woman's voice said, "You've reached the *Beat*."

"Hello, I'm returning a call from Caryn. This is Elizabeth Balsam."

"Elizabeth, hi! I'm so glad you called back. I'm Caryn, and I was calling you regarding a position we're looking to fill. Have you heard of our publication?"

Had I heard of it? Until I'd moved to the middle of nowhere, I'd devoured every issue of the trendy alternative newspaper.

"I have."

"Great! Then you may know that we are in search of a new features editor. You came to the attention of our chief editor, Marshall Boon."

"Really?"

"You sound surprised."

"Well, it's just—" I stopped. Wouldn't Marshall Boon have gotten wind of my disgrace? "I'm not at the *Free Press* anymore."

"And you're just the kind of unconventional risk taker Mr. Boon likes on his team. He'd like you to come in for an interview. Are you available sometime before Christmas?"

I was nothing but available.

"Yes. Though, just curious—how did you get this number?"

"It's on your cell's voicemail message."

Oh yeah.

"How did you get that number?"

"A friend of yours at the *Free Press* had it."

Desiree. She hadn't forgotten about me.

The details were settled in moments, and when I hung up the phone I couldn't help but smile. Somewhere in Detroit there was an open desk—and somehow I had to be sure I was the one who filled it.

It was dark outside by five o'clock. Nora and I ate our dinners by candlelight in our separate bedrooms. After dinner, I refreshed our stock of wood, then I lay on my bed in the flickering light of the fireplace I had thought I'd never use and began to strategize. I needed those photos. Now.

By the time I blew out the candles, it was snowing.

THIRTY-FIVE

Lapeer County, February 1965

Mallory Balsam arrived at the farmhouse on a bright, bitterly cold February day. Nora heard the car drive up, the front door open and shut, some murmurings down the stairs, and then footsteps outside the bedroom door. She wished she could disappear, just sink into the mattress and suffocate. Then, at the sight of the mother she hadn't seen in over a year, she overflowed into tears.

Mallory held her for a long time, rocking her as she had long ago when her little girl had a bad dream. When Nora ran out of tears, Mallory stood up and held out her hands. "It's time to take a shower," she said.

Nora slumped back on the bed she felt like she had been in for a lifetime. Every muscle was drained, every nerve ending dead.

"Get up, Nora. It's time to take a shower and do your hair and get dressed. Let's go."

Nora blinked up at her mother. "Just leave me alone."

"I'm not leaving this room until you get out of bed."

Nora groaned but did as she was told.

Mallory sat on a low wooden stool in the bathroom as Nora washed away three days of dirt and sadness.

"Time's up." Mallory turned off the water. She pulled back the shower curtain and handed Nora a towel. Then she left the room.

For the hundredth time that day, Nora placed a hand over the spot where her baby should be. Empty. Like her heart. Had she somehow lost that too when she was laid upon the hospital bed and pieces of her very soul were being scraped from inside of her? William hadn't stopped them. He hadn't even been allowed in the room.

Within an hour of her arrival, Mallory had Nora washed, dressed, and headed down the stairs to eat her first meal in days. Nora stared through her plate.

Her mother put the eggs on top of the toast, cut everything into bite-sized pieces, and held a forkful up to Nora's face. "You need to eat."

Nora took the fork and obediently put it into her mouth. Chewing felt impossible. She wasn't hungry. Just empty. "I hate this."

Mallory put a hand on her daughter's shoulder. "I know, honey."

"Why is this happening?"

"It happens to a lot of women, Nora. There's no reason for it."

The answer didn't satisfy, but deep down, Nora knew that no answer would.

"Come on, honey. Why don't you show me to my room?"

Mallory retrieved her suitcase from where William had left it in the front hall. Nora led her to the north bedroom.

"My, my! What is this?" Mallory asked in genuine wonder.

"It's a crazy quilt. I found it in a trunk in the attic."

Mallory ran her hand over the multicolored embroidery. "It's exquisite."

"I had to repair the seams in a few spots, but it looks to be in pretty good shape otherwise. I wish I knew who made it."

"You know who might know something about it? Your Great-Aunt Margaret. She lives in a nursing home in Detroit now, but she used to live here."

"Maybe I should visit her someday," Nora said. "She might know about a lot of things in this house."

"I'd go sooner rather than later, if I were you. She's in her nineties."

Mallory left the room and Nora let out a little sigh. The thought of going anywhere at all exhausted her.

A moment later, her mother was back and fishing in her purse. "I could go with you," Mallory offered as she copied an address out of a little book.

"We'll see," Nora said.

"Okay. Let's go get our coats."

"I said we'll see."

"We're not going to Detroit, Nora. We're going to the store. You're going to make your husband a real dinner tonight. Let's go."

They came home with all they needed to make lasagna and set about the long process of readying the dish for baking. It was such an involved recipe for two women who were not natural cooks that for a time Nora forgot that she was not going to be a mother in June. But at the expression of surprise on William's face as he walked through the door that evening to find Nora up and pulling a lasagna out of the oven, it all came crashing back.

During dinner, William and Mallory carried the conversation, each trying to engage Nora and then settling for silence when she responded with answers consisting of no more than three words strung together. Nora excused herself and retired early, leaving her mother and her husband to clean up the dishes. She pulled on a clean nightgown and crawled beneath the fresh sheets her mother had put on the bed. The sun was setting later and later in the evenings. She watched through frosted windowpanes as it sank behind the bare trees. The sky turned orange, then pink, then gray.

William came through the door, took off his clothes, and slipped into bed next to her. Nora tucked herself under his arm and laid her head on his chest. They exchanged "I love yous," but inside, Nora felt keenly that it was not enough. Love had not insulated them from pain. It had not saved their baby. It could not fix this. It could not fix anything.

Eventually William fell asleep, but for Nora the night was a long, lonely string of regrets and second guesses.

The next morning after a hot breakfast, William left for the job he had gotten in Flint—the job that would pay for the baby they were not having—while Nora and her mother lingered over coffee and talked of safe, mundane things. The weather, the house, her brothers.

"I'll never understand why Warner moved to Indiana," Mallory said. "There's nothing there."

"Maybe that's why he moved. For the most part I've been quite pleased with life out in the country."

"Your brother makes it sound very dull. They're turning into hayseeds out there. But I guess his mother was from kind of a hick town."

"Mom, that's not nice." Nora had only met her father's first wife once, but she'd seemed kind. More so than her own mother was at times. "Leigh's not a hick."

"According to your father, that was one of the reasons their marriage failed. She couldn't stand the city."

"I guess that was a good thing for you."

"I guess it was a good thing for you too. Otherwise you wouldn't have been born." Mallory winced as she said the last word.

"It's okay," Nora said, even though it wasn't.

"You know, you never can tell with things like this. Sometimes they can turn out to be blessings in disguise." At Nora's frown,

Mallory continued. "I'm sure you know it would have been hard to have a mulatto child. To go out in public with him and for people to know that you had . . . well . . . It would have been hard on the child too, to never know what he was or where he belonged."

Nora's fork clattered onto her plate. She stood up from the table and threw the plate into the sink, where it shattered. She walked out of the kitchen, leaving Mallory stunned at the table. Moments later, she reappeared with her mother's suitcase, which she placed by the older woman's feet.

Back in her room, she heard a car start up outside. Then the motor died away. And Nora vowed never to let her mother through her door again.

THIRTY-SIX

Lapeer County, May 1866

Mary bit down on her tongue for a count of ten. If she kept this up during the entirety of her mother-in-law's visit, she would have nothing left with which to speak.

"You mean to say the attic is full of them?" Catherine Balsam said with a note of horror in her voice as she gazed up at the ceiling in Mary's bedroom. "Like a colony of bats?"

Mary tasted the metallic tang of blood. "Why don't we get George and Jonathan now and go downstairs?"

"Where did this atrocious bed come from? What happened to the bedstead I gave you?"

"It's in another room right now."

"You don't have them sleeping on my bed, do you?"

"I have them sleeping on *my* bed, yes."

"But why would you replace that beautiful bed with this?" Catherine gestured at the bed in the same way she might have indicated to her maid that the dog had vomited on a carpet.

"This was a gift from a friend."

"A friend? What kind of a friend would inflict this on another person?"

Inside her apron pockets, Mary's hands balled into fists. "Let's go get the boys, Mother."

She walked out, leaving Catherine to follow. For all her discourtesy, Catherine Balsam doted on her grandsons, and Mary hoped they might keep her too busy for further commentary. At least the woman served as an adequate distraction from the uncomfortable pall that had settled over her household since Nathaniel's return. No words had been spoken about the letter that may or may not have reached Nathaniel on the front, nor about Nathaniel's alleged visit to a prostitute. But the weight of things left unsaid had squeezed out the joy that had characterized Mary's home during the war. The recent addition of Nathaniel's mother certainly did nothing to replace it.

That afternoon, Mary and Catherine planned to take the boys for a walk in the apple orchard Nathaniel had begun planting. Mary settled her mother-in-law in the back of the wagon with George and Jonathan and jumped up to the driver's seat.

"You're taking one of the only jobs they're fit to do, Mary."

Mary silently flicked the reins. If she kept the horses at a slow walk, the excursion would likely take until dinnertime.

Among the apple tree saplings, Catherine sat on a blanket with baby Jonathan and watched George collect petals from the ground while Mary flagged down Nathaniel.

"I don't think the hands should eat with us tonight—or any night until your mother is on the train back to Detroit."

Nathaniel looked grave. "I know. She is hardly tolerable."

"I don't understand how you could possibly be her son."

"She means well," he said weakly. "She has always been for emancipation. She just believes Negroes are fundamentally different than those of Western European stock, that the freed slaves should be sent to Africa. She can't envision a future America of two races."

"That couldn't be more obvious. I think we'd do well to keep the table white while she's here."

"I disagree," he said. "It's my house, after all."

His house? It had been *her* house longer than it had been his.

"Perhaps we could help change her mind," he continued.

"When has your mother ever changed her mind?"

He offered her a rueful shrug.

"I don't know how much longer I can take it," Mary said as she watched Catherine pull a fistful of petals from Little George's mouth.

"You're fine, Mary. Now I must get back to work if we're to get this row planted and staked before dinner." He kissed her forehead and walked away, leaving her to deal with the domestic issues he saw as her sphere and therefore her problem.

And it was a problem. As Lincoln's armies had marched north following the end of the war, thousands of freed slaves, now jobless and homeless, followed along with hopes for a future in a part of the reunited country where the cotton could not grow. Some of those sore-footed men and women had accompanied Nathaniel when he came home in July of 1865. There were now so many people living at the farmhouse that they had to eat in two shifts to use the dining room.

That fine evening, the men set up sawhorses and boards in the backyard. As the sun faded to its soft evening hue, the men brought every chair they could find from the house and carried out stacks of dishes. The women piled the table high with spring potatoes, greens, asparagus, peas, pickled eggs, and various cuts from the pig that had been roasted, including some with which Mary and Nathaniel were not familiar, but which the Southern transplants in their midst relished. The children tumbled around in the yard, occasionally snatching a bite off their mothers' plates. Little George and Simon snuck up behind people, poked at their sides, and laughed hysterically.

The large company of people that surrounded Mary almost made up for her mother-in-law. And it almost made up for the cold, businesslike manner in which Nathaniel had treated her since he discovered a strange bedstead in his bedchamber and learned it had been made for his wife by another man.

"Wasn't it enough that you named our son George? Must I sleep in a bed that man made?"

"We cannot refuse such a lavish gift and hope to retain his friendship or his services," Mary had argued. Whether Nathaniel believed her pragmatic reasoning or saw past it to her lovesick heart, Mary could not say. Either way, George remained, Nathaniel managed to sleep in the new bed, and Mary found her pleasure in raising Little George and Jonathan.

On most days, Mary would sit back and take in a scene such as the one before her in the yard with a deep sense of pride and gratitude. But on this evening, she kept her eyes and ears fastened upon Catherine in order to intercept the woman's rancor.

When Catherine complained about the breeze sending her napkin flying, Mary retrieved it for her and tucked it under her plate. When she fretted about the children running wild, Mary reminded her that they had been cooped up all winter and needed to stretch their legs. When she would not take a bowl of buttered peas from Loretta's hand, Mary took it and sent an apologetic look Loretta's way. When she nearly swooned at the sight of a dish of pig intestines, Mary wished she would just faint so they could take her back into the house and leave her there.

"When is she leaving?" she asked Nathaniel in bed that night.

"Just two more days, Mary. I'm sure you can manage that."

The next morning Mary prayed for forbearance and tried to put on a cheerful demeanor that might counteract her mother-in-law's dour one. By afternoon, she was sitting on the parlor rug with Little George and congratulating herself on her near-perfect performance. Angelica sat nearby, her nose in a book.

Catherine alternately brooded and cooed at little Jonathan until, without preamble, she said, "You ought to send these people on their way and hire some white workers, Mary. Even Irishmen would be more suitable."

Mary looked to Angelica, waiting for something shocking to burst from her mouth. But the girl kept her eyes on the page in front of her. Martha seemed to have finally gotten through to her headstrong daughter the value of holding one's tongue. But Mary, who had been holding hers all morning, felt she needed to speak at last.

"Mother, we quite like them here. They are our friends, and you don't send your friends away."

"Indeed, I understand that some are quite friendly." Catherine gave her a pointed look.

"Angelica," Mary said, "would you mind helping your mother in the kitchen?"

Angelica marked her place in her book and walked out of the room without a word.

Mary turned to Catherine. "Mother, you obviously have something on your mind, so I wish you'd just say it straight-out."

"Mary, you must know to whom I am referring."

"I'm afraid I don't. Is there a problem?"

"The only problem I see is that you seem to be overly familiar with that man George."

Mary's face grew hot. She felt not only Catherine's eyes upon her but Little George's and even baby Jonathan's. "I beg your pardon?"

"You needn't pretend to be surprised. Anyone could see you are flirting with him. It's positively vulgar."

"I'm sorry, but I must object to this incomprehensible accusation. I don't think I've said more than three words to George since you arrived."

"You're not saying it with your words but with your eyes. And your"—she shivered a little—"body."

Mary dropped her voice to a harsh whisper. "For Nathaniel's sake, I will not say what I want to say to you at this moment, but I will say this: Were it not for George, I very much doubt I would be here taking this abuse from you at all. I am sure that he saved my life when I lost my baby, and he most certainly saved this farm from ruin when your son went gallivanting off to war, leaving his pregnant wife utterly alone. So any looks you thought you saw exchanged between me and George were only those indicating the deepest possible respect and appreciation. As for your lewd comment about my person, I cannot account for it. It is most surely in your mind, which I'll allow may be failing at your age."

Little George giggled.

"Well," Catherine said, "I have never heard a less convincing speech in my life. I may be getting on in years, but I know a come-hither look when I see one. And I know that your manner of dress is too provocative for a mother of two. It borders on heathenish."

Mary forgot to whisper. "Provocative? In what possible way can this be considered provocative? Could a man be attracted to my chin? My little finger?"

"Look lower, my dear. What have you on your feet?"

"My feet?"

"It's positively scandalous."

"But nearly everyone at that table was barefooted after a hard day of work."

"I might expect that from the Negroes. I'm sure they are not used to shoes. But I do not expect such a state of undress from the woman my son married."

"I'll wear shoes or not wear them whenever I please." Mary realized she was shaking a finger at her mother-in-law. In Catherine's arms, baby Jonathan began to screw up his forehead, a sure precursor to a wail. Mary fisted her hands and pasted a pleasant expression on her face.

Catherine leaned in close and pointed at Little George. "Any woman who would name her firstborn son after a hired man in her household rather than her own husband, who was at war at the time and might very well have never come back alive, is saying something."

Mary had no response. As ghastly a person as she believed her mother-in-law to be, she knew that at that moment the woman was right. At Mary's silence, Catherine sat back with a superior air and turned her attention to baby Jonathan.

Mary got to her feet and walked outside for some fresh air. She leaned upon the water pump and tried to calm her frantic heartbeat. Who in the house might have overheard that conversation? If she were so transparent that her mother-in-law could read the situation in the space of two days, could everyone see it?

Just then, several men emerged from the barn carrying long wooden ladders, saws, and boards toward the house. Grateful for the distraction, Mary met them halfway.

"What are you doing with all of this?"

"Mr. Balsam gonna put a window in the attic," Sam said.

"No, we gonna do it," Gordon said. "Mr. Balsam just give us the okay and got us the glass."

Glass? After putting in the orchard? How much had that cost? They were doing well, but with so many hands to pay and mouths to feed, they could not afford extravagant purchases. Still, the workers did need a window up there or they'd all be cooked alive in the summer.

"I don't remember any deliveries."

"Mr. Balsam bring it with him when he come home from the war," Sam said. "They's picture windows."

What was a picture window?

"Where is Mr. Balsam?"

"Down in the barn."

She hurried down the slope and collided with Nathaniel as he was coming through the barn door. "Oh!" she exclaimed. "I'm sorry."

"Why are you in such a hurry? Is something wrong?"

"No," she said, catching her breath. "I was just curious about this window. The glass. Can we afford it?"

"It was free. A photographer gave it to me. Mr. Adams. He

was following our regiment during the last years of the war and taking portraits of the men to send home to their families. In fact, he took the likeness I sent to you. He fell ill very near the end and asked me to take charge of his equipment should he perish, which he did soon thereafter, poor fellow. So I inherited his entire wagon of equipment. Most I couldn't make heads or tails of. When I was in Washington, I sold it to another photographer, who was happy to have it at a good price. But he didn't want all of the glass negatives Adams had kept. Didn't know who any of them were. Since many were men from my regiment, I thought I should keep them, though I didn't know quite what to do with them. It was George who suggested we use them for the window. I thought it was a very good idea. The men will be able to gaze into the faces of those who fought for the Union and their freedom. It will let in some light and some fresh air."

"How fascinating," Mary said, her trouble with Catherine fading away. "May I see them?"

"They're over there." He pointed to three wooden crates sitting by the door.

Mary lifted a rectangle of glass from a straw-lined box. She held it to the sunlight coming through the door, and there appeared a young man wearing his Union uniform with pride. Because the image was a negative, his face and hands were black, his hair and mustache white.

"Did you know him?"

"That's Charles Sparks. Died at Petersburg."

She leaned the glass against the outside of the box and took up another. "And him?"

"Mitchell. Dysentery."

She picked up another. "And him?"

Nathaniel thought a moment. "McGibbins. Wilderness. Shot in the leg and died from the gangrene."

"Surely they did not all perish?"

"I haven't looked through them all, but I'm sure there are a few yet living. I imagine my likeness is somewhere in one of those boxes."

"Please don't use that one in the window. I'd prefer to keep it tucked away somewhere safe."

Nathaniel gave her a rare smile and seemed to regard her with a more generous measure of respect than he had of late. Mary was startled to find herself craving his favor. If he had received the letter meant for George, didn't it speak volumes that he hadn't confronted her about it? That he cared enough for her to keep her from shame and embarrassment? Wasn't that noble? Surely she could fall in love with him again if she tried.

"You don't think it's disrespectful, do you?" she said. "To use these as windowpanes?"

"I did think about that. But I've come to the conclusion that it would be worse to keep them hidden away in a trunk where no one would see them, no one would remember them."

She nodded. "I suppose." She replaced the glass in the box and got to her feet. "You are a good man, Nathaniel."

He smiled and grasped her hand. "And you are a good woman, Mary."

But Mary knew in her heart that it was not true.

THIRTY-SEVEN

Lapeer County, December

I woke sometime before dawn feeling as though I had fallen. The last echoes of some unnamed disaster rang in my ears. The cat was gone before I could even open my eyes, but he'd left some claw marks on my chest to remember him by. A solitary orange ember glowed in the fireplace, and the room was cold as the grave. I hurried down the front staircase in the dark to Nora's room and opened the door just as she was opening it, nearly knocking her over.

"Oh! I'm sorry! I thought I heard a crash."

"So did I."

"You're okay though?"

"Yes, except for the heart attack you just gave me."

"I'm so sorry. What was it?"

"I don't know."

"Give me your flashlight and I'll check."

Nora passed it to me with a shaking hand.

"Stay here. I'll be right back."

I crept around the parlor and the dining room and the kitchen, shining my light across every surface. I looked upstairs, in the attic, in the basement. Nothing was out of order.

"I don't know," I said to her as I handed her the flashlight. "It must have been outside. Maybe a transformer blew or something."

I built up her fire again to warm the room. With nothing left to do and with the adrenaline rush wearing off, I fed my own fire and crawled back into bed. Matthew remained in hiding.

The fire was dead again when I woke up. I pulled back my hair, which was grimy from two days with no shower, and went outside to see if I could locate the source of the noise from the night. There were a number of branches down in front of the house. One had narrowly missed the porch, another rested uncomfortably close to my car. The snow had stuck to the ice-covered branches, piling on more weight, flake by delicate flake, until it was just too much.

I walked around to the backyard. Then I saw it. The two great trunks of the catalpa tree had finally parted ways for all time. One leaned at an odd angle, the other lay on its side, its topmost branches reaching into the herb garden. Part of the fence had been smashed. A few broken branches lay scattered around the space, some stuck in the rosebushes, others flattening the oregano and the lavender.

All of my hard work lay beneath the wreckage of the tree Nora could do nothing to save.

The whine of a chainsaw echoed across the open field as Tyrese dismantled the fallen catalpa. When I had broken the news to Nora about her devastated tree, I'd expected her to grieve for the loss. She only said, "Tell William. He'll take care of it." Then she got back to work. I began to wonder whether I should be marking the frequency of her slips on a calendar.

Now Tyrese was replenishing our diminished woodpile with

the real William's tree. "Most of this has been dead for some time," he said, "so it should already be dry enough to burn. But I wouldn't keep stockpiles of it in the house if I were you. Dead trees are favorite homes for carpenter ants and termites. The cold will keep them dormant, but when the wood warms up inside, they'll wake up. So just bring in what you'll put in the fireplace right away. It'll mean a lot more trips in and out, but you don't want those in the house."

I nodded and imagined with some distaste the last sizzling moments of all the tiny bodies I would be feeding into the fireplaces. Did carpenter ants scream?

"Been pretty busy?" I said.

"Yeah. It's a mess out there. News is saying half the Lower Peninsula is without power. Says it'll be a week for some people. Do you two need somewhere to stay?"

"Do you have power?"

"No. But there are a couple churches that already have it back on, and they're taking people in."

"I doubt Nora would be interested. She's been obsessed with a sewing project. I don't think I could get her to drop it for even a day."

He went back to his chainsaw. I stacked the smaller logs and gathered sticks into bundles for kindling. Another hour went by before Tyrese had done all he could do. I was exhausted and my toes and nose were numb. I followed him back to his truck to see him off when it occurred to me that this special service was probably not included in the landscaping package Mr. Rich had devised for Nora.

"What do I owe you?"

He shook his head. "C'mon. Nothing."

"This isn't mowing the lawn."

"Don't worry about it. I'm happy to do it for you."

He was looking at me with such kindness in his eyes I wanted to cry. "Okay."

"Hey, what's wrong?"

I shook my head.

He put a gloved hand on my shoulder. "Don't say nothing. Because I know something's wrong."

Of course something was wrong, but I couldn't say what it was. How do you put into words the feeling that you're an adult and yet you are utterly lost and confused? How do you say that you don't know what to do with your life? That it feels like everything you've worked for is worthless and yet you don't know what else to do but more of the same? How do you explain the feeling that your life is over when there's nothing wrong beyond the fact that you lost a job? How do you say that out loud when innocent people are shot and killers go free and it feels like the very fabric of society is unraveling?

So I didn't say anything. We just stood there in the snow surrounded by sawdust, and a tear froze on my face.

"Let me take you out for breakfast tomorrow morning," he said. "Will Nora be all right on her own for a bit?"

I nodded and rubbed my raw cheeks. "Yes."

"Okay then. You meet me at the Roadhouse Diner—they do have power—at eight o'clock. And let's talk this out. Whatever this is. Okay?"

"Okay."

As I watched him drive away, I decided to tell him everything—about Nora, about Mr. Rich, about the camera and the photos, about Vic Sharpe, about the interview at the *Beat*—everything. And maybe if I could just say it all out loud, I'd know what to do with it.

THIRTY-EIGHT

Detroit, April 1965

Nora stepped around the open paint can on the porch. "Ugh. I'm glad this will be dry by the time I get back tonight."

"The smell might still hang around."

"But it won't be this bad."

William sat back on his heels and looked at the front door. "You sure about this color? It looks like raw salmon."

"It will dry orange. Look at the sample on the top of the can."

"You sure about *that* color?"

She smiled and patted him on the shoulder. "It will grow on you." It was the brightest orange she could find. She didn't normally gravitate toward orange, but somehow that was the color that had called to her at the hardware store. Her mother hated orange.

"I guess. At least it's on the outside where we don't see it much."

She laughed and walked to the car.

"Drive careful," he called after her.

Nora waved, pulled out of the driveway, and headed south. The drive was pleasant until she hit the traffic snarls of Metro

Detroit. Except for Christmas when she and William visited the Riches, Nora hadn't been back to the city. In December it had been covered in clean white snow. Now in early April the city was brown and dirty. Soggy paper bags and newspapers and discarded bottles congregated at the mouths of the storm drains as rivulets of last night's rainwater dribbled in beneath them. The sight made Nora yearn for the rebirth of the garden and the field of wildflowers around the farmhouse, but she thought wryly that William would find beauty amid these grim streets.

He had been taking his camera to Flint each day to photograph urban life and the people he worked with or saw around town. Nothing came of it. His ambition of selling photos of newsworthy things to the papers seemed all but forgotten. He and Nora read about the tumultuous events happening all across the nation as spectators rather than participants. For her part, Nora preferred it, but she wondered if she had somehow inadvertently snuffed out her husband's dreams.

"Do you like it here?" she had asked him one evening as they lay in bed.

"Of course I do."

"You know what I mean. Sometimes I feel like I completely derailed your life."

"You did. And I derailed yours."

She turned onto her side. "Do you miss living with your family?"

"Sure. Sometimes. Sometimes a lot. I miss my friends. Don't you?"

She knew the correct answer was yes, but she didn't feel it.

"Anyway," William went on, "this is where I belong. Here with you. This is where I want to live out my days. And when we're both old and gray and finally leave this earth, they can bury us in the backyard alongside Old Mary."

That was what he called her. Old Mary. Old Mary Balsam, laid to rest beneath the weathered gravestone in the garden.

And in a matter of minutes, Nora hoped to discover who she really was.

She pulled into a parking spot in front of a drab brick building. The nurse at the front desk directed her down a long corridor lined with doors. At room 127, she stopped and knocked lightly, then a little harder when there was no response.

She pushed the door open and poked her head in. "Hello? Margaret?"

Inside the institutional room, a shriveled woman sat hunched in a vinyl easy chair. Her white hair was so thin it looked like someone had set traces of cotton candy upon her freckled scalp. She squinted out the window at something Nora could not see.

"Margaret?"

The woman turned toward the sound.

"Who's that?" she said, her voice crackling like brittle paper left too long in the sun.

"I'm Eleanor Ri—Balsam, your great-niece. I'm Daniel's daughter."

"Daniel?"

Nora walked into the room and took an empty chair. "Your brother George's son."

"Oh, George!"

"I'm his granddaughter, Eleanor."

"Are you?" she said with palpable delight. "Well, isn't this a treat."

The old woman lifted a trembling hand, and Nora caught it in hers. Margaret held on even after the handshake was over, as though if she let go Nora might rush off to something else.

"Eleanor. I'm sorry, dear, but I don't remember you." Margaret's watery blue eyes looked past Nora as she talked.

"I don't know that we've ever met before. But you may know my older brothers, Warner and Richard."

"Oh, yes. Daniel's boys." There was a pause. "Who did you say your father was, dear?"

"Daniel Balsam. But I was born much later than my brothers and I have a different mother. My mother's name is Mallory."

The old woman shook her head. "I don't know. I can't keep it straight."

"Well, no matter. We don't have to know each branch of the family tree to have a chat, do we?"

She laughed. "No, we don't."

"I wanted to visit you to tell you I'm living in your old house."

"My house? On Kensington? With Ben's son? Oh my. You seem a little young for him."

"No, not that one." Nora stifled a small laugh. "Your childhood home in Lapeer."

"My heavens! Is that house still standing? No one's been taking care of it at all since Father died."

"Well, I'm taking care of it now." Nora gave Margaret's hand a reassuring pat. "Your father was Nathaniel Balsam, right? And your mother was Mary?"

"Yes, dear, yes." She paused a moment. "Though I didn't know my mother. She died not long after I was born."

"I'm sorry to hear that," Nora said. She waited for Margaret to speak again, but the old woman just stared into empty space. "Do you know if she quilted? I found a crazy quilt there and I am wondering who made it."

"Oh, yes. She made that. That was on my father's bed until my brothers moved him out of the house. She made that when he was in the war. Sewed it by hand."

"I found it in a trunk in the attic."

Margaret smiled. "I put it there, you know."

"You did?"

"Yes. When my brother George was closing up the house, I hid it away in the trunk. Men don't appreciate things like that. He would have just thrown it away or used it to cover some furniture and left it open to the moths and mice. So I put it in the trunk to keep it safe."

Nora smiled. "I'm so glad you did. It will probably please you to know it is being used again. It's on a bed in one of the guest rooms."

"Oh, that's lovely, dear. I've always preferred quilts to blankets. Especially now that I can't see so good. I can still feel the patterns. I used to spend hours running my fingers over Mother's quilt to find the bird tracks and the flowers and the spiderwebs. All the little secrets."

Nora looked down at Margaret's warm, gnarled hand in hers and imagined her as the sole girl among boys, bereft of a mother. She thought of the rift between herself and her own parents, and her heart ached.

"I'm so very sorry you never knew your mother."

"Influenza that year was very bad. But that's not what all of them died of."

"All of who?"

"The men in the field. I got it as a baby, but I survived. It made me weak in the eyes. But that's nothing, I guess, compared to all those men. And anyhow, I'm still here."

"What men?"

"The men who worked the farm. A lot of them got sick because they all slept together."

A light bulb flicked on in Nora's mind. "Did these men sleep in the attic?"

"Yes, yes!" she said in excited recollection. "The boys would play hide-and-seek up there. It wasn't fair to me because I wasn't allowed in the attic. That was the men's quarters. You didn't mix so much then as people seem to nowadays."

Nora considered this. "Was it common for farmhands to live in the boss's house?"

"It seemed common enough to me until those men came bothering us about it. They came once before I was born and again when I was just a little girl. I remember the one time. There was a lot of yelling, and they set the barn on fire again. The barn that's there now is the third one, you know."

"I hadn't realized that."

"It was very sad. I was very small, so it's hard to remember. I remember the animals screaming, though. I wish I could forget it. George got them out. Big George." She laughed. "Not my brother! He never wanted anything to do with Big George."

Nora tilted her head as though the motion might make all the parts of Margaret's scattered story line up into some sort of sensible arrangement of facts. "I'm sorry, but I'm having a little trouble following. Why would someone be so upset about people living in your house that they would set your barn on fire?"

"That did puzzle me too. My brother Jonathan said it was because they were Negroes. He had to explain to me what Negroes were, but I didn't understand. They were just my family. I figured out a little later that they had been slaves. Escaped from the South during the Civil War. When my father came home from the war and the farm was doing so well, I guess he employed quite a few of them. Some would stay for a season, collect their pay, and move on. Others stayed for years. Eventually the only one left was Big George. Everyone else moved out. That's who your grandfather is named after, you know."

Nora struggled to connect the dots. Her father had said that black people had ruined the family. But Margaret spoke of a family that seemed to embrace them. One generation was all it took to go from her grandfather being named after a former slave to her father disowning her for marrying a black man? It made no sense.

"Aunt Margaret, I hardly know what to say. I had no idea."

The old woman nodded slightly. "I'm not surprised. My brothers resented them—especially Little George. We got teased at school on account of it. As the boys got older, they seemed to think that the men in the attic were making off with money and land that should have been theirs. Father was very generous. Always giving them extra. He always made sure they all had nice presents at Christmas. I know George didn't like that at all. But then, George never seemed to like anything. Sourest person I've ever known. Once he moved to Detroit and the other two followed, they never came back to visit much. Just wanted to forget about the place, I suppose."

"What happened to all of those men who worked the farm?"

"Some saved enough to buy their own farms. Lots of them moved to Detroit during World War I. Lots of jobs then. But Big George stayed on. He ran the farm for Father. And there was a light-skinned Negro boy about my age who came around now and then. He'd help out in the fields sometimes. Steered clear of the house. Odd-looking boy. He had blue eyes. I'd never seen a Negro with blue eyes."

Margaret stopped to let out a raspy cough. Nora handed her a cup of water from the table near her bed.

"I stayed with Father until he got very old. Then the boys came up to the house and brought Father and me back to live with Benny in Detroit. Big George had died by then. Stroke, I think. Or heart troubles. We were heartbroken about the move. Couldn't stand the city." She sighed and licked her dry lips. "Wasn't much we could do about it. Being the youngest and a girl, I had no claim on the house. I couldn't live on my own with my bad eyes. I think my brothers wanted to sell it, but it was the Depression, you know. No one could afford a big house and all that land, and I don't think they wanted to let it go for a pittance. Then I guess they just forgot about it. Got busy making their money during World War II, building their own big houses. I'm glad it's being used."

After all her storytelling, Margaret looked worn-out. She coughed again and sipped from the cup. Nora felt a little guilty. She'd come for information and had certainly gotten more than she'd bargained for. But here was an old woman, her own flesh and blood, alone in a home, forgotten.

"I think I should let you get some rest now, Aunt Margaret, but I'd like to visit you again if you wouldn't mind."

"Not at all, dear. It's been nice chatting with you."

Nora pushed back her chair. "Would you like me to help you into bed for a nap?"

"No, no. I'll just rest here in my chair."

"Okay."

She started for the door but Margaret stopped her. "Eleanor, do say hello to the men in the field for me. It's been so long since I talked to them."

Nora frowned. "Of course, Aunt Margaret. I'll be sure to do that."

THIRTY-NINE

Lapeer County, July 1871

Mary took Nathaniel's proffered hand and stepped down to the platform at Lapeer Station. Seven-year-old George followed close behind, grasping Jonathan with one hand and Benjamin with the other. The train ride between Detroit and Lapeer was not an arduous one, but it had been taxing for Mary. The boys required constant watchfulness and frequent correction. Growing up on a farm had not prepared her boys for the more refined city life that Detroit had to offer. But when Catherine Balsam had invited her grandsons to the festivities surrounding the long-anticipated dedication of the new City Hall building on the Fourth of July, she couldn't refuse. The prospect of getting away from it all, even for a few days, was enticing.

The boys had seen little of their grandmother of late as she no longer traveled well. Illness had weakened her constitution, if not her tongue, and this limitation on Catherine's mobility had proven beneficial for the restoration of Mary's relationship with Nathaniel. Mary felt sufficiently chastened for her disloyal thoughts and temptations. She didn't require assistance from her mother-in-law to feel regret and humility. What she needed was to take control once more of her wayward passions.

To that end, she built a buffer around her heart and her person. She tucked all of the letters she had received from George into the hidden compartment in the trunk that had delivered him to her door all those years before. She wrote him no more letters and received none. She spoke to George through a proxy, whoever was handy at the moment. Often this turned out to be Little George. Each time she found herself tempted to think of George, she recounted to herself all of Nathaniel's many good qualities—his forbearance, his bravery, his fortitude, his principles about the equality of all men, his gentle hand with his children. Bit by bit, Mary found that she could love him. Not with the obsessive love she had felt for George, but love nonetheless.

The trip to Detroit was the first time their family had ever been alone together, without the company of the former slaves who had found refuge on their farm. Lacking a house full of people and problems to distract her, Mary discovered things about her boys she had not previously noticed. Her youngest, Benjamin, had taken to calling all adults by their first names as he did with the Negroes at home. Mary thought she might die of shame when he said to his grandmother, "Catherine, these are good biscuits, but not so good as the ones Mama Martha makes." Jonathan said little at all. Salutations, pleases, and thank-yous were all he offered most of the time. George, on the other hand, had an opinion about everything, usually a critical one.

As they loaded their luggage onto the back of the wagon for the trip home from the train station, Little George took one look at who was driving the horses and said, "Why are you here? Where's Jacob?"

Big George tucked a canvas over the top of the luggage and answered without looking at the boy. "Jacob's gotten himself some poison ivy on his hands. Can't control the reins until it heals."

Little George snorted his disapproval.

"How dreadful," Nathaniel said. "Where was it?"

"Got it when he was out in the woods snaring rabbits."

During the ride back to the farm, Mary stared out at the countryside. With every passing year, more of the land came under cultivation. Trees were felled, fences built, furrows plowed. Acre by acre, the outside world was encroaching on her little kingdom. Nathaniel looked upon this progress as proof of God's blessing. But to Mary, more people meant more criticism—and more danger. Every outsider who settled in the community was one more person to whom the Balsam way of life had to be explained and defended.

Just a few weeks earlier, Little George had come home from a trip to town with Big George, hot, angry tears running down his cheeks. "Henry Rutherford called me a nigger lover! He said I've got their fleas! And he said you and Big George—"

Mary clapped her hand over her son's mouth in horror before he could finish that sentence and dragged him to the backyard, where she washed his mouth out with soap and whipped his bare backside with a razor strap.

"I don't care that you didn't say it first," Mary said through his howls. "We do not talk that way in this family."

Half a dozen farmhands looked on as Little George was thus humiliated. The boy didn't speak to his mother for a week afterward, and ever since he had been more surly than usual with all of the farmhands, but especially with Big George.

Always Mary had been careful to ask George and the others to attend to a task. Nathaniel, used to commanding enlisted men once he became an officer, tended to order the farmhands around. Little George had clearly picked up on this method and had taken to giving orders like a foreman.

When the wagon rolled up to the house that evening, Little

George jumped down and walked around to the driver's seat. "Better get this all inside and then wipe down those horses, George."

"George!" Mary snapped.

"I told you I want to be called Jack," Little George said.

"Your name is George," Nathaniel said. "And you leave the orders to me, understand?"

"Yes, sir," the boy mumbled. "Come on," he said to his brothers. "We better get upstairs before Mother gives our beds away to more of them."

The two younger boys obediently followed their older brother up the front porch steps and inside the house.

"I'm sorry about that," Nathaniel said as he grasped one end of a trunk and Big George grasped the other. "I'm sure the lad is just tired after a long day of travel."

George nodded but said nothing.

Later that evening, Mary raised her hand to the doorknob outside the boys' bedchamber to kiss them good night. But Little George's voice on the other side of the door made her pause. It was difficult to make out what he was saying.

She opened the door. "What are you talking about in here?"

All three boys looked to their mother in the doorway. Jonathan and Benjamin looked as if they had just been caught with their hands in the cookie jar. George was calm, and Mary wondered if that was the slightest hint of a smile she saw playing at the side of his lips.

"Nothing, Mother. Just saying our prayers."

FORTY

Lapeer County, December

Tyrese waved to me through the window of the Roadhouse Diner as I pushed through the door and slid into the seat across from him.

"Am I late?" I asked.

"You're fine."

"I wasn't quite sure where this place was, and Nora's directions were on the strange side. No street names, but a lot of landmarks that I'm thinking just aren't around anymore. Except for going to the grocery store, she doesn't seem to get out of the house much."

"My grandpa is the same way."

The waitress came to take our order. When she walked back to the kitchen, Tyrese was staring at me.

"What?"

"That's a lot of food."

"I'm starving. I've been living on bread and water over there with the power out, and I'm making forty trips a day up and down the stairs with wood for the fire."

"Are you sure Nora's okay alone?"

"She's all stocked up with wood, despite your warnings about ants. She should be fine for a couple hours."

The waitress slid hot coffees in front of us, and I wrapped my hands around mine. "That feels so good."

"I told you there are some churches open if it's too cold."

"Don't worry about us. We've got a house full of quilts, an entire tree to burn, and a little cold never hurt anyone."

"All right," Tyrese said, rubbing his palms together vigorously. "Then let's get down to what's going on."

"I don't really know where to start. I feel like you're going to think I'm a horrible person."

"I doubt that. Just start at the beginning. Not like when you were born or anything, though I'd love to hear about that sometime. Just . . . start with what's got you all upset."

I took a sip of coffee. "Right. Here's the deal. I told you I used to work for the *Free Press*. Well, earlier this summer this old guy called me and asked me to meet up with him because he had something that he thought belonged to a relative of mine."

I filled Tyrese in on the details of that first meeting—the camera, the box of photos, the strange reticence on Mr. Rich's part to confront Nora with them himself, the suspicious football player son.

"You ate coney dogs with Linden Rich?" Tyrese said.

"Yeah, well, that's not really the point. Anyway, turned out that yes, I was related, and I got Nora's information from my dad's cousin who was all excited that I was going to visit her, and then *she* gave me the job of deciding whether Nora was just too old to live on her own anymore."

"Dang."

"Right? I mean, that's not fair to me. I didn't even know her."

"So what do you think?"

"About Nora?"

"Yeah."

"Well, that's kind of where these stories intersect. When I

came to live with Nora, she kept mentioning this William fellow. She said he'd planted the tree that fell down, that he tidied up the room I was going to stay in—which he didn't—that he mowed the lawn—which of course we know is actually you. Sometimes she talks about him as if he's long dead—she told me straight-out once that he had been gone for fifty years. And sometimes she talks like he's still around, like if I walked into the next room, there he'd be. William was James Rich's uncle. He's the photographer who took the pictures of the riots that Linden Rich didn't want to give me. But no one has ever come out and said he was dead, and my searching online turned up no death certificate."

Tyrese nodded. "I'm tracking with you."

The waitress came up with a tray full of food and commenced setting plates on the table. I was only a little concerned when the plates in front of me added up to four.

Tyrese pounded on the bottom of a bottle of ketchup. "So do you think this William is still around somewhere?"

"Maybe. My gut says it's pretty unlikely, but I guess it's possible. Nora said she didn't know what happened to him, but at some point he left and didn't come back. And at some point his darkroom in the basement was locked up." I took a bite of scrambled eggs.

"Why did he leave?"

"I don't know."

"Why lock the darkroom?"

"I have a theory about that. I found the key and I snooped around, and there were photos of a woman down there."

Tyrese talked around the food in his mouth. "A woman or *another* woman?"

"See, that was my thought. Like maybe he was having an affair and left Nora? But I don't know."

"She didn't know about the pictures?"

"I assume she doesn't. I haven't said anything about them.

And when I confessed to her that I'd gone in there without asking, she didn't ask what was in there. But she did say that *she* had locked it. She was talking about seeing things you can't unsee or something like that." I took a bite of hash browns. "I need to talk to Mr. Rich, don't I?"

"I don't know. That depends. What do you intend to do with the information he might share with you? Assuming he even knows, are you going to tell your aunt what happened? And if you do, how can you be sure she'd want to know? What if William's dead? What if he did run off with another woman? You want to be the one to tell her that?"

"I guess it might depend on what he could tell me." I dredged a piece of bacon in syrup and took a bite.

"But if he knows what happened to William, wouldn't he have told her already if they're family?"

"Maybe he's tried before but she won't talk to him."

Tyrese put down a forkful of eggs. "Okay, let's say he knows what happened and she wouldn't listen, so he tells you. Will she listen to you? And is it even something she needs to know at all? She's an old lady. Maybe she should be allowed to die in peace."

"You think not knowing what happened to her husband is peace?"

"Okay, maybe not."

I took a long drink of coffee. "Here's what I want, Tyrese. I want her to be able to die with no unanswered questions, no regrets. I have a lot of regret in my life right now and it sucks. I can't imagine how it would feel to have fifty years of wondering weighing on me. Something is going on with her, like she's stuck somehow. She abandoned sewing fifty years ago because, according to her, she didn't feel like it anymore. She stopped going to church. She rarely leaves the house, and she's slipping mentally more often than she was even two months ago. We hardly even talk lately. She seems depressed. For all I know, she's been depressed for decades. I'm hoping that knowing what happened to William could give her some closure."

Tyrese nodded. "I get it."

"So you think I should talk to him? Get the story, maybe even get him to bring the photos up and talk to her directly?"

"Sounds like it."

We ate in silence for a minute as I debated whether I really ought to go into all the other stuff that had been bothering me.

"You know," Tyrese said, "you still haven't told me anything so awful it would make someone want to cry. So, what else is going on?"

I swallowed a bite of pancake and felt it catch a little on the way down. "I have a job interview in Detroit in a few days."

He stuck out his bottom lip a little and nodded. "Good for you."

"I probably won't get it. I mean, I was fired from the *Free Press*."

"That doesn't mean anything."

"No, in this case it does."

I drained the last of my coffee, took a breath, and plunged headfirst into the events that made this extended trip to Lapeer County possible. I mostly avoided eye contact with Tyrese as I spilled my guts about my botched story, my deceptive relationship with Vic Sharpe, my ignominious exit. The few times I did venture a glance to see how he was reacting, his face was unreadable.

When I had nothing left to say and nothing left to eat, Tyrese paid the bill and took my hand. "Hey, that's all over and done. Maybe you'll get this new job and move back to Detroit. Maybe you won't. But all that business with that Vic guy, it's done. Can't change it. Can't let it hold you back. And anyway, everything happens for a reason. Sometime soon, maybe you'll look back on all that and see that it was the best thing that could have happened to you."

I smiled through tears of gratitude. "You're amazing, Tyrese."

Outside we parted ways, Tyrese to more storm cleanup and snowplowing, I to restock Nora's woodpile and prepare for my interviews—with both the *Beat* and Mr. Rich. As I headed down the road, my stomach lurched, protesting either the big greasy breakfast I had just consumed or my plans to meddle even deeper in Nora's personal life when I'd always been taught to mind my own business.

As the slate-gray clouds above began to shake out more snow, I told myself that it was my business. Nora was family, and I was there to help her. My parents didn't stop at tending to the bodies of the people they served along the Amazon. They also tended to their souls. I could bring Nora firewood and wash the dishes and do the laundry—but couldn't I also help to heal her broken heart?

FORTY-ONE

Lapeer County, August 1966

"Are you starting on a new quilt already?" William asked when he walked into the parlor. "Seems like you just finished one."

"I can't help myself. The Log Cabin quilt will be good for the second guest bedroom, but it just won't work on our bed."

"What's wrong with the one on our bed now?"

"I don't know. It just seems too stiff for that bedstead. Too straight and right-angley. That bed is so curvy and asymmetrical. I just feel like it needs something . . . different."

"What about that green and white one? The drunk one? That's all curvy."

"Drunkard's Path. It's the wrong size."

"Okay, well, what do you have planned?" He pawed through her basket. "Just yellow?"

"Yes, it's going to be all different shades. When all the little hexagons are put together, they should look like a sunset."

"Dang. How long is that going to take you?"

"At least fifty years."

He laughed. "Okay, baby. Looks good. Whatever you want to do. Though I did think that blue one was nice."

"It is. It's just not right for our bed. And I wasn't thinking of using it there. I just wanted to use up all those old shirts."

William shook his head. "See, I guess that's good. It did kind of creep me out."

"Why?"

"Those shirts were on dead slaves."

"Well, they weren't dead or slaves when they were wearing them, according to Aunt Margaret. They just worked in them. I think the history is what makes the quilt special. If it weren't for people like them, you'd have grown up in Alabama or Mississippi. Can you imagine that? We thought Detroit was bad."

"Come on, Nora. Not every black man in Detroit came from fugitive slaves. My daddy's parents came from Georgia during World War I, and Mama came up with her mother from Tennessee during the Depression. So I would have been born in Detroit all the same, even without the men who wore those shirts."

"You never told me that."

"You never asked." He glanced up at the ceiling. "Actually, my parents and grandparents would never talk about it much. But sometimes you'd catch them talking in real low voices—that's when you knew to listen up. And then you'd wish you hadn't spied because the next place you were going was bed. And you didn't want to dream about all that."

Nora's fabric and thread sat impotently in her lap. "What did they say?"

"Never mind."

"William, that's your family history, so it's our family history. Our stories are one story from here on out."

"It's not pretty."

"I'm sure it's not."

William sat down and took a long breath. "Problem is, I really don't know much for sure. There's so little to go on. I know almost nothing about Mama's family, and she's still alive to talk about it. She just wouldn't want to. And I could never ask her.

Best I can figure from all the clues I've had over the years, her daddy got lynched."

Nora gasped.

"Never could figure out why. But I don't think they needed much of a reason. Just someone claiming you looked at a white woman or didn't move off a sidewalk fast enough."

Nora felt sick to her stomach. It was one thing to know that lynching existed. It was quite another to have a family connection now with someone who had suffered that unthinkable fate.

"I know more about my father's father," he continued, "because my Uncle Chuck knew the story and told it to me. Grandpa was a sharecropper in Georgia. Sharecroppers would only get paid once a year after the cotton was all harvested and sold. But my grandfather's boss was always cheating, and lots of times he would tell the sharecroppers that they owed *him* money at the end of the season. That way he had a whole passel of slaves who weren't really slaves but they actually were, you see?"

Nora nodded.

"Most of them didn't know how to read or write, so they just had to go on the boss's word."

"Couldn't they challenge him? Take him to court?"

"Oh, come on, you can't be that naïve."

Nora was taken aback. "I beg your pardon?"

"A Negro couldn't take a white man to court."

"What?"

"Didn't they teach history in that fancy school of yours?"

Nora sighed. "Well, I guess they missed that part."

"I guess."

"So what did they do?"

"One night they hopped a freight train. They had to do it at night so the boss wouldn't send a posse after them to bring them back."

"But what grounds would he have for keeping them there? He couldn't just keep them against their will."

"Sure could. All he had to do was claim they owed him money and were skipping town without paying their debt. And he wouldn't just bring them back and put them back to work. He'd send a lynch mob to get them and teach them a lesson."

Nora sat back in her chair. "I can't believe that," she said, shaking her head. "That can't be true."

William looked incredulous. "Why not? Is it any less believable than two hundred years of slavery? You think people who had been buying and selling human beings and working them like animals would suddenly see the light and start treating them as equals? Open your eyes, woman."

Nora frowned. She didn't like being made to feel a fool. But it wasn't William's fault. "Why Detroit, then?"

"There were recruiters down in Georgia trying to get black folk to come up and work in munitions plants. I guess they got run out of town pretty fast by the bosses who wanted to keep their free labor, but word got around anyway."

Nora took a deep breath and let it out slowly. "It's amazing to think about all that had to happen to put you and me at the Detroit Artists Market at the same time. Even all the bad things. If your family had been treated better, if my father had treated you better . . . we might never have met."

A thoughtful smile crossed William's lips. "Yeah, I guess that's true. Mama always says that God doesn't make mistakes. Sometimes it's hard to believe that."

The phone rang.

William jumped up. "I got it."

Nora picked up her needle and thread and started to baste the little hexagon in her lap. She rocked the needle in and out, in and out, around the perimeter, until all six sides were secure. Then she put it in the tiny pile she had started on the side table and picked up another.

Faint murmurings floated out of the kitchen, but she couldn't understand what William was saying. She was just about to go see who he was talking to when she heard him run up the back stairs. She dumped the needle and the fabric into the basket and rushed up after him.

When she entered their bedroom, William was packing a suitcase.

"What's going on? Who was that?"

"Bianca. J.J.'s friend Rod got shot, and now J.J. is missing."

"Where are you going?"

"Detroit, where do you think?"

"Just tell her to call the police."

"Nora, it *was* the police. They shot Rod. And now there's trouble brewing down there." He stopped packing and looked at her. "J.J. got himself involved with some rough characters. Militants. Follow this Reverend Cleage character."

Thoughts of the man who had held a knife to her throat at the drive-in rose up unbidden.

"They've been agitating all summer. Since Watts. Looking to start something. J.J. may have been involved or he may not, but the fact is that these guys are stirring up trouble and he's throwing his lot in with them. He's not in jail as far as they can tell, but they don't know where he is. So I've got to get down there and try to track him down." He shut the suitcase and headed for the hall.

"Should I come with you?"

"Better not." He was halfway down the stairs.

"I could sit with Bianca and your mom."

"Baby, I've got to go *now*. If J.J. gets picked up by the police . . ." He didn't finish. Instead he planted a kiss on her cheek at the bottom of the stairs.

"Okay, but—"

"It'll be all right."

"Don't drive crazy!" she called after him as he hustled to the car. "And please call me tonight!"

"I will! I love you!"

The car roared to life and spit gravel out behind the tires. And then it was gone.

Nora went inside and picked up her quilt pieces again. She basted a few more hexagons, but soon she was so tense with anger she got sloppy.

Where did J.J. get off dragging William into his problems? William, who did his best to live at peace with everyone. William, who had been the bigger man and shaken her racist father's hand. William, who worked hard and didn't expect everything to be handed to him. And here J.J. took it all for granted. Bianca certainly had no control over him. It had always gotten under Nora's skin when J.J. would say something rude or disappear for hours at a time and his mother did nothing more than sigh. That boy needed a father.

While they were still in Detroit, William had tried to fill the gap. He'd taken the time to play basketball and take J.J. to movies. He'd even taken him to see Martin Luther King. What better figure could there be for J.J. to emulate? And yet all the boy had seemed to hear in that speech were the negatives. He latched on to the injustice and couldn't hear the solutions. He let the rage he felt grow and fester. He'd lashed out at Nora when she and William lived with Mrs. Rich. She had thought then that he must have just been annoyed that she was taking up too much space. Now she wondered if it was just because she was white.

The phone finally rang at eleven o'clock. Nora snatched it up on the first ring.

"Is everything okay?" she asked before William even had a chance to identify himself.

"Yeah, he's home now. But things are still heating up here. Cops swarming all over the place. Lots of arrests being made. But J.J. wasn't one of them."

A small part of her was disappointed. Maybe a night or two in jail was just what that kid needed to straighten out his life.

"When are you coming home?"

"I'll try to come home tomorrow."

"What about work?"

"I'll call my boss in the morning. It'll be all right."

She was quiet a moment. "So was he involved in this incident?"

"He says he wasn't."

"Do you believe him?"

"I guess."

"What does Bianca think?"

"I don't know. She doesn't know what to do with him."

"I know what I'd do with him."

William didn't respond at first. Finally he said in a flat voice, "I'll see you tomorrow."

Then Nora heard a dial tone.

FORTY-TWO

Lapeer County, October 1873

Mary watched the carriage heading down the lane with a bittersweet pang in her heart. It had been so nice to have Bridget and her little girl for the afternoon. The sweet baby's antics had given her such joy she hadn't noticed the time slipping by. But evening was approaching and Bridget had to get back home to her husband.

The last couple years had brought much change to the Balsam farm. As Little George's antagonism toward the Negroes grew, Nathaniel had decided that it was time for some of them to move on. He offered several of them small loans to start their own farms, and the men had jumped at the chance to become more independent and have something to offer prospective wives. Others left of their own accord and design. John and Martha Dixon had taken Angelica and little Elwin and moved to Cass City to open a store. Mary's accidental confidante Loretta had married and moved away with her new husband and her son Simon. Mary found herself the lone woman in the house until she'd hired Mrs. Farnsworth to help do the cooking and the wash. But Mrs. Farnsworth was all business and never had time to linger over a cup of tea with her.

Mary couldn't blame the poor woman. With more than a dozen men still in the house, besides the five Balsams, she had her work cut out for her. George was now nine and had begun to tag along behind his father in the fields. At seven, Jonathan wanted nothing more than to do everything his older brother did, and so Mary saw him less and less. Even little Benjamin seemed determined to be with the men rather than her.

In fact, Mary had begun to feel rather insignificant in the scheme of things. She recalled with a warm nostalgia the long-gone hardscrabble days when she had done everything on the farm, just her and Bridget and George toiling away. Now it seemed she was superfluous.

The farm had grown so large since the war that Nathaniel and a few of the hands sometimes slept at outlying barns during the busy harvesttime so that they could work until the sun went down and be at it again before the sun came up. All of the hard work had been paying off. The decimated South had need of nearly everything after Appomattox. Their fields and storehouses had been destroyed, their houses burned, their railroads twisted by Sherman's men. There were few options for them and therefore much money to be made by Northern farmers and entrepreneurs. A small part of her felt guilty for the high prices they were charging for such essential a commodity as wheat, but another part felt it was justified, part of God's punishment for a people that needed to atone for their sins.

That she benefited from it seemed somehow right to her. After all, she had given refuge to so many. Now she was reaping some reward. Her once simple house was full of nice rugs, handsome furniture, and fine china dishes from which the little boys were not allowed to eat. A new carriage had been purchased, new horses and oxen and mules pulled wagons and plows, and Mary could replace the fine dresses she had cut up in order to make her quilt during the long nights when Nathaniel was sleeping in an encampment in some Virginia field.

And yet, she felt empty. Her successful husband, her handsome young sons, her lovely house—none of it satisfied. After a few years of growing closer, Mary and Nathaniel had once again begun to drift apart. A fifth pregnancy had led to a miscarriage that devastated them both. There hadn't even been enough of a child to bury. After that, Nathaniel avoided his husbandly duties, waiting most nights to come to bed until she was asleep—if he came to bed at all.

"Mrs. Balsam?"

Mary turned around to find Jacob standing in the doorway.

"Mr. Balsam need me to go to town for more balin' wire, and Mrs. Farnsworth says we nearly out of flour and lard. So I'm gonna go pick those up. You need somethin'?"

Nothing came to mind, but she'd give almost anything right then to go to town and distract herself from her loneliness. "I think perhaps I'll go with you, Jacob. If I can convince Mrs. Farnsworth to keep an eye on the boys."

"It'd just be Benjamin. Little George and Jonathan is out with Mr. Balsam right now. They all stayin' out at the south field tonight. Those boys was excited, I can tell you."

"Well then, I think I can manage to get Benny taken care of, though I imagine he will be in a foul mood for being left out."

"I 'spect. Little George did pester Mr. Balsam about that somethin' awful. Wanted Benny along with them. 'Bout fit to be tied when Mr. Balsam say no."

"How odd. He normally doesn't care to have Benny tag along. Give me a few minutes."

"Okay, Mrs. Balsam. I'll bring the wagon up here."

Mary hustled into the house and headed for the kitchen.

"It's just Benny. He can help you with the dinner. He loves to cook, and it shouldn't be too difficult tonight. Jacob and I will be in town. Nathaniel, George, and Jonathan will be gone for the night, along with a few of the farmhands. I can't imagine you'll be having more than eight or nine for dinner."

"Is that all?" Mrs. Farnsworth said dryly.

"I sure would appreciate it. While I'm there I can look for a bolt of fabric for you. I know you wanted something red to make a new tablecloth for Christmas, and you don't want Jacob picking it out."

At this tempting offer, Mrs. Farnsworth relented. Mary donned her hat and retrieved her reticule. Jacob was waiting with the wagon when she went out the front door. He gave her a hand up onto the seat next to him, and she settled in for the drive.

"I'm ready now," she said when he didn't signal the horses.

"Just waitin' on—"

The wagon shook as someone hoisted himself onto the back. Mary turned in her seat.

"There you are, George," Jacob said, then he flicked the reins and the horses leapt into action.

Mary's stomach dropped, whether at the wagon's jerky motions or the sight of George sitting on a bale of hay in the back, she wasn't sure. George gave her a nod, which she returned before turning to face front. If she didn't look into his eyes, didn't speak with him or smile at him, she could pretend she didn't still love him.

The trip was quiet, with Jacob humming a tune in time with the horses' hooves. When they reached Lapeer, Jacob stopped in front of the dry goods store and George hopped off the wagon.

Mary went straight into the store and took her time looking at the fabrics, though there was just one red heavier-weight cotton that would be appropriate for a tablecloth. It still felt a little scandalous to buy cotton. But Mrs. Farnsworth said it would wash better than the alternatives.

After the clerk cut the correct length, Mary perused the store's other offerings. After a few minutes more, she saw through the window that Jacob and George had returned with the baling wire and were now rolling a large barrel of flour onto the wagon as well. She paid the clerk and started for the door.

"Why, Mary Balsam, I haven't seen you for an age," came a voice from behind her.

Mary turned to find Sadie Whittaker, the minister's wife, walking toward her with a small tin of straight pins in her hand. The women shared a quick embrace, and Mary pasted a smile onto her face.

"How have you been, dear?" Sadie said. "I've been so concerned since we didn't see your family at Easter services as we might expect."

"We've a minister at the farm right now leading our regular Sunday services, and we thought since he was qualified to serve the Lord's Supper that we wouldn't fill up all of the pews at church on Easter."

Sadie's face was a picture of concern. "You mean to say a Negro minister?"

"Yes. And if he is still with us at Christmas, we'll plan to worship at home then as well."

Sadie put the tin of pins down on a counter and grasped Mary's free hand in hers. "Mary, I have tried very hard these past years to be understanding, as has Reverend Whittaker. But I am deeply concerned about your family."

Mary schooled her features. "There's no need for concern, Sadie. We read the same Scriptures, worship the same Lord. We may sing some different songs, but I can assure you that we have been faithful to God."

"But not to his church," she admonished. "Mary, I know that years ago Reverend Whittaker passed on the concerns of some in the church about the Negroes you brought with you, but he didn't mean for that to drive your family away. What of your children? Don't you want them to grow up in the church?"

"The children worship with us, of course."

Sadie sighed and pressed her lips together. "Couldn't you and

Nathaniel come with the boys and leave the help to worship in their own way?"

"Why would we do that?" Mary asked, though she could guess the answer Sadie might give.

"It's just not . . . natural. The entire situation over there isn't natural, all of those men living there rather than living in their own homes. Why, they'll never learn to take care of themselves if you don't make them."

Mary clenched her jaw and weighed her response, but the door of the dry goods store opened before she could speak.

"Mrs. Balsam," Jacob said, "we ready now."

Mary forced a smile toward Sadie and pulled her hand away. "It was nice running into you today, Sadie."

She allowed Jacob to help her up onto the wagon. George climbed onto the back, Jacob flicked the reins, and the dry goods store and Sadie Whittaker faded into the distance.

"Was that Mrs. Whittaker you was talkin' to, Mrs. Balsam?" Jacob asked.

"Yes, it was."

"Are things well with her and the reverend?"

"I'm not sure. I assume so. We didn't talk about her family. She was far more interested in the state of mine."

"Oh? There somethin' wrong with one of the boys?"

Mary might have answered yes. Little George had been acting so strange and distant of late. "No, it's nothing like that."

"That's good. Mr. Balsam okay?"

"I believe so. Though I think you could tell me better than I could tell you. You see him far more often than I." Mary wished she hadn't said that. Nothing good could come of grumbling. "Mrs. Whittaker was actually sharing her concerns about us not returning to the church for Easter services. Though I can't see why she didn't just write me about it back in the spring if it has been on her mind since then."

"You tell her we had church?"

"I did, but she seems to think that must not be quite good enough for God."

Jacob laughed. "I guess God's all right with it. He seem to be blessin' us."

Mary smiled. "It would seem so."

They traveled in silence for a time, and then Jacob got to humming again. Mary recognized the tunes. They always put her in a happy mood and soothed her nerves on busy days. She missed hearing them in the house now that Martha and Loretta were gone. Mrs. Farnsworth certainly made no habit of humming.

Mary closed her eyes and focused on Jacob's song. Behind her George took up the harmony. The rich sound washed over her like a wave of sunshine, warming her soul and pulling the last vestiges of Sadie Whittaker from her mind.

Then there was a bump, a crack, and a sudden drop. Mary yelled out and the horses halted.

George leapt down from the wagon. "Axle's broke." He looked up and down the road. "Not sure if we're closer to town or home, but we'll have to take a horse one way or the other and bring back another wagon. We could rent one from the livery."

"Naw, we's closer to home than town," Jacob said. "I'll take the gray and ride on ahead, bring back a wagon."

Mary's heart began to beat faster. "George could go, Jacob."

"I know you don't like to ride, George," Jacob said.

"You're right about that," George said.

"He got thrown by a horse when he was a child," Jacob whispered to Mary to spare George's feelings.

"Mrs. Balsam and I will stay here with the goods," George said.

They unhitched the dapple-gray gelding. Jacob scrambled on top of its bare back and held to the bridle.

"Jacob, are you sure you can ride that horse with no saddle?" Mary asked.

"Sure as I am that this wagon ain't goin' nowhere fast. Don't worry, Mrs. Balsam. I'll be back within the hour."

With a click of his tongue and a light kick in the horse's ribs, Jacob was off at a trot with the sun at his back, leaving Mary and George standing by the broken-down wagon.

Alone.

FORTY-THREE

Detroit, December

On December 20, I mentioned in passing that I'd be gone most of the next day. Nora acknowledged this with a long, blank stare, leaving me with the unsettled feeling that she was trying to remember who I was.

"I expect William will be home soon anyway," she said.

Her increasing confusion tore at my conscience the entire drive to the downtown Detroit offices of the *Beat*. Though the power was restored, the cold weather seemed to have accelerated the decline of this woman I had been coming to love. How could I even consider leaving her for a job? And yet, how could I not? Who knew if any other opportunities would come my way?

I pulled up to the curb when ordered by my GPS. The same nervous energy I'd felt when I first arrived at Nora's house four months earlier boiled in my stomach. Then it had felt like the end of the road; now I had the thorny problem of options. Stay with Nora or get back to my real life. Watch an old woman slip into dementia or reclaim my dreams and start climbing back up that ladder. It seemed like such a clear choice.

I hung my coat and scarf on a rack that leaned to the left,

and Caryn of the phone call escorted me to a cramped room. Had the haphazard stacks of books and papers been shelved or filed in the pieces of furniture produced expressly for those purposes, there might have been room to walk around. As it was, the chair I was sure I should sit in was home to a messy pile of newspapers and a half-eaten sandwich.

I heard a toilet flushing, and a moment later Marshall Boon slid sideways through the door, tucking his shirt into his pants as he went.

"You must be Elizabeth." He shot his hand out to me. I tried to remember if I'd heard water running in a sink after the toilet flushed, but shook it anyway. "Have a seat."

At my hesitation he swooped into action, whisking away the mess. I perched on the edge of the chair to avoid a greasy spot that might have been mayonnaise.

He took his place behind a chaotic desk and regarded me with a thoughtful smile. "So, tell me a bit about yourself."

I recited to him my schooling and qualifications, emphasizing all of the important stories I broke at the *Detroit Free Press* before my disgraceful termination. Within minutes, I had made it through these credentials I'd spent a decade building and found myself with nothing more to say.

"And what have you been doing since you left the *Free Press*?" He said it as though I'd resigned of my own accord.

"I've been taking care of an elderly relative."

"Oh. Okay."

I was blowing it. Should I frame it as an investigation and tell him about the photos?

"Let me give you a clearer picture of what you'd be doing as the features editor."

For the next five minutes, Mr. Boon explained the job. I'd have my own regular column. I'd assign stories to other reporters and evaluate them when they were turned in. I'd have the freedom to take on any big story I wanted and the backing of

Boon himself when I ran into opposition. It was everything I could ever hope for and more, laid right in my lap.

"This is probably really stupid of me to say, but do you know why I'm no longer with the *Free Press*?"

He smiled at me. "Honesty. Good. The answer is yes. I know what happened. But if you were too risky for them, you're exactly the type of person I can use here. There are plenty of great writers out there. But I need someone with guts for this position. I want someone who will get in there and get the story, no matter what it takes. And I can promise you that you'd always—*always*—have my support."

I nodded.

"I want someone who won't take no for an answer," he went on. "Like this business with the police shooting back in October. No one has been able to get an interview with that cop. Police chief is blocking media at every turn. Think you could?"

"Yes." The answer came without thought. My journalism teachers had always told me to say yes every time someone asked me if I could do something and then figure out how to get it done later.

"I've reviewed your clips and I like what I see. Of course, I saw them when they originally ran. We have some other interviews lined up, but I'm going to be frank. I want you on my team."

I tried to keep the incredulous look off my face. I'm not sure I was successful. "Are you offering me the job?"

"Yes, I am. Do you want it?"

Yes. I did. Didn't I?

"And it doesn't bother you that I was fired?" I could admit it. Severance or no, Jack McKnight had sent me on my way before I threw that pen at him.

Boon smiled. "It's not like you got fired for embezzlement or for not doing your job. You got fired because an establishment newspaper can't afford to take the risks I can. They have to answer to the people who own them. And those people have to answer to the people who own *them*. No one owns us. The buck stops here." He pounded a fist on the desk, flipping an old coffee spoon into the air. "Anyway, if you hadn't gotten yourself fired, you wouldn't even be on my radar. Getting fired may turn out to be the best thing that ever happened to you."

Tyrese's words at breakfast the other day rang in my ears. Was this a sign?

Boon raised his eyebrows at me expectantly. My tongue felt like clay. I had to say yes. But I couldn't. Not yet. I had to make arrangements for Nora. When my parents called on Christmas, as they always did, I would tell them that Nora should move into assisted living because her mind was failing and she may not be able to take care of herself for much longer. Mom and Barb could work out the details. And I could get on with life.

"Can I have a little time to think about it?"

He frowned. "I can give you until the first of January."

"Great. Thank you."

We shook hands, and moments later I was bundled up and back in the car. I should have been elated, but I couldn't shake the feeling of a heavy weight on my chest. Why couldn't Marshall Boon have tracked me down before I'd uprooted my life and moved to the middle of nowhere?

I punched another address into my GPS and headed for my next appointment. Well, maybe you couldn't call it an appointment, since one party didn't know it was about to happen.

Mr. Rich lived on the edge of historic Indian Village, in the area where the houses got smaller and the cars got older. "For Sale" signs stood erect in a few snowy front yards, but the street did not seem to have many of the boarded-up houses and empty lots that still plagued so much of my once great city. I pulled to a stop in front of a modest brick house edged with snow-topped yew bushes. There were no cars in the driveway, but a lamp glowed warmly in the front window.

I looked up and down the street for activity and then chided myself. Pre-rural-eccentric Elizabeth would never have hesitated, even in the worst neighborhoods, which this wasn't. Country life was making me soft. I turned off the engine just as a sleek blue Mustang with white racing stripes and tinted windows pulled up in front of the house on the other side of the street.

A tall black man with short dreads stepped out. Linden. We locked gazes for just a moment before I looked away. I could still make a break for it.

No. He was already crossing the street.

I rolled down my window. "Hi, Linden. I was hoping to talk with your dad."

He put one gloved hand on the top of the car, giving it two firm knocks, like he was patting me on the head. "Dad's at work."

"What are you doing here?"

"Shoveling."

I looked him up and down, stopping at his obviously expensive dress shoes encased in rubbers. "A little overdressed for that, aren't you?"

He gave a little laugh. "I've got boots in the garage. You want to come in?"

"Will he be home soon?"

"Nah. He always goes out with a buddy for drinks after work since Mom died."

I quickly reconfigured my plan. "Do you have a few minutes?"

He looked at his watch. I stole a glance. Shinola. Detroit made. Not cheap.

"How about I shovel and you talk?" he said.

"I can help."

"All right then. Let's go."

I rolled up the window and followed Linden through the side door into the garage.

He handed me a snow shovel and gave me a once-over. "You aren't exactly dressed for this either."

"I was at an interview."

"Oh yeah. Dad told me you left the *Free Press*." He leaned against a worktable and slipped off his shoes. "Kind of surprised me."

"Me too."

"Another paper?"

I hesitated. If Linden thought I was no longer a journalist, he'd probably loosen his grip on the photos. I might walk away with them this very day if I played my cards right.

"I'm still unemployed." This was technically true.

"Mmm." He finished tying the laces on his boots, and we walked into the snow.

"I may have to rethink my line of work."

"Oh?"

"There are fewer and fewer jobs for journalists. Papers cutting staff."

Linden nodded, stuck his shovel through the ice-crusted snow, and began to push. I followed a couple steps back, picking up what escaped his blade. We got to the end of the driveway and walked back up for the next sweep.

"How's it going with Nora?" he asked.

"So-so. We were getting along, and I thought it was time to give her the camera. But it didn't go as well as I'd hoped. I think she was upset, though she didn't say anything about it. Then it was as if it never happened. We never talked about it again."

Linden stopped and stood up straight. "You tell her about my dad?"

"No, not a word."

He started shoveling again. I came along a few steps behind, shovel to the ground, trying to get through the heavy snow to the driveway that lay beneath.

"Linden, I feel like I need to know what happened between your father and Nora."

He pushed ahead to the end of the driveway. "He doesn't talk about those days much."

We worked in silence for a few minutes. And I let the silence work its magic.

"You know," Linden said as we pushed the last of the snow up in a mound at the end of the driveway, "I'd never even heard of Nora until Dad got the camera back. And I got the idea that the only reason I heard of her at all was because I walked in on him looking through those photos. Otherwise I don't think he'd have ever brought her up. I knew I'd had a great-uncle named William. I saw him in a couple old family photos with my grandma and my great-grandma. But I'd never seen a white girl in any of them. Dad never said William was married at all until I caught him with those riot photos."

"I thought you said I looked like her."

"Once the cat was out of the bag, Dad showed me some pictures my grandma had with Nora in them."

I followed Linden back to the garage to hand over my shovel.

"Come on in a minute and warm up. Dad's always got hot chocolate."

He stripped off his boots and led the way inside. I left my snow-saturated shoes on the doormat and sat down on the couch in Mr. Rich's living room while Linden busied himself in the kitchen with mugs and spoons and hot chocolate mix. On the wall to my right was a shrine to Linden, with framed news stories from his high school, college, and pro football days. I recognized a few of them from my time at the *Free Press*, though I'd never paid close attention to the sports section.

Linden came in with two steaming mugs and motioned to some coasters on a side table. I slid them onto the coffee table, and he settled down in the chair to my left.

"Your dad seems to be your biggest fan," I said.

Linden smiled. "Always has been. He's been an amazing father, especially considering he didn't have one."

A photo of a younger James Rich with his arm around a woman graced the side table.

"Your mom?"

"Yeah. She died six years ago. Breast cancer."

"I'm sorry."

Linden sipped at his hot chocolate. "Hoo, that's hot. Look, I'm sorry I can't tell you more about my dad's issue with Nora. I know it can't be easy on you out there."

"I didn't think you wanted it to be too easy on me, judging by your attitude back in July."

He laughed. "Yeah, well, I got to look out for my dad. And you were just an arrogant reporter who wanted to get her greedy little hands on something that wasn't hers."

"Arrogant? You're one to talk—"

"All right, all right, I'll give you that. Hard to stay humble in my business."

I felt a smirk grow on my face. "It's the Detroit Lions. I'd think that most of the time humility would not be a problem."

He gripped his chest. "Oh! Come on, now! Show some respect!"

We both laughed then.

"Look, at this point I'd happily send you back to Lapeer with those photos."

I hid my excitement in a sip of hot chocolate. Yikes. That was hot. "But?"

"But they ain't here."

"Where are they?"

"Dad's always been kind of paranoid about house fires. Or maybe it's not paranoia—a lot of places have gotten torched in this city. So he keeps anything valuable in a safety-deposit box at the bank. You going back tonight?"

"Yes. I could come back and get them another time soon, but honestly, I'm starting to think that it would be better if your father would just come to Nora's and give them to her himself."

"Oh, he won't do that."

"You didn't see her when I gave her that camera. This is his mission. He needs to man up and do his own dirty work. I'm tired of being the bad guy."

He looked thoughtful. "You might be right." He glanced at his watch. "Shoot, I gotta go."

I stood up too fast with my mug. Boiling hot chocolate sloshed over the rim and onto my hand. I sucked in a gasp of air and put the mug down hard on the table.

Linden jumped up. "Oh!"

"Ah! I'm sorry," I said.

He grabbed my wrist and rushed me into the kitchen. He flicked the faucet on cold, thrust my hand under it, and held it there.

"I'm sorry," I said again. I reached for a roll of paper towels with my other hand. "I better clean that up before it ruins the wood."

"You stay here." He released my wrist and took the towels from my hand. "Keep that hand under the water," he commanded from the living room.

A minute later he was back with a wad of wet towels. My hand was going numb under the frigid stream of water from the faucet.

"I'm sorry," I said a third time.

"No, I made it too hot. You okay?"

I turned off the water and pulled my hand out of the sink. "I'm fine."

"You sure?"

"Yes. Let me get my shoes and I'll be out of your hair."

Back at the door, I pulled on my cold, wet shoes. I'd be blasting the floor heater on the way home, that was for sure. I walked out onto the newly shoveled driveway, Linden following close behind.

"Let me talk to him," he said. "Just hold tight for now."

"Will you call me and let me know what he says?"

"Sure." He pulled out his phone. "Gimme your cell."

"It doesn't work out there."

"What? It ain't the moon! What kind of phone you got?"

"A good one. It just doesn't work out there. It's like some technological dead zone. I'll have to give you her landline."

Linden punched the number into his phone.

"Don't call after eight. She goes to bed early. And if she answers, just say you're Tyrese."

His eyebrows ticked up a notch. "Who's Tyrese?"

"My . . . friend." I crossed the street and unlocked my car. "Thanks for talking with me today. I know we got off on the wrong foot. But this was nice."

He smiled. "Yeah. Maybe you're not as greedy as I thought."

"Maybe you're not as arrogant as I thought."

He shrugged. "Maybe. I'll be in touch."

"I'll be waiting."

I got into my car and headed for the highway with a smile on my face. The smile vanished when I stopped for gas. Next to the door was a line of metal newsstands, reminding me what had brought me to Detroit today in the first place. I pulled into the stream of traffic heading north on I-75 and spent the next forty-five minutes telling myself why I should take the job Marshall Boon had offered. It was the only logical course of action. Linden would prevail upon his father to bring the photos himself. I would be released from my obligation to him. I'd let Barb know that Nora could use some assistance. I would be released from my obligation to her.

By the time I got back to the old white farmhouse with the faded orange door, I was resolved. I would take the job, move back to Detroit, and resume my real life.

FORTY-FOUR

Detroit, July 1967

Nora settled an afghan around Margaret's shoulders.

"Thank you, Evelyn."

Nora didn't correct her anymore. On her second and third visits it had taken so long to get through the exact same conversation about brothers and fathers and grandparents that she simply let her great-aunt think she was a nurse with time on her hands for long conversations. Sometimes she was Eleanor, sometimes Evelyn, and once Lisa.

No matter what Margaret called her or who she thought she was, the old lady loved having someone to talk to. Nora was happy to oblige. She had grown quite fond of Margaret, and with each visit she painstakingly put together the pieces of her family's past. There were still gaping holes. But she felt certain that someday Margaret would reveal the key to unlocking her father's mysterious comment years ago about black people ruining the family. It had to be more than mere resentment on the part of a few young boys who didn't want to be teased at school for their unconventional living situation.

"Where was I?"

"The attic."

"Oh yes, that's right. I wasn't supposed to be up there. The third floor was just for the men."

Nora nodded as though she had not heard this part of the story at least three times already.

"But I sneaked up there one day." The old woman wore a conspiratorial smile. "I went up there during the apple picking one year. The men and boys were out. Mrs. Farnsworth was busy making soup in the kitchen. And those boys had made me so cross. I was going to show them!"

She laughed, then seemed for a moment to forget that she had been talking. Nora's heart fell as she realized she might need to start over and get Margaret back on track. But the old woman recovered.

"No, I guess it wasn't all the boys. It was Little George. He was always mean to me. So I went up there to find out once and for all whether you could see faces in the window."

"Faces?"

"Yes, they were always talking about the faces in the window. I thought they were trying to scare me with ghost stories. So I was going to see if they were real."

"I've never noticed any faces in the window. Were they pictures someone had pasted up there?"

"Of course you haven't, dear. I'm talking about *my* house, not yours," Margaret said. She gave Nora a look that might suggest she was concerned about her nurse's mental acumen. "Anyway, they weren't pictures like you mean. They weren't pasted on the window, they were *in* the window, in the glass."

"I don't think I understand."

Margaret thought for a moment. "Do you ever take photographs?"

"No, but my husband is a photographer. He takes lots of pictures."

"Okay then. You know the little images, the ones on the little strip?"

"You mean the negatives?"

"Yes! The negatives. Long ago when cameras were much bigger, they didn't use those little strips. They used glass. And when my father came home from the war he brought a whole mess of these big glass negatives with him, and that's what they used to make the window. So each pane of glass had a portrait of a soldier on it. And those were the men in the window my brothers talked about."

"But I've never seen anything in that window," Nora objected.

"Dear, I think you're confused," Margaret said, patting Nora's hand. "I'm talking about my old house. The window was in *my* house."

"Yes, I'm sorry. Go on."

"They're long gone now. Faded away. The sun makes them disappear."

"But you saw them?"

"Only faintly. They were nearly gone by the time I saw them. And they were definitely gone by the time Father and I moved out. But I did see them once, even with my bad eyes."

She fell so quiet and so still that Nora almost called the real nurse.

"It made me sad to think of those men," she said finally. "The boys played at war. They pretended to shoot each other, and then they'd squirm around on the ground and go still. After I saw those men in the window, I couldn't stand watching my brothers play at war. It didn't seem a thing to play about. They used those stones in the field for their forts and hiding places, leaping and jumping all around on them. I didn't think that was right. George was always jumping on them. You'd think those stones were placed there just for their amusement."

"Ms. Balsam," came a voice from the door, "it's time for you to take your medicine."

The nurse gave Nora a pointed look. Further explanations would have to wait.

"Margaret, it was so nice talking with you. You've led such an interesting life."

"Well, I don't know how interesting it is"—she laughed—"but I do like talking. When you're busy living life, everything's a blur. It's not until you get to be my age and you've got nothing more to do than think that you start to see it for what it was."

"I'll see you again soon," Nora said.

"Okay, Evelyn. Come any time."

Nora drove home at a leisurely pace befitting a hot Sunday evening and tried to recall everything Aunt Margaret had told her. William would be especially interested to know about the faces in the window. But the moment she pulled up to the house, William burst out the front door, suitcase in hand, and ran to the car before Nora even had time to turn off the engine.

"Thank God you're home, Nora."

"Why? Where are you going?"

William opened the car door. "Detroit."

"But I was just there."

"And I'm glad you're not anymore," he said as he helped her out of the car. "Do you know what's going on down there?"

"Nothing seemed to be going on at all."

"There's a riot growing—a real one this time—and it's just a few blocks from Mama's house."

Her hand flew to her mouth. "Is she okay?"

"She and Bianca were going to go to Aunt Dee's, but they can't find J.J."

"Of course they can't."

William gave her a chastening look as he slipped into the driver's seat.

"I'm sorry," she said. "But you can't tell me you're surprised."

He slammed the car door.

"You can't go down there," she said through the open window.

"I have to."

She clamped her hands on the door. "No, you don't, William. You did your part last year. If he can't stay out of trouble, there's nothing you can do to make him. He's chosen his path in life."

"He's only sixteen, Nora. He doesn't know what he's doing." William pushed Nora's purse at her through the window.

"How are you going to find him in a city that size? Where will you even start looking? It'll be a needle in a haystack. I don't want you down there."

He put the car in gear and looked at his watch. "Baby, I have to go. It's going to be dark before I can even get there. I got the call from Bianca a half hour after you left. That was six hours ago. You know how much can happen in six hours?"

This felt like bad déjà vu. Nora looked at the sun beginning to sink in the western sky. It must be shining directly through the attic window. She thought of the ghostly images of soldiers that had once covered the glass, of the attic full of former slaves who finally got the chance to live free and be paid for their labor. She thought of her family's legacy of equality that had been twisted into bigotry over the last century, of that photo of her enraged father. And in her heart, Nora knew William needed to go. But she also knew he was not prepared to enter a riot zone.

"Wait, please. Just wait thirty seconds more."

"For what? I gotta go."

"Just wait!" she called over her shoulder as she ran into the house. She came back out a moment later with his camera bag.

"You think I'm gonna have time to take pictures?"

"These are the kind of pictures you always wanted to take, William. Important pictures. Pictures for the newspapers. So go find J.J. if you must. But don't miss this moment in time. When it's over, people are going to want to know what really happened." She pushed the bag at him through the window.

"Baby, I love you." He pulled her in for a kiss. "I'll call you as soon as I get him to Aunt Dee's."

"Okay." Tears welled up behind her eyes. "Don't forget."

"I won't. You know I won't. Love you, baby."

She nodded. He let his foot off the brake and pulled away. The car disappeared behind the row of pine trees. Nora heard it move into high gear. When only the sound of cicadas remained, she walked back into the house and shut the door.

Deeply unsettled, she turned on the radio and sat down to work on the binding of her yellow quilt. If she could get it done, it would be a nice surprise for William. When they had gotten home from church that morning, she had considered finishing the quilt once and for all now that there was only one last step. It would feel so satisfying to have it done and on the bed after her daily work on it over the past year. But William had convinced her to go visit Margaret again instead.

"You won't be able to go for another week if you don't go today," he'd said.

Now she wished she'd stayed home.

She turned the dial from station to station, but little news about the riot seemed to be leaking out. Just a "disturbance on Twelfth Street." Maybe William had blown it out of proportion.

By late in the evening, the binding was finished, the quilt was laid on the bed, and Nora was pacing. The cool green lights of fireflies blinked in haphazard patterns outside, and William still hadn't called.

That night, every little sound had her reaching for the phone. But it was never ringing. On Monday morning the news was still sketchy, but the tone had changed from detached to anxious. No one answered at the Rich house, and she couldn't find Dee's number. She needed a distraction.

Nora flipped through William's record collection and pulled out everything on the Motown label. Nothing drove away bad feelings faster than the Supremes, the Temptations, Stevie Wonder, and Gladys Knight. She turned the stereo up, moved the furniture to the margins of the room, rolled up the rug, and got down on her hands and knees with a pail of soapy water and a scrub brush.

When William came home, everything would be shining like new.

FORTY-FIVE

Lapeer County, October 1873

Mary looked down the road in either direction. "Are you sure there is nothing to be done?"

"Nothing but wait for Jacob," George said.

The bay gelding at the wagon tossed his head and stamped a foot.

"Oughtn't we try to get him out of the sun?" Mary asked. "It's warm for October and he's had a heavy load."

George unhitched the horse and led him toward the woods on the north side of the road. "We're not far from Pine Creek. Could give him a drink and get him hitched again before Jacob is back."

"Yes, let's do that. If you know the way."

"I know the way."

The forest was dressed in the fiery hues of autumn, made more brilliant by the sinking sun. The only sounds were of their footsteps upon fallen leaves. They walked due north until Mary could hear trickling water in the distance.

"There's the creek," George said. "Just ahead. Though with the dry summer we've had it won't be much."

"I can't believe I never realized you didn't ride."

"No, I don't care to ride."

"In all of your letters, that never came up."

Mary wished she hadn't mentioned the letters. They had been on her mind since she determined several days ago that she was once more with child. Her first instinct had been to tell Nathaniel, but after their last disappointment she held back. Instead, she took the letters out of their hiding place and pored over George's words to her during the years of their private yearning. The love she had for him blazed forth like a fire that had been long smoldering but not snuffed out.

When they reached the creek, the horse drank of the meager stream of water.

"It's so cool and beautiful here," Mary said. "I wish we didn't have to go back to the dusty road."

"We don't have to go right away." He looped the lead line around a low branch and left the horse nosing around the forest floor.

Mary walked a few steps along the creek and stopped. "We won't be lost, will we?"

George smiled. "As long as we follow the water we won't."

They walked in silence. Mary chose her footing carefully, her smooth-soled, heeled boots being far more suited to carpets and hardwood floors than roots and rocks.

"Do you know I haven't been out for a walk in the woods since I was a child?" she said. "Though I don't imagine those trees are there anymore. That part of Detroit is nothing but houses now." She snagged her foot on a root.

"Watch it, there!" George grabbed her arm and pulled her close. "You okay?"

Mary caught her breath and looked up into George's face. Twelve years had aged him gently. His once-shadowed eyes were ringed by fine lines, and as they met hers they still held the tenderness she'd seen in them at the kitchen door so many years before.

"I wish you would kiss me," Mary said, astonished that she had finally voiced her long-silent desire. She had revealed that yearning once before—in the letter that Bridget had mistakenly sent to Nathaniel during the last months of the war.

George hesitated but a moment, then pulled her closer and covered her lips with his own. Then he gently pushed her away. "I can't do this."

She stepped toward him. "George, please, I—"

He pulled back and gave her a hard look. "You know this isn't right. You shouldn't have allowed me to kiss you at all."

"I would allow it again."

She reached for his cheek, but he intercepted her hand and pushed it back toward her. "We shouldn't have come out here."

"George, I don't love him. I've tried. I even thought for a while that I succeeded. But I don't." She searched his face. "I love *you*. And I know that you love me."

"It doesn't matter."

Mary felt a tear trickle down her cheek. "I know he's been unfaithful."

George looked away. Had he known? What did the men talk about when there were no women around?

"Please," she said.

Then George buried his fingers in her hair and laid her down upon the newly fallen leaves. And beneath the veil of the silent trees, a decade of yearning came to an end.

"We been gone too long," George said without looking at Mary.

She didn't correct his grammar. How could she correct anything? She had expected to feel utter bliss at the fulfillment of her long-delayed desire, and so the swirling mixture of anxiety and shame in her stomach took her by surprise. What had she done? She buried her face in her hands and tried to steady her breathing. The trees that had hidden them from sight moments before now appeared to be witnesses to her crime. The sun filtering through the leaves was like the burning eye of God, the righteous judge from whom she would not be able to escape.

George led the way back to the horse. Mary conjured up an explanation of their tardiness for Jacob, who would no doubt be waiting for them with the other wagon. By the time they reached the road, the sun had dipped below the horizon, leaving a blush in the west that was swiftly being swallowed up by night.

But there was no Jacob and no extra wagon.

"He should have been back by now," George said. "Something must have happened."

George helped Mary onto the gelding's back and they started off down the road, which grew darker and darker. They had been walking nearly half an hour when the animal beneath her stopped. George clucked his tongue and tugged on the lead, but the horse remained planted.

"What is it?" Mary asked.

George shuffled around in the road, straining to see in the dim light of a crescent moon. Then his foot connected with something. He felt around in the dark. "My Lord!"

Mary slid off the horse and landed hard on the packed dirt road. "What is it?"

"Some poor soul left for dead."

Mary gasped. Together they pulled the unconscious man off the road and placed him on the horse's back.

She felt the man's ears. One whole, the other misshapen. "It's Jacob."

"Horse must have thrown him."

"How far are we from home?"

"Maybe another twenty minutes at this pace."

"Then we'd better get moving as fast as we can."

They started up again, each walking on either side of the

horse with a hand on Jacob to keep him from falling. It felt like an eternity, but eventually Mary spotted an orange glow ahead.

"Why, they must have every candle and lamp in the entire house burning to guide us home."

But as they drew closer they smelled smoke.

George dropped the lead and began running. "Barn's on fire!"

Mary hurried the agitated horse to the house and pulled Jacob onto the ground with a thud. She tied the horse to the porch railing, far enough away that he wouldn't trample Jacob, and rushed inside. "Mrs. Farnsworth! Mrs. Farnsworth!"

The cellar door burst open and Mrs. Farnsworth appeared, a crying Benjamin in her arms.

Mary reached for her son. "What are you doing down there? The barn is on fire! And Jacob is injured. Come!"

She peeled Benjamin off of her and set him on the steps in the hall. He screamed, his face crimson and streaked with tears.

"Stay right there! Mama will be back in a moment, I promise."

She rushed out the front door with her cook to drag Jacob into the house. When the feat was accomplished and Jacob lay on the settee, Mrs. Farnsworth ran into the kitchen for rags and water while Mary made a vain attempt to kiss away her son's tears as he screeched directly into her ear. She rocked him back and forth. Slowly, his high-pitched wails were replaced by a low and insistent whine.

Mary held Benjamin's small red face in her hands. "Benny, Mama must go help with the barn, do you understand? I am going to leave you here with Mrs. Farnsworth and I will be back soon, okay?"

Benjamin immediately resumed full volume. The look of betrayal in his eyes was more than Mary thought she could bear. Suddenly, Little George and Jonathan tumbled into the room.

"George! Where is your father?"

"They're all out back at the well with the pails. We saw the fire from the south field."

"Stay with your brothers."

She stood to leave. Jonathan dropped to the floor alongside his apoplectic younger brother and hugged him.

George hesitated. "Mother," he said, "I didn't know this was going to happen."

"Of course you didn't, George."

"They never said anything about the barn," he said as he choked back the first tears Mary had seen in his eyes in two years.

She gripped his shoulders. "What did you say?"

"They said they were just going to send them a message."

"Who? Who was going to send a message?"

Mrs. Farnsworth burst back into the front hall. "Boys, give me a hand!"

Mary heard the shouts of men through the open kitchen door. Her eyes lingered a moment on her eldest son, then she rushed outside. Horses, cows, and pigs screamed. Chickens were running and flapping across the yard. Sweat-slicked men had formed a bucket brigade between the water pump and the barn. Flames climbed into the night sky like the devil's grasping fingers. Mary looked around for a bucket and instead found the tortured features of a dead man. Sam. She could hardly hear her own screams for the noise.

"Mary!" Nathaniel's voice cut through the chaos. He caught her up in his arms. Immediately her treachery in the forest rushed back to her. "Where have you been?"

"W-we had some trouble on the road. Jacob's been hurt. George is—"

"There." Nathaniel pointed to the line of men with their sloshing and ineffective buckets. "What happened?"

"An axle broke, and Jacob went to get the other wagon and never came back. We went after him and found him unconscious on the side of the road."

She should have been there. Should have been home. Should have been faithful.

"Where is Benjamin?"

"The boys are all in the house. Oh, Nathaniel, what happened here? What happened to Sam?"

Nathaniel's face was grave. "He is not the only one. I've counted two others—Jim and Theodore—and I don't see Billy or Peter. This was no accident. Gordon said it was a group of men on horses with guns and torches. They may have caught Jacob along the road on the way here."

"But who would do such a thing?"

"Someone who wanted to send a message."

The old threat from Mr. Sharpe mingled in her mind with Little George's cryptic words and rare tears. They had not been tears of fear like those of her youngest son. They were tears of regret. And when all had settled down and life had somehow returned to normal, if it ever could, she determined that he indeed would regret whatever part he may have played in this night of terror.

FORTY-SIX

Lapeer County, December

Christmas morning dawned clear and cold. With a crackling fire in the parlor and fresh coffee in the pot, I tried to grasp the promise of this most joyous of days. But the decision I'd made about taking the job at the *Beat* and the phone call from my parents I knew would soon come competed to see which could throw me into malaise the quickest.

Nora and I exchanged a couple gifts. A matching necklace and bracelet for her. A sweater and a book about drying herbs for me.

After a late breakfast I caught Matthew regarding the decorated spruce with interest. "Don't you dare."

He feigned innocence by licking a paw.

Nora came into the room with a large box. "I meant to give this to you earlier. I had a feeling this morning that I was forgetting something."

"But you already gave me two presents."

"Pah." She motioned for me to sit on the settee. "Those were nothing special. This is what I wanted to give you."

She sat in a chair across from me, her eyes alight with mischief. She was completely present, more like the woman who had met me at the door in August with a warm hug and a welcoming smile than the one last night, who had wondered aloud about when William planned to shovel the driveway.

"Can I open it?"

"What do you think I brought it out here for?"

I tore into the box and gasped. "Is this—is this a quilt?"

Nora smiled. "This is your quilt."

"You made me a quilt?" I all but squealed. "That's what you've been doing all this time?" I pulled it out of the box and began to unfold it.

"Yes," she said. "I'm sorry I've been so preoccupied. I wanted to get it done in time for Christmas. Recognize the fabrics?"

"I picked these out! You had me picking out fabric for my own quilt, you sneak!"

Nora laughed.

"Can we lay this out somewhere so I can see it all at once?"

"If we move the furniture there will be enough space here."

"Let me get this coffee out of here first. I think I'd faint if it spilled on this."

A few minutes later the coffee was safely in the kitchen, the furniture was hugging the walls, and Matthew was in another room sulking about the disturbance. We laid the quilt on the floor and stood back to admire it.

I put a hand to my mouth. "It looks just like the garden."

"I'm so glad you can see it. It is your garden, not as it is now but as I think it will be in a year or two when your hard work is rewarded and all of the plants fill in. Sometimes it's hard to see the end from the beginning. But good work and good soil will eventually bear good fruit."

My eyes moved across the kaleidoscope of colors representing the pinks of roses, the violets of mint, thyme, and oregano flowers, the chartreuse dill, the silvery leaves of artemisia and lavender, the grays and tans of the pebbled pathways. In the center was a large circle of varied greens, and within the circle were two dark gray shapes. The gravestones.

"How did you even begin to design this?"

"I'll admit it was a challenge to figure out how it would all go together. I drew it out on paper first, matched colors, started cutting, and hoped for the best."

"Sounds like a true creation."

She smiled at me. "Yes, I suppose it is."

I traced the tiny quilting stitches. "It's perfect." I gave her a gentle hug. She felt so small.

"I don't know if you'll want that on your bed or not. I know you like the yellow one. But I thought if you did we might make you some new curtains to match it. They would be a good first sewing project for you."

"For me? No. I don't sew."

"So you say, but once upon a time, I didn't sew either. Everyone starts from square one, and I intend to teach you how to sew now that you've gotten the garden under control."

"I don't know. Did I ever tell you about the washcloth I knitted?"

"Sewing is nothing like knitting."

I knew my face was betraying a serious dearth of enthusiasm. What Nora didn't know was that she couldn't teach me to sew when I was back in Detroit and she was tucked away in a nursing home.

She scooped up my hand and squeezed it. "Elizabeth, I'm getting old, and I have a house full of supplies and a list of faithful clients who will need to find a replacement once I'm gone. Why not just try it and see? You might fall in love with it. It just might be what you were meant to do. How are you going to know if you don't take a chance?"

The phone rang.

"That'll be my parents." I escaped to the kitchen, grateful for the reprieve from Nora's earnest eyes.

"Hi, Mom. Merry Christmas." I peeked back into the parlor and then pulled the phone cord as far from the door as I could.

"So how are things going with Aunt Nora?" Mom asked after the perfunctory greetings. "Barb wrote and told us all about it, though I was hoping to get a letter from you . . ."

"It's going pretty well. We get along, and I've been able to help her out quite a bit." I relayed the story of the ice storm and the power outage and the hauling of all the firewood.

"Thank the Lord you were there for her!" Mom said. "I'm so glad God worked this all out."

"Yeah, well, about the other thing, though."

"Yes?"

I lowered my voice to just above a whisper. "Unfortunately, I think Barb was right. I've noticed it more and more the longer I've been here. She has these moments where she isn't really in the present. She talks about people who aren't here as if they are, and she gets confused."

"Oh my. That's such a shame." The line was quiet as my mother passed this information on to my father. "So what would you recommend?"

"Me?"

"You're the one who's there and can assess the situation. Do you think she needs twenty-four-hour care?"

"Maybe not yet, but I think she will at some point soon."

"Mm-hmm. And what are your thoughts on that? Is it something you can handle on your own?"

"Me?" I said again, a little louder this time. "I'm not a nurse."

"It doesn't sound like she needs a nurse. Just someone to lighten her load and keep her safe."

"But, Mom . . . I kind of got a job offer. In Detroit."

"Oh." She let the word hang there. "And you're taking it?"

I sighed. "I don't know. My brain keeps telling me it would be stupid not to."

"And what is God telling you?"

"He doesn't . . . I just don't hear him like you do. And anyway, if he's supposedly orchestrating all of this, if I've been offered a job, doesn't that mean I should take it?"

My mother was quiet a moment. "Sweetie, why do you think your father and I spent so long living in Detroit when we'd been called to the mission field?"

"I don't know. I guess I just figured it was so I could go to a real school."

She laughed. "You think the Detroit public school system was our top choice for you?"

"Uh . . ."

"Elizabeth, we had several opportunities to return to our mission work as you were growing up. But we stayed because we saw that there were needs close to home. We wanted to be there for Grandma as she battled breast cancer and for Grandpa as he dealt with diabetes. It's not that we didn't yearn to get back to fieldwork. And it's not that doors to mission work weren't opening. There's no one right path that if you make the wrong choice you're sunk. Whatever you choose to do, God can use that. Life is always a winding path. It's only in retrospect that it appears to be a straight and inevitable one."

"That's not helpful, Mom. Sometimes I wish I didn't have a choice."

She laughed again. "But you do. So think hard, pray on it, and make that choice with open eyes."

We chatted a little longer and they filled me in on the goings-on in the Amazon jungle. When I hung up the phone and walked back out to the parlor, the magnificent quilt still covered the floor. Nora sat staring at the Christmas tree and stroking Matthew's head. Backlit by the light streaming in the window, her thinning white hair looked like it might blow away.

Everything I could see in this house and everything that still lay hidden from me—all of it would be gone without Nora, sold off to pay for her care. The antique furniture, the paintings, the quilts. Every plate, every book, every lamp would be sold to bargain hunters or thrown away. The graves would be reclaimed by the earth. The garden would succumb to weeds. The land would be sold off to developers. The cots would finish their days in a landfill. The trunk would be opened with a crowbar and its contents pawed through by strangers.

Worst of all, no one would know what had happened here. With no artifacts, there would be nothing left to spark the questions that had to be asked if the stories were to be told. The slaves who had risked their lives for freedom and found shelter beneath this roof would be forgotten. The women who had created such stunning quilts would be lost. The identity of the woman in the photographs in the darkroom would never be revealed. Nora was the last defense the past had against the relentless onslaught of time and decay.

And I was Nora's last defense.

FORTY-SEVEN

Lapeer County, July 1967

Two days and William still hadn't called.

News was officially out on the disturbance in Detroit. Buildings were burning, stores were looted, hundreds of people had already been arrested, and rumors were spreading of rooftop sniping and police brutality. The National Guard had been called in, but the situation only deteriorated all the more.

Where was William in all this?

Nora picked up the phone, hesitated a moment, and dialed Diane's number. They hadn't spoken in years, but she was running out of options. It rang three times, four, five. Nora hung up. She knew who she needed to call. But she couldn't. The last time she had seen her mother was when she had all but thrown her out of the house two years before.

She made herself dial. One ring. Two. Then Nora heard her father's voice.

"Daddy? I need your help."

"Nora? Nora, what's wrong?"

"I—I need you to come pick me up."

"Where are you?"

"I'm at the house in Lapeer. I need you to come pick me up right now, please."

"Lapeer? What are you doing up there?"

"Mom can explain. Just please come get me. I have to get to Detroit."

"You don't want to come down here. Haven't you seen the news?"

"William's there and I haven't heard from him and I'm afraid something happened to him."

Silence. She hadn't meant to say his name.

"Please, Daddy. Please."

"Okay. But I'm bringing you back here to the house. You are not going to go out looking for that man in this."

"Thank you." She'd figure out how to look for William once she was there.

Nora packed two suitcases, one for her and one for William, then walked downstairs to wait on the front porch. By the time her father pulled up, she felt as if she might throw up from the potent combination of heat and anxiety.

Daniel Balsam climbed out of his black 1967 Corvette Stingray. Nora would not rush into his arms, no matter how much she needed someone to hold her up at that moment. Then he took a step toward her. The first step.

"Was that door always orange?"

"No."

He looked at the two suitcases sitting on the porch steps. "Those aren't going to fit. The smaller one might."

"I didn't know you'd be driving a Corvette."

"I always drive a Corvette."

She sighed. "Come in a minute while I figure this out."

Nora laid the suitcases on the settee and began redistributing their contents.

"This is incredible," Daniel said. "It's exactly as I remember it."

Nora snapped the smaller of the two suitcases closed again. "Did you spend much time here as a child?"

"Not much. My father never wanted anything to do with the place. But I went with my Uncle Ben and my cousins a few times."

Daniel took the suitcase outside and shoved it into the small space behind their seats. "Barn still out back?" he asked as he pulled away.

"Yes." Nora fiddled with the radio.

"You don't need that. They don't know anything. I can tell you that the city is going up in flames and the idiots are shooting at the firemen trying to put it out. They're burning down their own neighborhood. They're trying to get the Army called in, but that fool Cavanaugh will have to do some serious politicking to get any help."

Nora was quiet.

Daniel turned his attention to the road. "Where does his family live?" he asked.

"A few blocks from where it started. Twelfth and Seward."

"Are they still there?"

"I hope not. William said his mother and sister were going to his aunt's house."

"Where is she?"

"Somewhere off Linwood. I don't know." Nora tried to read the side of his face. "Have you heard anything else?"

"All I know is that it's a mess."

She felt like he was holding back. But perhaps that was best. Knowing the extent of the destruction wouldn't put her mind at ease. They were quiet for a few miles, but the air hung heavy with unanswered questions.

"How did you even meet this guy?" her father finally said.

"I already told you. Apparently you weren't listening very well."

"Or maybe something more important drove that information out of my head that day," he said meaningfully.

Nora sighed. "I met him at an art exhibition. He's a photographer. He takes very telling spontaneous portraits." She gave him a harsh look. "Shows people as they really are, when they aren't posturing."

Her father nodded. "And photography is how he makes his living?"

"No. He works for GM in Flint."

"In a factory."

She hated that he assumed it. "He makes good money. We're doing just fine."

"No need to get defensive, I'm just asking. Just wondering how this guy managed to turn your head at all."

"You're so superficial, Daddy."

"Maybe I am, but it's not that. We raised you smarter than that. Why give up your family and your home and your car for a guy who works on the line and takes a pretty picture?"

She folded her arms across her chest. "You were the one who took all of that away. And anyway, not all his pictures are so pretty. That's what got my attention at first. A certain photo he had taken of an angry businessman just a moment before he attacked him." She saw his eyes narrow almost imperceptibly. "He told me that the man actually destroyed his camera."

The car began to accelerate. She pushed a little further.

"It so happens that I recognized the man in the photo, and I didn't think the photographer should have taken it, much less displayed it, so I offered to buy him a new camera in exchange for it. It's funny, you know? If that man hadn't smashed his camera, I never would have talked to him in the first place."

"I see," he said stiffly. "And what did you do with this picture?"

"I still have it."

He turned toward her. "What?"

"Daddy! The road!"

He swerved back into his lane. "Why wouldn't you have destroyed it?"

"Because I wanted to keep looking at it."

"Why?" he practically shouted.

She wheeled on him now. "At first I was trying to find something that would prove it wasn't you. And when I finally accepted that it was, I kept looking at it so that the hate I saw in your eyes for the man I love would become hatred in my heart for you, so that it wouldn't feel so horrible to have been thrown out of my own family."

He cursed under his breath.

"You asked," she said.

"I'm sorry I did."

Nora shrugged and turned to look out the window. For several minutes, all she could hear were the tires on the road and the thrum of the V8.

"I'm not proud of that moment," Daniel finally said. "I lost my temper on an already bad day, and I took it out on him because it was convenient."

"Would you have done the same thing if he'd been white?"

"I'm not going to play that game. What's done is done. I can't go back in time and change it."

"If you could go back in time—"

"Nora—"

"If you could, would you have thrown me out of my apartment, taken my car, and kicked me out of your life? Was that just a bad day you were taking out on me?"

Daniel stared straight ahead.

Nora looked hard at him. "Daddy, what did you mean when you said that black people ruined this family?"

FORTY-EIGHT

Lapeer County, June 1874

Chest heaving, Mary looked down to the end of the bed, hoping that Anna, the midwife, and Mrs. Farnsworth would announce that the baby who had just emerged into the world was a girl. But instead of smiles and tears of joy, she was met by wide eyes and slack mouths.

Mary pulled herself up into a sitting position. "What? What's wrong?"

Mrs. Farnsworth covered her mouth and sat down heavily in a chair.

Mary was frantic now. "What?"

"The baby is fine and healthy," Anna began. "It's only . . ." She trailed off and lifted the squalling infant up, allowing Mary a clear view.

Mary emitted an almost inaudible gasp. The child had light brown skin, a wide nose, and tightly curled black hair.

"But—how?" she managed.

"I'm sure you're the only one who can answer that question," Mrs. Farnsworth said.

Anna hastily swaddled the baby and brought him up to Mary's chest. "Put him on your breast to stop his crying."

"But I—" Mary began.

"Quickly!" Anna commanded. "Unless you want your husband to hear it and come running to see what is clearly not his child."

Mary did as she was told and the baby's crying ceased. She hardly dared make eye contact with the two women who now looked upon her as what she undeniably was—an adulteress. Her sin had found her out, and now her husband would be shamed, her children mocked, her marriage shown to be a farce.

Now more than ever the community around her would turn on them. She thought grimly of the graves they had dug last October, of the six large stones that had been taken from the wall at the end of the drive and dragged by oxen, one by one, to the heads of each grave to mark the spot. Was such a fate to await this poor bastard child? What might Mr. Sharpe and his thugs do to George? Mary knew in her heart that it was she who had seduced him—practically begged him to commit this sinful act. Yet he would be the one to bear the blame—and the punishment.

Anna's voice drew Mary back into the moment. "This is what we will do. Yesterday I delivered the baby of that prostitute on the outskirts of town—Margaret. I told her I would find a place for the child."

"No, no," Mary pleaded. "No, I—"

"I take this baby boy with me today and you stuff your dress, make it look as though you were not yet delivered. Mrs. Farnsworth, tell Mr. Balsam it was a false alarm and the baby is not yet born, but that Mrs. Balsam must remain in bed, undisturbed. Meanwhile, I'll get the baby I delivered yesterday—"

"No!"

"—and tomorrow at nine o'clock you will send for me. I'll give the baby whiskey to keep her quiet and bring her in the same basket I use to take this baby out. Then Margaret's baby will be yours and no one beyond the three of us will know."

Mary could hardly believe what she was hearing.

Mrs. Farnsworth stood. "I'll get a basket and some blankets straightaway." She rushed from the room, shutting the door behind her.

"Anna, I will never—"

"You will, my dear. Because if you don't, you will have destroyed your entire family, past, present, and future."

"But you don't understand. Nathaniel has been with that—"

"Mr. Balsam is not the issue here," Anna said. "You are. Now then, the moment this baby falls asleep, I'll take him out of here."

Mary gripped the child tighter. "What will happen to him?"

"I haven't figured that part out yet. But this at least will save your family from public shame. I'll find a suitable home for him, I promise."

"But couldn't I find a Negro woman to come work for me and pretend the baby is hers? Then I could—"

"Mrs. Balsam, get ahold of yourself! This is the only solution to your problem. You're lucky this other woman's baby looks enough like you and Mr. Balsam that the switch might possibly go undetected. And even if someone did suspect, it would be better to be suspected of philandering with a white man than a Negro."

Mrs. Farnsworth swept in with a large basket filled with blankets, a bottle of whiskey, and an eye dropper.

"I thought it best if we gave this one something as well, Anna. He cannot make a sound as you leave."

Anna reached for the baby lying contentedly against Mary's chest.

"Please, wait," Mary entreated through tears. "Just for a moment. Please."

"It will only make it harder, Mrs. Balsam." She dipped her

finger in the whiskey and pried the little mouth from Mary's breast. He sucked Anna's finger as she quickly transferred his swaddled body to the basket. Mary bit her fist to keep from crying out. Mrs. Farnsworth dripped whiskey into the corner of his mouth with the dropper. The baby soon relaxed, stopped suckling, and fell asleep.

Mary's thoughts raced to search out some other plan, some other way. Anna covered up the basket and peeked into the hallway, then she and the basket disappeared. Mary thought she might hyperventilate. She heard Little George's voice in the hall and her heart froze. Then Anna's muffled voice. Then nothing.

Mary let a quavering breath leak out from between her lips. Gone. Her baby. George's baby. Gone.

The next few minutes were a blur. Mrs. Farnsworth cleaned her up, changed her bedding, and helped her stuff her dress.

"I'll keep everyone out of here," she said. "This would only convince someone from the doorway if you remain under the covers."

At nine o'clock the next morning, Mrs. Farnsworth sent the children away, told the men to stay out in the field, and sent the young stable boy rushing for the midwife again. Anna carried the same basket. The baby inside was a small girl with light reddish-brown hair and blue eyes who had no idea that she was a trick being played on the world. The child did look remarkably like Nathaniel, a thought that made Mary retch. The man who had fathered this child likely lived nearby, perhaps with a wife and legitimate children of his own. Like Nathaniel. She tried to comfort herself with the thought that at least the poor little girl would not be raised by a prostitute. But how could she stand in judgment? At least a prostitute did not hide her sin.

"You will have to pretend you are in the travail of labor until this baby is awake enough to cry," Anna said. "If no one hears anything from this room, no one would believe you had just borne a child."

Mary wondered how much dignity she would have to forfeit to cover up her transgression. "I can't do that with you both in here watching me."

"I'll sit watch outside the door," Mrs. Farnsworth offered.

"I must stay," Anna said.

Mary closed her eyes to shut Anna out, to shut the world out, and began to groan. It felt at first as though she were an actress playing a part in a sordid play. But at some point, her cries of agony became genuine. She cried out for her impossible love, for her betrayal of her husband, for his betrayal of her, for her selfishness, and for the baby who had been stolen from her. In her sorrowful moans were all the words she felt she could not utter aloud before God or man, her full confession and cry for forgiveness. Finally her cries were joined by the mewling whimpers of that pitiful baby in the basket, and the deception was complete.

Nathaniel came in first, smiling and cooing over the tiny baby girl upon his wife's breast. "What shall we call her?"

"You name her," Mary said flatly.

Nathaniel thought a moment. "What about Margaret?"

"What?"

"Margaret."

"How can you even suggest that?" Mary realized she was glaring at him, but she couldn't stop. How could he propose the name of the woman whose bed he had visited instead of her own?

"What do you mean?" he asked. "What's wrong with Margaret?"

"The only Margaret in this town is not fit to speak of. And don't think I don't know why you chose that name."

Nathaniel's eyes clouded over with anger, a sight made more terrible for its rarity. "You would sit in judgment of me? You, who named our firstborn son after a slave? A slave you wished would ravish you all the time I was picking worms from my rations so I could maintain some ghost of my humanity?"

The letter. He had gotten the letter.

"This baby's name is Margaret," he said. "And her middle name shall be Catherine. And we will never speak of these things again. Do you understand?"

Mary nodded and whispered, "Yes."

Nathaniel schooled his features, tugged at his cuffs, and left the room.

Jonathan and Benjamin came in next, smiling over their new baby sister. Benny especially took a shine to her and would not leave until Mrs. Farnsworth suggested that there were cookies down in the kitchen waiting for him.

Little George came last. He looked at the baby with an expression bordering on contempt, and he would not look at his mother at all.

Their relationship had been even more strained than usual since the night of the attack. Not wishing to bring shame to the family, Mary had kept her suspicions of his involvement to herself. Instead, she developed her own personal system of justice, meting out punishments for every small infraction, assuming the boy would know why, even if she didn't exactly.

"Don't you like your little sister?" Mary said.

"Not my sister," he mumbled.

Mary's mouth fell slightly open, and beads of sweat began to sprout from her upper lip. "Of course she's your sister."

Her eldest son's stormy expression was a mirror image of his father's not twenty minutes before. "I'm not stupid, Mother." Then he turned and walked out of the room.

FORTY-NINE

Lapeer County, December

"Thanks for doing this," Tyrese said. "I know it's not the way most people want to spend New Year's Eve."

"We're glad to help," Nora said, patting his hand. "Stop acting like you pulled us away from some glittering party somewhere. This is Lapeer, not New York."

"I know, I know. But most people wouldn't want to work on spreadsheets and order forms any old day, let alone a holiday." Tyrese turned to where I sat drowning in plant and seed catalogs. "And this isn't the most romantic place to ring in the New Year."

Nora gave me a knowing look and then went back to following lines of minuscule text with a magnifying glass. Tyrese turned back to his computer screen. I went back into the shell of private misery I'd been living in for the past ten days. Tomorrow I was supposed to call Marshall Boon to tell him whether or not I would accept his generous job offer.

The big clock on the nursery's office wall kept cruelly ticking off the minutes I had left before I'd have to tell Nora and Tyrese of my decision. I was powerless to stop it. I'd spent much of my life in high gear, wishing clocks and people would hurry up. Now there was almost nothing I wouldn't do to slow time down.

When I'd gotten Tyrese's call a few hours before, I'd actually jumped at the chance to get out of the house and help him play catch-up. His father had been down with acute tonsillitis for a week, leaving Tyrese to cover all of their plowing customers on his own. He hadn't had time to finish their orders for the coming season, and the end-of-year deadline was bearing down on him.

"Would you mind if I brought Nora?" I'd said.

He'd hesitated just a moment before saying, "Of course not. With three people we just might finish before midnight."

"Oh, it will take that long? She usually goes to bed pretty early."

"No problem. If she wants to get some shut-eye, we can just set up the couch in the break room for her. A couple years ago we had an employee sleeping on it for a week after her parents kicked her out of the house. It's really comfortable."

Nora and I arrived at Perkins Nursery at 6:30 p.m. with a pizza and got to work, matching Tyrese's scribbled notes to products, reading item numbers out loud, and checking species off lists while he maneuvered through order forms from a dozen different vendors.

As 8:30 p.m. rolled around and Nora began making mistakes, she decided to call it a night. Tyrese retrieved some bedding from a cupboard and lost himself once more in catalogs as I spread blankets and fluffed pillows.

"This is better anyway," Nora said as she took off her reading glasses and settled in under the covers. "No one wants a third wheel on a night like this."

"A night like what?" I snickered. "We're ordering fertilizer and seed packets, not slow dancing in front of a roaring fire."

Nora shook her tired head slightly. "Real romance happens when you least expect it. That's what makes it romantic. I fell in love with William on a couch very much like this one after

I'd embarrassed myself at an awkward lunch, made thoughtless comments about his neighborhood, and tripped on the sidewalk and bloodied my knee. I did everything wrong."

I smiled. "My mother would say everything happens in God's time, I guess."

"Maybe." She shut her eyes. "But if God had asked me anything about it, I would have told him he was mistaken."

I frowned. "Why?"

"William was the right man, all right. But it was the wrong time, that's all. Good night, Elizabeth."

"Good night."

I shut off the light, closed the door, and leaned heavily on the other side of it. Was she right? Did God get things wrong? Did his clock and our clocks just not match up, like how the clock in my car was four minutes faster than the one in the kitchen? Whose clock was Marshall Boon's job offer running on?

Tyrese and I pounded out the remaining orders over the next few hours until there was only one left. I looked at the clock. 11:29 p.m.

"We're going to make it," I said.

"Yep. I just gotta run through to the back greenhouse a minute and double-check how many seed geraniums I already have planned."

"I'll come with you. I need to get out of this chair."

"Grab your coat."

We walked through the front showroom, the gardening equipment room, and the front greenhouse, flicking on each light as we went. The back greenhouse was where seasonal workers prepped seed trays and planters, where thousands of tiny brown seeds swelled and split and became tiny green plants that would be offered to customers starting in April, even though the last freeze date for the region was in late May.

Clipboard in hand, Tyrese counted off the trays of seed geraniums, his finger punching the air in front of him, the mumbled numbers adding up under his breath. My boots scuffed along the soil-strewn floor, leaving trails of bare concrete behind me like the gravel two-track drive that had first led me to Nora's doorstep back in August. The chill air smelled of promise, of gardens that would soon be planted and watered and tended.

I thought of my own little plot of land, the garden I had worked so hard to renew. Of Nora's beautiful quilt. Of Mary's silent grave. Mute testimonies of our family's story, a story I had known nothing about until just a few months ago. A story I was in the middle of right now.

If everything really happened for a reason, then I must have lost my job at the *Free Press* so that I would be free to come to Nora's—to deliver Mr. Rich's photos, to assess Nora's independence for Barb, to help her through the ice storm. But that was all for other people. Was the *Beat* God's way of telling me my work here was done? Was any part of his so-called plan for me?

I watched Tyrese scratch notes onto his clipboard as breath streamed from his lips in a white cloud.

"Don't stay in Lapeer for me or even for Nora if what you really want to do is be a journalist."

His heavy shearling-lined leather coat was marred by a year's worth of dirt from transferring living things from one place to another.

"You'll never be happy that way."

All the things he worked to grow in this cavernous space reached their full height and beauty in gardens he would never see.

"You've got to do what's right for you."

I felt something inside of me shift and click, like the right key in the right lock.

"Hey," I said when the clipboard dropped to his side, "I think I've made up my mind about that job."

He turned guarded eyes on me from across two long tables filled with seed trays. "Yeah? And what did you decide?"

FIFTY

Bloomfield Hills, July 1967

Nora made a conscious effort to close her mouth as the Corvette pulled into the driveway at her parents' house. "Aunt Margaret isn't Mary Balsam's daughter?"

Over the past couple years, Nora had felt a growing connection with her sweet great-aunt, despite Margaret's confusion about who Nora was. Now she realized that Margaret's understanding of their relationship was more the true nature of things. They were unrelated, disconnected souls sharing an hour here and there.

"Does she know this?"

"I have no idea." He opened the car door and stepped out onto the driveway.

Nora scrambled out of the car. "Did Nathaniel know?"

"Whether he knew is anyone's guess. There's no one left alive beyond Margaret who might know. I shouldn't even have told you."

"Did Big George know?"

"Big George?"

"That's what Margaret called him to differentiate him from your father."

Daniel pulled the seat back forward and retrieved Nora's suitcase. "I never spoke to that man. Whenever we came around, he and that younger colored fellow made themselves scarce."

"But if Margaret did know—"

"Leave it alone, Nora. Better to let her die in peace."

Nora chewed on the inside of her cheek as they walked through the foyer. "Have you heard from Wanda?"

"She's fine. We told her to stay home until this all gets sorted out."

She started up the stairs with her suitcase, then stopped. "Do I still have a room here?"

"Yes. But don't shut yourself up there. The *Free Press* is on the veranda—and so is your mother, I imagine. You need to come apologize to her."

"For what?"

"You know what, Nora. She told me about her trip to Lapeer after you and I spoke on the phone."

Nora continued up the stairs to her old room. It was just the same as ever. She was not. Gone was the girl who had listened to those records, drawn those pictures, played with those dolls, talked on that phone. She had been replaced for a few years by a woman who knew what it was to enjoy an impossible love. And now, looking in the vanity mirror, Nora saw only a woman who was unraveling.

She sat on the edge of the bed. Tears she'd held back when her father stepped out of that black Corvette now trickled down her wind-dried cheeks. Nora hadn't cried since her miscarriage two years before. When she'd lost her baby, the source of her sadness had been clear. But now she struggled to parse the emotions swirling within her. She wasn't crying for Margaret's ignominious origin or for Mary's devastating mistake. She wasn't even crying about William's silence over the past two days.

She was crying over how easy it was to be back in this house, this room. About how simple it had been after all to call her father. About how she knew that when she saw her mother on the veranda, all it would take to patch up their relationship was a glance. This was her family. As much as she had told herself that William was all the family she needed now, that he was enough, he wasn't. She wanted the love of her parents too. And now she was so close to reconciliation with them that it scared her. It should not be this easy. It should not even be possible.

Could she embrace the woman who had called her dead baby lucky? The man who, it seemed, would exile her all over again? How could those things be forgiven? What was she even doing here?

Nora wiped her face with the back of her hand and picked up the phone. She dialed Mrs. Rich's number, then Bianca's work, then one of William's old friends, the only other number she could remember. On the third ring, someone picked up.

"Lowell?"

"This is Marvin. Who's this?"

"I'm Nora Rich. I'm William's wife. Lowell's friend William."

"Yeah, I know Will Rich."

"Do you know where he is? Have you seen him or heard from him at all? He went to Detroit on Sunday night to look for his nephew and I haven't heard from him since and I'm worried something's happened and—"

"You got to slow down. Listen, there's lots of people missing right now. He'll turn up. Probably just got picked up by the police for being in the wrong place at the wrong time. Out after curfew or something. Paper said thousands of people have been arrested. You call the station?"

"Which station? I don't even know who to call!"

"Calm down, girl. I can call around for you if you want."

Nora flopped back on the bed in relief. "You would do that?"

"What's your number?"

Nora gave him her parents' phone number.

"Where you at?" Marvin asked, no doubt puzzling over the non-Detroit number.

"Bloomfield Hills."

"Bloomfield! What you doing up there?"

"I'm at my parents' house."

"Psh. That's right. You the white girl. Where y'all been?"

"Lapeer. Listen, please call me as soon as you can. Even if you can't find out anything, please call me so I know you tried. I'm going crazy."

"Whole city's going crazy, girl—wait, what's your name again?"

"Nora Rich."

"Got it. Listen, Nora Rich, I'll give you a call soon as I can."

They hung up and Nora breathed a small sigh of relief. Something, at least, was being done.

Now it was time to face her mother.

She found her parents on the veranda in the exact positions they had been four summers earlier when she and William had come to break the news of their marriage. Now the memory threatened to undo her. Where would she be now, at this very moment, had she not married William? She might still be on the veranda, she decided, but the stark black-and-white photos of billowing smoke that graced the newspaper lying on the table beneath her mother's drink would hold no special terror for her. She would look at them much as her parents probably had, with a scornful eye and a tongue quick to lay blame, then toss them aside to be gathered up later in a basket by the hearth. Yesterday's news to start tomorrow's fire.

Without looking at her mother, Nora slipped the papers from beneath the glass and took a seat in an empty chair. She searched each photo for a figure that might be William but came up empty. Jagged words leapt out at her—snipers, looters, chaos, shots, flames, curfew, troops, destruction. As she sat on the veranda on the hot, still day, it was as if she was reading about the war in Vietnam. But she knew that if the wind turned she'd be able to see the smoke.

When she looked up, her parents were staring at her. Then she heard the phone ring. She rushed into the house, snagging the phone from the cradle on the fourth ring. "Hello?"

"Nora?"

"Bianca? Oh, thank God."

"Someone named Marvin gave me this number for you. I tried calling you at your house an hour ago, but no one answered. We're at my boss's house on Buena Vista right now."

"Who? Is William with you?"

"No. Mama's here."

"What's going on? Where is he?"

"I don't know. We saw him Sunday night at Aunt Dee's, but just for a few minutes. We had to get out of there because the house next door started on fire."

"What about your house?"

"It's gone," Bianca choked out.

"Oh my. No word on J.J. either?"

"He's being held in the Wayne County Jail. I only know where he is because our minister is there trying to get word to people. They ain't even processing anybody. Don't even know who they have. Just throwing them all in together like animals."

Nora heard Bianca's voice catch.

"Pastor said he'd been beaten pretty bad."

"He'll be okay, Bianca. He's just a kid. They bounce back fast." Nora didn't want to be insensitive, but J.J. wasn't her real concern. The kid's arrest made William's desperate trip into this war zone futile. "Did your pastor talk to J.J.? Did he say anything about William?"

"He couldn't talk to him! He was lying against a wall unconscious! Pastor almost didn't recognize him!"

Nora had to pull the phone away from her ear at Bianca's

agonizing groan of despair. Then the choked sound of her weeping faded away.

"Nora?" came Louise Rich's steady voice.

"Mama, what is going on over there?"

"Sweetie, it's bad. We just in shock. Nobody knows nothing. I just don't know what to do. We got people out looking for Will. I'll call you as soon as there's word, but right now we got to pray. You understand? We got to pray like never before. You pray with me now, all right?"

Nora squeezed her eyes shut to hold back the tears.

"Lord, hear us now," Louise began. "Hear us as we cry out to you. We know you know where our Will is right this moment. We know you see him, that you're looking at him even now. We're trying to trust you with him, but it's hard. We're trying to leave him in your hands, but it's so hard to do. Lord, bring him back to us. Bring him back even today, even this very hour. Hear our prayer as you heard your own Son's voice as he cried out to you on the cross. Amen."

But Nora could not say "amen." Because all she could think about was what Jesus had said upon the cross: *"My God, my God, why have you forsaken me?"*

"Nora, honey, we've got to trust. He got a plan and he don't make mistakes. I'll call you again, sweetie."

They said their goodbyes and Nora replaced the handset on the cradle. She looked up to find her parents standing in the open doorway, her father's face looking grim, her mother's streaked with silent tears.

"Oh, sweetie," Mallory said.

Nora gathered her anger up inside her chest and locked her heart against their sad eyes. "I don't need your pity."

She walked back upstairs into her old room and slammed the door.

FIFTY-ONE

Lapeer County, June 1875

With great effort, Mary raised her eyelids. Nathaniel's face came into shaky focus against a background of blurry colors. Baby Margaret wiggled in his arms.

"Mary?"

He sounded like he was outside, speaking through a closed window.

"Mary, can you hear me? The doctor is on his way."

Margaret did look remarkably like Nathaniel.

"Mary?"

She closed her eyes.

"Mary?"

Oblivion.

Mary opened her eyes. Mrs. Farnsworth sat next to her with a bucket at the ready.

"Mr. Balsam is sending someone to hurry the doctor along."

"George," Mary whispered in a hoarse voice.

"You want to see Little George?"

Mary shook her head. The movement made her dizzy and she began to heave. Mrs. Farnsworth thrust the bucket at her, making it just in time. She let Mrs. Farnsworth wipe her mouth with a cloth.

"Big George."

"Ma'am, I—"

"Please?"

The housekeeper let out a long sigh. "I'll get him."

Mary closed her eyes, but her head still spun. When next she opened them, George's face filled her vision, looking so much like the man who had stayed at her bedside that fateful night when her first baby died—her real baby girl.

"Mrs. Balsam?"

"George," she whispered.

"I'm here."

She smiled. "You're always there." She moved her fingers. "Hold my hand."

George stood up and closed the door. Then he took her hand in his.

"I need to tell you something."

"Save your strength."

"George, we have a baby."

A look of panic came over his face, and he glanced at the closed door. "No, ma'am, we don't."

"Don't call me ma'am."

"Let me get you some cold water."

"That day in the woods. I wasn't with child. I thought . . . But I was wrong. But after . . . The midwife switched them. Took our baby boy away. And gave me the baby of Nathaniel's prostitute."

George was shaking his head. "You're not thinking straight."

"He's out there. Someone has him. Mrs. Farnsworth knows. Please forgive me."

"No, Mrs. Balsam."

"Please forgive me. Oh, God, I'm so sorry. God, please forgive me."

"Shhh," he soothed.

"Anna knows where he is. You need to find him. Little George knows. Somehow. Figured it out. Maybe saw the baby in the basket. I don't know. Clever, dreadful, spiteful boy. It would have been better if he had been the one born dead."

"You don't know what you are saying."

"He helped them." She began to cry. "Those awful men. The fire."

"What are you talking about?"

"Somehow. I don't know. Wanted you all gone. Please forgive me." She squeezed his hand. "I love you, George."

Mrs. Farnsworth opened the door. George snatched his hand away from Mary's and put it in his lap.

"Mrs. Balsam needs her rest."

He stood up. "Of course."

Mrs. Farnsworth placed a wet rag on Mary's ashen forehead. When the housekeeper straightened, she did not try to hide her contempt. George didn't need to ask her anything. He left the room and reentered a world that had been irreversibly altered, a world in which he was the father of a lost son.

Mary tried to feel comforted by the cool rag, but the sensation of spinning out of control would not abate. She remembered the strange look Little George had given her at the dinner table that night. He had not looked her in the eye since baby Margaret's arrival. Until that very evening.

She'd seen him in the herb garden earlier in the day, digging up weeds, a punishment she had meted out for some small breach of protocol, though what the infraction was she could not call to mind. It didn't matter. They both knew the real reason.

Jacob had been talking to him in his new voice, courtesy of missing front teeth and a broken jaw that hadn't healed correctly.

"Carepul wi dat. Dat ain't no parsnip. You best burn dat. Don't let da pigs get at it. Dey be dead bepore you know it."

She hadn't seen what he'd done with the plant as she returned to the task of mending a torn shirt for Nathaniel.

No. It was Big George's shirt.

Big George.

"No, that one is for you, Big George," her son had said as the man set the plate in front of Mary.

"You should serve your mother first," Big George had replied gently.

Roast chicken, spring peas, baked parsnips with butter and herbs. Mary loved parsnips. She had snuck a bite from her plate even before everyone had sat down, before they had said grace.

What had she seen in Little George's eyes?

The convulsions returned and Mary felt her throat closing. She struggled for breath. She heard Mrs. Farnsworth's strangled cry for Nathaniel.

Then she was swallowed up by the darkness.

FIFTY-TWO

Lapeer County, March

I stood at the calendar and peeked ahead. Just one more day until April started.

The first day of spring had come and gone in a flurry of snow, followed by a week of constant rain. But March 31st had dawned sunny. Birds were nesting, brown grass was visible, some intrepid herbs were pushing up their first leaves in the rich garden soil—scouts that would report back to the subterranean infrastructure about whether it was safe to emerge.

"Oh, just turn it," Nora said as she walked into the kitchen. "Let's start April a day early."

I did as directed, happy to see that she was having a good day. "Coffee?" I asked.

"Yes, that would be lovely."

"Great. I have something I want to talk to you about."

I went about the task of brewing our standard half pot of coffee, set everything on a tray, and took it into the parlor. Matthew had situated himself next to Nora on the settee in a spot of sunlight, his orange fur radiant, one green eye squinting up at me. I buried my fingers in his hot fur.

"It's been ages since I felt that warm. Maybe I need a fur coat."

Nora poured the coffee, revealing a shake in her arms that had not been there before. "What do you have on your mind?"

I gathered my thoughts. It had been far more difficult and taken far more persuasion on Linden's part than I'd anticipated to get Mr. Rich to agree to come out to the farmhouse. Linden first called in January with the news that his father wanted nothing to do with my scheme. But I would not be dissuaded. As Marshall Boon had said, I was tenacious. By mid-March I had finally gotten James Rich himself on the phone to hash things out.

"It's not that no one tried," he said. "Nora shut down and shut herself away after it was clear that William wasn't going back to Lapeer with her. She wouldn't talk to anyone about it, and she sure wouldn't want to talk to me—ever."

"Mr. Rich, I don't think you quite understand. Sometimes she talks about William as if he's still here. There have been a couple times lately when I've walked into a room and she's been talking *to* him. If you could just tell her what really happened, maybe she'd understand and she'd be able to make her peace. You said you've been carrying around a burden for years. Well, that's your burden. Not mine. I can't lay it down for you. You need to lay it down yourself."

A long sigh. "Would you mind if I brought Denny with me? Just for support. I know you two didn't hit it off, but . . . I can't do this alone."

"I don't mind at all," I said, knowing I'd won him over. If he wanted to bring along an interpretive dance troupe or Chinese shadow puppeteers to tell the story, I would have agreed.

And now, next Sunday, he would be here.

I stirred the cream into my coffee and tried to calm my racing heart while Nora waited for me to talk. "I've arranged for a visit from someone who has information about the family to come and talk with us. I figured since we're both so interested in family history, it might be beneficial to hear some parts we don't know much about."

"My, my, that sounds intriguing. Where did you find this person?"

"He found me. He happened to notice the Balsam name in the newspaper and realized he knew someone with the same name."

"Who is this mystery man?"

"I can't say yet." I stood up to avoid Nora's suspicious gaze and tried to change the subject. "I should put this pot back on the burner so it doesn't get cold."

Nora followed me into the kitchen. "I have to say I'm pleasantly surprised at how interested you are in this sort of thing."

"Why?" I said as I replaced the carafe. "Isn't everyone interested in their family's history?"

"Plenty of people don't give it a second thought, and some would rather keep it under wraps." She looked thoughtful. "Sometimes I wonder if it would have been better that way."

I said nothing. Give the subject space.

"I remember talking to my old Great-Aunt Margaret about her experiences in this house," Nora finally said. "It was like pulling at a loose thread, trying to release it from the past so that this thread at least would not be lost to the ravages of time. I tried to weave it into my own story, to see how *then* fit into *now*."

Nora seemed to be looking through me as she spoke.

"You get to my age and you wish you had a chance to step back to see the whole, to see what you've made of your life and what you've made of theirs, to see if you've honored their memories or redeemed their faults. But you never can. Time never stops and allows you to *know* anything." Her eyes shimmered with unshed tears.

"If you don't want to talk about it—"

"Don't be silly. If we don't share what we know, it dies with us. And ultimately that's not fair." She seemed to be trying to convince herself. "The more we know, the better."

One week later, I sat at the front window and stared at the gap in the pine trees where I knew a car would soon appear.

"That won't make our guest show up any sooner," Nora said as she set the table in the dining room.

"I know. I'm just excited."

Actually, I was anxious. I was nervous that he wouldn't show up. And nervous that he would.

"Help me with the salad and take your mind off it."

Chopping vegetables did little to allay my anxiety, but it did manage to pass the time. At one o'clock, just as we had arranged, Mr. Rich rang the doorbell.

"Go sit down in the parlor," I commanded. I slid the pocket door between the front hall and the parlor closed and tried to quiet the voice inside me that was whispering, *This is a very, very bad idea.* I opened the door and found myself eye to eye with a well-dressed James Rich and, behind him, an even better-dressed Linden Rich holding a dingy old cardboard box with a yellowed handwritten label.

"Hello," I said quietly, but with a smile on my face. "I'm so glad you're here."

"Have you prepared her for this?" Mr. Rich asked in a low tone.

"I told her someone was coming to tell us about some family history."

"But you didn't tell her who?"

"I didn't think I should. I didn't want her to tell me to cancel it."

He and Linden exchanged a glance. I heard the pocket door slide open behind me.

"Elizabeth?"

Nora stood in the parlor doorway and looked past me to the two men in her foyer.

"Aren't you going to invite them—"

She put a hand on the door frame to steady herself. "William?" she whispered. Her eyes were fixed upon Linden.

"Why don't we sit down?" I said.

I took one of her arms and guided her back to the settee. The men situated themselves in chairs across from us.

"No, you're not him," Nora said.

"No, ma'am," Linden said kindly.

"Nora," I said, "this is James Rich and his son Linden. I believe you know James?"

She furrowed her brow a moment, then her contemplative look became one of furious resentment. "Yes. I know him."

Mr. Rich looked down at his hands. "I know I'm the last person you want to see, Nora. But your niece was adamant I come talk to you."

"Elizabeth, what would give you the idea that I would ever want this man in my home?"

She stood up, so we all did.

"Wait, Nora. I think you need to hear what he has to say. I think it would help."

"Help what? All you've done is dredge up something that would have been better left buried." She walked out of the room. Across the hall the bedroom door slammed.

"Please sit down," I said to the men. "Let me talk to her."

I entered Nora's bedroom without knocking and shut the door behind me. She was sitting on the quilt she had told me she never sat on, her face in her hands.

"I'm sorry," I said as I sat down next to her. "But I'm concerned about you. You talk half the time as if William is dead and half the time like he's still living in this house. I thought that if you would just listen to what Mr. Rich has to say, it would help you.

Wouldn't it be better to know the truth and have closure than to keep wondering?"

She dropped her hands. "Elizabeth, I know he's dead. I've always known."

It was my turn to be confused. "Then why lock yourself out of the darkroom? What were you afraid of seeing in there?"

"I wasn't afraid. I didn't go in because I knew it probably contained the last photos he would ever take. That once I saw those, there wouldn't be any more. He'd never run up those cellar stairs again with a handful of prints and ask me what I thought of them. And that man sitting in my parlor right now is the reason. He's the reason William went to Detroit that day. He's the reason he never came back. He's the one who destroyed my life. Everyone said it would be William. But it wasn't. It was J.J."

I sighed. "I just wanted to fix this."

"Some things cannot be fixed—they can only be endured. I'm not upset with you. But I don't want to talk to him. I know everything he has to say."

"No you don't. He's the one who gave me the camera to give to you. And that's not all there is. Something else turned up, something of William's that has been buried in an evidence room somewhere. He came all this way so he could give it to you."

She was shaking her head.

"Nora, please. That man out there has been wanting to be reconciled to you for fifty years. He's the one who has been paying Tyrese to cut your lawn, not some stupid government program. He wants to apologize, make amends. Would William have wanted you to be at odds with him for the rest of your life?"

"No," she admitted. "He wouldn't have wanted that."

I plucked a tissue from the box beside her bed and handed it to her.

She wiped her nose, took a deep breath, and stood up. "I'll

let him say what he's come to say, but that's all. I can't promise forgiveness."

I hugged her gently. "Thank you."

She sniffed and smoothed out her clothes. When she walked into the parlor, Mr. Rich and Linden stood up.

"I'm sorry, J.J.," Nora said. "That was very rude of me. You came a long way today, and it's only right that you have a chance to say what it is you've come to say. We have lunch ready, so please follow me into the dining room."

When everyone was seated and served, Mr. Rich took a sip of water and cleared his throat. "This isn't an easy story to tell, and it won't be an easy story to hear."

FIFTY-THREE

Detroit, July 1967

The shattering glass sounded like freedom. Like breaking out of an exhibit at the zoo. J.J. had always resented the way the city treated his neighborhood. Like a beast that needed to be contained. If they wanted to treat him like an animal, he'd show them what an animal did when it was on the loose.

"C'mon!" Arnold shouted. "Let's hit the liquor store."

J.J. looked through the large picture window he had just broken. "Hang on, man! I'm gonna get me some new shoes."

They climbed through the window and picked their way across the shards of glass to the stockroom. Arnold began pulling shoeboxes off the shelves at random, dropping them on the ground in a heap.

"Don't do that!" J.J. said. "You're mixin' them all up. How am I supposed to find my size?" J.J. ran his finger along a row of boxes until he found a size 10. He opened it up and pulled out the shiny black leather shoes inside. "Dang. I ain't never had a pair of shoes this nice before."

"Man, you can't run from the cops in those. Them some church shoes."

"I don't care," J.J. said as he removed his old sneakers. "I'm sick of secondhand. C'mon, hurry up and take some."

"Psh! I ain't out for shoes. I'm gonna get me some beer and make me some bombs."

J.J. retrieved the brick he had thrown, and they stepped out onto the sidewalk. The mayhem to the south sounded closer. People were milling around now, nervously looking down the street to see what they were in for.

J.J. noticed a woman watching him from a porch. "Come on in and shop till you drop!" he called.

She narrowed her eyes. "Ain't you Bianca's boy?"

J.J. let out a low curse. "Let's go!"

Around the corner they came upon Arnold's target and heaved their bricks through the glass. It came crashing down in a sparkling shower.

"Love that sound!" J.J. shouted.

Inside they stuffed their pockets with candy, cigarettes, and lighters, and filled one box with liquor bottles and another with beer.

"Don't we need a bunch of cloth to stick in them?" J.J. asked.

"I know where we can get some."

They hid the heavy boxes in the tall weeds behind some trash cans and took off running again.

"There!" Arnold shouted.

They hopped a fence and landed hard on the other side, where sheets and baby diapers were strung on a clothesline. Arnold started to pull a diaper off the line.

"Not that," J.J. said. "That's cold, man. Use the sheet. We can tear it up easier anyway."

They yanked the sheet down. On the other side of it hung a yellow floral sundress and a line of women's undergarments. For just a moment, J.J. was distracted.

"C'mon, help me with this," Arnold called from the ground. He was biting at the sheet and tearing off long strips. They looked like the bandages J.J.'s grandma rolled with the church ladies for the Red Cross.

"That's enough," Arnold announced a minute later, and he grabbed up the handful of fabric strips. "Let's go."

When they were back on the sidewalk, Arnold took off at a run for the stashed liquor bottles. J.J. looked back at the house, where a girl he knew sat in the front window. They locked eyes for a moment before J.J. turned and ran after his friend.

Heart pounding in time with his new shoes hitting the pavement, J.J. thought about the girl and the brassieres he'd seen hanging on the line next to that yellow dress. He tripped on Arnold as he came around the back of the liquor store. Rum splashed out of the bottle in Arnold's hand and onto his bare arm.

"Watch it, man!"

"You sure you know what you're doing?"

"Sure. I seen it on the news."

They opened up four bottles, soaked the strips of torn-up sheet, and inserted them into the necks.

"Let's go," Arnold said.

"No houses," J.J. said.

They ran back out to the street and scanned the shops.

"That one," Arnold said, pointing.

He found a potted plant by the door and chucked it through the store window. Then he lit the fuse and tossed it through the open space into the little grocery store. It broke against a shelf and sputtered into nothing.

Arnold cursed and shouted. "Gimme another one." He tried again with the same ineffective result.

"I thought you said you knew what you were doing."

J.J. heard the sound of laughing behind him and turned to find a boy not much older than himself grabbing his stomach in scornful delight. "Fool!" he shouted. "You need gasoline to make a Molotov cocktail!" Then he kept walking up the street with a spring in his step.

J.J. leveled an exasperated look at Arnold.

"Shut up. How was I to know?"

"You saw it on the news," J.J. mocked.

"Forget the Molotov cocktails then."

Arnold sent another brick sailing through the window of a record shop. The boys worked their way down the street until J.J.'s throwing arm was sore. Then they went back for the beer. The street teemed with people shouting and looting and throwing rocks at the line of police that had moved up from their spot near Clairmount where the rioting had begun more than twelve hours earlier. In full view of the police, young men, black and white, and even some women were carrying off televisions, speakers, boxes of laundry detergent, coats, couches, guns, and loaves of bread. Shots were fired here and there, but none of them came from the police.

"Why ain't they doing nothin'?" J.J. asked a man emerging from the liquor store with his own box full of booze.

"Can't shoot back. Orders. So get what you want while the gettin's good!" The man walked on down the street, bottles clinking all the way. J.J. wondered if the man knew about needing gasoline.

"C'mon, J.J.! I'm gettin' me a color TV!"

Arnold ran into an electronics store they had spared on their earlier tour of the street because they liked the guy who ran it. But someone else had broken in, and now hordes of people jostled for the goods inside. J.J. swallowed down a pang of conscience. That guy never did anything to him.

A few minutes later Arnold resurfaced carrying a turntable. "TVs all gone, but I got this!"

"You already have a record player."

"So?"

J.J. shook his head. "You stealin' somethin' you don't need from someone you like."

"Hey, I didn't break the window, man. Everything's gonna be gone from that place anyway. Why shouldn't I get my piece?"

"That ain't what this is about."

"Yeah, what's it about then? You so smart. What's it about?"

"It's about Rod. Remember? It's about black power. It's about showin' them we ain't gonna take it no more. It's about takin' control of our own destiny. Didn't you ever listen when we was at those rallies with Derek? This is bigger than gettin' some stuff for free."

"Oh yeah?" Arnold looked at J.J.'s gleaming shoes, which were already scuffed from climbing fences and running down cracked sidewalks.

"That's different. That guy makes you feel like scum every time he catch you lookin' in the window."

"Oh, I see how it is. Even when you steal you's better than me, huh? Go home, J.J. Go on home to your mama and show her your shiny new church shoes. I bet she'll be real proud of you and your principles."

Arnold turned away. J.J. looked at his feet and wished he had his old sneakers back.

The riot closed in around them, enveloping them in a smoking cacophony of sirens, screams, and shattering glass. To the south, the sky was black.

As the sun set late Sunday night, J.J. stared at the smoking rubble of his house. Up and down the street, chimneys rose up like factory smokestacks, like that photograph of the aftermath of Sherman's march to the sea he'd seen in his history textbook. While he and Arnold had spread the mayhem north, others had spread it south. His house was gone, and he had no idea whether or not Mama and Grandma had escaped or if they'd been consumed by the flames. He sat down hard on the garbage-strewn street, pulled his knees to his chest, and wept.

"J.J.?"

He looked up to see a tall man closing in on foot. "Will?"

"Thank you, Lord," William said into the smoke-choked sky. He threw his arms around his nephew.

J.J. stuffed his tears back inside. "Where's Mama and Grandma?"

"Aunt Dee's. I'm taking you there right now. Had to leave my car a few blocks away. But we're not far. We can get there on foot. Better get going. It's getting dark." William put his camera up to his face and snapped a few photos of the wreckage.

"What you doin'?"

"Capturing history, kid. Nora's idea. Already got three rolls done. Got three more ready to go. Hey, back up a minute."

"Don't take my picture."

"C'mon."

"I said don't take my picture."

William let his camera hang from the strap around his neck. "Okay, man."

"Let's go," J.J. said.

"We can skip over to Linwood on Virginia Park. Better avoid Twelfth."

They trotted down Seward and took a jog in the road, William stopping to snap a photo every few minutes, then catching up. When they turned the corner onto Linwood, they stopped short. The conflagration that had started three blocks to the east was already consuming that street as well.

"I don't know, man," J.J. said. "You really think we can get through all that?"

"I guess we have to."

"What if they had to leave Aunt Dee's?"

"We won't know until we get there. But they're expecting us. And I need to call Nora."

They hurried through streets flooded with people—concerned neighbors checking on each other, looters bringing their stolen goods home to their families, police officers watching over the proceedings with anxious eyes and itching trigger fingers. The man with the box of liquor was right. The cops offered little resistance to the rioters, who were taking full advantage of this mandated restraint.

They cut through yards and stopped in shadowy alleys as the rioters ran by and more police poured in, called back from their summer vacations. What sunlight had been breaking through the shroud of smoke that covered the city had finally disappeared below the horizon. With no light and no flash, William wound up his finished film, inserted a new roll into the camera, and tucked it back into his bag. But when they neared Taylor Avenue, the light from the fires was so bright that he took it out again.

A volley of shots rang out, followed by the sound of a helicopter taking off.

"Let's get outta here," J.J. said. "I ain't heard so many gunshots all day. Cops musta got the okay to shoot."

William shook his head. "National Guard. I saw them rolling in earlier. Whole line of tanks. They're all up at your school."

"Man, we gotta go that way," J.J. moaned.

William put the camera back in the bag. "Then we better just go and get it over with."

The farther they went, the more obvious the presence of the Guard became. Tanks creaked down streets, lines of men in drab uniforms carrying rifles marching behind. J.J. felt that every one of them must know about his shoes.

A long column was nearly past when a guardsman near the end of the pack spotted them. "Hey! You there!"

William put his hand out in front of J.J. to stop his forward motion, then pushed his nephew behind him. "What?" he said.

The guardsman trotted over to him, followed by another. "What you got there?" He was pointing to William's bag.

"Camera."

"Just pick that up?" The man shifted the rifle on his shoulder.

"I've had it for four years."

"That so?"

"Yes, sir."

J.J. seethed inside to watch his uncle call this guy *sir*. He couldn't have been more than a few years older than J.J. himself.

"You want to take it out of the bag for me?"

William pulled the camera out and handed it over.

The man slung his gun across his back, dropped the lens cap to the ground, and held the camera up to his face. He spun the focus ring. "You there, what are you hiding back there?"

J.J. stepped out. "Ain't hidin'."

"Well, come on out here then. Move in a little." He waved his hand at them.

William and J.J. stood close together.

"Say cheese!"

Click.

His companion laughed. "Take ours now."

The first man handed the camera back to William.

"Look mean," the second guardsman told his partner.

The young men put on the expressions of hardened war veterans. William adjusted the settings, focused, and took their picture.

A shouted order filtered back through the noise.

"We gotta go, man." The second man started up the street.

"Hey," said the first, "if you make it out of this alive, look me up so I can see that picture." He began to run after his companion. "Name's Ryan Sharpe! From Davison!"

William retrieved the lens cap and put the camera away. "Maybe you should carry this, J.J." He handed the bag to his nephew. "Run and hide if it comes to it. Can't lose those pictures."

J.J. slung the bag across his shoulder.

Twenty minutes later they made it to Aunt Dee's house. Or what had been her house. In the orange glow of the fire and the spinning red lights of the fire truck, J.J. could see that the house was past saving. Half a dozen firemen were spraying three burning houses with fire hoses. Each was attended by two guardsmen. There were too many fires and not enough men or equipment to put them out. J.J. thought of the fires he and Arnold had tried to start earlier that day and was grateful for the ignorance that had kept their faulty Molotov cocktails from working.

"Hey, you! Back up!" a familiar voice shouted. It was the guardsman who had stopped them less than a half hour earlier.

"Here, give me that." William reached for the bag on J.J.'s shoulder.

"Hey!" came another shout.

William put his hands up. "It's just the camera."

A shot rang out from a window behind William and J.J. The guardsmen returned fire. J.J. ducked and ran, straight into a waiting guardsman who knocked him over the head with the butt of his rifle. He fell to the ground and felt blood oozing down his forehead and into his eyes.

The last thing he saw was a bullet rip through William's body as cinders from Aunt Dee's house rained down around them.

FIFTY-FOUR

Lapeer County, April

As Mr. Rich drew his story to a close, I looked down at my plate, surprised to find it empty. I didn't remember eating anything.

"Are you sure you're remembering that name right?" I pressed him. "Ryan Sharpe? As in, Judge Ryan Sharpe?"

He looked grave. "I'll never forget it."

My mind raced. Ryan Sharpe had been in the middle of a firefight that resulted in the deaths of at least two men—a supposed sniper and a firefighter. "What happened to William?"

Mr. Rich looked over at Nora. "His body was never found. The city started a project to locate missing people in the months following the riot, but lots of people were still unaccounted for. We held a memorial service that fall, without a body. But we can't know for sure what happened. My belief has always been that his body was burned. That entire block was destroyed."

"I never found a death certificate when I was looking into it," I said.

"After seven years of being missing, Nora could have filed to have him declared deceased," he said. "She never did."

Nora was shaking her head and staring at the tablecloth.

Mr. Rich nodded at his son, who pushed the box toward his father.

"These are the photos that William took that night," he said. "Everything I had on me was collected as evidence. I'm sure they thought I had stolen the camera, though if they stopped a minute to think about it, they'd know a camera that nice wouldn't have been sold in any of the stores in that neighborhood. Someone at the station had the film developed, probably thinking they could use the photos to identify looters." He pushed the box toward Nora. "They're really yours. I think you'll want to see them."

Nora made no move for the box. With every fiber of my being I silently begged her to open it. If there was truly a photo of a young Ryan Sharpe just minutes before the firefight that could place him in the proximity of the incident . . .

Mr. Rich leaned in. "Nora, I know you hate me. I don't blame you. You have every reason to. If it wasn't for me, William would never have been in Detroit that day. I was angry. All I could see was how life had done me wrong and would continue to do me wrong. But I have regretted the rash words and actions of my youth since that day—bitterly regretted them. Only I can't change them. If I could go back in time, I would, but I can't. I can only move in one direction—forward. I wish you could do the same. I wish you could forgive me."

Nora looked at him with tired eyes. "There are three people in this world I have not been able to forgive. My mother, my father, and you. It would have been easy to forgive my parents. I was so close the day I came looking for William. It took a force of will to keep myself from doing it then, or any time in the years that followed. Even when they deeded this house to me. Even when they died. It took effort and sacrifice not to forgive them. But it has cost me no great effort not to forgive you."

Mr. Rich pursed his lips and shut his eyes, looking very much like a man on the verge of tears.

"I want to," Nora continued. "I do. I don't want to be an angry old woman. But . . ."

Mr. Rich nodded and regained control over his emotions.

"Nora," I ventured, "maybe Linden and I should give you two some time alone."

Linden was out of his chair in a flash. We walked through the kitchen and out the back door. I took a deep breath of spring and leaned on the remains of the woodpile Tyrese had created with William's tree.

Linden put his hands in his pockets. "Man. This is rough."

I nodded my agreement.

He looked up at the house. "This is a cool old place. You're lucky to live here. It's hard to see everything falling apart all over Detroit. Places from my parents' childhood—houses, schools, the places they worked—all getting wiped off the map."

"I know. The history of millions of people, just rotting away until some wrecking crew comes to put it out of its misery."

"Or some hipsters buy it and turn it into a brewery."

We were both quiet a moment, reflecting on the struggling city we called home. The city Vic Sharpe had been investing in. The city he was helping to save. I thought of Mr. Rich inside the house, doing the hard work of reconciliation. Maybe I needed to call Vic.

At the sound of gravel crunching under tires, I headed for the front yard, rounding the house just as a pickup emblazoned with the Perkins logo pulled up. My stomach did a flip when I saw Tyrese at the wheel.

He rolled down the window. "Special delivery." He was smiling as he said it, but his eyes strayed to Linden.

"Are you working on Sundays now?" I stepped up on the running board and gave him a kiss.

"Not normally. But I'm glad I got here when I did. Before Linden Rich ran off with my girl."

I laughed and jumped down to the ground.

"No, no, man," Linden said, approaching the cab of the pickup. "It ain't like that."

The men clasped hands through the open window.

I craned my neck to see into the bed of the pickup. "Is that my tree?"

"That's it," Tyrese said. "A beautiful three-year-old catalpa."

"Oh! Bring it around back!"

Tyrese and Linden fought with some rope and dragged the tree down onto a dolly as I led the way to the spot I had picked out for it.

I looked at Linden's impeccable Sunday clothes. "I don't suppose you want to help us plant this."

He smiled. "Sure."

For the next hour, the three of us dug, carried, poured, positioned, and covered. As the work progressed, I shared with Linden the history of his great-uncle—my great-uncle, I now fully realized—planting the first catalpa, of its struggle to survive only to succumb to the ice storm, of my work restoring the garden and the graves. I told him about Mary and Nathaniel, and about the cots in the attic and the men and women who had found shelter here. All stories Tyrese had already heard, but he seemed content to hear them again.

By the time the tree was snug in the ground, we all sported rolled-up sleeves, dirty hands and knees, and soiled shoes. I stood for a moment in the chill spring air and regarded our small accomplishment—one tree planted in good soil. It was young and supple. It would weather the storms to come in a way the old tree could not. It might live beyond my lifetime.

What might change in that time? Would things be better? Or worse?

"I should go," Tyrese said. "Give Nora a hug for me."

Linden hung back a little as I walked Tyrese back to the truck.

"Now don't go falling for that guy," Tyrese said.

I smiled at the thought that he could be jealous. "I won't. He's practically family, anyway."

Tyrese and Linden shared a wave, and then the pickup slowly inched back through the pines and onto the road.

Back in the kitchen, Linden and I removed our shoes, and I took a good look at him. "I think your clothes might be ruined."

"That's what dry cleaners are for."

"They won't clean your shoes."

"They're just shoes. It'll come off. And if not, it's a good excuse to buy new ones."

We crept to the dining room, but no one was at the table. The box of photos was gone, but the lunch plates were still there. I started to stack them.

"Leave those, Elizabeth, and come in here," came Nora's voice from the parlor.

Nora and Mr. Rich were on the settee, open box between them, photographs covering the coffee table.

"Come in here and look at these," she said.

"We're kind of dirty."

"What? Why?"

"Linden was helping me in the garden."

"Heavens, you just met him and you're putting him to work?"

"I was a willing helper," Linden said. "And this isn't the first we've met."

"Never mind the dirt," Nora said with a dismissive wave of her hand. "Just come look."

Linden and I pulled chairs in close to the coffee table. Among the photos spread out before me were a few of what you might expect when looking at photos of a riot—burning buildings, abandoned cars, groups of agitators facing down the police. But most were close-ups of individual people. Given the situation in which they were shot, they had to be candid, but many had the quality of portraits.

"Look at this." Nora handed one to me. A small black girl stood on the sidewalk, watching men push a mattress out of a second-story window and into a waiting pickup truck below. Behind the men, the block was going up in flames.

"Are they stealing it?"

"They're saving it."

I picked up a close-up of an elderly woman through a window, the trail of a tear running down her dark cheek. In the glass, a reflection of a house burning across the street. Then a frightened young boy holding a fat white cat, its legs looking for solid ground. I shuffled through photo after photo of boys and old men, mothers and grandmothers, displaying the full range of human emotion from despair to anger to heights of ecstatic mania. The one thing missing was joy.

"He was an amazing photographer."

"Yes, he was," Nora and Mr. Rich said in unison.

"This is the best work I've ever seen of his," Nora said in a voice thick with emotion.

I came to the last two photos. In one, two young white National Guardsmen looked steely-eyed at the camera. One of them was most definitely Ryan Sharpe. His expression was almost identical to one in a formal portrait I'd seen of him that had been taken right before he left for Vietnam. In the last photo, two black men stared out of the past. In the eyes of the younger was anger mingled with fear. In the older, a quiet strength.

"That's J.J.," Nora said. "And that's William."

My first glimpse of William Rich, a man whose ghost had haunted my aunt for fifty years. The man behind the lens. He was strikingly handsome and exuded confidence and dignity and grace.

He was the genius behind the photos I'd just seen, behind the ones down in the darkroom. Eyes that saw past the surface of a person to what was deep inside. The beauty and the pain. History being made. It wasn't the fires burning around them that captivated me, but the ones William had exposed burning within them, the interior crucible of past and present that would make them into new people, different people. One moment in time that would define all the moments that came after.

"These really should be in a book," I said when I could speak again. "And I'm not saying that for the reason you're thinking, Linden."

"He always wanted to make a book," Nora said.

"Too bad they're such small prints."

"All the negatives are there," Mr. Rich said, "in an envelope. You could have someone make more prints of any size you wanted."

"Actually, you could do that right downstairs—"

Nora looked up.

"If you knew how," I continued feebly.

"I know how," Linden said.

"You do?"

"Sure, it's a hobby of mine. Always done digital, but I was learning manual on Uncle William's camera. I'm not as good as he was, but I'm coming along. You've got a darkroom here?"

"It hasn't been used in decades," Nora said. "I'm sure the chemicals wouldn't work."

"Probably not. But do you mind if I take a look?"

Nora rubbed her forehead. "I suppose you may as well. After looking through all of these, I guess there's no reason to hold back any longer."

I retrieved the key and showed Linden to the basement. He had to hunch over the entire way to keep from hitting his head on the low ceiling. Inside the darkroom, he pulled the chain of an overhead light I hadn't seen before. It glowed a dim red. He sat on the stool so he could straighten his back and took stock of the room, fiddling with bottles and opening drawers I hadn't noticed during my candlelight expedition.

"It's pretty dusty down here," he said. "We'd have to clean everything first, but I don't see any reason we couldn't try it out. Probably need to get new developer and stop and fixer. There's an enlarger and a chrome dryer."

"That thing dries them? I thought people hung them up. There are some right behind you."

He spun around on the stool. "These weren't hanging up to dry. They're just for decoration."

"How do you know?"

"They're glossy. When they're hung dry, they end up with a matte finish. These were just here for William to look at." He took down one of the photos. "Wow, she was beautiful."

"I kind of thought that maybe the room was locked because William wanted to keep these photos a secret, but it turns out Nora's the one who locked it."

Even in the dim red light I could see that Linden was looking at me the same way he had when I ate my coney dog with a fork.

"What?" I said.

"That's Nora."

"No it isn't."

"Yes it is, just look at her."

"How can you tell?"

"It's her eyes. Same blue eyes. Remember? You've got them too."

"How can you tell the color of someone's eyes in black-and-white?"

"I may be an amateur, but I know what blue looks like in a black-and-white photo. Anyway, I told you I've seen photos of her. And that is undeniably Nora."

I was quiet a moment. "Do you really think we could make a book of his photos? Not for me. For him. Those photos up there are pictures of an event that changed Detroit forever, and no one has seen them. And he didn't take them for no one to see them."

Linden held up his hands to stop my arguments. "I get it. Really. I think someone might be interested in publishing it. Maybe Wayne State University. William deserves recognition for his talent and his sacrifice." He pointed at me. "*William* does."

I nodded. He was right. Those photos were not my ticket to

a Pulitzer or a new job or even one byline as a freelance journalist. They were William's legacy. And I was no reporter anymore.

But Desiree was. And there was still justice to be done in the case of Judge Ryan Sharpe.

I started pulling the other photos down. "Let's take these up to Nora."

Emerging from the cellar, I waved Linden ahead of me and took a quick detour through the kitchen. I dialed Desiree's number.

She picked up on the second ring. "Elizabeth!"

"No time to talk now, but be on the lookout for a pic from me in the next week."

"Of what?"

"It's your ticket to the front page."

"My ticket?"

"Some possible evidence in the Judge Sharpe thing."

"Really? Then why wouldn't it be your ticket?"

Through the dining room I could see Nora, Mr. Rich, and Linden still studying the photos that blanketed the coffee table. If I went back to Detroit, I would never be a part of that scene.

"Because I'm staying in Lapeer."

"What? You don't want to live in Lapeer. Elizabeth, this is your way back in! It's your chance!"

"Maybe it's my chance to get back into being a journalist. But it's not my best chance at happiness."

"But I can't take credit for your story."

Linden beckoned me into the room with a tilt of his head.

"It's not my story anymore," I said. "Maybe it never was."

We said our goodbyes and I hung up the phone. Then I walked into the glow of life and love that began at Nora and spread like sunlight throughout the parlor.

I held out the photos that had been hanging in the darkroom. "Aunt Nora, when was the last time you saw these?"

FIFTY-FIVE

Lapeer County, April

I watched Linden's Mustang disappear beyond the pines and felt an upwelling of joyful satisfaction such as I'd never felt before.

"Thank you, Elizabeth."

I turned to see Nora sitting among the sea of photographs. In her hand she held the last photo ever taken of William.

"I think you were right," she said.

"About what?"

"This did help." She placed the photo of William and J.J. atop the rest of them. "I shut the door on this part of my life long ago. I shut out my parents and William's family and God, and I tried very hard to shut out the memories. Just like I shut up that darkroom."

I sat down next to her.

"The way I was brought up, you didn't talk about your problems. You didn't allow yourself to become the object of pity. So I kept it all to myself. But it seems like lately it all wants to get out. And now I feel like I'm finally seeing this life for what it was."

I put my hand on hers. "And what do you think?"

"I think I've spent the majority of my life mending things for other people while I've been walking around in tatters. Today has me wondering what the last fifty years might have been like if I had forgiven my parents and forgiven J.J. Maybe I would have been happier."

"Maybe," I said. "But then I never would have met you, and where would that have left me?"

She put her other hand on top of mine the way old ladies do. "Long ago I believed that everything happened for a reason," she said. "That everything that happened before led you to where you are now, and so it all had a purpose."

I sighed. "That's what my mother always says."

"I think she's right. I couldn't believe it for years and years after William died. But now that I've gotten to the other side of it all, I have to believe there must be a plan. We just can't see the whole picture. Our lives are like this." She held up the photo of William and J.J. "On its own, it doesn't mean anything. You can't look at this one picture and understand what has happened in this country, or even what happened during the riots. But when you add them all up"—she put it back on the table among the others—"then you start to see. There are always hard parts. But so many of those things—later you realize that were it not for them, something else wonderful could never have happened."

"Hey, Aunt Nora," I ventured, "I wonder if I might show you one more surprise?"

She put a hand to her mouth to stifle a yawn. "I'm not sure I could handle another surprise."

"It's nothing big. It's outside."

She acquiesced with a tired smile and followed me into the kitchen to where my dirty shoes sat on the mat. I picked her windbreaker off the peg by the back door and helped her into it. The sun had nearly set, but there was enough golden light filtering through the distant trees to guide our steps across the muddy backyard. When we drew close to the little tree, I didn't even have to explain.

"Oh, Elizabeth."

"It's a catalpa, just like the one William planted for you. I thought maybe you'd miss the other one."

"You are so thoughtful." She stood with her arms crossed over her stomach and smiled.

I put my arm around her and pulled her close. "So now you have your tree back."

"No. This one is yours. You planted it, and you'll be the one to see it grow." She turned to look at me head-on. "You know I want you to stay, don't you?"

"I told you I was staying. I'll stay as long as you'll have me."

"No, I mean stay here, when I'm gone. I want you to live in this house and keep its memories. I still have more to tell you, and there are more mysteries to solve. I never did get to ask Aunt Margaret some of my questions. She died just a few months after the riot. Did I ever tell you about the window in the attic?"

I shook my head.

"Now there's a story for you."

The next Sunday morning I came downstairs to find Aunt Nora dressed to the nines in a pale pink suit, heels, and jaunty pillbox hat.

"Wow. Did you make that outfit?"

"Long, long ago. But I understand from my clients that vintage is in."

"I wish I could sew something like that."

"You will. You're learning fast. We'll get you onto lined jackets in no time. But now we better get on the road."

The parking lot at Mr. Rich's enormous Baptist church was packed. I let Aunt Nora out at the front of the church, where her door was opened by a well-dressed black gentleman who offered his arm to her. Two more men stood a few feet away, holding the doors of the church open. I thought of the simple hut my parents were worshiping in with poor farmers and fishermen and smiled. What a strange and wonderful family we were all part of.

I parked and hiked back to where Nora waited in the foyer with Linden, who then guided us through the river of beautiful people streaming into the sanctuary. I kept an eye trained on Nora, hoping that the carnival atmosphere wasn't too much for her. It was nearly overwhelming me. I felt practically naked as one of very few white women, and the only woman in sight not wearing a hat. But she seemed calm and delighted to be shaking hundreds of hands and hugging strangers.

The music was soul stirring and full of genuine joy. The minister spoke of redemption and rebirth. All around me I heard murmurings and shouts and affirmations, "all rights" and "uh-huhs" and "amens." I felt as though I were making up for missing a year of church all in one morning. I also felt that I had something I needed to do.

When Linden and Mr. Rich left to retrieve the cars, I placed Nora in the care of some women and stole away to a quiet corner of an empty classroom. I pulled out the phone I had silenced for the service and dialed Vic Sharpe's number. After the third ring, I prepared to leave a voicemail. Then the ringing stopped.

"Elizabeth?"

"Thank you for taking my call."

"What can I do for you?"

I took a breath. "I just wanted to say I'm sorry. For everything."

The line was silent.

"Vic?"

"I'm here. I—thank you, Elizabeth. I appreciate that."

I wasn't sure what else to say.

"Look," he said, "maybe I should have gone about all this a

little differently. I let my anger get the best of me. If you want your job back—"

"I don't."

"Really?"

"Really. I have a better job now. A better life. I'm good."

"Okay. Well, let me know if there's ever anything I can do for you."

Everything happens for a reason.

"Vic, have you ever thought of investing in the arts?"

"I'm listening."

Several minutes later, I met Nora at the lobby door.

"You sure seem to be in good spirits," she said.

"I am."

I had much to be thankful for. I was also grateful that I had been wrong in my assessment of James Rich when I first saw him walking into the Lafayette Coney Island. He wasn't wasting my time. He was there at exactly the time he needed to be.

Maybe God was in control. Maybe there was a plan. And maybe, just maybe, he had written me in there somewhere too.

The next morning, I sat down to another sewing class in Aunt Nora's crowded workroom. Matthew smirked at me from the doorway. But his smug disapproval would not deter me. There was a house full of fabric waiting to become something useful, something beautiful, something that some young woman generations down the road would find, unfold with rapturous wonder, and use as her own doorway into the past.

Epilogue

Lapeer County, Some Time Later

One hot August morning, much like the day I had first come to live in the old farmhouse, Aunt Nora didn't get out of bed. I found her lying peacefully, unmoving, beneath Mary Balsam's colorful crazy quilt, and I knew at once that she was gone. I pulled a chair over to her bedside, took her cold hand in mine, and wept as I never had before, much as anyone would weep over the loss of their best friend. I would miss her terribly, even the her she had become.

Ours was an unusual friendship. The closer we got, the farther we drifted apart. The hints of confusion I had noticed when I'd first moved in had grown over the next year, until she forgot who I was. Strange snippets of long-ago conversations crossed in her mind with the one she was having at any given moment. It was hard at first to keep up, but eventually we settled into a rhythm and followed her rippling thoughts wherever they led.

Sitting there at her side, I recalled the last odd chat we'd had just the night before. It had started with me updating her on a few clients who had detailed requests I couldn't quite fulfill with my still-intermediate sewing skills. But it quickly devolved into something else.

"I used to make beautiful clothes," Nora said.

"Yes, I know."

"I used to quilt. What ever happened to that yellow quilt?"

"It's at the foot of my bed. Do you want me to go get it?"

"You know there's a bed in this house that was made by an escaped slave."

"Really? Which one?"

"I think it's in the back now. They moved it there after Mary died."

"The bed in my room was Mary Balsam's bed?"

"I don't know what room you're talking about."

"I'm sleeping in the back bedroom. By the attic stairs."

She looked at me as though I had spoken in another language. "I don't understand you. I don't know what you're talking about. I don't want to talk to you anymore."

I let it go and hoped that maybe she'd bring it up again. It did no good to try to steer our conversations. It was like trying to steer a train.

Now I would never have the chance to hear any more about it.

I called Mr. Rich, and simple funeral arrangements were made. After a call to Tyrese's friend in the legislature, I managed to get permission to have Nora buried in the backyard by the catalpa tree.

When the guests had all gone and Tyrese had hugged and kissed me one last time, I shut the front door and wandered from room to room in the huge, empty house. In Nora's bedroom, Matthew was lying on the bed.

"You know you're not supposed to be up here." I picked him up. He twisted out of my grasp and ran off, leaving a clump of orange fur behind on the crazy quilt. I picked it up and then ran my hand over the embroidered designs, looking for more.

Instead I found a large, hard bump. There, secured by thread at the end of a chain of stitches, was a lever lock key.

The long-forgotten trunk in the attic flashed into my mind. Nora had hidden the key to the darkroom in a drawer. Had she hidden the key to the trunk in Mary's quilt? Though it felt like I was slicing into the *Mona Lisa*, I snipped the threads that held the key and walked, trembling, up two flights of stairs into the attic.

By the glow of a bare light bulb, I knelt before the trunk and slid the key into the lock. It turned.

Inside, a rolled-up paper sat upon a green silk lining, awaiting discovery. The dried rubber band fell apart as I tried to remove it, and the paper was stiff. I unrolled it to reveal a large black-and-white print of the angriest man I'd ever seen. I thought of all the beautiful and poignant pictures I had seen as Linden and I collected the materials for the book of our great-uncle's photography. In all of the prints and all of the negatives, I had never seen this one. Had William taken it? It certainly bore his distinctive mark. Why, out of all the amazing pictures he had taken, would someone keep this unpleasant one packed away for posterity?

I searched the back for some notation of the subject, but it was blank. I'd have to see what Linden made of it, but the oversized coffee table book billed as *The Definitive William Rich Collection* and financed by Vic Sharpe would forever be incomplete.

I set the print back in the trunk, bumping it in the process. The lid slammed shut, startling a mouse that scampered out of a hole, over my bare foot, and across the floor, where it disappeared. Strange. If a mouse had been in the trunk, I would have seen it. I lifted the lid again. No droppings, no stains, no shredded fabric. No mouse.

I pushed my finger into a hole on the outside and wiggled it around. I couldn't see anything moving on the inside of the trunk. I ran my fingers along the inside bottom of the trunk until I found a slight indentation just big enough to get a fingerhold. I pulled and the bottom came loose, revealing a large, shallow compartment filled with shredded paper.

I picked at a piece of it. It looked very old. Then I saw slanted writing and a fragment that said *Love, Geo.*

"No!" I cried aloud.

How long had these letters been here, intact, before mice got to them? Had they been here when I moved in? Had Aunt Nora known about this secret compartment? Had she been able to read them before they were destroyed? I nearly started to cry as I sifted through the mess. It wasn't fair. This had all been hidden away so that it would one day be found. And now it was gone.

For one crazy moment I thought maybe I could work it all out, put the pieces back together. At the very same moment, I knew it would be impossible. Nevertheless, I scooped up the mouse's nest and packed it gently into a large ball. This old house was finally ready to give up the rest of its secrets, and I was going to do whatever it took to preserve them. Because if I didn't, no one would.

Aunt Nora had been wrong when she said that history was written by the victors, for the victors in one generation may turn out to be the villains of the next. And the only way to get closer to the truth was to refuse to quit searching for it. All it took to lose one's history was a single generation that didn't take the time to learn it and pass it on. I would do my part to keep it alive.

With the nest removed, I spied one more item in the bottom of the secret compartment. The photograph was small, not much more than two by three inches. The heavy cardstock edges had been chewed by the cursed mouse, but the image was clear and haunting and incomprehensible. A light-skinned black boy of perhaps five or six years old looked into my eyes out of the distant past, seemingly pleading for someone to acknowledge him. To make him known. I flipped over the photograph. Written in fine script in ink that had faded to brown were the words *our boy*.

I didn't know who this boy was or how his photo had managed to escape destruction. But I did know one thing.

He had blue eyes.

Author's Note and Acknowledgments

It was 2012 when I first started thinking about the story that would become *We Hope for Better Things*. It was before a string of highly publicized deaths of African American men and boys at the hands of white police officers. It was before the murders of nine black worshipers in a Charleston church. It was before white nationalism was making national news—again.

As I researched, wrote, revised, and sought publication for *We Hope for Better Things* for the next seven years, I was constantly reminded of its unfortunate timeliness. This novel was not written as a response to those events. It was written in the midst of them, born out of my own struggle to comprehend the scope, understand the roots, and empathize with the victims of racism in America. It was an attempt to reckon with something that could not be reconciled.

I am well aware of the dangers of writing about such a subject. I am aware of the possibility that I have gotten something wrong. I am aware of the pitfalls of writing characters of color as a white woman. I have striven to faithfully and respectfully represent every character, whether white or black, male or female, protagonist or antagonist. I have done my best to avoid stereotypes and cultural appropriation. I have vetted the story with African American friends and been the grateful recipient of their critiques.

I am also aware that good intentions are not good enough. Like all human beings, I am fallible. And while I don't mind if readers are uncomfortable with or offended by my work, I want it to be for the right reasons. If it was because I fell into an offensive stereotype, please accept my sincere apology. If it was because the story made you see something in yourself that you don't like, please accept my invitation to explore that further, to confront it, and to repent of it.

In bringing the world of *We Hope for Better Things* to life, I am deeply indebted to several writers and researchers for their fine work, including Isabel Wilkerson (*The Warmth of Other Suns*), Sidney Fine (*Violence in the Model City*), Herbert Shapiro (*White Violence and Black Response*), Marilyn Mayer Culpepper (*Trials and Triumphs: The Women of the American Civil War*), Hubert G. Locke (*The Detroit Riot of 1967*), Mark Binelli (*Detroit City Is the Place to Be*), Courtney B. Vance (*Rebellion in Detroit* podcast), and others.

Many thanks to those who read early drafts and offered their kind critique and advice, including Valerie Marvin, Debra Dawsey, Mary Bowen, Booker T. Mattison, Nancy Johnson, Twila Bennett, Orly Konig, Noel Harshman, and Dr. Meghan Burke. To my wonderful agent, Nephele Tempest, my enthusiastic editor, Kelsey Bowen, and the whole team at Revell Books, thank you for taking a chance on a new writer with a complicated story in a tough market. To Jessica English, thank you for your keen eyes and light hand when it came to copyediting this beast. To Michele Misiak and Karen Steele, thank you for your ideas, energy, and expertise in spreading the word. To Cheryl Van Andel, thank you for your patience as we wrangled over the cover. And to David Lewis, thank you for saying in one breath that you loved this book and that it made you uncomfortable. No one could give it higher praise than that.

Special thanks to my parents, Dale and Donna Foote, who not only shared invaluable firsthand accounts of growing up on both sides of the tracks in the Detroit area in the 1960s, but who have offered continuous encouragement in all of my endeavors for the past thirty-nine years.

My deepest gratitude goes to my husband, Zachary Bartels, my best friend and stalwart supporter. He has celebrated with me in my small triumphs and has comforted me in every disappointment along the way. I am truly blessed by a gracious God to have this man as my partner in life and love.

And to my son, Calvin, who was only four when I started working on this book and ten when it finally found its way to bookstores. Growing up an only child with parents who are both writers must be odd. So often Mom and Dad are mentally in other worlds, letting nonessentials (like laundry and grocery shopping) go as we perfect places and people that exist only in our minds. I am beyond delighted that your imaginative life is as vivid and engaging as ours, and that you value and enjoy reading as much as we do. You may not know it yet, but you are a storyteller too. And whatever you will be when you grow up, I hope that you will always maintain your imagination.

Because unless we can imagine a better way, we'll never work to make it a reality.

READ ON

FOR AN EXCERPT OF

AN ENGAGING NEW NOVEL FROM ERIN BARTELS

• • •

Coming Fall 2019

ONE

Most people die only once. But my father is not most people. He is a monster.

He first died on a Wednesday in November 2001, when his sentence was handed down—*We the members of the jury find Norman Windsor, on three counts of murder in the first degree, guilty; on the charge of extortion, guilty; on the charge of obstruction of justice, guilty; on the charge of conspiring with enemies of the United States of America, guilty.* And on and on it went. Or so I imagine. I wasn't there. The teenage daughters of the condemned generally are not present at such events.

Now, seventeen years later, he will be executed. It's the first thought I can separate from my dreams this morning, though I've tried for weeks as the date approached to ignore it.

I dress quickly in yesterday's clothes without turning on the news. I don't want to see the mob hoisting signs, the guards standing stone-faced at the prison entrance, interviews with grim relatives of the dead. All I want is for this day to be over, for that part of my life to be over. So I shut the past in behind the door, descend the creaking stairs, and emerge as always in the back room of Brick & Mortar Books, where my real family resides in black text upon yellowed pages, always ready to pick up our conversation where we last left off.

"Good morning, Professor." The African Grey parrot offers his familiar crackly greeting.

"Good morning, Professor." I open the cage door, wondering not for the first time who is imitating whom.

The Professor climbs onto the perch above the cage and produces the sound of a crowd cheering. I change his paper, refresh his water, and give him a terrible used pulp paperback to shred into ribbons. Every morning is the same, and there's comfort in that. Even today.

I know the store will be dead—even more so than usual—but I can't afford to stay closed on a Saturday, even if it is the day after Saint Patrick's Day in River City, Michigan. I have never understood why the feast day of an Irish saint is so popular here, as nearly all of the Catholics that settled in the area have unpronounceable surnames that end in *ski*. Maybe they all just need a big party to forget the misery of March for a day. Even the Lutheran church three blocks south canceled services so that its members could walk in tomorrow's parade. And many of those same people who will paint their faces green and don blinking four-leaf clover antennae as they march down Centerline Road instead of going to church were on this side of the river last night, guzzling green beer and kissing plenty of people who aren't actually Irish, despite T-shirts asserting ancestry to the contrary.

Of all the storefronts on this section of Midway Street, there are only five that do not serve alcohol: a pet salon, a custom lighting store, a bank, an aromatherapy shop, and my bookstore. Every other business along this quarter-mile spur of Midway is a bar, making it the destination of choice for about half the sleepy city on any given weekend and about eighty percent on Saint Patrick's Day. Not that the high traffic translates into high sales for me. They stay in the bars. I stay in my sanctuary. I've never been much of a socialite, which most people would find understandable if they knew my story, or a drinker, which most people would find surprising if they knew the same. Some might claim that the reason my store ended up on the street with the highest percentage of dart boards, pool tables, and broken beer bottles in the city is nothing more than an accident of real estate availability.

It has always had the taste of fate to me.

Armed with more than a few years of experience with the aftermath of Saint Paddy's, I pull on a pair of bright yellow rubber gloves—*Ladies and gentlemen of the jury, Exhibit A: the gloves Mr. Windsor wore when carrying out the strangulation of Mr. Lambert*—and head toward the front door with a triple-thick garbage bag and a broom.

But there's another matter to attend to before I can clean up all the trash. A woman is slumped against the door, her back to me, her head buried in her arms.

I knock on the glass near her ear. "Hey!"

She doesn't move.

Back through the store, through the maze of boxes in the back room, through the metal receiving door out to the alley. A stiff breeze whips up a torn paper shamrock chain, along with the stench of beer and vomit. I hug the east wall of the store, passing beneath the pockmarked remains of a mural of a billowing American flag. I stop. There, on the very lowest white stripe, is a profane word scrawled in black spray paint. I add the removal of the word to my mental checklist and keep walking.

The wind hits me hard as I turn onto Midway. Long shadows cast by light posts in the rising sun point toward the spire of St. Germain Catholic Church, just visible over the tops of the still bare trees, and graze the edge of the woman's coat. She is curled up tight, as if she were developing inside an egg. Glittery green shoes poke out beneath her black parka. Her bottle-blonde hair, streaked with green dye, was probably stunning last night. Now it is matted down around her face.

I poke her with my broom. She shrinks a little farther into her egg.

"Hey, wake up!"

Slender fingers push back the bird's nest of hair. One brown eye squints up at me. "Hey, Robin. There you are."

Sarah Kukla is as slim as she was in high school, but as I hoist her to her sparkly feet she weighs three hundred pounds.

"I was knocking. You never answered."

Her breath almost makes me drop her back onto the pavement.

"I can't hear knocking at this door when I'm upstairs. You should have called."

Leaning her body against mine, I manage to open the front door and dump her into a threadbare armchair. Her parka falls open, revealing black fishnets under an impossibly short green dress that looks like it was sprayed onto her body. Her cheeks and nose glow red. Her emerald eye shadow smudged with black eyeliner makes her look more like she had dressed for Halloween than Saint Paddy's.

"Where were you last night?" I ask.

"Everywhere," she moans.

"Come on. I'll take you upstairs. You can wash up and get some coffee."

Even a massive hangover cannot hide Sarah's surprise at this offer. In my seven years at 1433 Midway, I've never invited her or anyone else up. But I can't send her back home to her son like this. Anyway, I do have a human decency clause in my unwritten personal privacy policy. I'm not a monster.

"Let me get The Professor back in his cage. If I'm not around for too long he chews up good books."

The parrot is not impressed by this break in his routine and lets me know with a sharp bite on my thumb. I don't grudge him his irritation. I kind of wish I could simply bite Sarah's thumb and send her on her way.

Somehow we make it up the steep staircase and into my apartment, where she looks around with an expression that grows ever more disappointed. "It's so plain."

"What were you expecting?"

"I dunno. It used to be—" She looks away. "Never mind."

She slouches onto the couch, kicks off her shoes, and pulls a fleece blanket over her head. Soon her snores are drifting back to the kitchen. I don't have the heart to wake her when the coffee is done, so I creep back downstairs to gather in the remains of last night.

Each new gust of wind brings me more confetti and cigarette butts skidding along the concrete like staggering drunken partiers. I tuck it all into the trash bag along with broken glass, wadded-up tissues, and a single black shoe. I'll have to do it again in a few hours when the wind brings more. It doesn't bother me like it used to. It's just part of the rhythm of this place.

A sharp beeping ceases, one of those sounds you don't notice until it's gone. In the silence left behind I realize that the ice on the river has finally melted. I know it without looking. Rivers have voices, and this morning the Saginaw is grumbling.

At the end of the street, a tow truck ascends the boat launch at Marina Five, dragging the rusty blue pickup I saw still parked on the thinning ice yesterday. The last of the ice fishermen leans toward the truck, hand at his heart, as one might hover over a dead body to search for one more breath, one more twitch of the eyelids, something that might indicate that there was still time to tell him you loved him. Only there wasn't.

No, he's just getting a pack of cigarettes from his breast pocket.

I watch until all that's left of the story is wet gravel. Next year it might be a Jeep or an ice shanty. It will probably be in February rather than March—winter had lingered so long this year. But it wouldn't be nothing. This too is part of the routine—when the ice gives way, when what was solid ground suddenly cracks and shifts and turns deadly.

There had been a tow truck in my father's case, pulling a black sedan from a different river—*May I direct your attention to Exhibit B?* It was anything but routine. I saw it splashed across the front page of the *Boston Globe*, read the gruesome details in neat columns of text that left leaden dust beneath my fingernails. I didn't go to school the next day.

When I can't fit even one more stray sequin into the bag, I tie the plastic handles and stretch my back. That's when I see it, in a skeletal crab apple tree on the other side of the street—the first robin. Spring. All signs point to it. A winter, no matter how long, cannot last forever. The longed-for bird tips his head at me and lifts off against the wind. I deposit the trash in the alley dumpster and fish out my scrub brush and graffiti remover—it's not the first time—and get to work on the wall.

Half an hour later I turn on the lights and let The Professor back out of his cage. Ignoring his muttered cursing, I flip the "Open" sign and settle down behind the cash register with a hundred-year-old copy of *Aurora Leigh* as company.

The spine crackles and the sweet perfume of time drifts up to my nose. The lines slip under my eyes like a mother duck and her brood slipping down the river. Word by word, Aurora lives and loves as she first did under Elizabeth Barrett Browning's graceful pen.

Three quiet hours later—not even a visit from Mr. Sutton, the only customer I could call a regular with any integrity—the bells on the front door jingle.

The Professor squawks, "Hello!"

"I got the mail," comes Dawt Pi's heavily accented voice as she rounds a shelf. "I thought you were going to put that sign out."

She tucks her tiny purse under the counter before reaching

up for The Professor. The bird edges over and makes his way down her arm to her shoulder. He'll spend the next half hour carefully preening her straight, oil-black hair. He never does this to me. If he sat for more than a couple minutes on my shoulder, I would probably end up missing half my ear.

"What sign?"

"That sign. You said you were going to put it out. On the sidewalk."

I put down my book. "Sorry. I was a little distracted this morning."

"I will get it." She retrieves a chalkboard easel nearly as tall as she is and a box of colored chalk from the back room. "You want me to do it?"

I know she is still not confident about the peculiar spellings of her adopted country's language, so I love her for offering. "No, I can do it. What did we decide?"

"Hardcover one dollar, paperback fifty cents."

I sigh. We will lose money. Still, I kneel at the easel to write out the words I hope will draw people into my beloved store. The past few years have been tough, but I'm determined to weather the storm.

"You want to look at this mail? There's a package for you."

I stand back up and tear open the large padded manila envelope Dawt Pi slides across the counter to me. It's obviously a book. I carefully unwrap the brown paper from around it to reveal a vivid red and white dust jacket adorned with a stylized carousel horse beneath a bold yellow title.

"Oh my."

"What is it?"

I can hardly breathe when I see the copyright page. "Oh my."

"What?"

"It's a first printing, first edition *Catcher in the Rye*."

"Is that good?"

I shouldn't expect a recent refugee from Myanmar to know

better, but I give her an incredulous look all the same. "This could be worth a lot." I flip over the envelope. No name, just a return address in California. "Why would someone just send this to me?" Starting at the back of the book, I flip through the pages. "Oh no."

"What?"

"There's underlining. That'll affect the value. Though it's in pencil, so we could . . ."

The moment I see the coffee-ring stain on page twenty-three, I drop the book on the counter.

"What?" Dawt Pi's now exasperated voice cuts through the fog that is swiftly gathering in my mind.

The bird on her shoulder voices his own question. "What does our survey say?"

But I can only manage one word in response.

"Peter."

Erin Bartels has been a publishing professional for seventeen years, most of that time as a copywriter. She is also a freelance writer, editor, and book coach, and a member of Capital City Writers and the Women's Fiction Writers Association. When she's not writing, she can be found wandering through the woods with her camera, painting landscapes in both watercolor and oil, or reading with a semi-spastic Chihuahua mix on her lap.

Erin lives in Lansing, Michigan, with her husband, Zachary, and their son, Calvin. *We Hope for Better Things* is her first novel.

Check out her newsletter, blog, podcast, and more at

ErinBartels.com

@ErinBartelsWrites  @ErinLBartels  ErinBartelsAuthor